the STONES of CAMELOT

the STONES of CAMELOT

by
Brian Stableford

A Black Coat Press Book

ISBN 1-932983-69-4. First Printing. February 2006. Published
by Black Coat Press, an imprint of Hollywood Comics.com,
LLC, P.O. Box 17270, Encino, CA 91416. All rights reserved.
Except for review purposes, no part of this book may be re-
produced or transmitted in any form or by any means, electronic or mechanical, including photocopying, recording, or by
any information storage and retrieval system, without permission in writing from the publisher. The stories and characters
depicted in this novel are entirely fictional. Printed in the
United States of America.

For Jane

Introduction

1

Hello. My name's Amory; I only have the one.

I don't know how old I am.

If you were to pass me in the pedestrian precinct, or stand next to me on the platform at the railway station, or catch sight of me sitting on the grass in the Cathedral Close, you might take me for thirteen, but I'm older than I look.

I'm small for my age in any case—everyone was in the days when I spent my childhood in the Convent of Saint Syncletica, somewhere on the road to the west—but I've also spent a lot of time in other worlds.

I say "somewhere" because I've walked the modern road that follows the same route all the way from Winchester to the Great Ridge and back again without being able to identify the spot on which the convent stood.

I say "the road to the west" because that's what we called it, though not in what you'd call English. We'd lost the Roman names by then, for the road and for the towns it once connected. It was the road to Camelot, but we didn't call it that, and it wouldn't be very helpful if I called it that now, because you have no idea where Camelot was. History was another of the things we'd lost with the Romans, although we didn't know it, because we'd lost the idea of history along with the thing itself.

In the other worlds where I've spent time, the flow and pace of life is very different. If there were days in the land of the fair folk, one day there could be a year or more here; if there were days in the Dark Land and years in Faerie, one day in the Dark Land could be a year or more there.

You have such wonderful ways of keeping track of time that I can guess, within a hundred years or so, how long I was away from your world the second time I was taken out of it, but I'm not exactly sure how much time went by for me.

Let's say, for the sake of argument, that if memories were merely something to be counted and added up, I'd probably be entitled to think of myself as sixteen, going on seventeen.

If quality counted as well as quantity, I'd be prepared to believe myself a good deal older than the average boy my age, but I guess I'm not alone in thinking my own experience unusually rich and varied. By your standards, it might seem absurdly narrow, given that so much of it was spent in slow and stagnant worlds, where the hectic pace of yours would have been unimaginable.

I couldn't have figured out your world in a hundred years, if I hadn't had magic to help, but one of the benefits of being away so long is that you come back fully charged with potential. I write your hideously complicated language like a native, don't I?

Well, perhaps not exactly like a native, but hopefully well enough to make myself clear.

At sixteen, I'm the same biological age as someone born in 1989. While I was with the fair folk for the second time, though—especially while I was in the Dark Land—more than fourteen hundred years went by in this one: a century, or thereabouts, for every year I spent in Arthur's kingdom of the Britons. I don't know for sure how long I was with the fair folk as a changeling, so even with the aid of history I can't tell which century I was born in, let alone what year, but it was probably a little while after the year that you'd call 500 A.D.

We wouldn't have called it 500 A.D., of course. When we numbered our years we counted from something people could remember. The nuns who raised me were Christians but they didn't have any idea when Christ had been born. Like everybody else in the neighborhood, the Sisters of Saint Syncletica thought of the year I was laid on their doorstep as the fifth year of Arthur's reign as King of the Britons, and the year when Merlin took me for his apprentice was the sixteenth.

They didn't know any better. They didn't even know that they were ignorant. Most of the people I knew, especially

Merlin and Mother Leocadia, would have been appalled if anyone had told them that they were living in the "Dark Ages". Mother Leocadia couldn't read, and Merlin never wrote a book, but neither of them thought that their dependence on legend was a bad thing, or that writing could possibly be the basis of an "Age of Enlightenment".

I can see why you think differently, though. That's one of the reasons why I'm taking the trouble to write my story down. I wouldn't want it to be lost. It's not the main reason, though. The main reason is that I got hooked on story-telling while I lived in Cokaygne.

The fair folk loved to listen to my tales of Arthur, Merlin and the knights of the round table, and I became fond of telling those tales. I was an accomplished liar then, so I made a lot of them up, but I don't have to do that any more. The truth is more than strange enough to amaze and amuse a modern audience.

Maybe writing it all down will help me to figure it out a little bit better and help me decide exactly what I'm going to do with my life now that I'm here, but anything of that sort will be a bonus. My first purpose is to let you in on the secret of what really went on in Camelot, and how it came to fall and vanish. It's a story that only I can tell, not merely because I happen to be the sole survivor of those distant times, but because I was the only person, even at the time, who knew the whole story.

Well, maybe not the whole story. A lot happened after I left, and Lancelot didn't take the trouble to fill me in on a lot of the details when he came to Cokaygne to kill me, twenty years later. Also, a lot happened before I ever got to Camelot, and I have to admit that Merlin wasn't the best teacher in the world when it came to matters of newsworthy detail. Then again, I could only be in one place at a time while I was actually living in Camelot as Merlin's spy, and the gossip to which I listened so carefully wasn't always completely reliable. Even so, there are things I know about the fall of Camelot that no one else knew, even at the time—things that are vital to an accurate understanding of the collapse of Merlin's dream.

So, even if I don't know the whole story, I know enough to know that without hearing my story, no one else could possibly know the half of it—certainly not Thomas Malory, so-called knight, or Chrétien de Troyes, cleric for hire, who had to rely on sources that were very unreliable indeed.

There's a lot that even I have to guess, but I trust my guesses far more than anyone else's, because I was actually there.

You'll be interested in my story, I know. My world was the stuff of legend then, and it still is—which makes it even more familiar to you, in a funny sort of way, than the worlds before and after it, which are far better illuminated by history. You still know enough about it to get a grip on it, even though everything you know seems unreliable because nothing was written down at the time.

The images you have of them might be mistaken, but Arthur, Merlin and Lancelot are all familiar to you, in a far more intimate way than any of the victorious vandals who tore Camelot down and scattered its stones, or any of the petty kings who reigned in Arthur's wake, and in his stead.

2

Before I start my story, though, I'd like to introduce myself a little more fully. If you're to understand my viewpoint as well as my tale, you need to understand what a strange fellow I am.

Try to imagine, if you will, how different my situation is from yours. I was a creature of three worlds before I arrived in yours; now I'm a creature of four.

Legend, however badly corrupted it may have been in the intervening fourteen or fifteen hundred years, still provides you with an approximate insight into my world—a way of stepping into my shoes, to see Camelot as I saw it, and understand Camelot as I understood it. You have a little knowledge of the world of Faerie too, and will understand easily enough what I have to tell you about the land of Cokaygne. The Dark Land is a slightly different matter, but, like my master Merlin, you know the myth of Orpheus, and you have a wealth of literature that deals with strange worlds.

I had no such resources when I was hurled into your world: nothing at all to prepare me for what I found.

Even Merlin, who fancied himself as a prophet and had the kind of second sight that could discern something in the mists of the future, never had the least inkling of the kinds of magic you take for granted.

Not that he'd have admitted it, of course. If Merlin were here instead of me—and what a conspiracy of chance and choice it was that gave the opportunity to me, his stupid apprentice, and not to him!—he wouldn't admit that it's more than he could ever have imagined. When he visits as a ghost, in fact, he boasts that this is exactly the world he wanted to build, with not a single feature that he wouldn't have included in his plans—not even atom bombs and global warming.

His ghost is a liar, though. Merlin made plans of Camelot for the stonecutters and their laborers, and he sketched the round table for the carpenters and joiners, but he never made a plan of anything like this—-and not just because we had no paper then, and parchment was too expensive even for a king's magician to waste.

Merlin imagined himself the architect of the world that would emerge from Camelot, but even if he had succeeded in his dream, he couldn't have begun to imagine the twenty-first century. He would have loved every one of the miracles that I love—baked potatoes, flush toilets, widescreen TV, pale blue plastic buckets, soluble aspirin, ornamental fountains, left-handed screwdrivers, privet hedges, Sainsbury's supermarkets, and so on—but he couldn't have foreseen any one of them, any more than I could. His ghost gives that away, every time he loses his temper and shouts at me, as he used to when he was alive, calling me "stupid fool!" or "wretched changeling!"

and telling me that "if I still had magic to waste, I'd turn you into a toad!"

He still repeats all his old catch phrases, even though he's been dead for fourteen hundred years. He never visits anyone but me; Tom Rhymer came into the Dark Land with me, but Tom didn't come out with the ability to see ghosts.

"Every man may know his future," Merlin used to say, when I asked him whether he was sure that I really was a rejected changeling—and why, if so, I had been thrown out of Faerie instead of being allowed to grow up there. And then he'd add: "but none may know his past."

At the time, I used to think that it was a rebuff: a cruel refusal to give me a straight answer. I know better now. Merlin meant that I ought not to waste my time in thinking about a past I couldn't remember and couldn't understand. He meant that I ought to look forward instead of back, to consider what I ought to make of myself rather than what accidents of past happenstance had given to me in the way of a bad beginning.

I suppose, in a way, I'm still ignoring that advice. Writing my story, in Merlin's eyes, would be looking back instead of looking forward, turning my back on the wild and wonderful world of modern magic instead of hurling myself wholeheartedly into it.

I don't think so. I think writing my story is a way of hurling myself into the modern world. After all, it's not as if I'm using a quill pen, or scratching away on ragged parchment. What could be more wonderful than typing? And what could be more wildly wonderful than typing into a computer? All stories happen in the past, but all tellings are addressed to the future.

It's not the boy who scurried like a busy rat through the walls of Camelot who's writing these pages but a creature of four worlds—including yours. I couldn't tell the story properly if I weren't.

I can see, now that I've spent time in your world and learned the meaning of the word psychology, that Merlin's saying wasn't just advice. It wasn't just something he used to say to me, when I pestered him about my dubious origins. It was something he used to say to himself, as a spur to his own ambitions and a vital item of his faith.

He was an old man when I knew him, and one of the things he meant by "every man may know his future" is that we all know that we'll grow increasingly decrepit with age, unless or until death arrives to claim us, and that we must make our plans accordingly. He meant, too, that no matter how young or old we are, we still have influence to wield over the shape that the future will take—not merely our own future, but the future of others, and the future of the world. He meant that every action we take is a cause, whose effects might be small or large, negligible or infinite, good or bad.

As for "but none may know his past"—well, he too had been with the fair folk, and had been disconnected from the flow of this world's time in consequence, but that wasn't what he meant at all. He meant that the forces that make us what we are, to start with, are a complete mystery: a mystery hidden in the forgotten events of infancy and the dabblings of one's ancestors. And so they are—even for you, who have history, archaeology and genetics as well as legend to tell you where you came from, and how.

I didn't know that then. I never made the kind of reply to my master that might have convinced him that I wasn't such a stupid fool, or a wretched changeling, or a toad in human form, as he thought me to be.

All I could say for myself, then, was: "If I'm a changeling, why did the fair folk throw me back? What was wrong with me, that they should repent of having stolen me?"

I didn't say it in English, of course, and I admit that my translation is very free, but I'm a writer now, in a world that has paper and ink in glorious abundance, and fabulous machinery to facilitate its distribution. I hope you'll forgive me for needing to make the boy I used to be—who couldn't read, although he wasn't as stupid as he seemed—sound more articulate than he knew how to be.

Sometimes, when he was in a particularly good mood, Merlin would condescend to admit that he simply didn't know the answers to my questions.

"When I first saw you," he told me, once, "I could feel the magic in you, although you could not feel it in yourself and let it ebb away unused—but that is not proof that you were stolen from your crib by the fair folk. None has been seen in these parts for eleven summers now, as much to my relief as my regret, but the flight of years is nothing to them, who do not age as we age, nor mature as we mature. You might only have been touched as you lay on your sleeping mother's breast by some passing elf, moved to a moment's curiosity."

"But I wasn't at my mother's breast for long," I reminded him. "Whether I went by way of Faerie or not, I was with the Sisters of Saint Syncletica before I was weaned—and what you felt as magic, Mother Leocadia perceived as sin."

I had no memory of the first time Merlin had come to see me, although he told me on the second occasion that he had come before. It seemed to me then that it might have been Merlin's interest that set the sisters against me, for they lacked the kind of sensation that would have allowed them to feel magic in me, but I dared not say so to him. I dared not say: "You should have taken me with you when you first saw me rather than leave me to play the devil's child in a nunnery for nine long years." That would have seemed ungrateful, and he was not a man to tolerate much in the way of ingratitude.

He might have guessed what I left unsaid, though, for what he said in reply to my remark was: "If Mother Leocadia saw sin in you, sin there was and is. I do not care about that. Your slyness is useful to me, as long as you are careful to lie, spy and steal on my behalf. If Mother Leocadia had told me that you had become a virtuous child, fit only for the church, I would have rejected you myself."

How much truth was there in that, I wonder? At the time, I assumed that Merlin had taken me for an apprentice because of the magic he had felt in me when I was a baby—magic that had left its imprint on me, even though I had never knowingly worked a spell or cast a curse.

Now... I don't know.

If Merlin hadn't come to see me in the convent soon after my abandonment there, drawn by rumors of my changeling nature, then he certainly wouldn't have come to see me thrice more, or summoned me to Camelot to be his servant—but the magic that had once been in me might have had nothing to do with it. I might simply have been a convenient age, and free of any potentially inconvenient family ties. Perhaps he really did want to replace honest Harl, his former apprentice, with a more sinful boy, who would take to eavesdropping like a duck to water, and spread rumors very cleverly, without ever suffering the least pang of conscience.

If it hadn't been for me, Merlin would have been lost. His legs had grown weak, and without stronger legs the secret passages he had inscribed in the plans of Camelot's four towers would have been almost useless to him. Anyone could have fetched his meals from the kitchen and carried his slops to the cesspit, but he needed someone to serve as his eyes and ears who could walk without making a sound, remain motionless for hours on end, and draw true inferences from surreptitious glances and hasty mutterings.

If it hadn't been for my careful observations, Merlin might never have known that everything he held dear was imperiled by Guinevere's affection for Lancelot—and if it hadn't been for my cunning as a messenger, he might not have been able to place as many obstacles in the way of their affair as he contrived to do. The dream of Camelot might then have died long before I killed it with my carelessness.

Had I not been so preoccupied with my own mystery, I might have played an even greater part in his schemes than I did—but I hadn't learned to look forward instead of back. I couldn't forgive Mother Leocadia for what I saw as persecution—and if the cause of that persecution was my expulsion from the land of the fair folk, after one of them had taken the trouble to steal me, I couldn't forgive that either.

I yearned to know the truth. I burned to know the truth. What a stupid fool I was!

I know the truth now. Yes, I had been a changeling, stolen from my crib on the instructions of Morgana, whom Merlin called Morgana le Fay. Yes, I had been returned to the world far sooner than the majority of my kind. No, it wasn't my fault. I hadn't been tried and found wanting; I was merely a pawn in a scheme, plucked at random from the world.

I know all that, now—and I know, too, that if I had known it then, I might have acted very differently when Morgana came to Camelot. But if I had been more content as a child, or as Merlin's apprentice, I wouldn't be here now. I wouldn't be able to tell you the bare bones of my story, let alone to employ the insight of four worlds to the task of putting flesh on the bones.

If I hadn't been such a stupid, spiteful and ungrateful fool then, I wouldn't be such a knowledgeable, thoughtful and magically wise fool now. And that's the kind of fool this story needs, as a teller and a hero.

Part One
The Convent of Saint Syncletica

1

I don't know how I came to be Christened Amory. Christened I certainly was, for there was no one to give me a name but the Sisters of Saint Syncletica. Mother Leocadia must have chosen my name, but in choosing it she broke with the convent's tradition, which was to recycle the names of Christ's apostles endlessly. In the normal course of events, I should have been a John or a James or a Simon or a Thomas.

I dare say, although I can't actually remember, that the names of John, James, Simon and Thomas had already been used within the convent. Even so, there must still have been an apostle or two to spare. There were never more than sixteen children in the convent while I was there, and no more than two in three of those were boys. By the time I was old enough to remember, there was a John, a James, a Simon and a Thomas, all four of them older than I was, but some of them must have arrived afterwards, because foundlings come in all sizes. Had I taken my turn, I'd surely have been entitled to one of those names—or if not them, Matthew or Andrew, Philip or Bartholomew.

The likelihood is that Mother Leocadia knew from the first that I wasn't cut out to be a disciple. Perhaps she thought of naming me Judas, but couldn't bear to do it.

Why Amory, then?

Perhaps she believed that there was a saint called Amory, whose legend she had heard from one of her followers. It isn't impossible. After all, who would ever have guessed that there were saints named Syncletica and Leocadia, had their names not been preserved—at least for a little while—in such holy places as that shabby convent on the road to the west?

I can only guess, but I do know that Mother Leocadia had more Latin than any of her sisters. She might have called me Amory because she thought me a love-child, and amor is Latin for love. On the other hand—and this seems far more likely—the root she might have had in mind is that which gives rise to the word amoral, meaning not customary, or not right.

If so, she was correct. From the very beginning, I was no slave to custom. From the very beginning, I was a rebel and an outsider.

All the successive Johns and Jameses, Matthews and Andrews disliked me. So did the Judiths and the Marthas, the Hannahs and the Ruths, not to mention Sister Dorcas and Sister Claire, Sister Anne and Sister Catherine. In retrospect, I can see that they didn't treat me exceptionally badly. Had they done so, I would probably have died, as many of them did while I was part of their company. At the time, though, my treatment seemed quite bad enough. Though I worked no harder than anyone else, and was punished only a little more often and more harshly, it seemed terribly unjust that they talked to me so little, never comforted me as they comforted one another, and often referred to me, even to my face, as "devil's child" or "elvish castaway". I thought them cruel, and I thought myself harassed.

Whenever I watched a Simon or a Hannah die, of the pox or the measles or some ague without a name, I thought that it served them right. I never said so, but was glad to think of their anguish and pain as punishments for all the sly and nasty things they had said about me.

I hadn't the power to curse them, but if I had, I'd have used it. I'm glad, now, that I hadn't.

It was nothing personal. It was merely a way for my fellow orphans to draw much-needed bonds a little more tightly between themselves. It seemed intensely personal at the time, though, and I hated it. The Thomases and the Bartholomews were small for their ages, and when I fought those no older than myself I could give as good as I got in a fair fight—but I was one and they were usually more. When I did give as good as I got, I had to bear the blame for most of the damage done in the eyes of the sisters.

I was full of sin, and tangibly so.

If there ever was a Saint Amory, I wonder whose patron he might have been. I can't believe that he was the patron of changelings.

I never believed Mother Leocadia or Sister Catherine when they told me how fortunate I was. I measured fortune according to the nearness of the day when I would be free of them.

Now that I've lived a while in your world, though, I understand a little better exactly how fortunate—and exactly how unfortunate—I was. You would have considered my circumstances utterly wretched, but the miracle is that I had any circumstances at all. The miracle is that there actually was a door at whose step I might be left, and that when the door was opened to discover me, there was not the least hesitation as to what should be done with me.

In spite of the fact that I was marked for a changeling by the cloth in which I was wrapped and the basket in which I lay—both of which were obviously elvish in manufacture—the sister who opened the door took me in, and found me a breast at which to suckle.

You might be surprised that a wet nurse could be found in a convent, but the picture the word conjures up in your mind is one more recently designed. In those days, it was not merely orphan children who were outcasts from society, in need of a community to harbor them. History tracks the adventures of empires, armies and conquests, giving the impression of an ordered and organized world—and, indeed, the existence of armies and the need for their supply meant that there was always a community ready to absorb fit and healthy young men—but for the great majority of ordinary people there was no order but family and village. The strong and the skilled could always find new places in towns, but a weakling who lost a family might struggle to find a new place in a village, and a weakling who lost a village was in dire straits. It was not at all unusual, in those days, for families and villages to be all-but-obliterated by disease, famine or violence.

Before there were Christians in Britain, such weaklings must have died in even greater numbers—but the Romans brought all the religions of the empire with them, including the ones they affected to despise, and when the tide of Roman civilization went out again, the Christians and their legends remained.

I can still remember Mother Leocadia telling us the legend of Saint Syncletica, as she had heard and understood it. I doubt that it is the version contained in any modern book of legends, but this was several centuries before any legends were committed to parchment.

"Syncletica lived in a village in Armenia," Mother Leocadia told us one wintry evening, as we sat in a circle on the frosty earthen floor, while she stood with her back to the cooking-fire. "One day soon after the harvest had been gathered, marauding Turkmen came, armed with scimitars, to steal the produce of the harvest and all the livestock in the village. The men made ready to defend their grain and their animals with pitchforks and spades, eating-knives and scourges. They asked the women to fight with them, with broom-handles and cooking-knives, frying pans and distaffs, but Syncletica spoke to the women, saying: we are Christians; let us pray to the Lord for deliverance. And so the women prayed, instead of fighting.

"The Turkmen outnumbered then men of the villages, and they were skilled in battle. They overwhelmed the defenders, and slaughtered every man and boy-child in the village. Then they seized the women and the girl-children, and raped every one of them before loading their carts with the produce of the village, leading the animals away, and setting fire to all the houses. The fire devoured everything the Turkmen had left behind.

"Some of the women wanted to rebuild the houses, gather whatever roots remained in the fields, and plant a new harvest, even though they feared that they would starve before

20

the shoots would sprout. But Syncletica was visited by an angel as she slept, who told her to lead the women away into the barren mountains. They walked for six days and six nights, with nothing to eat but what they scavenged along the route, and nothing to drink but what they found in trickling streams. In the end, they came into a high valley so barren that there was nothing at all to eat or drink, although it slopes were wooded, and no prospect before them but steeper slopes, also densely wooded.

"We shall rest here today, Syncletica said.

"We shall die here tomorrow, said her followers.

"During the night, there was an earthquake in the mountains above them, which brought down landslides, but the valley in which the villagers hid only trembled. A herd of wild goats, terrified by the earthquake, ran into the valley and remained there, too exhausted to run any further, until the women caught and tethered them. The next day, a stream diverted by the movements of the earth flowed into the valley, and shoots began to sprout from the earth it dampened to either side of its course.

"Here we shall stay, Syncletica said. Here, the Lord will provide for us.

"Nine months later, every woman of child-bearing age gave birth, within a span of days so narrow that none could be sure whether the child she bore was her husband's, or a rapist's.

"We shall treat them all equally, Syncletica said. And when they are grown they shall go out into the world, to carry the word of the Lord. And we shall replenish our own numbers by welcoming other women and children fleeing from the plain below.

"And that, children, is how the Order of Saint Syncletica was founded, and how news of it was carried through the world, so that others might copy Saint Syncletica's example."

Perhaps it is true that Christianity thrived in a pagan world because Christ was and is our only redeemer, but to anyone who lived as I lived before I went to Camelot, the essence of Christian charity was the provision of places for people who had none: places where women and children could come together and form communities irrespective of birthplace or family.

I estimate now that the Sisters of Saint Syncletica were two-thirds widows and one-third spinsters, but any virgins among them would have been exceptional, and the number of new arrivals was always compensated by a more-or-less equal number who died, or found new places in the greater world by making new marriages. Perhaps one in three of the children raised there had been borne by the sisters themselves, having been conceived in various circumstances, but there was no discrimination in the convent against the children of rape or foolishness, and none in favor of orphans dutifully taken in, whose ancestry was unknown—except, of course, for me: the devil's child; the castaway of Avalon.

2

It was Sister Dorcas who told me that I was "the castaway of Avalon". She had been born on the edge of the forest that was now the Royal Protectorate, and had seen more elves than all the other sisters put together. She was certain that the elf who had brought me to the convent must have come through the gate of Avalon.

"There are gates throughout Britain," she once told me, "but none is as wide as the gate of Avalon. Men stray through all of them, from time to time, but only the gate Avalon is big enough to swallow a horse and cart as well." She said it as if she were entitled to feel some pride in the fact.

"Next time I run away," I told her, "I'll go back there, to where I belong."

"Don't talk like that," she said. "You don't know what you're saying. Anyway, you'd never find the gate. The elves know where it is, right enough, for they ride through it to hunt whenever they feel the urge, and sometimes to trade for trinkets, but humans and horses only stumble upon it by accident, and they have only to step across the threshold to be stricken by an awful fear and dizziness that makes them want to flee. The only ones who get trapped in the other world are those so stupid or unfortunate as to be incapable of finding the way back... and the babies stolen by the elvish women, because they have none of their own."

Sister Dorcas always called the elves by their proper name, and called their world "the other world" or "the Land of Light". She never called it Faerie, that being a word imported by the Romans. I doubt that she ever heard the name of Cokaygne, which is what the elves call the region beyond the gate of Avalon; although she had seen elves, she had never dared to talk to one.

Mother Leocadia, on the other hand, never hesitated to call the other world Faerie, and she was always enthusiastic to tell me that there was a Land of Darkness as well as a Land of Light, and that both were instruments of the devil.

"The land where the sun always shines is but bait in a trap, Amory," she told me, when it was reported to her that I had boasted of my intention to run away to the other world at the first opportunity. "They take babies there occasionally in order that they may become the devil's emissaries, leading others to destruction with tales of fabulous fruit and easy living. But there are gates within that realm as well as gates without, which lead into eternal darkness, where sinners are cut off forever from the light and love of the Lord."

How did she know that? It was mere rumor, of course, but how had the rumor got about? It certainly hadn't been spread by any elf in Cokaygne. Perhaps Merlin had taken others into his confidence long before he ever mentioned Tom Rhymer to me—but the likelier explanation is that there were gates that led from earth into the Dark Land in those days, which scared those unlucky enough to stumble into them far worse than the gate of Avalon.

Had I known then what I know now I might have said to Sister Dorcas and Mother Leocadia that stopping the sun in the sky was not the devil's prerogative but the Lord's, who had done it in order to give Joshua the time he needed to complete a massacre—but they would only have whipped me for insolence, even if they had heard the legend. They had no scripture of their own to which reference could be made, of course. Not one of the sisters could read, so they were entirely dependent on legend. The bishop in whose diocese the convent was located must have been the custodian of some written scriptures, and might well have been a clerk himself as well as a master of clerks, but the sisters knew nothing but what they had committed to memory. Much of that they did not understand; they sang mass in Latin, but only one or two of them had the slightest knowledge of that language; for the remainder, it was all mere incantation. All they knew of the gospels was contained, for them, in legend. All they knew of the saints, and of the nature of their order, was contained in the stories they told, not merely to one another but to us: the little children chance had thrown their way, whom Christ and the example of Saint Syncletica had instructed them to suffer.

The legend of Saint Syncletica was not the only one that Mother Leocadia liked to tell us, and perhaps not even her favorite. Had she had her own choice of the kind of convent she would like to be in, she would have chosen to be an Acemite.

According to the legend of the Acemites, it was Mary Magdalen who had founded the first women's convent of all, in the desert to the east of Jerusalem. There, in the Convent of the Acemites, mass was sung perpetually, the nuns working in shifts to keep the song going from dawn to dusk and dusk to dawn, through winter and spring, summer and autumn, year after year after year. According to Mother Leocadia, the song of the Acemites had already been maintained for twenty lifetimes and more, in spite of lootings, rapes, burnings, impalements and all the misfortunes that might be visited upon defenseless communities of women in a cruel world. Every now and again it had to be carried away from its current habitation by a group of escapees—more than once by a single Acemite—but the song had never ceased, and had always found more voices to join in, and take up the burden before it fell silent.

Mother Leocadia loved the idea of a perpetual song, but she had a terrible voice. That was the bitterness she took out on the world, and on me.

The Sisters of Saint Syncletica sang mass once a day and spent the rest of their time in more prosaic pursuits. Even so, their entire lives were, in a symbolic sense, a continuation of the glorious song of the Acemites—as ours would be, they told us, when we went out into the world as Christians.

When the song of the Acemites fell silent, Mother Leocadia assured us, the world would end. Is it still going on, do you think, in some forgotten corner of the world?

Whenever Mother Leocadia told us the story of the song of the Acemites, her dark brown eyes would linger on me just a little longer than anyone else, and she would touch her forefinger to her whiskery chin. I was the changeling, the devil's child, whose original sin had been compounded with the taint of elvish magic. In spite of my tainted origins, though, Mother Leocadia counted me a Christian, and required a Christian's duty of me. I had been saved, in her reckoning, and it was now my duty to become a bearer of the symbolic song, as she was.

I had been nine years in the convent, and believed that my time of release would not be long delayed, when I first plucked up the courage to answer back to that expectation. It was not to Mother Leocadia but to the far less fearsome Sister Letitia that I spoke.

"There must be another song," I told her, "which the fair folk sing. They love music, Sister Dorcas says. Even changelings returned to earth must carry that song with them, no matter that they cannot find the tune. One day, I shall hear it again, and follow it home to the Land of Light."

If soap had been less precious, Sister Letitia might have washed out my mouth with soap and water. If I hadn't already been set to work for every hour that was not taken up by religious observance, I would doubtless have been given a heavy penance. As things were, I was only whipped—and that lightly, lest I be rendered incapable of dutiful labor—and forced to submit to an exceptional catechism from Mother Leocadia.

3

"Do you know what special snares the devil devises for children like you, Amory?" Mother Leocadia asked, when I had proved that I could give the answers I had learned by rote to more familiar questions.

"No, Mother," I admitted, "but I dare say they're made of finely-drawn wire, and very cleverly set."

"The finest wire in the world," the superior assured me. "The thread of faery silk. Do you know why they call the fair folk fair, Amory?"

I shall have to improvise more than usual in rendering the consequent dialogue into what you call English, but most of the parallels work as well now as they did then. "It's because they're so fair of face, Mother," I replied. "They don't catch the smallpox, and are not marked by its legacy as we are."

"Are you sure that is why?"

I wasn't, and my silence betrayed me.

"Might it be because their hair is fair, like the Saxons?"

I had never seen a Saxon at that time, and couldn't remember ever having seen an elf, but even a boy of nine or ten years is heir to the mysterious common legacy that constitutes what "everybody knows".

"No, Mother," I said. "The fair folk are as dark-haired as you or I, if not darker, although their eyes are paler."

"Might it be that they are fair in their dealing, honest traders with a sense of justice?"

"No, Mother," I replied. "They pretend to be honest, as all tradesmen do, but they've an eye for a bargain, and a taste for one too when they take a fancy to human baubles and playthings. They don't often come through the gate of Avalon as traders, but when they do, they haggle masterfully. They'll cheat you if you aren't on guard, so people say."

"So people say," she echoed. "But might it be, do you think, that fair is merely a local corruption of fatere, which is soldiers' Latin for enchantment, and the source of the word Faerie?"

Latin, good or bad, was not something that "everybody" knew. I said nothing.

"Well," she said, "might it be that they are called fair folk because fair is a word that might mean many things or nothing at all? Might they be called the fair folk precisely because they are not at all fair, even though they pretend to be? Might it not be that we call them what they are not in order to show that we know how deceptive and treacherous they truly are? Might it not be, above all else, that we call them fair because we understand that they are the living embodiment of temptation, allowed admittance to our world from their lesser one in order that they may play the part of imps, to tease, torment and test us, by persuading those of us who lack faith to turn their eyes away from the one true Light?"

The answer to that, clearly, was supposed to be yes—but I said nothing.

"You are in danger, Amory," Mother Leocadia informed me. "I do not know whether you were ever in Faerie or not, but I do know that the devil takes a closer interest in you than in any other child within these walls. Do you know that the king's magician has been to see you twice?"

"Yes, Mother," I said. "I remember the second time, and he told me then that it was not the first."

"He has sent word that he is coming again. Are you smiling, Amory? Does that news delight you?"

"No, Mother," I said. It was a lie.

"We owe our livelihood to two authorities, Amory," she told me. "It is the church which won us the privileges we have, but the land on which the convent stands, and the fields we farm, belong to the estate of Winterslow, whose lord holds that manor by permission of Arthur, King of the Britons. The rights we have to gather food and wood in the forest are also granted by him, at the bishop's request. We owe our thanks to both—but we should not confuse the two. One day, perhaps soon, the Lord of Winterslow will be baptized, and every other knight that owes allegiance to Arthur, along with the king himself, but in the meantime..."

"Arthur is a fair man, Mother," I dared to say—and, having begun to speak, dared not stop. "Not blond, to be sure, but honest in his dealings, and his justice is even-handed. And yet they say that he is half-brother to Morgana le Fay, a queen in the land of the fair folk, and that the magic within him by virtue of that half-brotherhood allowed him to pull the sword Excalibur from the stone and claim the throne of Britain."

It was Sister Dorcas who had reported to me that "they" said all of this, and she had assured me that it was probably all lies. Mother Leocadia made me the same assurance, with even more confidence, once she had closed my rebel mouth with her forefinger. "It is a tissue of fanciful lies," she said. "Merlin's work, all of it. He is the only magician in the court, and it was his power that made the omens favor Arthur, who has no kin among the lords and no prejudice to unbalance his judgments. Whatever compact Merlin may have forged between Arthur and the elf Morgana is immaterial now that the old man's magic is on the wane. Were Merlin out of the way, Arthur's conversion would be certain—and that is what I pray for, Amory, every day and every night. Merlin is the devil's instrument, my child. If he asks for you, I cannot refuse—but you can, and should."

"How can I, Mother?" I answered, defiantly. "If he comes here with the king's authority, and you can't deny him entry, who am I to say no if he wishes to take me away?"

"You are a wicked boy, Amory," she told me. "You taunt me, when you should be ashamed. If you say no to Merlin, he will let you be. He will not want an unwilling servant. Do not think for one moment that he will treat you any more kindly than we do, or work you any less hard—and remember that ours is the road to salvation, his the road to oblivion. If you must needs grow weary on either road, who but a fool would take the road to ruin?"

I know now what I could have said to her by way of a brave reply, but it's a writer's privilege to have second thoughts, and I mustn't yield too often to the temptation to improve my cleverness. I said nothing—and resented my whipping all the more for the fact that it only made my labor more painful, instead of earning me a day of idleness upon my bed of straw.

To add insult to injury, Mother Leocadia was wrong. When Merlin came, a few days later, it wasn't to ask me to be his apprentice. I had no opportunity to spite her by accepting his invitation gladly.

4

Merlin looked me up and down, and sighed. He obviously thought that I was too scrawny, as yet, to serve his many purposes—scrawnier, at any rate, than his present apprentice, poor but honest Harl.

While Merlin looked me up and down, I looked at him in like manner, and found him equally disappointing.

His hair was white and thin, and the flesh of his face was very meager upon the bones. His blue-green eyes seemed perpetually to be weeping, albeit very slowly and not at all mournfully. His hands were stiff and gnarled.

All that was only to be expected, I suppose, but it was his clothing that made the worst impression on me. He seemed remarkably drab for a man of magic who had been in the Land of Light far longer than I. He wore no elvish silk, nor even any good human linen. His jerkin and trousers were grey, and his hat too. He wore slippers instead of boots. He was better dressed than any of the sisters, of course, but that wasn't saying much at all.

Because the convent was so close to the road I had often seen knights riding by, and squadrons of men-at-arms, and sometimes ladies in carriages. I had seen the Bishop twice and the Lord of Winterslow once, albeit at a distance, and all of them had been clad in better and brighter plumage than Merlin's travelling garb, despite that he was Court Magician to the King of the Britons and the second power in all the land.

Most of the carriages I had seen on the road were better than the one that had brought him to the convent, which was little better than a haycart. Their horses had been sleeker, and more elaborately harnessed. His cart bore the king's colors, of course, but they were carelessly draped over the side rather than mounted on a pole. He seemed to me to be a slovenly man, with insufficient pride in his station and appearance.

Even so, when he asked me whether I would like to be his apprentice, when I had grown a little older and stronger, I said: "Yes, my lord—if I don't run away to Avalon before then."

He looked down at me with what was meant to be tolerant expression. "Well, he said," if you can find your way to Avalon, and pass through the barrier without vomiting overmuch, I suppose you might find the Land of Light to your liking. But you're too big to be a human doll, and you have no skill as a musician or a craftsman, so the elves might not have much use for you. If you were my apprentice for a while, you'd be certain of a better welcome in the future, if Cokaygne is where your desire and destiny leads."

"Is Cokaygne what the elves call the Land of Light, sire?" I said.

"Cokaygne is but a region, like Britain," he told me, "but it's all that those who pass through the gate of Avalon ever see of the immeasurable Land of Light."

"Well, sire," I said—or perhaps I only wish that I'd said it—"Cokaygne will be enough for me. If you think I need to be educated before I go, perhaps you ought to take me as your apprentice now, for I'm not wanted here—and too many convent children die of disease and starvation for me to be content to stay."

"Harl is more useful to me that you could be, for a year or two," he told me," but the time will come when I can send him back to his family and let you take his place. I'll come back for you then, never fear—and in the meantime, you've just enough elvish magic left in you to keep you alive."

So I was doubly disappointed, and would have been doubly disappointed even had I known how narrow, precarious and badly clad Arthur's Britain and Merlin's dream actually were.

Nowadays, of course, every person I pass on the street is better dressed than King Arthur himself could ever have imagined—even homeless beggars wear sturdier cloth, tailored to a standard that would hardly have been imagined in Arthur's day—but steel needles and cotton thread are two among a millions miracles that all seem trivial to you.

If I could go back whence I came, wearing the clothes I'm sitting in at this very moment, I could pass for such a lord of magic as the world had never seen... but that's the stuff of daydreams.

I was an eavesdropper in the making even at that tender age. I left the caterpillars unmolested in the cabbage-patch in order to crouch beneath Mother Leocadia's window when the wizard spoke to her before returning to his silly carriage.

"He is not ready yet," the old man said, with a wheezy sigh, "but I shall come again when he is older. Keep him safe for me."

"I can only do so much, sire," Mother Leocadia told him. "He is a willful boy, and those who are hard to control are hard to keep safe. If you were to instruct him to be more obedient..."

"I'm sure that will not be necessary," Merlin told her, his voice as dry as summer kindling. "Do what you will—but remember that you must answer to me for anything that harms him."

"I will do what I can," Mother Leocadia told him, coldly, "but he is forever babbling about running away to seek the fair folk, and this is no prison."

"Nor should it be," said Merlin. "Even if he does run away to look for them, he will surely not find them, and will then return a little wiser—and if the elves were ever to seek him, nothing you or I could do would keep him from their grasp."

I had no difficulty visualizing the expression on Mother Leocadia's weather-beaten face when he said that. "I shall pray for him," was what she said aloud, "As I pray for you and the king. But he should not stay here very much longer, for we have taught him all we can. He is ripe for apprenticeship in some honest trade, or for labor on a better farm than ours."

I heard a clink of coins then, and realized that my labor was paying double for my keep. I smiled at that, albeit mirthlessly. It reassured me that I was more precious than any of my fellows or my many mothers would ever condescend to let me know—because and not in spite of the fact that I was reckoned as a devil's child.

5

Mother Leocadia had told Merlin that the Sisters of Saint Syncletica had taught me all they could. I'm not so sure of that, but they'd certainly taught me all they cared to teach, and they held nothing back from me that they gifted to my fellow orphans.

The sisters couldn't read or write, but they could count and calculate mentally, and those skills they taught us. They also taught us to pray, and to sing—in both of which respects, I must confess, I showed far less aptitude. Outside of that, their lives and ours were consumed by daily labor.

When I walked the modern road that follows the course of the old Roman road to the west, I saw what you now call farms, and how they are worked. I saw tractors and ploughs, harvesters and haymakers. I saw cows and pigs and sheep. All those things, as you will understand, seemed miraculous to me. But I've seen nothing more miraculous than a field of wheat, except perhaps a potato-field. To see such rich grain growing in such abundance, untroubled by weeds and insects seemed far more magical to me than any of the fields and orchards of Cokaygne, which had all the magic of Faerie to assist their fruitfulness.

I couldn't see the fertilizers and the pesticides that helped the wheat-fields grow unmolested, any more than I could see the changes in social organization that had gathered little farms into vast ones fit for heavy ploughs and tractors, or the generations of careful selective breeding that had found such prodigious strains—but I could see how much more powerful that sort of magic was than the similarly hidden processes controlling the produce of Cokaygne.

The altogether unmagical farm which supplied the living of the Sisters of Saint Syncletica and their orphan children was very mean indeed by comparison.

We had wheat, of a sort. We had corn, too, and in place of the bountiful potato we had beets and turnips—but we had nothing like the fields that you take for granted. We had no plough, let alone an animal capable of pulling it. We prepared our ground ourselves, as best we could, with what implements we had, which were not many. We had iron, although we had no foundry or smithy, but our iron was as precious as it was poor. Sharp points and blades were difficult to maintain, and the corruptions of rust were irresistible. So our fields were tiny, and our yields were poor. Most of what we grew fed our chickens and our goats—our bees, mercifully, fed themselves, though they were horridly inconvenient in other ways—and most of what we ate for most of the year was mere bulk, tasteless at best, consumed to persuade our guts to desist from aching.

We couldn't have lived had we not had the right, graciously granted by the Lord of Winterslow at the request of the Bishop, to take wood and produce from the forest. That was a precious right, not granted to many and always grudgingly. You might think that limitation vicious, but that's because you think of a forest as something wild and natural, which everyone should have an equal right to plunder. That isn't true now, and it wasn't then.

Winterslow Forest wasn't enclosed by fences, nor was it worked as intensively as the Lord's tenant farms—many of which did have ploughs of a sort, and oxen to draw them—but it was the product of many generations of careful artifice, because it was itself the source of all artifice. Wood was our fuel, and wood the substance of our buildings. In the towns they had bricks, and neat-cut stone, and even we had more kinds of clay than you can easily imagine, not only for making pots but for sealing walls and plugging gaps—but the framework of our artifice was wood, and the framework of our society was the rules determining who could cut and gather wood, and where, and when.

There was more to the forest than wood, of course. There were many kinds of animals in the forest, which could be trapped and eaten. There were multitudinous plants, which could be gathered and eaten: nuts, fruit, mushrooms—but none of them grew by accident. Once, perhaps, they had, but generations of foresters had fostered the useful and discouraged the useless. The clearings and coppices were ragged, but they were managed and maintained by all kinds of rough-hewing. The bushes and trees that put forth edible fruit were assisted; those which put forth poison were not.

It may seem hardly possible that mere dozens of men could have so much influence over thousands of virtually-trackless acres of trees and their undergrowth, but those dozens of men had been exercising their quiet influence for generation after generation—and the lord's forest really was the lord's forest, in dire need of the protection he extended in return for the privileges he enjoyed.

The rights we had, as members of the convent, to gather wood and scavenge for food, were vital to our existence. In a bad winter, they were what kept us from starvation. In a good year, the foresters would even give us the benefits of rights that we did not have, bringing us meat that we were not allowed to kill. What favors they obtained from the sisters in return I honestly don't know, but Syncletican pottery was said to be good by the standards of the region, and Syncletican tailoring was clever when the sisters had sturdy but slender needles with which to work. The Bishop had a brewery, and a forge, so his company of clerks must have found it far easier to obtain comforts, but I now have every reason to believe that we lived quite well by the standards of the day—perhaps as well as many families and villages. Nor was the convent ever looted, or burned, or subjected to any random massacre—which circumstance demonstrates well enough that Arthur's rule was no mere pretence or ragged compromise.

But it all required hard labor.

The fields had to be kept free of weeds and pests. Stores of every kind had to be maintained and protected from pests. Animals had to be fed and milked, protected from predators and parasites, slaughtered and butchered. The buildings had to be maintained: the house, the barns, the privies. Water had to be fetched four or five times a day; the kitchen fire had to be kept around the clock; the cooking-fat and stock-pot had to be preserved and renewed—and, above all else, the forest had to be foraged for all the materials it supplied.

By the standards of the day, we were all weaklings, women and children alike—but that didn't mean that we had any less far to walk in order to gather the necessities of life, not were the burdens we carried any lighter.

Mother Leocadia had told Merlin the truth; I did babble about running away to search for the fair folk. Everyone babbled about running away, but not everyone could embellish their daydreams as I could. When I actually did run way, though, I ran away in exactly the same manner as everyone else. I had nowhere to go. How could I have found a portal into Faerie, even if there were portals to be found within the parts of the forest where we were permitted to scavenge?

I "ran away" five times, always in the height of summer, when the nights were warm—except that I didn't run away at all. No matter how determined I was to travel as far as the forest where the gate of Avalon was to be found, I never got that far. I never got out of Winterslow Forest. I didn't have the stamina, or the means of feeding myself along the way.

All I did, in effect, was to stay in the forest for a while longer, instead of carrying my immediate burden home. Twice I stayed away for three days, once for four—but every time I set out for a more distant destination, I was forced to turn back. I could only run while the forest could supply my needs unaided, when there was no need for shelter from cold or rain, and while my legs would consent to carry me—but even when I stuck to the paths rather than braving the undergrowth, they wouldn't carry me very far.

The only real difference between my desertions and those of my fellows was that I was only once in company; on the other four occasions I ran from the other orphans as well as the sisters. The others never did that; they always stayed out in twos or threes, unable to bear much in the way of solitude.

Like daily labor, "running away" was part of the normal pattern of our lives. We were whipped for it—and rightly so, for it was a manifest failure of our duty to the company, which had to do without the burdens we did not carry back—but it was an expected and perfectly usual dereliction. It was our way of introducing a second Sabbath into the week, in weeks that could tolerate a second Sabbath. Without ever being wholly conscious of it, we operated in shifts, so that our temporary absences would never cause more than minor inconvenience to those who stayed behind and had to work a little harder because we were not there.

6

I did search Winterslow Forest for portals to Cokaygne, though. After all, I had to find something to occupy my time and mind while I was free, and Faerie remained the refuge and ultimate destination of my dreams, even though I had neither the strength to run as far as the gate of Avalon, nor the wit to find it if I had.

Sister Dorcas had told me that smaller gates than Avalon were often concealed in hollow trees and in caves behind waterfalls. She had never seen one herself, of course, but she had heard every teasing tale that travelers through her neighborhood had ever told. So I searched our local forest for hollow trees and caves behind waterfalls, although I soon found out that there were no waterfalls in Winterslow capable of hiding anything larger than a rabbit warren.

I also searched for mysterious standing stones that might have been ancient pagan altars or markers for overgrown tombs. Sister Claire, who was descended from Romans born in Greece, often told us stories which included such artifacts, as did Sister Anne, who had had a grandmother from the Scottish isles. I had no shortage of rumors to guide my searches. Even my fellow orphans had tales to tell, and although they usually went out of their way to exclude me from their designated audiences, that didn't prevent me overhearing what they said to one another.

You'll be unsurprised to learn, however, that I never found anything in Winterslow resembling the magical doorways featured in the tales I had overheard.

The Sisters of Saint Syncletica didn't think of tales of Faerie as true legends, of course. True legends, in their reckoning, were legends of Christ, the apostles and the saints. You might not recognize much of what they were convinced they knew about the life of Christ, the acts of the apostles and the heroism of martyrs, because you not only have written gospels but a Bible that instructs you as to which written gospels are reliable and which are merely apocryphal, but the Sisters of Saint Syncletica were merely one conversational company in an endless series. They only knew what they had been told— but they knew all that they had been told, and had no reference book against which it might be checked. They tried to be discriminating, but the only means they had of sorting the intellectual wheat from the chaff was faith. Whatever fitted with their image of Christ they believed; whatever did not became the substance of mere amusement or the devil's wiles.

It isn't surprising that as well as telling us all they had been told about the substance of their religion, they also told us other tales, for the sake of amusement or alarmism. Even if

37

they had been stricter censors than they cared to be, we would still have heard at least some of the other lore, for we orphans had traditions of our own, tales handed down from child to child without the need for adult intervention. Fortunately, we weren't reduced to that.

Even Mother Leocadia, who thought of all elvish lore as the devil's business, wasn't unprepared to tell us what she insisted on calling "faery tales", even if she did feel obliged to use the excuse that she was doing so only to provide us with evidence of the devil's wiliness. Most of the other sisters needed no such excuse; they took it for granted—and assumed that we too would take it for granted—that faery tales, unlike true legends, weren't to be taken seriously. This wasn't because they doubted the existence of the fair folk, but because they doubted their relevance to the business of salvation.

Some of the tales I heard in the convent still exist in your world, in books that I have recently learned to read—though most of them, I think, go unheeded there. Sister Letitia told us the tale of the child Elidor, who was allowed into Faerie to play, until the day he stole a golden ball and was banished forever. Sister Anne told us the tale of Tom Linn, who was taken into military service by an elvish queen until the day arrived when he was to be paid as a Faerie tithe to the devil, at which point he was saved by the intervention of a good Christian maid. Sister Catherine told us that Tom Linn was also known at Tom Rhymer, and had served his elvish mistress as a minstrel rather than a fighting man, and was still waiting for the Christian who would save him.

At the time, I had no way of knowing which tales had a grain of truth in them and which had not, or where the grain of truth might be in those that had one—but experience eventually showed that I wasn't entirely a fool to take them as seriously as I did.

Mother Leocadia sometimes scolded the other sisters for telling us tales as well as true legends, even though they were following her own example. The difference was that her status as Mother Superior compelled her to dignify her tales with educational value. For one thing, she imported more devils into them than they could reasonably contain, but she also tried much harder to explain the geometrical relationship of Faerie to our world.

Mother Leocadia couldn't think of Faerie, as you might, as a world displaced in "another dimension" so she imagined it as a world "within" our own. She didn't know that the Earth is spherical, but she did think of the greater world containing the Earth as a sphere, because she saw the sky rotate about the Earth, as if the stars were painted on a spherical ground. She had, in consequence, a vague apprehension of Faerie as a second inclusion within that cosmic sphere, enclosed within our world and thus cut off from our sun and stars. She pictured it as partly dark and partly lit—perpetually but not warmly—by its own strange light-source. She also believed, although I don't understand exactly how or why, that somewhere in the depths of the earth there was an ultimate void, terrifying in its abysmal emptiness.

"It is because of this inferior position of their world to ours," Mother Leocadia told us one day, when our entire company was seated on the grass as the summer twilight waned, "that the fair folk are so envious of humans. We are nearer to God and to his firmament, and those of us who are worthy of that closeness shall be resurrected to share the Kingdom of God with Christ when he comes again."

It was a Martha, not me, who asked: "Is that why the fair folk steal babies, Mother Leocadia? Because they envy us?"

"Yes," said Mother Leocadia, positively. "That's why they steal little children—and older children too, on occasion, when they become aware of one who has a particular talent."

"And is that also why they always leave their human lovers, Mother Leocadia?" asked a Judith, emboldened by her friend's example.

Mother Leocadia never liked to hear talk of lovers, so she frowned—but she answered nevertheless. "The fair folk are incapable of love," she said, imperiously. "Sometimes, they pretend to love human beings, but always in a spirit of mischief. They are handsome, and easily persuade humans to fall in love with them, when the whim takes them—but they excite passion only to disappoint it, to leave its victims bereft and ruined."

She was looking at me as she said that, so everyone else looked too. It was grotesquely unfair; the kind of passion she was talking about had not the slightest influence on my desire to live in Cokaygne.

It was embarrassment at that suggestion rather than any other motive that persuaded me to ask my own question. "Why does time pass more slowly in Faerie than it does here, Mother Leocadia?" I asked.

She looked at me more suspiciously than before.

"It is a diabolical trap," she said, confidently. "The fair folk seek to delay as many humans in their own company as they can, in the hope that Christ will return while their victims are distracted, and will return to earth to find that they have forsaken the opportunity to be judged."

"And why would that be unfortunate, Mother Leocadia," I asked, "for those whose judgment would have found them wanting?"

Her frosty tone belied the warmth of the evening. "I should have said that they would lose the opportunity to be found worthy," she said. "Their failure to appear before the Seat of Judgment would not, of course, prevent their being condemned in their absence."

I wasn't brave enough to say what I thought of that, which was that as long as they didn't know that they'd been condemned—and even more so if they did—they might be perfectly happy in Cokaygne. Fortunately, a Thomas intervened, to ask why the fair folk came so rarely into our world if they were bent on our seduction, and why they never stayed for long.

"Because they cannot long abide the light of God's firmament," she told him, "because it is the sight of God himself, who knows that they are soulless. Although human weapons cannot kill them—even iron ones, which they shun—they

40

shrivel and die if they remain separate from their own world for too long."

I realize now that none of what she said was entirely false, though none of it was literally true. It was all corruption of honest reportage, some of it deliberate. Somehow, I always knew that. Somehow, I always believed, long before I was conscious of having any beliefs at all, that although there was some truth in what the Sisters of Saint Syncletica told me, they had got it all wrong.

Perhaps it was magic that protected me from their persuasion, and perhaps it was only wishful thinking—but either way, I survived it, and never let go of my determination to return one day to the world beyond Avalon, when the time was ripe and the opportunity arrived.

7

The two years that passed between Merlin's penultimate visit and my appointment as his apprentice weren't as hard to bear as the nine that had gone before. I was impatient to be gone, but I was more confident that all I had to do was wait. My fate was fixed, and it was a fate with as much glamour attached to it as any imaginable in the convent. Other boy-children were taken to work on the land, or to bear arms; the best destiny any James or Matthew could hope for was to be apprenticed to a stonecutter or a thatcher, by which means he could learn a skill that would always be in demand. I, by contrast, was to go to Camelot—not merely to the town but the citadel—where I would be a servant to the court magician.

No one in the convent had any higher ambition than to be servant to a good master. No boy ever dreamed of one day being found to be a misplaced gentleman, heir to an estate; no girl ever dreamed of marrying a knight, let alone a prince. Going through the gate of Avalon to dwell with the fair folk was a plausible ambition by comparison with either of those.

That I was destined to be a magician's apprentice didn't make me any more popular with my fellows, of course, but now that I was older than all but one or two of them, and as capable of doing harm as any, I was treated with much more respect. As I became stronger I was given more work to do that required brute force—including tasks that even Sister Anne and Mother Leocadia might have struggled to accomplish—but for that very reason it seemed to me more dignified work than picking caterpillars, stirring pots or emptying chamber-pots.

Being predisposed towards arrogance, I began to develop a certain swagger—but even the thinnest of the sisters never hesitated to thrash me if I went too far. They weren't afraid of me, because they had strength in numbers and the Lord on their side—and because they knew full well that I had to wait meekly until Merlin came to fetch me. If I ran away in earnest, I would become a vagabond.

You might think that because our homes were so mean, it would be no great penalty in my native land to be homeless, but you'd be wrong. To be homeless, in my native land, was to be an outlaw—which not only meant a law-breaker but someone who had no protection under the law. To be homeless, in Arthur's Britain, was to starve, or live by theft until you were hanged or stabbed or beaten to death by anyone who cared to do it. Unprepared to be a vagabond, I had either to curb my unchristian behavior or accept occasional beatings. I compromised as best I could.

There were compensations. As the Jameses and the Johns, the Judiths and the Ruths, the Simons and the Bartholomews were replaced, one by one, the inheritors of their names learned to think of me as half a magician already, and thus as a source of alternative wisdom. When the smaller children wanted reassurance that not everything the sisters told them was unchallengeable, they came to me. I didn't set out to become the devil's advocate, in perpetual opposition to Mother Leocadia, but circumstance urged me in that direction, and it was an opportunity I wasn't about to refuse. I had sense enough not to play the devil's part too actively, by pouring scorn on "true" legends, but I felt fully entitled to play with the others. I was, after all, the only person in the convent who had ever been in the Land of Light.

Little by little, the other children acquired the habit of addressing their questions about the other world to me in preference to Mother Leocadia. No matter how much they disliked me, the new Matthews and Thomases, Hannahs and Marthas, were always curious to know exactly what benefits I had derived from my now-long-distant sojourn in Faerie.

I did what any child would do under such circumstances. I made up lies. I hoped, as I did so, that my lies might become the tales the survivors would one day tell to their own children, stressing that they came from someone who had really been to Faerie, and were thus more reliable than any others. Perhaps a few of them did—but the faint echoes I've found in your libraries might have been started by any of a thousand other liars.

"Is it true that the food in Faerie is sweeter than honey?" a wayward Peter or a doubtful Thomas would ask.

"Yes," I would say. "Sweeter than sweet, and more delicious than the most perfect apple you can imagine."

"Is it true that the fair folk can fly?" a starry-eyed Eve would inquire

"Yes," I would say. "On wings more gloriously decorated than the brightest butterflies.

"Is it true that the fair folk dance with the devil, and let him do worse to them than twirl them in the dance?" someone would whisper, as we all lay abed in the darkness.

"Yes," I would say. "And you cannot imagine how wild the dances are, or how much worse are the things they let the devil do to them."

All nonsense, of course. I knew that none if it was true when I said it; I didn't need to wait for the proof I eventually found, when I was finally allowed to return to the land of Cokaygne.

"Have you ever found a portal in Winterslow forest?" a simple Simon or a jesting James would ask.

"Yes," I would say. "I've found several—but when I asked to be admitted, their guardians told me that I must first serve an apprenticeship in King Arthur's court, under the protection of the great Merlin, so that I might go to Faerie as a magician. Only a man who is already a magician can hope to learn enough in a few days spent in Faerie to come back with power that he can preserve—and I'm to be a magician even greater than Merlin, when my day comes."

That was nonsense too, alas—but that, I confess, was hopeful nonsense, even if it did earn me the occasional beating from dutiful sisters desirous of teaching me the folly of pride. Had they believed me, they would not have dared. Had they even had the imagination to wonder whether I might be right, they could have used their tricks of calculation to determine that it simply was not worth the risk. Alas, they had not—and what's even more regrettable is that if they were ever punished for their saintly temerity at all, mine was not the hand privileged to deliver vengeance.

If the Sisters of Saint Syncletica could see me now, they'd have to admit that I am indeed a greater magician than Merlin ever was. They would be quick enough to point out, though, that everyone is now a greater magician than Merlin ever was, not excluding the foundlings in the orphanages and the beggars by the roadside. They'd be quick enough, too, to recognize that no one, in your world—however wretched his condition—ever has to work for a single hour as hard we had to toil from dawn till dusk, every day of the year. We all had to do that, even as children—even when we ran away.

Sometimes, I imagine the children asking me questions about this world, instead of Faerie.

"Is it true that the food in the future is sweeter than honey?" a greedy Martha might ask.

"Yes," I say. "Sweeter than sweet, and more delicious than the most perfect apple you can imagine."

"Is it true that the people of the future can fly?" a wide-eyed John might inquire.

"Yes," I say. "On wings of steel, wider than those of the vastest bird you can imagine.

"Is it true that the people of the future dance with the devil, and let him do worse to them than twirl them in the dance?" someone might whisper, in the silence of the night.

"Oh yes," I say. "And you cannot imagine how wild the dances are, or how much worse are the things they let him do to them."

"But have you ever found a portal in the new world?" a tremulous Teresa might ask—and here the game must end, because in spite of all my adventures, and all my lies, I haven't.

8

When Merlin did come for me he arrived without forewarning, in the same glorified haycart as before, pulled by the same lumpen horses. I was collecting water at the time, from the stream in the forest, and was so bowed down by the yoke across my back that I didn't catch sight of the cart until I was within a dozen yards of the horses.

The driver was waiting in his seat, with a burly guardsman beside him; they looked at me as I looked at them, but there was no curiosity in their eyes. They hadn't been speaking to one another; having found themselves with nothing to do for a while, that was exactly what they were doing.

I couldn't imagine that they would be willing or able to fight like heroes should their king's magician happen to be attacked by brigands, but I couldn't imagine, either, why brigands would bother attacking such an ill-stocked cart when there were others on the road fully-laden with wurzels or barrels of bitter ale.

I drew myself up as straight as I could, to pretend that two leather buckets fully charged with water was no burden at all to one such as me. I carried the buckets to the kitchen and set them down without spilling more than I could have spit, and then I went to Mother Leocadia's room—which she called

45

a cell, although it had far more room in it than any of the sisters had in the alleys between their pallets, let alone the children who slept three or four to a mattress.

Merlin was waiting there, sitting in the only chair that the convent possessed, except for the mercy-seats in the chapel. A stout staff lay across the wizard's lap, but it was a walking-stick, not a magic wand. Mother Leocadia didn't seem to mind that the magician had usurped her petty throne; she was probably glad of the opportunity to tower over him.

"Amory," the magician said, hoarsely. "Your time here is done. Have you possessions to gather?"

"None," I told him. "Everything I use in my work belongs to the convent."

"The clothes in which you stand belong to the convent," Mother Leocadia pointed out, "but I doubt that your master thought to bring you fitments of your own."

She was right about that—but Merlin had a pouch tied to his girdle, into which he reached a claw-like hand. He plucked out a copper coin, and placed it in Mother Leocadia's hand. He didn't ask about the silken sheet that had been wrapped around me when I was abandoned at the door, or the basket in which I'd been set. They'd been sold long ago, and nothing was reckoned to be owed to him or me on that score.

"Well then," he said. "Better help me to my cart, boy. My hands are still steady but my legs have begun to creak."

I lent him my arm to pull himself upright, and my shoulder on which to lean.

He was less of a burden than I'd feared, for he'd grown a little thinner as well as a little weaker since I'd seen him last. We walked slowly and awkwardly, but not without a certain pride.

"You're smaller than Harl," the great magician observed, "but you fit more neatly under my arm. You'll do, on that score."

By the time we reached the road there were twenty people gathered in front of the convent to watch us go. Perhaps I should have bid them some formal farewell, or offered them my thanks, but I only looked at them as coldly and as indifferently as the driver and his companion had looked at me—as if their interchangeable names were nothing to me, and that once they were out of sight I would never think of them again.

I did think of them again, far more often than I had expected. I think of them still, though only collectively, as a peculiar crowd. I rarely pronounced their names—except, I suppose, for Mother Leocadia's—and I rarely pictured their faces. I forgot by far the greater number of them, as individuals, but I never forgot them as a company. They live on in my thoughts as a kind of swarm, ceaselessly at labor, humming all the while about their wooden hive: gathering, gathering, gathering, utterly preoccupied the while with wax and honey...but they did live on, and have never left me. I'll know the children's names as long as I know the names of Christ's disciples and a handful of virgin martyrs, even though I can't fit the names to faces.

Mother Leocadia felt obliged to put on a show for the sake of the others.

"Goodbye, Amory," she said. "Always remember the legend of Saint Syncletica. There's work for you to do in Camelot, if you care to put your mind to it."

"There'll be plenty of work for him to do in Camelot without spreading the gossip of the Church," Merlin told her. "You've done your work, Leocadia. It's time for Amory to do mine, now."

"If Amory does the Lord's work well," Mother Leocadia observed, craftily, "your work and his will one day be the same."

Did she really hope that I would become a missionary in Camelot, charged with the conversion of the king's wizard—and then no doubt, the king himself? Of course not—but she couldn't resist the temptation to pretend that one as humble as she might have launched a chain of causes that could transform a kingdom. Perhaps, in her way, she did; and perhaps she would not have been entirely displeased with the eventual result.

"Goodbye, Mother Leocadia," I said to her, more for fear of being left out of the conversation than in obedience to any sense of duty. "Remember me in your prayers."

"I shall," she promised, severely. "Have no fear of that."

I climbed up into the cart, and sat down. I raised my hand in a final salute.

They all saluted me in return as the cart pulled away. I told myself that they were only glad to see me go, hopeful that they would never see another like me. It was probably true, but just for a moment, I would have been glad to be wrong.

1

Merlin's cart wasn't handsome, but it was solid of construction, and its wheels spun tolerably smoothly. The road helped in that, having endured very well since the last of the legions marched eastwards along it, never to return. The awning that provided shade from the summer sun was ragged at the edges, but it served its purpose, and the interior was comfortably padded, at least in the place where Merlin sat, with his back supported by the wagon's high flank. I had taken up a position opposite to his, so that I could meet his eye.

"The old witch was right," he growled, when the convent passed out of sight behind us. "I should have thought to bring you a shirt and britches—and a hat and belt. You're as mangy in your coat as a rat-catcher's dog."

"The fellow who had these clothes before me looked only a little better, master," I assured him. "I've done my best to cherish them."

He gave me a wry smile then—I was still new to him, still interesting. "I suppose they'll think they trained you well, to call me master without being told," he said. "Can you count and calculate well?"

"I can," I told him, "and I can tell a lie with a straight face, too, though that isn't one of them."

His eyes narrowed slightly and the ghost of the smile faded into uncertainty. "That's good," he said, "but the art of lying has little to do with keeping a straight face—the art of lying is knowing when not to do it, and how to mingle truth and lies effectively. I can teach you that, but you'll have to be honest with me if you intend to learn."

"I do, master," I told him. "I've waited a long time for you to take me away. I wish you'd done it when you were last here."

"You weren't ready," he told me. "You're a handswidth taller now, and a good deal broader in the shoulders. You'll need that muscle, to fetch and carry up and down the steps to my garret. You'll soon be cursing the day I took you away from the soft Earth and the level land to place you in a world of cold stone steps—but a magician must have his lonely tower, filled with mysteries, lest other men should not look up to him, and tremble in awareness of his nearness to the lowering stars."

He sounded contemptuous, not only of those "other men" but also, more than a little, of himself. He obviously found the weakness of his flesh offensive—and I understand why, now that I know how robust even human flesh becomes while it abides in Cokaygne. That summer was the eighteenth of Arthur's reign, and Merlin had been ten years out of Cokaygne before he put his boy-king on the throne, so twenty-eight years had passed since Merlin had come back through the gate of Avalon. For twenty of those twenty-eight years he had been a superman, full of the magic of the Land of Light, but for the last eight he had deteriorated at the same rate as any man of his advanced age. What a fall it must have seemed, to a man of his bold and future-fixated kind!

At the time, though, I could only take note of his dissatisfaction, and wonder whether I would take the brunt of it. "Stone steps must be hard on your slippered feet, Master," I observed, carefully.

"They would be," the old man agreed. "That's why they'll be harder on yours than you'd like, as you relieve me of the necessity of climbing them. But there are compensations. You'll discover soon enough that of all the apartments in Camelot, mine is the only one that offers no opportunities at all to spies and eavesdroppers. You and I, Amory, are the only men in Britain who have the privilege of privacy."

I couldn't help replying to that by glancing at the broad backs of the taciturn driver and his silent companion.

"Not here," Merlin agreed. "We cannot speak of secrets here—but when we are at home, we shall have secrets a-plenty between us, and abundant time to talk them over. Can you keep a secret, Amory? That's an art more precious than lying, and harder by far to master."

"I hope so, master," I told him. "So far, I've had none to keep—except, of course, for the sad truth that I had none to keep, which I was careful not to betray."

I hoped to make him smile again, but he frowned instead. "Perhaps I should have given you one to keep," he muttered. "I could have done that, when I was here before."

I had no answer to that, and he didn't brood on it for long. "Mother Leocadia tells me that you got lost in the forest five times," he said. "That speaks of a certain carelessness, does it not?"

"I was never lost, master," I told him. "I stayed away on purpose."

"Searching for portals to Faerie?"

"Perhaps I was, master," I told him. "But I knew how unlikely it was that I'd find one, just as I know that if Morgana le Fay wanted to change her mind again, she could find me wherever I might be."

His eyes narrowed to mere slits then—but he was facing southwards, and the sun was moving ever westwards, and it's not impossible that its harsh light had pierced a hole in the awning to make him squint.

"What do you know about Morgana le Fay?" he asked, his voice slurred into a croak by phlegm in his throat.

"What everybody knows, master," I told him. "That she is queen in Faerie, or at least that part of it that borders Britain. It must have been by her command, must it not, that I was left at Mother Leocadia's door twelve summers ago? It was twelve, wasn't it, master? Several passed before I learned to count."

"This is Arthur's kingdom," Merlin retorted, ignoring my request for confirmation of the length of time I'd passed in the convent, "but that doesn't mean that he gives the order every time a babe is abandoned to the charity of the wilderness."

"Yes, master," I said, humbly. "What I meant to say is that I know nothing whatsoever about Morgana le Fay, except what people say about her—and that everything they say is very probably a lie. I wouldn't trust any man's word on such a matter—except, of course, for yours."

He was still watching me from behind his eyelids. It didn't seem to me that there was any mischievous ray of sunlight playing on his face now. He was watching me, studying me, weighing me up. I realized, for the first time, that there was a puzzle in me that he had not quite solved. He had no idea why I had been abandoned at the convent, or by whom.

"If we are to share secrets, Amory," he said to me, eventually, "we must trust one another. I could have found a servant in Camelot to replace Harl, very easily indeed. There are a thousand boys in the remoter parts of Britain who'd happily leave their homes for a chance to be my apprentice—but I chose you. I chose you a long time ago, knowing that I would have to wait for you to grow into the job. Do you know why I chose you?"

"No, master," I said. It seemed simpler, and far safer, than hazarding a guess.

"Because you're older than you look," he said. "Perhaps only a few hours older, but perhaps far longer. I too am older than I look. Much older. Do you understand what I'm saying?"

"Yes, master," I told him. "You were in Faerie. You know Morgana le Fay. I don't know how long you were there, but the stories I've heard say that you were born when the Romans were at the height of their power in England—that you've traveled with their legions, and conversed with at least one emperor. Some say Claudius, some Hadrian, and some say both."

"The stories exaggerate," Merlin said. "I certainly never supped with Claudius, although I had some slight acquaintance with one of his skilled engineers. I never marched with any Roman legion, although I was offered the opportunity—and I labored in the building of a Roman road in consequence of my refusal. I was considerably older than you are now my refusal. I was considerably older than you are now when I was taken into Faerie. When I came out again, I seemed only a little older than that—but centuries had passed, for the inner world was very quiet at the time."

He paused, but I said nothing, so he went on. "I was in Morgana's company for seven years, but I aged far less than that, in physical terms. Mentally, on the other hand, and magically... when I say that I am older than I look, I do not simply mean that time moved swiftly while I was away. I came back a very different man. More different than anyone knew or understood—including Morgana, who only acquired the surname le Fay and the rank of queen when I decided to build her a reputation. I think you may be a good deal older than you look, Amory, and a good deal older than you feel, but you mustn't flatter yourself with delusions about the queen of Faerie, for the land of Cokaygne has no monarch. They do things differently there. I think you might be an exceptional child, even though you have kept the secret well—from Mother Leocadia and her sisters, perhaps even from yourself—but if you are exceptional, it's not because you were rocked in your cradle by an elvish noblewoman."

I wanted to believe him. I wanted him to be right. I wanted to be more exceptional than Mother Leocadia had ever been able to imagine. I wanted to be more exceptional than I had ever dared to dream—but I was, as Merlin had judged, a secret even to myself. It was one that he never managed to penetrate, and proved far more difficult for me to unravel than I could ever have imagined.

2

I suppose that if he had suspected the truth about my secret, Merlin might have killed me rather than taking me into his household. Mercifully, there was no way he could learn the truth from me, no matter how hard he tried, because all I wanted, at the time, was to join my fate with his. I wanted to learn from him, and play my part in his schemes as cleverly and as honestly as I could. I wanted to be a good servant to a good master, and I expected Merlin to be the best master in the world. He was, after all, supposed to be the greatest magician in Britain, and the greatest there had ever been.

"I shall be as good a servant to you as I can be, master," I assured him, in all sincerity. "I hope, and believe, that I might be a very good servant indeed, for I have always felt that the land of Cokaygne has left its mark on me, even though I have no memory of anything that happened to me there."

Merlin nodded, pensively. "Good," he said. "We shall do our best. We shall continue my work, together. If you can add more to my art than an ordinary boy, so much the better. If not—well, you've a strong pair of legs and a keen wit. Even at worst, you'll do."

I never saw him in such a good mood again. Perhaps I had a premonition of that, or perhaps I was merely too eager to have the question answered, but either way, I mustered all my courage to say: "Master, there is one thing I have always wondered." I left off there, in the hope that he might be intrigued. If he asked me what my question was, I thought, he would be far more likely to feel an obligation to answer it.

"What?" he asked.

"All my life," I said, "I've been told that I must have been expelled from Faerie because I was taken for a changeling, and then found wanting. But that isn't the only possibility, or so it seems to me. It seems to me that if you spent seven years in Faerie, and were not the only human there, then human children might be born in Faerie, to human parents. Perhaps, in that case, I was never stolen, and never rejected. Perhaps I was cast out for another reason entirely. Perhaps..."

I stopped than, having said more than enough. I waited for his answer, which was slow in coming.

"There is no childbirth in the Land of Light," he said, eventually. "The fair folk are exceedingly long-lived, and none bear children, even to replace one of their company who dies. They allow themselves the occasional luxury of stealing children from our world, most of which they hold for a while and then give back. Those who grow to adulthood in Co-kaygne become as sterile as the fair folk. Even those who stay for seven years... no, Amory, I cannot tell you what you want to hear. I dare not say that it is utterly impossible, but I think it extremely unlikely that you were born in Cokaygne."

"But they say that Arthur is Morgana's brother, master," I whispered.

"Even as a lie," Merlin told me, his voice growing harsh, "I did not mean that to be taken literally. Yes, I arranged a meeting between Morgana and Arthur, long before he became king. Yes, Morgana pledged her support to his cause in return for a trivial favor—a rare gift indeed, from an elf to a man. Yes, there was talk of brotherhood between our two realms—but that was mine, fine rhetoric to win pledges of allegiance from the lords of the land. Servants' gossip always exagger-ates, and sometimes takes literally that which was only a fig-ure of speech. I would rather the rumor died, and would stifle it if I could. You were not to know, but I ask you now not to repeat it again. You must learn to guard your tongue, Amory, if you are to serve me well."

"I'm sorry, Master," I said, honestly. "I didn't know."

"And you have much to learn," he conceded, "that you will not learn unless I instruct you. I don't blame you, child. You mustn't be afraid to speak to me."

But he did blame me—perhaps not then, but on many another occasion when I didn't do what he wanted because I didn't understand what he wanted, because he hadn't ex-plained what he wanted in a way that I could understand. He gave me abundant cause for resentment in the weeks and months to come, and soon forgot that any failure on my part might be the result of a failure on his. For the remainder of that journey, though, I was new to him, and he was very con-scious of everything I didn't know, and forgiving of my igno-rance.

It was a good journey, and a happy one, all the more so because I had so little to do. I fetched and carried for him, but when the driver and the guardsman sought to give me orders too he told them to desist. He told them that I was his servant, not theirs, and that it was their work to see to the horses and the cart, as well as their own needs.

I was never so lightly worked again, because the cart—unlike the tower, as he had warned me—had no steps. Attending to my master's needs while we were on the road was very easy indeed, and I had cause soon enough to rue the weakness that kept him from going abroad in it more often. To me, the journey to Camelot was leisure: a chance to see the world.

I didn't realize at the time that it would be my only chance to see that particular world, but I couldn't have stared any harder if I had, or understood any more of what I saw.

The road became much busier as we came closer to Camelot, but I had been watching such traffic pass the convent grounds all my life, and a mere increase in density was not enough to make it interesting. The villages through which we passed were far more surprising.

I had roamed far enough abroad from the convent to see half a dozen neighboring hamlets and obtain distant glimpses of a couple of larger villages, but I had unthinkingly taken their configuration and distribution for the norm, and it was not until Merlin's cart had progressed a good way along the road to the west that I realized my mistake. Farms and houses are not like handcarts and carriages, striding chapmen and mounted messengers; density makes a great deal of difference to their aspect and their significance.

I figured out soon enough that the stretch of the road on which the convent stood must be one of the most frugally populated, and guessed immediately afterwards that the sprawl of Winterslow's patchwork forest had kept a different kind of world at bay. I had gone a hundred times, usually with Sister Letitia or Sister Ruth, to what they called "the market", and had in consequence thought of a market as a scrappy thing, a local and grudging exchange of goods, after long-winded but desultory haggling, between a handful of neighbors. On the road to the west, I saw what markets really were, and gradually came to understand that the whole road was, in a sense, a series of markets, which drew goods from the north and the south in order to redistribute them to the west and the east.

Because Camelot lay to the west, the bulk of the goods went westwards—and it was the flow of goods, I belatedly realized, that determined the fact that the road was called "the road to the west". The fact that Camelot lay in that direction was certainly the underlying reason, but if that had been the only reason the road would indeed have been called "the road to Camelot". The people who traveled it called it "the road to the west" because they carried their produce hopefully in that direction; it was the arrow of their livelihood.

I saw more traders' stalls in a single hour on the road to Camelot than I had seen in my whole life before. I saw more cabbages and turnips, more beets and radishes, more eggs and carcasses than I had ever expected to see in a lifetime—and when I had studied the houses and the farms more carefully, I understood why. I understood that the human world was not a forest, with little clearings here and there where people tended a few cramped fields or grazed their animals in a narrow meadow. There were, to be sure, trees in the distance wherever there was rising ground—but alongside the road, there was something very different. Alongside the road, there was a long and gaudy ribbon of human society, of prosperity, of artifice, of order.

You would not have seen it that way. To you, it would have seemed dreary, primitive, coarse, chaotic—but you would have seen it through the lenses of industrial civilization, and this was the Dark Age, the long twilight of Roman culture and the bloody dawn of Saxon expansion. This was a moment poised on an edge, whose preservation would have been the salvation of British civilization and British history, instead of a precipitation into the near-oblivion of half-stifled legend.

I saw that. I don't say that I understood it, then, but I did see it, and knew enough to marvel at it even though I didn't know, as yet, what civilization and history were.

3

Merlin watched me as I studied the roadside. He guessed why my eyes were growing wider, and my brow more thoughtful.

"It's high summer," he told me. "Bellies are full; everything is plentiful; the day is warm. If every day were like this one, ruling the world would be an easy matter. In the depths of winter, when the ground is hard as iron, the cold seeps through the soles of the thickest boot. The road tempts marching men then, not hawkers and idlers."

"I don't like winter, Master," I agreed. "When the stores ran low, we used to yearn for spring—but there was always a while to wait before it replied to our yearning."

"The winters have been fairly mild, of late," he said. "The summer's bounty cuts both ways. The English Saxons have done well, and there are rumors of war in the distant east. More settlers will come, and more—and they will move west before they move north. Even the Welsh are thriving, waking up to the fact that the world beyond their borders has changed. It will soon be necessary to make allies of them, if they are not to become actively hostile. If that were not bad enough, what remains of Rome has embraced the Church; where once it sent forth legions, now it dispatches fishers of souls in almost equal quantity."

"Is that a bad thing, master?" I asked, a little hesitantly. I didn't know how deep the gulf might be that separated him from Mother Leocadia, and he had trusted her to look after me well enough to suit his own purposes.

"Not in itself," he answered, "but it is a complication. The King of the Britons must be everyone's king, or he is likely to be no one's. A realm in which tribes follow various gods is governable—but a realm in which one god's followers are bent on the obliteration of all others is a very different matter. In high summer, contentment is everywhere—but when winter comes, resentments harden like ice on still water."

"In Faerie, they say, it is always summer."

He scowled at that. "This is our world," he said, without confirming or denying the rumor. "This is our business, now. The past is gone, the future waits—and winter with it. That is where our hope must lie. I should have brought you a new suit, so that you might step into your new life and leave the rags of the old where they belong. And I should be quiet, while you look about you and learn—there'll be time enough to teach you what it means."

There was, indeed, time enough—especially when winter came and we spent long hours huddled over his little hearth, keeping the dark at bay with flickering candlelight. But Merlin never talked to me again in the kind and earnest way he did as we journeyed to Camelot. For a time, I thought that I must have disappointed him somehow, but now I realize that the summer sun had its effect on him too. His spirits were high that day he came to fetch me; for all his forebodings, he felt well in himself. He felt strong, although he was not; he felt that the flask of his youth was not yet emptied, although it was. He was on the road to the west, travelling hopefully with his produce. Once he was back in Camelot, I think it became clear to him that he had left it for the last time—that a prison door had closed behind him, locking him in.

On the road, I was his companion, a secret he had nursed for a dozen years, a seed planted long before and only now coming into flower. Once we were back in Camelot, however, I was the servant who brought him food and news, and carried away his chamber-pot. I was necessary to him, and he resented that. I was his eyes, his ears, his shadow... and he envied me all those faculties that he could no longer reserve to himself.

Had I known what was to come, I might have made more of the brief opportunity gifted to me by the summer sun, but I didn't. I looked about me, until I became bored with the end-lessness of the road, impatient to see Camelot. Boredom was a luxury of sorts, but it was not one I knew how to enjoy.

When dusk fell and we stopped for the night I was disappointed that we did not stay at an inn, but merely bedded down by the roadside. At least I got to sleep on the cart with my master, though, while the driver and the guardsman lay down on the bare ground.

I didn't expect to sleep so easily in such strange circumstances, given that I'd hardly done a stroke of work all day, but travelling is curiously exhausting, even when one sits upon a cart, and I was woken less than half a dozen times by unfamiliar noises.

On the second day of the journey I saw a nimble thief pursued by a stallholder, who couldn't catch him. I saw children screaming in frustration, in a way that I had never imagined it possible for anyone to scream who was not in mortal agony. I saw a knight ride by with silver mesh sparkling on his leather armor, with his squire staggering behind his horse, bowed down by the weight of the shield that bore his coat of arms, and a train of servants in livery. I saw men-at-arms with iron helmets and half-pikes, swollen with self-importance as they stood guard at a crossroads. I saw a goose-girl whose face was red and wet with tears because her flock was panicked by the crowds.

I broke fresh bread with my new master, and ate a slice of salted beef, and drank ale from a tankard. It was all new, all surprising... but in the end the newness of it all was overwhelming, and my capacity for surprise shriveled into near-indifference.

I longed to see Camelot. I wanted nothing except to arrive—but like the spring when winter supplies run low, Camelot was in no hurry to loom up on the horizon. The steady clop of the horses' hooves became irritating in its ponderousness, and I grudged them every pause they took for water and oats.

When the citadel finally appeared, though, my heart quickened again. It was visible from a long way off, although the hill on which it was built was certainly no mountain. Its towers were not quite as tall as I had imagined, nor its flags as gaudy, but it was built of paler stone than any of the fortified houses we had passed on the road. It was roseate in the glow of the descending sun, which hung above it as if in obedience to its overlord's command.

"There's your new home," Merlin said. "Will you like it, do you suppose?"

"It's the most glorious sight I've ever seen," I assured him. "To be any man's servant in such a place would be a privilege. To be yours, master... well, I'd rather be that than the king's."

"Arthur was my apprentice once," he said, mildly, "but I was always grooming him to be my master. I can't make you a similar promise—but I can say this. If you serve me well, you'll be Arthur's servant when I'm gone, and you'll be as vital to him as I am. Magician or not, you'll be his confidant. Remember that, whenever you think I'm using you cruelly. Only be patient, and you'll be the first servant in the nation."

He meant it, and it was true. If I'd stuck with him to the end, I'd have been the first servant in the nation, if there'd been a nation to be first servant in—but it wasn't long before began to dream of the Land of Light again. When Merlin used me cruelly, it was with thoughts of Faerie that I comforted myself, not thoughts of a better station in Camelot—but while its towers stood up high against that ruddy sky, radiant with health as we came towards it along the road to the west, I wanted nothing more than to be part of it, safely held within its fabulous stones, an aspect of its magnificent architecture. Weak though he obviously was in body, Merlin seemed a titanic schemer, a penetrating seer.

"This is all I have ever hoped for, master," I lied. "I shall never want anything more."

Part Two
Camelot

1

Four towers were visible from the road at first, all broader than I had expected and not as far apart, but their arrangement was not precisely square, nor were their heights identical—the contours of the hill had imposed their own imperatives. One of the towers was soon lost to view, however, being obscured by the other three as we came closer. The road which led to the castle steps ran northwards from the road to the west, which headed further on towards the sunset once Merlin's cart had turned aside.

There were hills to either side of the road hereabouts, and I saw other towers on their crests, but they were not the towers of castles—they were slender structures built from wood, bearing garlands of fluttering pennants

"Signaling towers," Merlin said when he saw me looking at them. "A castle needs early warnings as well as strong walls. The sentries in the nests can see for miles. They receive signals by coded flags from similar towers by day, and warning from beacon-fires by night."

"Which tower is yours, master?" I asked him, returning my gaze to Camelot.

"It's a slender one, not visible from here," he told me.

"The one that faces west?" I suggested, that being the one that I had briefly glimpsed before the others eclipsed it.

"No," he said. "Mine is the one that breaks the pattern. It's neither as wide nor as high as the ones that mark the corners. Its stairs are narrower." He did not add: "though not as narrow as the hidden ones you'll be treading in secret, nor as dark." The driver and the guardsman were not to be let in on that aspect of my service; nor was I, as yet.

"There must be a great many stairways in the citadel, Master," I observed, studying the steps that led up to the castle gate. I couldn't guess how many people lived in the castle, or how may more might flood into it were it ever besieged, but I could see how inconvenient it must be to carry everything its inhabitants might need up that stairway. The architecture might have been better designed, I thought, if carts could be driven through the gates—but I realized quickly enough that where carts could easily be driven, siege engines could easily be driven too.

"There are stairs a-plenty," Merlin agreed. "When I drew the plans for Camelot, I was a great believer in stone steps and spiral staircases. I was nimble then, and did not realize what a curse they would be to anyone old or infirm. I loved the idea of flights of steps, whether straight or spiraling. Even Roman roads must respect the lie of the land, but steps are roadways into prisoned space, which lift us from the earth into the sky. If only our legs did not become weak... I hope that you will learn to love stairways, Amory, for you'll have a miserable time in Camelot if you can't."

"Better stairways than rickety ladders, Master," I said. "In the convent's barns, the lofts had no stairs, nor guard-rails either. A boy once broke his leg in a fall, and died soon after. A mercy, Mother Leocadia said, for he'd have been a cripple. Sister Barbara tried to set the bone, but couldn't do it."

"It's skilled work," Merlin observed. "If you fall on my stairs, you'll be lucky not to shatter your head—but you'll never lack for a wall to brace yourself against."

I had to help him up the steps to Camelot's gate, although the burly man-at-arms would have been more use to him in such an open space. Mine was the duty, and mine the work. No one came down to greet him, although the castle steward, Sir Kay, was there to bid him a passing welcome. Kay was the first of the knights of the round table that I saw, and the one I saw more often than all the rest. He was always busy in the courtyard, directing the ceaseless flow of goods and containers in and out of the gate.

Merlin's tower was, as he had admitted, far slighter than the others. Nor was it really a "tower" at all, since it grew out of an intersection of two thick walls like some strange excrescence: a parasitic annex to the northernmost of the four main towers, the broadest of them all.

He was right about the stairway, though; it was very narrow indeed—unnecessarily so, it seemed to me, even taking the relative slenderness of the whole structure into account. It took us a long time to get up to Merlin's attic.

On first sight, the attic seemed sumptuous to me, and crammed with treasures—but I had nothing with which to compare it, having always known that the apartments in the convent were meager by any standards. I had never seen a bed before, and only one chair, so Merlin's were bound to seem sumptuous until I saw the knights' apartments. I had never seen curtains, wall-hangings or a carpet, and my experience of tables, shelves, trunks and screens was limited to ill-constructed objects that had been improvised rather than designed. What Merlin did have, however, that was not outshone by the possessions of his richer neighbors, was a very impressive collection of bottles, flasks, jars and mortars, mingled with all manner of implements and instruments whose functions I couldn't even begin to guess—and which only became clear to me by very slow degrees. He also had a shelf of what seemed to be quintessentially magical objects, including skeletons of birds, the skins of snakes, cloven geodes, seashells, pendulums, colored minerals and polished fragments of what looked like black glass—although I found out soon enough that they were as purely decorative as the embroidered hangings.

I was disappointed to be told that I was not to sleep at the foot of my master's bed, but in a hole of my own at the top of the stair: an alcove hollowed in the wall, with a shelf for a candle and no curtain, and a mattress whose complement of straw was much depleted.

"You'll get a new mattress as well as new clothes," Merlin promised. "My advantages won't seem so great when you've peeped into the rooms where others receive their visitors. The apartments of Camelot are said to be the richest in

64

Britain, and I worked as hard to give them that appearance as to give them that reputation. You'll understand why soon enough."

It was the simple truth. Every wall of every apartment in Arthur's citadel was hung with carpets, tapestries and embroideries of extraordinary beauty and complexity, and the rooms themselves were cleverly divided by carefully crafted screens. Guests placed in such well-decorated rooms were invariably delighted by the gaiety of the hangings and the artistry of the screens, as well as their remarkable capacity for quelling draughts. The knights and their ladies had long grown accustomed to their surroundings, and took less pleasure in them, but were grateful nevertheless for all the inbuilt finery.

The guests and the knights might have been a little less pleased, I suppose, had they known that the carpets and tapestries had more functions than the obvious, but all the builders who knew the secrets of the citadel were long gone by the time I arrived. When Merlin introduced me, little by little, to Camelot's hidden coverts and myriad spy-stations, I became one of a very select company indeed.

When Merlin supplied me with a new suit of clothes, the day after my arrival in the castle, he secured me a soft but very serviceable undershirt and a sturdy shirt to top it off, with two sets of comfortable hose. He also gave me a jerkin and a sleek pair of trousers, for more occasional wear. He wouldn't let me have a pair of boots, though. I was to have slippers like his, because slippers like that made no sound on secret stairs, provided their wearer was careful.

I learned quickly enough to be very careful indeed.

Merlin procured me a new mattress too, as he had promised, and instructed me to give the old one to the ragman. He obtained a broad-brimmed hat, and an overcoat—even though I would not need the latter item for at least two months—and a fine sturdy belt with a capacious leather pouch. He gave me a candle-tray of my own, and a knife of my own, and a box for spells and tapers, and a copy of his signet ring to wear at all times, as a badge of my station as his designated deputy in matters of commerce and law.

For the first time in my life, I had property. I was a man of substance. More than that: as Merlin's servant, and Merlin's apprentice, I had a position in the castle that was higher than those of two hundred lesser servants. For every man and woman entitled to command me, it seemed, there were two that I was fully entitled to command! The Sisters of Saint Syncletica had taught me calculation well enough to realize soon enough that the ratio was somewhat less favorable than it seemed, but the vast majority of those who were entitled to command me never deigned to notice my existence—while I, for my own part, was ever ready to notice every last one of those I was entitled to command.

It wasn't so easy in practice, of course. The circumstances in which I was fully entitled to command the humbler castle servants were exceedingly limited, and the servants in question were very skilled in the art of making excuses, so the power I had in theory usually melted away in actuality—but that was not the point. The point was that I had a presence in the little world of Camelot that I had never had in the Convent of Saint Syncletica, not merely as Merlin's shadow in the walls, spying on anyone and everyone, but as myself, in the open, where everyone could see who deigned to do so.

I was no longer a boy, but a man. I was no longer a rejected changeling, but a person with a place of his own, in the greatest citadel that legend had ever known.

I was still the devil's child, of course, because Merlin was widely reckoned as the devil's favorite instrument—and not just by Christians, by any means—but even that was a considerable advantage. A devil's child is an inconvenient thing to be when the devil's empire is so far away that he might not even exist, but when the devil's favorite instrument is close at hand, and court magician to the King of the Britons, there's a great deal to be said for being under his wing.

Can you imagine how happy I was, during those first months in Camelot, in spite of my master's rapidly worsening temper? I doubt it. I was, after all, merely a servant—and that's a rather pitiful thing, in your reckoning. I slept on a straw mattress in a hole in a wall, and commanded almost no one, in spite of my apparent right to do so. What a miserable wretch I would have seemed to you!

In my world, though, I was as near to glorious success as a thousand men in every thousand-and-one could ever hope to be, and even you must catch your breath a little at the thought that I was in Camelot, knowing more of Merlin and the knights of the round table, at that particular moment in time, than any other man alive. Admittedly, the moment escaped the lax grip of history, and slipped into the mercurial dust of legend—but I'm returning it as I write, am I not? I'm bringing it back into the light of print—and who else could do that but me?

Who else, even if he had followed Morgana into Cokaygne, as I did, and followed Tom Rhymer into the Dark Land, as I did, could have brought back to history all the secrets that I and I alone obtained? Tom's with me still, but he'll never write a book like this, because he was never in Camelot. I wasn't only in Camelot but within Camelot; its secret passages were my true home. I spied on Kay of Lancaster and Lancelot du Lac, Gawain and Gareth of the Isles, Bors of Falmer and Sagramore of Dunwich. I even spied on Arthur and Guinevere, although the station looking into their marital chamber was one that Merlin reserved entirely to himself—unwisely, so it turned out, given that the one secret we were slow to penetrate, and were never able to address, was Arthur's deepening anxiety about his marriage. They hadn't been married very long when I arrived in Camelot—four years, I think—and the servants had enough goodwill towards them not to sharpen their gossip overmuch, so the extent of Arthur's private humiliation never became evident in public, even to me. Everything else, however, was mine to find out, and I delighted in the opportunity.

I was happier to be in Camelot, for the remainder of that summer, than I ever was again—even when I lived in the Land of Light, where misery is an exile, or the Dark Land, where sublimity replaces beauty, or when I first came here, flush with magic, and began to understand the kind of world into which I had come.

Then autumn came, and winter, and Merlin became more oppressive and more irritating with every day that passed. When summer came again, I was still reasonably content, but I wasn't as happy as I had been before... and when winter came a second time, the last vestiges of my happiness froze in the northerly wind.

2

I thought at first that only Merlin and Arthur knew the true extent of Camelot's secret passages, until I learned them too—but I deduced before that first autumn faded away that even Arthur did not know their true extent.

The King of the Britons knew that the hangings in every single one of his guest-rooms were so contrived as to conceal narrow coverts in the walls, or to mask holes through which inquisitive eyes might peer and inquisitive ears catch whispers, but he didn't know how many peepholes there were into his knights' apartments, let alone his own, nor how they might be reached.

Arthur had spies of his own, whose paths occasionally crossed mine as we jostled for space in the castle's secret ways, but there were passages that Arthur's spies did not know and would never have found, no matter how hard they searched. There was good reason for the fact that Merlin's "tower" was packed into a corner where thick walls intersected, and why its own stairs were even narrower than the slenderness of the structure required them to be.

I wasn't let into these intimate secrets quickly, and can't be certain even now that I was let into them all—but one thing of which I'm sure is that I soon had sole access to a few coins of vantage that Merlin could no longer reach, and thus had powers of discovery that were mine and mine alone.

Throughout the first half-year of my service, Merlin usually went with me into the secret corridors he had constructed. Sometimes, when he was sure that the glimmer could not give us away, he even let me bring a candle to light our way. On such expeditions he would pause at every peephole and every listening-post, and comment on its usefulness.

"Here is the armory," he might say. "Armoires learn a good deal about the men they fit out—not as much as body-servants but more than food-servers. It's no use listening while noblemen are making inspection of their wares, but when the noblemen have gone again their tongues flap like pennants in a gale."

Alas, I was never much interested in armourers. I took more heed when he said such things as: "Here is Gawain's reception-room, which is the most important after Arthur's, no matter what Lancelot might think. Lancelot is a stray from Less Britain, which is really part of Gaul, but Gawain is an English Briton through and through. He has far better blood than Arthur could ever claim, even with my lies to aid him. Gawain's loyalty is worth more to Arthur's throne than a dozen errant heroes come to lend a little glamour, or a hundred petty Percevals ambitious to reclaim what they consider their fallen families' due. When Gawain dictates letters to a scribe, you must listen to what he says. When he receives a messenger, you must listen to what he hears. When he converses with a visitor—even a woman—you must listen to their chitchat."

That was how I was introduced to the knights of the round table, one by one, over the space of a year. Four out of five of them I saw for the first time through one of Merlin's peepholes, and never saw at close range in any other place. I saw them in their finest clothes and in their nightshirts. I saw them posing, and I saw them drop their poses. I saw them with their wives and I saw them with their serving-maids. The only part of them I saw but rarely was the part they liked to parade before the world: the part that bore arms; the part that pretended to be a hero.

I went to the tourneys like everyone else, but precisely because everyone else was there and I was a servant of relatively small stature, I saw hardly anything at all. I knew when a favorite unhorsed a rival because I heard the crowd gasp in delight. I knew when a less accomplished warrior took a tumble because I heard the crowd jeer. In all my time in Camelot, though, I never got close enough to the front to see the clever thrust that did the work. I Heard the twang of bowstrings during contests of archery, but I never saw the arrows hit the targets.

I never saw the knights of the round table practicing swordsmanship in the open, although I saw common men being drilled with swords and bows whenever I stepped into the open air. On the other hand, I did see them practicing alone, thrusting at shadows. The one thing I can say for sure about knightly prowess in combat is this: every knight that ever took a seat at Arthur's table looked exceptionally elegant when he was thrusting at an invisible opponent, and never lost a duel against a figment of his own imagination. In fairness, though, I never saw Lancelot fencing with shadows; I had no reason while I was in Camelot to doubt that he deserved his reputation as the finest swordsman, archer and lance-wielder in the kingdom—but he was far younger then than he was when I finally saw him in action at perilously close range.

I had not been three months in Merlin's employ before I began to think that I knew Arthur's knights better than Arthur did—perhaps better than anyone did. My knowledge seemed all the more delicious because it was entirely one-sided. They never saw me at all; they didn't even know that I existed. I lived three parts of every day like a rat scampering through the partitions of Camelot's walls, wedged into narrow and pitch-black crevices, with my eyes pressed to holes no bigger than a gimlet might make—but even when I left that world within the world and stepped out into the light, I was invisible to the knights of the round table. They hardly ever saw me, because I was beneath their notice.

Even when I had messages to deliver to their faces, and replies to collect, the knights of the round table didn't see me. Although mine was the voice that spoke the words, they only heard the messages. The knights of Camelot listened to Merlin when I spoke to them, and replied to Merlin when I waited to hear their replies. If I had occasion to return again to their presence with further intelligence, after an absence of an hour, they stared at me blankly, until I reminded them that I was Merlin's apprentice, the bearer of his news and his ring. They were knights, after all; I was an instrument without individuality, like one of your telephones or post-it notes.

There were only two exceptions to this general rule. One was Kay, the steward, who counted all the castle servants as part of his own stock, and kept track of them accordingly. The other, strangely enough, was the king himself.

I was sent to carry messages to Arthur long before Merlin deigned to show me how to spy on him, but rarely. It wasn't necessary to go very often, because the two of them met so frequently on a regular basis. Arthur was the only nobleman who ever came to Merlin's apartment, more often than not by a secret corridor. Perhaps it was the fact that he passed my alcove so frequently, on clandestine errands of his own, that made the difference in the way Arthur regarded me, although I was never allowed to be in the room when he and Merlin talked.

I only had to remind King Arthur twice that I was Merlin's new apprentice before he learned my face—and I only appeared before him twice more before he spoke to me as myself, and not as Merlin's ear. But I rarely had occasion to approach him on a formal basis, and months passed between the few messages I had to deliver. It wasn't until my second year in Camelot was about to begin that his appearances in Merlin's apartments became rarer, forcing Merlin to send me to him more frequently—and it was on one such occasion that he broke protocol by speaking to me confidentially, almost as if I had already acquired Merlin's status.

He was in his council chamber when he did it, surrounded by his courtiers. The round table was in the council chamber, but that was where he sat to confer with his knights, maintaining the illusion that he was the first among equals. In order to address the petitions of common folk, and to judge their disputes, he placed himself on the Seat of Judgment: a throne in all but name, stationed against the most extravagantly decorated wall of the chamber, beneath the place where Excalibur was mounted. Although he sometimes wore the elvish sword that he had pulled from the stone on ceremonial occasions, and used it for the initiation of new knights to the Order of the Round Table, it was usually set above the Seat of Judgment, as a symbol of his authority. So far as I know, it was never used in combat in the human world.

On days when Arthur occupied the Seat of Judgment he did so from noon until the day's business was complete, and messengers had to wait their turn. On the occasion when he spoke to me, I had to wait for much longer than usual, although I didn't mind at all. The message seemed trivial—Merlin had received a letter from an agent in the ranks of the Bardic Order, concerning the plans and projects of one Taliesin, who might soon become a useful friend—so there was no reason for impatience, and I was always glad to observe the operations of the court from a comfortable position. The room emptied once the last formal petition had been heard, save for two guardsmen, two ushers and two of Arthur's personal servants. Arthur seemed very tired, and I couldn't have blamed him for regarding me sourly as I finally stepped forward to take up a few more minutes of his time, but the expression in his face as he looked down at me was apologetic; he knew how long I had been waiting. He heard me out, and thanked me. Then he said: "Do you have any other name but Amory?"

I was struck dumb by astonishment. He waited for my reply. The King of the Britons actually waited for me to say "son of..." and give my father's name. No commoner had ever done that.

"I have no other, your majesty," I finally admitted. I must have blushed scarlet, for it was tantamount to confessing that I was fatherless, devoid of family: an item of human jetsam even among my own kind.

Arthur nodded his head, fingered his neatly trimmed beard, and glanced around the room. There were only six people present, only one or two of whom had taken the trouble to listen surreptitiously to the message I had come to deliver, and even they wouldn't have bothered to listen further when they heard that it only concerned the Welsh. Even so, the King of the Britons, leaned a little closer, and lowered his voice to a whisper as he spoke to me from above, so that no one else might hear what he said to me.

"Nor have I, Amory," he murmured. "Nor have I."

Then he straightened up again, and said in a voice that could be heard in every corner of the room: "Thank Merlin for his news, Amory. Tell him that I will call on him, and bring a scribe, that we may send a polite greeting to this Taliesin, and assure him of our friendship if he will assure us of his in return."

When I turned away, I was so confused by what had happened that I almost bumped into Sir Lancelot, who was just coming into the room on some errand of his own. You, I suppose, would say that he almost bumped into me, but it's a servant's duty to avoid such collisions, and my reaction was belated. My upper arm brushed his elbow as I tried to escape the contact.

Lancelot might have glanced at me then, and kicked me half across the room with his polished boot, but he didn't. To anyone else, it would have seemed that he was exercising generosity, extending courtesy to an inferior by way of condescension, but I saw the flicker of his gaze. I saw him look at his elbow, to see whether any dirt had come off my sleeve on to his. I saw that his first concern—his one and only concern—was with the possibility of contamination.

You'll probably think it remarkable that there was none. You know that I had but one full suit of clothes, and that I

73

spent my life scurrying through dark and narrow corridors. You must have assumed that I was filthy. In fact, the nooks and crannies into which I squeezed myself were far less dusty than you might imagine. The stones of Camelot were very solid, and such mortar as was used to seal them did not easily crumble. The intervals between them were virtually lifeless, devoid of spiders' webs and rats' nests. Much of your dust is the residue of human skin and human hair, but there was very little of that in Merlin's secret world. My work wasn't as filthy as you might think—and although I had but the one shirt, it didn't go long unlaundered, any more than my hands and face went long unwashed.

There was no contamination. Lancelot's sleeve was unsmeared—and once he had taken note of that, the incident became utterly unimportant, not worth the trouble of a kick or a cuff—either of which might have had the result that he was trying to avoid.

I had never liked Lancelot, but that insignificant incident made me like him even less. Everyone else liked him, because he was a great warrior, tall and handsome, and very charming among his own kind, but I never did.

3

When I took the king's reply to Merlin I didn't tell him that Arthur had asked me my father's name, or what he had said to me when I told him I had none.

That night, there was singing and dancing in the hall. There was a whole company of musicians, with drums and pipes and stringed instruments I couldn't name. The balladeers took turns with courtiers who had party pieces to perform— mostly comedy turns, given the rough quality of their voices. I had been pressed to service at dinner, but once the meal was cleared I was free to watch, and that I did. For once, I was not crammed into a cavity or crouched behind a tapestry; I stood with other gawkers in a shadowed gallery, easily visible to anyone who cared to look up. None did.

I had no commission from Merlin. I was free to watch the singers and musicians, or admire the ladies in their gowns, or follow the steps of the dances. I could have relaxed, and let my eyes rest, not watching in any meaningful sense at all. Instead, I watched Lancelot, with the keen eye of a practiced spy.

Why? I don't know. He had done me no harm, and had in fact refrained from doing harm when he might have. It would have been more understandable had I watched the king, admiringly—but I watched Lancelot, alert for any slip, any secret, anything to his discredit.

I had seen him alone in his apartments, but only in passing. Merlin was not much interested in him, for he had no spies or correspondents, no dubious friends or shady schemes. In private, Lancelot had always seemed relaxed, more comfortable with himself than most of the others who had seats at the round table. I had no reason whatsoever to expect that I would see something while he was in a crowd, wearing his public face, in the yellow glare of two hundred candles.

I didn't know then how remarkable it was that I could track Lancelot's gaze so easily, at such a distance. I had always assumed that everyone could see as well as I. It wasn't until I arrived in your world, and saw spectacles for the first time, that I realized how very variable the quality of human sight is, and how exceptional my own keen vision must have been in a world without any but the crudest lenses. Merlin knew, I suppose; he had checked my sight the second time he came to see me, just as he had checked my girth, although he had not made it obvious what he was doing—but I doubt that even Merlin knew how keen my sight really was. Perhaps it was a gift of nature, perhaps the last lingering legacy of my first adventure in Cokaygne.

Either way, I thought nothing of the fact that I could track Lancelot's gaze from the other side of a long room, looking down from a gallery. It was not unusual to me. Nor was it unusual to me that I could read the intent of his eyes just as easily as I had read the meaning of his gaze when he looked down at the elbow he had brushed against my upper arm.

He looked about him as any man might. Unlike me, he looked at the singers as they performed, the dancers as they twirled, the knights with whom he conversed. He admired the ladies in their finery, one by one and each in turn. He wasn't a man preoccupied, let alone a man possessed. It's conceivable—perhaps even probable—that he wasn't consciously aware of the pattern of his glances, or of anything therein that might betray him.

I saw, though, that he looked more often than he might have done at the queen, and that whenever he looked at her his gaze lingered longer than it might have done, especially when it happened that she met his gaze. It always seemed, perhaps even to him, that their gazes met by accident—but I wondered as I watched whether there might be an intelligence in our eyes that precedes the intelligence of our thoughts, and leads us on before we know it.

I watched Lancelot's eyes catch and hold the queen's— and I watched him caught and held in his turn, never for long, but repeatedly, again and again and again, as if their little accidents were marking time more accurately than any burning candle or beating heart.

I disliked Lancelot, but I wasn't deceived by that dislike into thinking him more responsible for what was happening than he was. Guinevere was the angler, he the fish. Guinevere was the opportunist, he the opportunity. He was a victim, but he was ready to be one, and willing to be one. I watched as he was seduced, and watched him glory in his seduction.

You might think that any man might have done the same; Guinevere, after all, had the reputation of being the most beautiful woman in the land, and I had seen none, even in Camelot, to challenge that reputation. She was, however, the queen. Even if Arthur was disappointed in her—and I didn't know, at the time, that he was—she was the queen. Lancelot could and should have lowered his eyes.

When I was certain of what was happening, I began to measure Lancelot in a different way. It wasn't easy. I had grown up among women, but I had always been a stranger. The Sisters of Saint Syncletica were by no means immune to passion but I had never learned to place myself, imaginatively, in their shoes. Everything I knew about the affections and desires of women I had learned in a matter of twelve months, as a spy in Camelot's walls, and it was little enough—but I knew enough to understand why Lancelot was reckoned an unusually attractive man by the castle's serving-women, and why the voices of the ladies of the court changed slightly when they spoke of him. It wasn't so much that he was taller than the average, with a clearer face, nor that his voice was accented with a pretty purr, nor even that he moved with a grace and style that few of his peers could duplicate. It was his mastery of expression that gave him power over he admiration of others: his way of making manifest his pride, his affection, his generosity. He was easily readable—which is not at all the same thing as being honest.

In that, he stood in total contrast with King Arthur. Arthur was as tall as Lancelot, and although his face was by no means as clear it was neatly formed. Arthur had brighter eyes, blue-grey instead of dark brown, but they were not nearly as expressive. When Arthur moved, he was far from graceless, but he was more economical in his movements than Lancelot, and more reserved. Arthur was a hidden man—which is certainly not to say that he was anything less than honest, but merely that he was not at all obvious.

None of that was a fault, or a disadvantage, especially in a king—but when I paused in watching Lancelot to study Guinevere more closely, I soon deduced that Guinevere saw in Lancelot a very welcome contrast to her husband. I realized that Guinevere had become detached from her husband, not because she had tired of him—although he had doubtless become familiar in four years—but because she felt that she had never been attached as closely as she might.

Perhaps I ought to emphasize that no one married "for love" in those days, as you pretend to do. They didn't do anything else "for love" either, if they could help it. They recognized the possibility of reckless infatuation, but they considered it a kind of madness: a disease dangerous to social order, to be avoided or ignored if at all possible. They were more successful in that than you can probably imagine, given that you have a very different attitude—but they were human, as you are. They knew their duty, but couldn't always keep it. They tried to do their duty, but couldn't always contrive it. They knew the cost of failing in their duty, but sometimes had to pay it.

It wasn't like that for Guinevere and Lancelot. They were fully conscious of what they were doing as they looked at one another—and fully conscious, too, of what they might do. They were not being borne away by any kind of irresistible force. They were making a choice.

On the evening of the day that Lancelot's elbow brushed my sleeve, I saw into his mind, and knew, at least as well as he, how fragile his determination was to keep the pledge of allegiance he had given Arthur in every last one of its details. And I saw, too, that Guinevere was ready and willing to take advantage of his weakness.

4

Looking back now, with the advantage of centuries, I can't say that the knights of the round table were better men than most. On the other hand, I won't say that they were bad men either. A spy never sees a man at his best, and shouldn't be too contemptuous of the failings that all men have. The knights of the round table were certainly no more spiteful than their captains or their armourers, and no more licentious than their stewards or their grooms. If they were vain and haughty, and envious of one another, it was because they could hardly avoid such attitudes—and if they were sometimes cruel, it was because they lived in a world where cruelty was common-place.

Gawain was the best of them, in my opinion. He understood the wisdom of what Merlin had done in putting a king in place who had no land of his own, no family feuds to continue, and no connections to favor: the kind of king who could take his place at a round table, requiring no place of privilege, making honest judgments as best he could. Gawain was prepared to do his utmost to protect that order, and to defend it against any threat from within or without. In that purpose, he could count on the active assistance of two brothers and four cousins, and also of Kay and half a dozen more—not quite a clear majority around the famous table, but clear enough in the absence of manifest opposition.

What opposition there was to Arthur's rule was by no means manifest in the first year that I was in Camelot. What opposition there was, in fact, seemed to be directed at Gawain and his clique rather than the king, and may well have been continuing disputes and resentments that went back to Roman times and beyond. What I was slow to realize, however, during the long months when Merlin patiently showed me the secret stairs in the western tower and the southern keep, the kitchens and the cellars and the ladies' tapestry-room, was how fragile a man King Arthur was. I never saw Arthur in private conference with anyone except my master, nor did I ever see Arthur in his nightshirt, nor alone with Guinevere; those peepholes Merlin reserved to himself.

Once I had seen Lancelot exchanging excessive glances with Guinevere, however, I took care to observe the queen whenever I could—and since I could not look at her in private, I watched her in public, in the throne-room and the tapestry-room, the ballroom and the gardens. I might have fallen in love with her myself, keeping watch on her with such concentration, but if I had I would simply have waited for the madness to pass. I didn't. I decided, on due reflection, that I liked Guinevere even less than I liked Lancelot, for all her prettiness. She was even more vain than he, and haughtier. She loved being the queen of the Britons more than she loved being Arthur's wife—and was, I think, contemptuous of Arthur's less-than-noble birth. She was a true aristocrat, from top to toe, and knew her worth as a symbol of Arthur's authority too well to concede him much authority over herself.

She didn't seem to care at all that she had been married four years without bearing a child. She had no desire to nurse an infant, and no particular interest in ensuring the succession to the throne of Camelot. She would even tolerate mention of Mordred within her hearing, which few others would do. Mordred had come to Camelot long before I arrived, claiming kinship with Arthur, and had not been kindly received. Perhaps his claim was true, and he really was related to the supposedly kinless king, and perhaps not—but in either case, he had badly misjudged the likely attitude of Camelot to his claim. He had been banished, although rumor had it that he had gone no further than the Saxon lands, and few people dared speak his name in the castle. Guinevere was the exception—but I don't think she did it to annoy Arthur. If she sought to annoy anyone, it was Merlin, whose influence over Arthur she resented. She had not known the wizard when he still had magic enough to terrify, and rarely lost an opportunity to disparage him to the ladies of the court.

In spite of her waspish manners, though, Guinevere was widely liked. She was beautiful, and she was very feminine; her smile was infectious. It wasn't the delightful quality of her smile that caused me to watch her so closely, though, nor even the conviction that my vigilance was vital to the future of Camelot. It was, I suppose, the simple triumph of discovery. The detection of Guinevere's determined passion for Lancelot, and his willingness to return it, was the first real secret that my spying had uncovered.

Alas, it was not so easy to persuade my master that I had made the calculation right. He had tested my sight and my wits when he had visited me in the convent when I was seven years old, but the standards he had set were lower than the ones I was now beginning to set for myself.

"You're just a boy, after all," Merlin said, when I laid my evidence before him as explicitly as I could. "How can you read a woman's eyes? A queen's eyes! You're a fool to imagine such things, and a knave to waste my time with them when I have Taliesin's reinvigorated Bardic Order to think about, and the Abbot of Glastonbury pestering me, and the Saxons always lurking in the east!"

My second autumn in Camelot was well advanced by then, and the weather had turned cold long before the winter snows were due. Merlin's temper had shortened with the days. He seemed to find it difficult to keep warm, no matter how I stoked up his fire or swathed him in coats and blankets. What horrified him more than anything else, I think, was the possibility that he would have to go creeping through the lightless corridors himself, up and down stairs so narrow that he would have to stand sideways to drag himself through the narrowest gaps, to press himself between slabs of increasingly icy stone... perhaps only to discover, after weeks of careful investigation, that I had merely made a mistake.

"Do you think, master, that because I was raised in a convent, I know nothing of female lust?" I asked him, although it wasn't such an absurdity as I tried to make it seem. "Well, perhaps I knew less than I should, sixteen months ago. It's only now, looking back, that I can understand words I heard spoken then, and gestures made. But you know what an education I have had since I came to Camelot. I've kept watch on Lancelot, as well as many others, on your instruction, and I've kept watch on the Lady Enid and the Lady Vivien. I'm not a fool any longer, if I ever was."

"Have you seen them kiss or caress? I do not mean a polite peck on the glove—I mean a kiss, or something like."

"I don't say that they've kissed, as yet," I told him, "let alone anything more—but I do say that if and when they do kiss, neither of them will want to stop at that. Already, when they meet in the courtyard or on the dance-floor, there's a definite hesitation, a lingering exchange of hungry glances. It will be deep midwinter soon enough, master—there will be no tourneys, no fairs, no expeditions for any purpose but necessity and the hunt, and knights don't seem to like hunting in dreary weather. We'll all be cooped up, and the amusements of the great hall are more likely to draw them closer together than distract them, even when Arthur is present, as he cannot always be."

"If this is an invention of your fevered brain, you wretched changeling..."

"If it is, then I'm sorry, master—but I know that you would not have me hold my tongue for fear that you might think I have made a mistake, when I'm certain in my own mind."

He had to nod at that. I poked the fire, and sighed at the thought of fetching more firewood, and arguing with the custodian of the store. We needed more water, too—although I could probably have collected all we needed simply by hanging a bucket out of the attic's narrow window every morning and every night.

"If you're right," he murmured. "Then we must do our utmost to prevent it. This is worse than Glastonbury's machinations, and worse than the sum of all the rogues and hoarders who'll try to hold the castle to ransom for its supplies when the frosts come."

"Is it really so difficult, master?" I asked. "Lancelot is a foreigner, after all. Would it matter if a whisper in the king's ear led to his being sent away? That's what needs to be done, isn't it? And you do have the king's ear."

"If only it were as simple as that," Merlin complained. "Yes, if the possibility were real, even if it were less than certain, then Lancelot should go, and quickly. If he could only be persuaded to go of his own accord..."

"I doubt that he would do that, master," I said,

"So do I," Merlin agreed, his voice sour as well as hoarse.

"The king could invent a mission for him easily enough," I pointed out. "Which is to say, that you could, on the king's behalf."

"I could easily invent one," Merlin agreed, "but persuading the king that the invention was a good one is a different matter." His sour tone told me that I was a fool to think that the king might be easily convinced to send Sir Lancelot away, without a very good reason. Given that Merlin couldn't possibly tell him the true reason, he would have to invent a false one—but if Arthur realized that it was false...

I began to see why the matter was not as simple as I had hoped.

5

In the days that followed, I pursued the question further. Once Merlin had been convinced by my insistence that I was right, he encouraged me to do so, although he became increasingly irritated by the awkwardness of the problem.

"It shouldn't matter that Lancelot stands so high in Arthur's favor, master," I said, when his annoyance became infectious. "Can't you invent an errand that only a trusted man could do—something so delicate as to require a friend as well as a hero?"

"I can invent the errand and suggest the hero," Merlin said, "but the king has been the king too long to be as pliable as once he was—and of all the people that dislike me, there is only one who dislikes me more than Lancelot does."

There was no one he could possibly mean but Guinevere.

"Well," I said, "if Arthur is blind to his friend's faults, perhaps he deserves to be cuckolded. I dare say they'll be exceedingly discreet. The king need never know."

It was a reckless thing to say, although I didn't understand quite how reckless it was. Merlin threw his walking-stick as if it were a spear, and caught me painfully on the thigh. "Imbecile!" he cried. "Cretin! Idiot child! Bring me back my stick!"

When I brought it back to him, he used it as a club, and beat me across the shoulders before I could retreat out of range.

I didn't apologize, nor did I protest. I waited for an explanation—and watched while I waited, to see if I could read the reason for his anger while his guard was down. I couldn't. Merlin wasn't a readable man; he was more securely hidden than Arthur.

"The one thing Arthur must have, if he is to keep his crown indefinitely, is universal respect," the wizard croaked, eventually, drawing his disordered blankets more tightly around him and clutching at the collar of his coat. "He has no land and he has no family, and no one believes any longer that he has powerful magic at his disposal, or the good will of Elfland. Only a man such as he could have united the quarrelsome factions, and I doubt that he could have done it by any other means than the theatrical, but all that was a long time ago. Now, there are threats from without as well as within, and the threat within is far more subtle than any common treason. If Arthur loses his reputation for perfection, no matter how, the balance of power will tip all the sooner. And that is not to take count of Arthur's response, if he ever finds out that his wife has seduced the man he counts his closest friend."

"But if Arthur exiled Lancelot before anything could happen..." I began.

I was interrupted. "Exile, you say! Away, away with him! Yes, of course, if that could be contrived... but you do not know what Arthur is. I do, because I made him. If he found out that Guinevere and Lancelot... even before they had exchanged a kiss, if he were certain of the intention... well, it would take more than my diplomacy to calm him, even if I were still in my prime. And if someone else found out before him, and the rumor ran around before it reached his ear, that would be ten times worse. The moment anyone finds out..."

He paused to cough and spit, then took several deep breaths before continuing, having moved on a little in his thoughts in the meantime. He was speaking as much to himself as to me. "I have made him very sensitive to the notion of honor," he whispered, "and he thinks of Lancelot as a man of honor. Perhaps he's as big a fool as you are, but I cannot blame him for becoming so fond of a stranger, when he must be so careful in the treatment of all his nearer subjects. He thinks himself an outsider, exactly like Lancelot... and he is an outsider, for no one but an outsider could have done what he has done, with my hand to guide him. If only..."

He stopped. I remembered what Arthur had said to me when he had asked if I had another name, and believed that I understood why he had said it. I waited for Merlin to continue, but this time he hadn't paused to cough or clear his throat. I had to prompt him.

"If only what, master?" I said.

"If only he were not afraid of me, Amory," he said, softly, after a minute's hesitation. "If only he were prepared to make a friend of me."

"I thought..."

"You never thought, imbecile! Never!" His voice was loud again now, but he could not shout as Kay or Gawain might have shouted; his wrath exploded in a screech, like some kind of mad bird.

I waited for him to calm down—and then I waited for him to speak. Eventually, he said: "I was an outsider too, but I came from another world. He was my apprentice before I made him a king, and he was always in awe of me. He still is—and he's never been able to bring himself to count me a friend. He wanted a friend more like himself: a man of breeding and ambition, but no home; a man with charm and natural authority, but no immediate kin or ready-made household. He sees himself reflected in Lancelot, a little more clearly than he sees himself—and Lancelot, alas, sees himself reflected in Arthur, a little less clearly than he sees himself. They are so alike that they might destroy one another...but not so alike that Lancelot would exert himself to the utmost to prevent it happening. If you still pray, Amory, pray that this silly infatuation is an illusion that will wear off before it becomes damaging— or that I can a find a way to slow its progress until one or other of them finds another distraction. If we are forced, in the end, to get rid of Lancelot, we must be careful to see that the break is clean. If he were to go to Mordred..."

"Is Mordred so dangerous, master?" I asked, quietly.

"In himself, no. As a Saxon pawn, perhaps. At present, the Saxons want to maintain peace between their land and ours; they're not disposed to question Arthur's claim to be king of the Britons, or the implication that he is therefore king of all Britain. But they haven't killed their as-yet-unwanted guest, nor are they likely to. And their kinsfolk keep coming, fleeing the front where Rome's last fragment is clinging to the vestiges of empire. If only I still had Morgana's ear! An elvish archer, a single subtle shot! The assassin would be back in Faerie before the Saxons knew that their guest was dead. And the Saxons respect the fair folk—they're not like churchmen. They'd simply bow their heads and accept the judgment of the Other World."

"And would she also send an archer to put an elf-bolt in Lancelot's back for you, master?" I asked him. "If you were to ask her as a friend, that is."

He made as if to throw the stick again, but desisted. "She was never my friend, imbecile," he muttered. "She was never anyone's friend. But she has her own ideas, her own preferences, and while she thought that her aims and mine were in concert..."

He stopped again. He really was an exceedingly annoying old man.

"But she doesn't think so now, master?" I prompted him. He wanted to be prompted. Perhaps he would tell himself, later, that he was testing me, but he wasn't. He was a cold and lonely old man, with winter looming, and I was the only company left to him, except for Arthur's occasional visits. If he didn't talk to me, he could easily pass a day without talking to anyone.

"No one knows what she thinks," he murmured. "She hasn't been seen in these parts for as many years as you've been alive. But if she keeps watch on our world, she probably believes that I betrayed her—that I obtained her help under false pretences."

"Did you, master?"

"Of course I did! Do you think I could have obtained it by honesty?"

"I don't know, master," I reminded him. "You've never told me how you fared in Faerie, or why you came back, or how you persuaded Morgana to help Arthur to the throne. Since that day we rode along the road to the west in your cart, you've been occupied with more immediate matters."

"While you, I suppose, are still brooding about your own expulsion from the land of Cokaygne?"

"No, master," I said, dutifully. "I put it out of my mind."

"Good—except that, had you only been old enough to sit up and take notice, you might have a better idea than I of Morgana's opinion of the realm I've carved out here. As things are... I do not think that she would be altogether pleased with me. I can only hope that she cannot care sufficiently to do anything about it—but she is not an Arthur or a Lancelot—she knows that she has only to distract herself for a little while and we shall all be dead and gone. The fair folk are not as petty as we are. And she owed me something, I think, for what I was to her."

I had been thinking hard while he said all this, and was ready with a guess. "You told her that you would make something of Arthur's kingdom that would please her," I said, "but it was a lie. You only intended to make something of it that would please you."

This time, he did throw the stick, and accurately too. I howled in pain.

"Idiot!" he screeched. "Miserable cretin! Do you think I have no higher motive in all this but to please myself? Do you think I returned from the land of peace and tranquillity to this vale of trouble and tears to satisfy a whim? You probably think Lancelot is a fine fellow, then, and a true hero! You probably think Mother Leocadia a potential saint, and yourself a potential magician. Have you not realized yet that I am trying to save the world?"

From what? I would have said, had I not been hurt so annoyingly. From the Saxons? The Welsh? The Church?

I know now, of course, from what he was trying to save the world: from chaos; from the Dark Age; from the reversal of progress. I might have known then, had I only cared to ask myself the question more seriously, but I resented his manner. At that particular moment, he was merely the man who beat me with his stick and called me fool, and I had not wit enough to do anything but strike back at him with mockery in the silence of my private thoughts.

6

Merlin did set out, very earnestly, to find ways of keeping Lancelot and Guinevere apart when winter set in. They had to be small things, which could only be temporary solutions, but that was all he could do without showing his hand. He couldn't ask Arthur to send Lancelot as an emissary to Gaul or Cornwall without making a convincing case for the appointment. He had to maintain the impression that he was merely making trivial suggestions, of no real significance.

I didn't dare to repeat my suggestion that what Merlin had suggested as a fate for Mordred might also be applicable to Lancelot. Even if Merlin had been able to send me through the gate of Avalon to ask his former friend Morgana for the gift of an elvish assassin, I doubt that he would have done it, even to get rid of Mordred. It would not have been a wise move even if he had been unscrupulous—success would have required not merely that the intended victim would be dead, but that the assassin would escape and that there would be no further repercussions of the bargain—but Merlin had his scruples, no matter how devious his methods might be.

I had scruples too. I would have been reluctant indeed to undertake a mission to procure an assassin, let alone to play the assassin myself by slipping poison into someone's cup.

Although the Sisters of Saint Syncletica had labored long and hard to persuade me that lying was sinful and would exclude me from resurrection in the Kingdom of God, it had never occurred to me to take the judgment or the promise at all seriously—but the commandment against murder had always seemed a very different thing. Even if Lancelot weren't such a fine fellow as everyone thought him to be, he certainly didn't deserve an assassin's dagger in his back.

By contrast, I could and did take considerable pride and delight in the subtle war of attrition on which we actually embarked.

Merlin mentioned to Arthur in passing that the noble students in fencing and archery needed more expert demonstrations to set them a good example, and might benefit from the assignment of personal mentors. He proposed that the new couriers needed more help with their Latin, such that a man a little more civilized than the average rude Briton might easily provide. He advised that if the king were intent on bringing down a particularly fine stag of which rumor had been heard, then he ought to make sure that he had his most reliable friends about him while he tracked it down. He pointed out that if Kay needed more help in impressing his will upon the reluctant merchants who were supposed to keep the castle well-supplied even in the bleak midwinter, then he ought to have the more frequent assistance of a man of proven presence and charm.

It was not only Lancelot for whom Merlin thought up little tasks to keep him occupied; he found small vocations to take up Guinevere's time in the intervals. Nor was it only Arthur he used an as instrument. He sent messages to Gawain and Kay suggesting things that ought to be done, but would require more pairs of hands than they had readily available. Neither he nor I ever said "you might ask Lancelot" in so many words, but Merlin was a master of indirection, and I was a good apprentice. He directed rumors too, not in Lancelot's direction or Guinevere's, but in the direction of certain other ladies of the court, who had always liked Lancelot but had never quite plucked up the courage to pursue him actively. They, I think, were the most useful obstacles of all.

Alas, we were swimming against the current. Frustration, it seemed, only served to inflame the regretful understanding that grew in the lovers' furtive glances.

We did a deal of good by accident, for the winter became very harsh very quickly, and most of the tasks Merlin devised really did need doing. The king did bring home that stag eventually, and increased his reputation in consequence, as well as providing a fine meal at a time when even the finest poachers in the realm were often hungry. For all our hard labor, though, the situation never improved; it merely grew worse more slowly. Eventually, the queen and her admirer found opportunities to meet in private, where they talked excessively of love—albeit in the noblest possible terms, acknowledging the impossibility of consummation while taking pride and pleasure in their own sweet torment.

Did they actually achieve the impossible? I don't know for certain, but I assume so. Merlin couldn't keep them busy forever, not could I watch them incessantly—and even if I had been present when they took the final step, I would have been impotent to interfere. The nights of deep winter are exceedingly long, and darkness makes a fine cloak for treachery.

Lancelot and Guinevere's incipient treason wasn't the only canker that grew slowly worse as the snow lay thick upon the ground and the bitter wind gnawed away at Camelot' walls. When the thaw came and the roads became passable again, Merlin's correspondence with his agents in Caerleon began to devour good parchment at an unhealthy rate, and the court's official correspondence with the Bardic Order was almost as greedy. The Abbot of Glastonbury had better uses for his supplies of parchment, but his messengers became increasingly tiresome as they presented his fulsome respects and listed his increasingly urgent pleas for attention and co-operation.

"There is nothing else for it," Merlin told me, eventually. "We shall have to deal with them here. They must be invited, as honored guests, to make formal agreements. The trouble is that any compact we make with one will limit our opportunities for making agreements with the other. They must know that as well as I do, and neither will take it kindly if the other is invited first, since we have been in correspondence with both for several months."

"Which of them is the more dangerous to Arthur's cause, master?" I asked, meekly.

"We cannot afford to have either against us, if it is avoidable," He replied. "Both might make a very useful contribution, if they can be persuaded to help us."

"Which has the larger army?" I asked.

"Neither," he said. "The druids are not fighters any more than the priests. Either might lend a blessing to someone else's army, but could not raise one. It is not armies that concern us here—it is attitudes and aims. We all have the same goal, I think—but the abbot and Taliesin have widely different ideas as to how it might be attained. Even the Saxons want a lasting peace, and prosperity for all, if it is achievable—but winter has been hurtful, and we have yet to see whether summer can fully repair its wounds. If the new planting season goes badly..."

I have to confess that I didn't understand the complexities of the situation. Unable to read, I couldn't tell what Merlin wrote or what news he received in written form, and his explanations—when he cared to offer them at all—were often vague. I thought I understood well enough what the Abbot of Glastonbury might desire of Arthur and the world, because I knew what Mother Leocadia desired, but the Bardic Order was a complete mystery to me.

The Welsh, Merlin had informed me, had never been fully subdued by the Romans, although it was the Romans who had built Caerleon. When the Romans withdrew the legions, the old order had reasserted its grip on the territories that now lay unprotected, but I had only the vaguest notion of what that order was, or how ambitious it was to extend into England, or what methods it was likely to use in the attempt.

That didn't stop me trying to play my part, though; I was determined to be a good apprentice.

"The Christians are already here," I pointed out. "There are Christians in the town and in the castle, and Christians in the Saxon lands too. I dare say that there are Christians even in Wales. They aren't very numerous, but they're determined. Surely you ought to give them first consideration."

"Don't preach to me, son of Leocadia!" he said, testily. "I know how insidious they are. I know how they conquered Rome—and I know what that victory is likely to cost the empire. I know the past as well as I know the present, and there's no man in the isle of Britain better able to see what potentials the future holds. Don't think that kneeling through a few hundred masses sung by twenty ancient widows and semi-retired whores, in a language none of them can understand, gives you any insight into the ways and wiles of the church. Wretched changeling! You'll be telling me next what Morgana le Fay will do to make sure that all our compacts come to nothing!"

"Will she, master?" I asked.

He waved his stick at me. "She won't do anything!" he said. "She doesn't care! But Taliesin cares what becomes of Britain, and the meddling monks of Glastonbury care too. I've half a mind to invite them both at once, to sit them down with one another, and see if we can all make a compact."

"Master," I said, with a sigh. "I can't spy on two enemy camps at the same time."

"They aren't enemies, yet," he retorted, "not even to one another, no matter what their differences are. It would be complicated, I'll allow—but complication can be useful, and if Arthur could pose as a peacemaker between the two, as a pragmatist who persuaded Christians and druids to let one another be—what a reputation he'd have then! But if it were to go awry..."

"It might help to keep Guinevere busy," I pointed out. "A queen playing hostess has little time to spare. Has Taliesin a wife, perchance?" I knew that the Abbot had not; Mother

Leocadia had explained the church's views on priestly marriage.

"No, more's the pity," Merlin said. "Bards and druids are worse than priests when it comes to exclusive mysteries. Even so, duties of hospitality... and we should have to make room. One party could be accommodated without inconvenience, but two at once... we should all have to accept a certain amount of cramping in our quarters. Servants everywhere... but so much confusion might serve as a shield and distraction as well as a deterrent. Curse complication! If I had not grown so old so quickly... but a man is still a man, no matter how much time he spends in Faerie. Sometimes I wish I'd followed Mad Tom after all."

"Who's Mad Tom, master?" I queried—but he only thumped the end of his staff on the floorboards.

"None of your business, fool! We have no time for idle chatter. Have you filled my inkwell? Have you replaced my quills? Have you scrubbed the leaves of parchment for reuse? You must take a message to Arthur—and one to Kay. Let me think. What are you waiting for? Get moving!"

His orders were unclear to say the least, but I did as I was bid, and got moving.

7

There were quills enough on the shelf, but all the parchment we had was covered in letters and blots, and most of it had been scratched and scrubbed so thin that it was hardly there at all. As soon as I had filled the inkwell I set to work to contrive something my master might be able to write on.

"We need a fresh supply," I told him, when I finally handed over the result of my labor.

"So we do," he said. "Time was when parchment was one of the few items whose price did not go up in winter, but that was before the Christians started scribbling away. No scrubbing and scraping for them—not more than once, at any

93

rate. Once the page is full of holy writ, they bind it up and store it carefully away. Imbeciles!"

The fact that the convent had possessed no books had not prevented Mother Leocadia explaining the value of holy writ and its preservation. I knew, too, that the Romans Merlin admired so much had been very fond of making and keeping books, so it did not seem to me to be overly bold to say: "Writing that's made to last must have its advantages, master. A man like you might write a worthwhile book himself, so that men might benefit from your wisdom for as long as copies could be made and stored."

"You think so, do you?" he said. "For as long as copies could be made and stored... but how long is that, in a damp land where rot runs riot if you turn your back? In desert Egypt, so it's said, even papyrus lasts for years—for whole lifetimes, if safely entombed—but this is Britain. Mark me, Amory, there's no way to make wisdom safe but to transform it into action. Memory lies; speech corrupts; parchment decays. Nothing lasts but the effects of what we do, and even that may be obliterated soon enough, if time is unkind. I don't need to be remembered, Amory, or to be the stuff of legend, or to have my name preserved in ink for the children of your children to marvel at. What I need is to make a difference in the world, to be the architect of its enduring order. Now, listen to me well, for this is what you must say to Arthur, and to Kay...and afterwards, I have some other things for you to do."

He always had more for me to do. A message here, a message there; now go to this station, or to that; watch what is done and remember what is said. And don't forget the chamber-pot on your way down, or my supper on the way up, and the firewood too...

It could have been worse. Had I been a common servant, I'd hardly have had time to think, and when I had time to think, I'd have spent it mooning after some scullion girl, or gaming with dice. As a wizard's apprentice, I had a great deal of time when I was forced to think, and think hard, about all manner of matters of which common servants never even dreamed.

I was becoming a good apprentice, even though I never learned magic.

As you will have deduced from the stirring speech I've just reported, Merlin had no books of magic spells, and not much in the way of occult wisdom. He brewed a good many potions, for all manner of customers, and brewed them cleverly enough, but all his recipes were in his head and he never attempted to concoct an elixir of life or a truth serum. He cast the occasional spell, for purposes of public display, but all his incantations were improvised.

I asked him, when he was in a good mood, whether such products as the elixir of life and truth serum really could exist.

"Oh yes," he said. "Not a doubt about it. In Faerie, the power of wishing really can prolong life indefinitely, and provide a panacea for all ills. Morgana's potions always worked—on humans, at least—and when she dealt cards or looked into an obsidian skrying-glass... well, she always saw something. The future yet to be forged by chance and choice was mere mist, but she had skill."

"And you could do all those things, master, when you first returned from Faerie?"

"Some," he agreed.

"And if you went back?" I said. "Could you renew your power? Your youth?"

"If I went back," he told me, sourly, "everything I'd built here would fall apart. Men have died searching for the gate of Avalon, waiting in the forest for the elvish huntsmen to appear, in the hope of following them home... but even if I were sure that I could find the gate, and survive the shock of passing through it, I could not leave my business here. It is too important."

And suppose it falls apart anyway? I thought—but dared not say. Suppose that Caerleon and Glastonbury can't be reconciled? Suppose that the Saxons can't be appeased? Won't

95

you howl in anguish, then, when you remember that you might have returned to the world of magic?

I didn't understand him. No matter how hard I tried to be a good apprentice, I didn't understand why he had consented to become the man he was.

I learned a little about poisons from Merlin, more than a little about the easing of pain, and a great deal about spying and lying—but I didn't learn anything from him that you would think of as magic. Paradoxical as it might seem, though, I never doubted that he really had been a great magician, and I was proud to be a great magician's apprentice.

I never told any of the other servants that I hadn't learned any of his magic; on the contrary, I was very ready to help them believe that I had.

Despite Merlin's fits of nasty temper, he always kept it in mind that I was his heir as well as his instrument. No matter how irritable he became, and no matter how many times he called me a fool, he knew that if his work were to be carried forward after his death, I would be the one to do it. There was no one else who could. He didn't love me for that—in a way, he was resentful of it—but he recognized the reality of the situation. No question I asked went too long unanswered—even such trivial questions as the identity of "Mad Tom".

Mad Tom was Tom Rhymer, whom Merlin had met in Cokaygne. He was a singer and a player, one of several human playthings favored at one time or another by the elf Morgana, although he lived alone when Merlin knew him.

"Why was he mad?" I asked Merlin, when he eventually condescended to enlighten me on the subject. It was late one night, and the weather was cold enough, even though it was spring, to make him wrap himself in blankets and pull his collar tight at the neck.

"Because all men go mad who spend too long in Faerie," he told me. "Time passes strangely there as well as slowly. The bounds between waking and dreaming are harder to maintain. Madness isn't altogether a bad thing in a musician, I suppose... but even a musician can't always be lost in his art.

Like me, Tom was human enough to feel restless even in Co-kaygne, but he never wanted to come home. He thought that he might recover his lost wits in the world on the far side of Faerie, the Dark Land. He wanted me to go with him, to find the shadow folk who live there and ask them questions."

"Ah," I said. "But you wouldn't go, being too wise a man to heed a lunatic."

"It wasn't as simple as that," Merlin told me, with a sigh. "I was interested in the secrets of the Dark Land too, and not just for curiosity's sake—all the more so because Morgana was so adamant that I shouldn't go. In the end, I let Tom talk me into going through the portal—but it was worse than passing through the gate of Avalon. I was certain that I'd go mad myself, and I turned back from the threshold. Perhaps, if Tom hadn't been mad, he wouldn't have been able to go on. If he hadn't been mad, he'd surely have turned back when I did... but he didn't."

"What became of him?" I asked.

"I don't know. I never saw him again. Did you ever hear the legend of Orpheus?"

"Was he a saint?" I asked. I couldn't recall any of the Sisters of Saint Syncletica ever having mentioned him.

"He might be one by now, given the church's penchant for appropriation. No—in the beginning, he was a musician, like Tom: a great musician, good enough to charm the beasts of the forest—and the dead too. He went into a Dark Land, not unlike the one that lies beyond Cokaygne, in order to ask that his dead wife might be returned to him."

"And was she?"

"He was told that she would follow him home, provided that he did not look back until they had returned to the light. Can you guess the rest?"

I thought about it for a few moments. My newly found expertise in the art of lying had given me some insight into the method of legendry. "He came out and looked back," I said, "but she was still within, so he lost her again."

"So you have heard it!" he said, inexplicably disappointed by my cleverness.

"Not that I can remember," I assured him, although I couldn't suppress a twinge of conscience. Had I heard it, from Sister Claire? I wasn't sure. "What has it to do with Mad Tom?" I asked. "Is it because you turned around too soon, do you think, that he was stranded?"

Merlin shook his head slowly. "I hope not," he said. As denials went, it wasn't very convincing. He paused before going on "He was very adamant, you see, that it would take two of us to penetrate the heart of the Dark Land, and then to return in safety. I was never sure why he was so insistent... but how can I tell what rules apply to the navigation of that lightless space? How can I be certain that Tom wasn't doomed by my failure. He no longer had my wit and wisdom to aid him, you see, because I hesitated on the threshold, and wouldn't go on. I waited outside, of course, but he never came out. Who knows? Perhaps, if I had only been there with him, we might each have won our heart's desire. No, that's nonsense... but when you grow old, Amory, you too will look back over your life, and you will not be able to prevent yourself from wondering. No matter how wise you become, you will always wonder whether some foolishness that you did well to avoid might not have led you to the gold at the rainbow's end."

"I see," I said—although, to tell the truth, I didn't.

"If you never return to Cokaygne, Amory," he went on remorselessly, "and all the more so if you were never really there at all, you will always wonder, when you grow old, whether you might not have become an architect of worlds, if only you had managed to find that portal in the forest at the right time and returned to the human world with magic in your flesh—but the fact that you're bound to wonder doesn't mean that you should spend your life searching for a portal you might never find, or might only find too late. Do you understand what I'm trying to tell you, Amory?"

"I think so," I said. "You're telling me that it's better to be sensible, even though there's bound to come a day when I'll wish I hadn't been."

"More than that," he said, grimly. "I'm telling you that you must be sensible, and always make plans, even though there's bound to come a day when you'll wonder whether you might not have done better to go mad."

I thought about that, and then said: "As you might have done, if you'd stayed in Cokaygne any longer than you did."

"Yes," he said.

"Except," I dared to say, "that now you've grown old, you can never be entirely sure that you didn't stay a little too long."

He might have thrown his stick at me for that, or made the screech of his anger echo from the ceiling—but he didn't. He just looked at me, as if in bitter disappointment.

It wasn't me that had disappointed him, I realized. It was the fact that what I'd said was true.

8

Merlin was in a good mood, by his standards, when the invitations to Camelot were sent out to Taliesin and the Abbot of Glastonbury. I wouldn't say that he was optimistic, but he seemed to take a certain relish in the challenge that he had set himself. He tried with all his might to reinvigorate himself, that he might be ready to rise to the occasion—but his good mood faltered soon enough, then plunged abruptly into dark anxiety, of a kind that I had barely glimpsed before.

He took his frustration out on me, as usual, but he also took it out on himself, muttering angrily at every little failing of his flesh and every hesitation of his scheming, no matter how understandable or prudent.

Had the court's messengers been able to ride more quickly, and had the guests responded with greater alacrity, Merlin's mood might not have blackened to such a terrible extent. No matter how rapidly time flows in our world, distance slows the pace of progress.

The messengers had a bad time of it, even though it was spring; the rain was heavy and relentless, and even the roads the Romans had made became difficult; the rest became rivers of mud. The same downpours made the recipients of the invitations pause before sending their thanks, and pause again before they set out, hoping for signs of an easier journey. When they eventually set out, they traveled more slowly than they or anyone else desired.

Merlin had dispatched the letter to the Welshmen some time in advance of the other, not because he favored them in any way but because they had further to come. His hope was that both parties might arrive at the same time—but the weather put paid to that. Glastonbury, as a lake town, was partially flooded and deeply enmired, but that did not prevent the abbot and his priests making better progress than the bard and his druids. They arrived in Camelot three days ahead of their rivals, and were delighted to discover their advantage—which they attributed, of course, to the will of God.

They were not alone in that, for there proved to be more Christians in the town and the castle than I had estimated. When the abbot advertised the masses he proposed to celebrate, within and without the castle walls, and the monks' willingness to hear confessions and grant absolutions from sin, the response was more enthusiastic than I, or my master, had anticipated. Nor was the abbot the only one who was inclined to take a lesson from it. Ordinarily, it was a matter that Arthur would have discussed with Merlin and no one else, but it was raised at the round table by no less a man than Gawain of the Isles.

I was crouched behind a screen at the time, and glad to be so comfortable; I always liked it far better when I had that luxury, instead of being crammed into a crevice between two walls of stone.

"It seems that half my servants are begging time to go attend mass, sire," Gawain said to the king. "And time for private prayer as well. I hesitate to forbid them, since they seem to be trying to cultivate a finer virtue, but I am not sure that their loyalty to this new cause will not diminish their loyalty to me—and hence to you. I would be grateful for your advice, sire."

"And I," said Bors of Falmer—and Sagramore of Dunwich added his own voice to the chorus before Arthur had time to reply.

"I have spoken to Merlin," Arthur said. "His opinion is that it is a fad. The common people are always vulnerable to fashions and novelties. Last winter was hard and spring has been miserable. The townsfolk are hungry for distraction. It is not significant."

"Your majesty is doubtless right," Gawain conceded, "but the analysis does not solve my problem. How indulgent should I be in letting my servants follow the fad?"

"If I may say my piece, sire," Lancelot put in, "it seems to me that servants will welcome any excuse to shirk their duties. This new enthusiasm for prayer has less to do with cultivating finer virtue than avoiding work. Boundaries have to be set."

Lancelot du Lac was a fine one to talk of setting boundaries, I thought, although his cynicism in the matter of cultivating finer virtues was understandable.

"The abbot is our guest," Arthur pointed out. "We cannot appear to be setting bounds to his freedom when we summoned him here."

"That is understood, sire," Gawain agreed. "The abbot must be treated with all due courtesy. I am only asking for your guidance in dealing with my own servants."

"If our business with the abbot could be conducted at a swifter pace, sire," Sagramore observed, "that might help us all."

"It might, indeed," Arthur agreed, "but the requests that the abbot has made must be balanced against requests made by others, and it will help the abbot understand our position if he and I can sit down at the same table as Taliesin—just as it will help Taliesin to understand our position if he can sit down with the abbot. Their pleas are contradictory, and if our judgment is to be seen to be even-handed, they must each be made fully aware of the other side of the balance.

"Will druidry become a fad as well, sire when the bard and his fellows arrive?" Bors asked, letting a little irony show in his voice. "Will those of my servants who have not asked for special privileges on account of being Christians ask for their equivalent, in the name of fairness? And will my Christian servants then attempt to convert their druid fellows, and vice versa? When you sit down at a table with Merlin, Taliesin and the Abbot of Glastonbury, your majesty, you will doubtless behave like civilized men, and take polite note of the irreconcilability of some of your aims, and be respectful of the need to compromise. I am not so sure that the common folk will approach the problem in the same kindly spirit."

"With all due respect sire," Lancelot said, "I am not convinced that the abbot and the bard will approach the problem in a spirit of compromise either."

"Then it will be our business to persuade them, will it not?" Gawain was quick to put in. "The knights of the round table will set the necessary example, and demonstrate the value of courtesy and compromise. That is what our code requires of us, and what we require of ourselves."

"It is what we require of our servants, too," Arthur pointed out. "We require tolerance of them, and must provide them with models of tolerance. But our ultimate aim is order, and we must also provide an example of good order. If we are to provide our guests with powerful evidence of the value of courtesy, we must demonstrate the alliance of courtesy with strength. We must be firm with our servants, and with our friends. We ought to be grateful to Gawain for raising the question, and grateful for the frankness of its discussion. We must ask for a little patience, and a little tolerance—but not too much. This is a critical time in our affairs, and we must be very careful indeed if we are to preserve our unity and our strength. If we can all stand together—knights and farmers, serfs and tradesmen, Britons, Welshmen, Christians and Saxons all allied in the cause of order and justice—we might build a nation in this island finer than all of Rome... but if the thread of our patchwork society once begins to unravel, the whole garment might fall to rags."

It was at such moments that I could see why Merlin had selected Arthur to be his kingly instrument, for Arthur was capable of playing the king to perfection, when he was seated at the round table. If he had only been consistent in every aspect of his life... but no man is. Every man has his seasons; none is free of the internal weather of passion and mood. Every man who is wise in one matter can be foolish in another; every man who is strong in one relationship can be weak in another. So it was with Arthur, and with Lancelot, and with Merlin, and with me.

9

When I reported the knights' discussion to Merlin he was pleased to hear what Arthur had said. "What a statesman I made of him!" he exclaimed, taking all the credit for himself. It was, I suppose, his due. Arthur was a statesman, and Merlin was his maker—but there were things that Arthur was not, which Merlin could not have made him. He wasn't the kind of husband who could inspire adoration in his wife, but nor was he the kind of husband who could expect anything less.

"Bors was wrong, though, wasn't he?" I said to Merlin. "There are no druids in Camelot castle or Camelot town. If Taliesin had arrived before the abbot, he could not have provoked the same response. The Christians have the advantage."

"You would think so, I suppose," Merlin told me, gloomily. "Perhaps I should have taken you away from the convent the fist time I saw you, and found you a foster-mother in the town."

"No, master!" I protested. "I'm not taking the abbot's part, or adopting the Christian cause. I'm trying to be a good apprentice, to weigh the situation honestly. The Christians are the stronger party, it seems to me—and there are Christians in the Saxon lands. If Arthur can't strike a fair balance between the Welshmen and the abbot, or can't persuade one or other of them that the balance really is fair..."

Merlin thumped the floorboards with his staff to shut me up.

"Enough!" he said. "Your business is to look and listen, not to make policy. One architect is enough to make a castle strong; two can only weaken it."

"Am I wrong, master?" I complained.

I wasn't, and he knew it—but conceding the fact didn't improve his temper. "No," he admitted. "Our pagan Britons may offer petty sacrifices to the same gods as the druids, but not with the same devotion and intensity. Oppression by the Romans has left the Welsh with a siege mentality, and I fear that they might not bend, even though they must see as well as you do that they are the weaker party. Alas, the abbot has not only seen that, but is determined to press home his advantage. It will not make for easy diplomacy."

Taliesin's party arrived the next day, in pouring rain. They were unhappy and bedraggled, and when Kay had given them quarters they disappeared from view to dry their clothes and collect themselves. I was in the courtyard as they passed through, as were a hundred other gawkers, and I felt sorry for them. I saw the Abbot of Glastonbury watching from his window, and knew that eyes less keen than mine must have perceived his smile, but what perturbed me more was to hear the mocking remarks rippling through the crowd,

Merlin had told me that in the days before he went to Faerie, no one thought the words "Welsh" and "Briton" contradictory, but it was obvious as I listened to the castle servants gossiping with the hawkers and grain-carriers that no one in Camelot town thought of Wales as a natural adjunct to Arthur's Britain. Whenever the Welsh were mentioned, the tone in which the word was pronounced was little different from the tone in which they would have said "Saxon" or "Gaulish". The druids seemed foreign to the people of Camelot, in a way that the church, imported relic of Rome though it might be, did not. Without the loyalty of the Welsh, though, how could Arthur ever become an authentic King of Britain, rather than a tokenistic King of a few self-styled Britons?

Merlin was angry with me when I went back up to his attic, because there were a dozen tasks he wanted done that I had not had time to start. I was running up and down the stairs for the rest of the day, fetching and carrying. We still needed wood to keep the fire blazing, no matter that winter was supposed to be done. We still needed candles to light his long meditations and discussions, despite that the equinox was past and the days were getting longer. We needed food, though food was almost unobtainable, given that Kay was desperately anxious to secure every scrap for twenty miles around, driving prices in the markets to unprecedented levels.

Nothing I did was satisfactory to my master, in circumstances like those. Whatever I brought him was inadequate as well as late.

"Cretin!" he cried, for the tenth or twentieth time that day, when I brought his supper. "I've a world to make, and you expect me to eat this rubbish! A scavenging rat would pass it by, in the certainty of finding something better in any silo or compost-heap in the realm." And he struck at me with his stick.

I dodged the blow, which made him even angrier, and determined to hit me twice as hard—which, when I finally obeyed his order to be still, he did.

"It's all I could get, master!" I protested, not bothering to add that it was better by far than my own wretched fare.

"Then you're useless! Do you expect me to believe that Lancelot's servants have brought him such a meal as this? The Lady Enid's skivvies would be offended by such noisome mush. Tomorrow I must face the hardest day of my life, and you give me this!"

He knew that he was being unfair. Was it my fault that the winter had been long, or that whatever stores of wheat and rye had lasted through it had been rotted in the granaries by

105

leaking rainwater? Was it my fault that the sheep in the pens and the chickens in the runs, not to mention the rabbits in the meadows and the boar in the forest, had had as bad a winter as humans huddled in their hovels? How could I compete with servants who were directly responsible to Kay, or even the lifelong friends with whom they had grown from infancy? To be Merlin's apprentice was no help at all in making friends in Camelot, and his name no longer had the power of command that it must have had when he had strode the castle corridors like a man of power and strength. He knew all that, but he beat me anyway, for lack of anyone else to beat. He was master of the world, in his own opinion, but the only servant he had within ready range of his stick was me.

I had never had the habit of praying, and had left the Convent of Saint Syncletica swearing never to pray again, or even to pretend to pray—but I prayed that night for a better master: a kinder, more understanding, more cheerful master, who would be grateful for all that I did in his service. I didn't address my prayer to God, or to Christ, or to any of the saints whose names I knew. I simply prayed, to make myself feel better, and didn't expect that my prayer would be heard.

Mercifully, the next day dawned clear and blue. The rain clouds had vanished over the north-eastern horizon; there wasn't a trace of them left. The wind was blowing from the south-west, warm and dry. It was obvious that the day would be good, and I took it as an omen: a fine day for fine diplomacy. I couldn't find a better breakfast for my master than the supper I had taken him after dark, but I knew that it would look better in the sunlight, and the water was fresh. I helped him dress himself and managed not to be unduly clumsy.

Then we waited, knowing that the official summons would come. He became fretful, but he made every effort to suppress and conceal it, practicing for the time ahead. I can't say that he was kind or cheerful, but he did seem more understanding.

"You must go to the Welshmen's apartments as soon as you have helped me to the conference," he told me. "Taliesin will have one of his druids with him, for propriety's sake, but this is to be an intimate meeting and the rest will stay behind. I need to know what impression they have formed of the way things stand in Camelot. I need to know how much of their petition they expect to be granted, and how much they will settle for without taking irredeemable umbrage, They will be circumspect, of course, but they will have made a careful investigation of their quarters by now, and concluded that there is no place for a spy to hide; we must know what they have to say while they are still hopeful, and we must know what they will say when Taliesin comes back to them with news. Forget the monks, for now. We know where they stand. You must be sharp, Amory—miss nothing, judge cleverly."

"Yes, master," I said. "I'll do my best—but when I heard them speaking in the courtyard yesterday, they used a good many words I didn't know, and their pronunciation is strange."

"Their language is purer than ours," Merlin told me, gruffly. "Less polluted with Latin borrowings and scraps of the Saxon tongue. Listen hard, and you will understand perfectly well."

"Yes, master," I said, although I was not so sure.

When the summons finally came, I helped him down the stairs. By the time we reached the throne-room, he was no longer prepared to be seen leaning on my shoulder, so I walked the last few paces behind him, before racing ahead to open the door for him.

He swept through it with all the grandeur he could muster, and I could only hope that he seemed more a magician to Taliesin and the Abbot of Glastonbury than he seemed to me.

10

If the Welshmen had not been so difficult to understand, or the day had been as damp and dreary as the one before, I might have stayed longer at the post to which Merlin had assigned me. The dark and narrow space in which I was confined wouldn't have seemed so uncomfortable had I not been able to see the sunlight streaming through the window of the druids' room, but the slanting rays were a sharp reminder of what I was missing, and the conversation seemed as dull as it was opaque. The new visitors talked a good deal about Camelot, in less than generous terms, but had little or nothing to say about their own schemes—and in the end, I grew impatient, and decided that I was in dire need of a drink of water and a bite to eat.

I wasn't welcome in the kitchens, but Merlin was known to be in the council-chamber with Arthur, exercising his tongue for Camelot and Britain, so I was granted a little more respect than usual. I obtained a piece of bad bread, and a cheese that wasn't entirely unpleasant. I took them to the castle gate, and went out on to the steps, where I cold sit in the sunlight and feel quite unconfined. I had finished the meal, but was still sitting there, when I heard the cries begin.

"A rider!"

"See the rider!"

"Look at the rider!"

There was nothing at all unusual about a rider approaching Camelot. I knew immediately that there must be something else, to warrant anxious cries of that kind. I stood up abruptly, and leapt up three steps to the level of the gate. I could see the road to the west, but there was no one on it. The rider was approaching across country, from the south-east. His horse was galloping strongly, and could not have been moving for long at such a breakneck pace. The man was slumped down, his face upon the horse's neck, so that the object embedded in his back was pointing vertically upwards, like a flagpole.

The colors it bore, though uncommonly bright, were no pennant; they were the fletchings of an arrow.

The man wasn't dead. Realizing that he had come close to Camelot he tried to raise his head, craning his neck to look forwards. I could see his eyes, though I doubt that there were many in the crowd who could.

The horse was still obedient to his touch, without the necessity of a whip. It slowed as it approached the town, but the agitated crowd did not make it shy away. It seemed to know where it was going—and perhaps it did, if it had served messengers before. The man wore no livery, though; he was not one of Camelot's couriers, nor was he wearing any other badge of protection.

Merlin's couriers wore no livery, of course, but the injured was not one of the messengers to whom I had carried letters in the past. I couldn't remember ever having seen him before.

The horse came to the foot of the stairway leading to the castle gate. The injured rider made as if to dismount—but the effort was too much. He slipped and fell, and I was momentarily convinced that the impact would kill him.

I ran to help, taking the steps three at a time. Although there were a hundred people in the street and a dozen more on the steps, I was the only one who didn't hesitate—and as soon as the others saw me moving so quickly and purposefully, they decided to leave the responsibility to me.

The man had fallen sideways, and had not driven the arrow any further into his back, but the edge of a step had left an ugly stripe on his forehead, and his eyes were dazed. He was older than me, but some might still have reckoned him a boy rather than a man.

He tried to speak as soon as he saw my face draw near. His lips formed the ghosts of three or four consonants, but I could make no sense of them.

I put my hand beneath his head, to support him, but I didn't know what else to do. I looked behind, imploring help.

The crowd in the street pressed forward, but those who weren't townspeople were farmers and husbandmen bringing provisions to the overcrowded fortress; there was no one there who knew what to do, if anything could be done, to preserve the fast-ebbing life.

Two men-at-arms came running down the stairway, and made as if to take the man up and carry him to the gate—but they halted when Kay's voice boomed out, saying: "Leave the man be, or you'll kill him for sure."

I was never so glad to see the steward as I was then. He must have been working within the shadow of the gate, doling out coin to the carriers and sending servants scurrying hither and yon with the produce he bought.

He arrived at my side, and knelt down with me.

"Do you know this man?" he snapped at me.

"No, sire," I answered.

The words must have cut through the wounded man's dizziness, for he made an evident effort to focus his eyes—not on me, but on Sir Kay of Lancaster. Kay wore no armor, nor plumed cap, but he was obviously a man of quality, and the wounded man tried to reach out to him with his right hand, to pull his ear close to his lips.

Kay didn't wait to be pulled. He leaned as close as he could, to catch the whisper.

It was a very faint whisper, but an abrupt hush had fallen on the crowd, who were agog to hear anything that might be said.

"M... sage... for th'kin," the dying man gasped, trying with all his might to make the most of his remaining breath. "M... m..." Then, it seemed to me, he changed his mind. Instead of the word he had been trying to pronounce he pronounced another, which began with the same consonant. "M... rcy!" he finished, no longer addressing Kay at all, but whatever god it was to whom he prayed.

And then he died.

My hand was still supporting his head. I felt the muscles in his neck relax before his hand fell back and his bowels relaxed.

Sir Kay let loose a curse, but I was speechless. It was by no means the first time that I had seen someone die, but the others had all been children—and they had died abed, expectedly.

I laid the man's head down on the stone step, very gently, and drew my hand away.

Kay was already done cursing. He was leaning close to my head now "What did he say?" he growled. "Before I came, what did he say?"

"Nothing, sire," I assured him. I met his eye frankly enough, but he was looking at me with a strange expression. He didn't believe me. It was almost as if he thought I'd been waiting on the steps to receive the messenger.

The crowd was muttering now, although most of its members were keeping their voices low, unenthusiastic to be heard by Sir Kay or the men-at-arms. One voice spoke up, though, saying: "I know the fletchings on that arrow! 'Tis elf-shot!"

"Hold your tongue!" was Kay's immediate response to this. "I want facts, not fancies. From what direction did the rider come?"

He should have known better than to tempt fate like that. No sooner had one voice said "the south east" than half a dozen were shouting "Avalon! From Avalon!"

Kay was not an even-tempered man at the best of times, and these were not the best of times for a castle steward. Even so, I was surprised to see him grab the collar of the dead man's shirt and shake him, as if he might somehow rouse him from the silence of death. He cursed again, deeply offended by the courier's impoliteness in refusing resurrection, after offering such a tantalizing part-explanation of his presence. Then he collected himself, and looked for the two men-at-arms.

"You can take him now," he said.

They were not as enthusiastic as they had been before, now that the poor fellow had shit himself, but they managed to pick up the corpse by the shoulders and the boots, and began to make their way sidewise up the stairway.

They could go no further—the gate was blocked.

"Get out of the way, imbeciles!" Kay roared. "And send a messenger to the council-chamber. Arthur must be told."

Told what? I wondered. I was glad that Kay hadn't thought to send me on that particular errand, until I realized why. His thick hand dropped on to my shoulder, and took a painful hold.

"You come with me," he said, "and hold your damned tongue till we're indoors."

He had pushed through the crowd in time to see me with the dead man's head cupped in my arm. He didn't believe my assertion that the messenger hadn't said a word before he arrived. I knew better than to struggle or protest against the injustice of his doubt. I let him drag me up the steps, across the courtyard and into the barbican, where the guardsmen had set the body face down on the floor.

The arrow was still sticking up, like some insulting gesture.

11

Sagramore of Dunwich arrived before Arthur, and Arthur before Gawain, but they were so close together that they ran into one another's ankles when Sagramore stopped dead. The Abbot of Glastonbury and Taliesin were not far behind. I supposed that Merlin must be on his way, but that no one had offered him a shoulder to lean on.

"He said that he bore a message for you, sire," Kay told the king, "but he died before he could tell me more. This boy was at his side before me, though."

Arthur looked down at the body before he looked at me, and I saw his expression darken slightly—but whether he knew the messenger or whether it was merely the sight of the arrow that distressed him I couldn't tell. When he did look at me, though, he recognized me immediately. "Amory," he said. "Did you hear what the boy had to say?"

I was too anxious to take note of the way he had phrased the question. "He didn't have a chance to say anything, your majesty," I reported. "He was stunned when his forehead hit the stone step. He was incapable of speech, until Sir Kay put an ear to his lips."

Sir Kay made to cuff me, but Arthur raised a hand to stop him. "The boy is telling the truth, Kay," he said. "I know him—he would not lie." I was delighted to hear him say it.

Gawain and Sagramore were peering down at the cadaver. "He wears no livery," Gawain observed. "Who bears a message for the king, without the badge of its sender? He has no signet on his finger."

"Remove his belt!" Sagramore instructed one of the men-at-arms. "He must have a signet-ring in his pouch.

The belt was removed from the body, and the pouch from the belt. Sagramore opened it, tipped it upside-down over the palm of his left hand. He shook out three copper coins, and nothing else.

"The arrow's elf-shot, sire," volunteered the soldier who had removed the belt. "Everyone says so."

"He rode from the direction of Avalon, sire," his companion put in, not wanting to be outdone.

"It might be elf-shot, sire," said Sir Gawain, looking at the arrow dubiously. "It certainly wasn't made by any fletcher in Camelot."

"It's no British arrow, that's for sure," murmured Sir Sagramore, holding his nose as he knelt down to take a closer look.

"Ask Merlin, sire," I dared to say—the king, after all, had admitted to knowing me, and trusting me. "He will know."

"Where is Merlin?" Arthur asked, looking round.

Mercifully, Merlin was just arriving at the door, having come as fast as he could. He looked around resentfully, seeming not at all grateful to find me in the thick of the action.

"The boy died before he could tell us what his message was, or who sent him," Arthur said to his magician. "The arrow is our only clue."

Merlin knelt down beside the body, not bothering to hold his nose. He seemed deeply perplexed. He looked up before speaking—at the king, at Kay, at Gawain and Sagramore, and finally at me. I'd never seen him quite so puzzled. In the end, he had to be prompted.

"Is it elf-shot?" Sagramore asked. "Never seen its like, myself."

"It looks like elf-shot," Merlin said, cautiously. He reached out and gently worked the arrow free from its lodging between the ribs, so that he could examine its head as well as its fletchings. It was not an easy thing to accomplish, given the weakness of his fingers, but he did it without requiring my help. "Not iron," he said, as he looked at the point. "Black glass—of a kind that's certainly found in Faerie, but used in our world too."

"In magicians' skrying-stones," Sagramore observed, with a slight sneer.

Merlin seemed mildly surprised by the implied insult, but only said: "In skrying-stones and many other things. Then again, it's not so very long ago that arrows like this were being traded in local markets. Human archers prized them very highly."

In archery tournaments, I knew, the competitors were nowadays issued with identical arrows made by the castle fletcher, but that hadn't always been the case. In any case, my master had only said that the arrow looked like elf-shot, so I reserved my judgment as to where it might have come from, and who might have fired it.

It seemed to me that Merlin was being discreet in other ways, too. He turned the body onto its side, but he was using his own body almost as if it were a shield, hiding the messenger's face from the knights. Perhaps, I thought, he was trying to protect their delicate sensibilities—but I could see easily enough, and was astonished by the appalling suddenness with which the corpse had lost its appearance of youth. The young man's beard was still ragged and wispy, the hair still dark and slightly curly—but the face was ashen now, and quite horrible. Merlin picked up the dead man's right hand, and examined it closely, but I had no idea what he was looking for. I was out of my depth.

Merlin returned the body to its former position. "We'd best hide him away," he said. "Did anyone in the crowd recognize him?"

"There was a deal of muttering," Kay told him.

"What about his saddle?" Merlin asked. "Was there a bag attached to it?"

"No," Kay said. "But the saddle's ours, and the horse too. Anyone could see that. They'll work out soon enough that he was coming to you. Why was he coming to you, Merlin?"

"He wasn't," Merlin said, his eyes flaring with anger at Kay's lack of diplomacy. "Or if he was, I have no idea why."

"That's enough," the king said, decisively. "We should not stand over him like this, arguing amongst ourselves. There are things that must be done. Go away now—we'll discuss the puzzle later, in the proper place."

Gawain seemed surprised by that, and Kay shook his head in frustration, but they were both aware that Taliesin and the abbot were looking on, and that the rider's purpose and fate were private business.

Why, I wondered, had Kay assumed that the messenger had been Merlin's man? A rider bearing a message to the king should have been carrying a badge of his identity, whereas one of Merlin's spies would not, but it seemed more likely to me that whatever badge he had carried had been stolen from him, and that he had been shot afterwards, as he tried to escape from the robbers. Would common thieves have been armed with elf-shot, though? It seemed unlikely.

Arthur had turned to his guests. "I think it might be wise to halt our conference for an hour or two," he said. "We need to collect ourselves. Gawain, can you take care of the body?"

"Yes sire," Gawain assured him.

As Arthur turned away to usher his guests out of the barbican I finally shook myself free of Kay's restraining hand. He made no objection; I think he had forgotten that I was still his prisoner.

"Thank you, Kay," Merlin said to him, although his politeness seemed a little strained. "Amory, will you help me back to my apartment?"

He waited until we were safely back in his attic, with the door shut behind us, before he rounded on me and said: "What do you know that you did not tell them, Amory?"

I had been expecting the question, and had my answer ready. "One thing only, master. Kay heard it too, but did not think it worth mentioning. The man died trying to pronounce a word beginning with the letter M. It was only when he knew that he could not spit it out that he gave in, and asked his god for mercy instead."

"Is that all?" Merlin complained.

"Master, I said, "I can only hear what others speak. I cannot conjure information from the empty air."

"Very clever," he snarled—but he was standing up, using his staff for support, and didn't try to strike me with it. "You did not, by any chance, form an opinion as to the vowel that would have followed the M?"

"I couldn't be sure," I said, "but if I had to guess what word he was trying to say, once the voice in the crowd had identified the arrow as elf-shot, I'd probably make the same guess as the crowd."

"If guessing is not plucking information from the empty air, what is?" Merlin muttered. "This is all so stupid! What could the boy have been doing? Well, fool, since you think yourself so clever, what do you think he was trying to say?"

"He was shot with an elf-bolt," I said. "He was riding from the direction of Avalon. The rumor must be flying around the town at this moment that he was trying to say Morgana. Perhaps he was. Did you know him, master? I didn't, but..."

"You never met him," he said, cutting me off, "and I doubt that Sagramore remembered his face. Gawain might— and Kay certainly did, although he should have known better than to ask that question. I don't suppose it matters—the servants will known him, and the rumor will be all around the castle by nightfall that he was bringing news to me from the gate of Avalon, and was shot by elves—perhaps by Morgana le Fay herself. Damn the boy!"

"Who was he, master?" I asked, quietly. I was trying to be patient.

"Your predecessor," he said, shortly. "His name was Harl. He should have been safe in the bosom of his family, learning to be a farmer. Evidently, he had other ideas as to where and how to seek his fortune. But why was he riding to Camelot so urgently? And who wanted to stop him badly enough to put an arrow in his back?"

"So Kay was right," I said. "What he intended to say was that he had a message for the king's magician, but slurred the two words into one."

"You're the one who heard what he said," Merlin retorted. "Is that your judgment too?"

"I can't tell," I admitted. "But I doubt that he'd have galloped to the gate if he hadn't been on the point of death. He'd have come in secret."

"I certainly trained him well enough to do that," Merlin agreed. "Too well, it seems—whatever he's been doing since I gave him leave to go, he's kept it secret even from me." He collected himself suddenly, and clipped me round the ear, for no reason at all. "You've got work to do, boy," he said, with altogether unwarranted contempt. Without pausing for breath, he listed a dozen things he wanted me to do—but as soon as I turned away to begin he changed his mind again, and stopped me. "Wait," he said, remembering the mission on which he'd sent me forth that morning. "What did you learn from Taliesin's druids?"

"They're nervous men, master," I told him. "They're intimidated by Camelot. They don't like the Abbot of Glastonbury, and fear that he has plans they'll like even less. They're afraid that Arthur might intend to be baptized a Christian. But of their own plans, I learned nothing. I hope that you fared better with Taliesin himself."

Clearly, he hadn't. "We had no time for anything more than an elaborate exchange of guarded courtesies," he muttered. "We were just about to get down to business when Kay's messenger arrived. If someone arranged that display on the steps he has an acute sense of timing—and more cunning than seems likely."

"Cunning, master?" I echoed. "Do you think that cunning could have determined that Harl would die at Camelot's gate, having voiced no more than a single syllable of his alarm?"

He saw my hidden meaning readily enough. "No," he said. "But I doubt that it was magic, either. Morgana loved to play games, but not like this." Even as he said it, though, his face clouded with doubt. He hadn't seen Morgana for many years, and he had deceived her when he saw her last. He didn't trust his own judgment that she didn't care enough about his petty treason to take reprisals.

"The Saxons must have heard about your invitations to the Abbot and the druids, master," I ventured to say. "They must feel alarmed by the possibility of a three-way alliance. They might think that it's in their interest to disrupt the conference. They might have wizards of their own, subtle enough to hatch a scheme like this."

"They might," Merlin agreed.

"And the Saxons might have been interested to talk to Harl when you sent him away," I suggested. "They might have thought him a useful source of information, about Camelot and you. Did Mordred know Harl, by any chance?"

"For a boy who cannot pluck information out of empty air," Merlin said, dryly, "you seem remarkably willing to try. You have work to do, remember—get on with it."

"Yes, master," I said, meekly. I knew that I hadn't conjured anything out of the empty air that he hadn't already conjured for himself. He had been darkly anxious before, but he was desperately confused now, almost as far out of his depth as I was. I knew that he'd need very tender treatment

118

indeed, if his evil temper were not to rebound on me with greater ferocity than ever before.

12

The conference resumed after an hour's delay, and didn't break up before nightfall. I had plenty to do, because Merlin thought of half a dozen further tasks for me while I was helping him down and up the stairs again. When he came back again, assisted by one of Arthur's servants, he seemed quite exhausted as well as very sullen. Obviously, things had not gone well.

When I tried to ask him what had happened, he sent me away to bring his supper—and when I brought it, he cursed me for its inedibility and told me to go to my bed early. Ordinarily, I would have been glad of the opportunity to rest a while longer than I was usually allowed to do, but too much had happened during the day. My thoughts were still buzzing in my head, and I decided to make a brief excursion to the so-called servants' parlor, to see what gossip I could pick up about the Christians, the Druids and my unfortunate predecessor.

Most of the servants had no more than a corner to sleep in, of course, but their hierarchy was extensive, and included its own petty aristocrats, who had a drinking-den of their own where they gathered to chat when their work had all been delegated to their inferiors. In theory, I might have won a place in it myself had I only taken the trouble to ingratiate myself with the right people, but I was content with my observation-post within its walls.

Merlin had been right about the servants recognizing Harl—and about their jumping to the same conclusion as Kay. "Merlin has half a hundred spies of whom we know nothing," one of Kay's assistants, Hereward Wyke, opined. "He only pretended to send Harl home. He sent him to Avalon instead."

"And the fair folk caught him spying," Gracchus Manus the brewmaster put in. "That's plain."

The third party to the discussion was Lud, one of the armourers." No one can send spies through the gate of Avalon," he said, contemptuously. "And anyone foolish enough to wait in the forest might wait for years before seeing an elf emerge."

"But Merlin knows the ways of Faerie," the brewmaster objected. "Who knows what compacts he made with Morgana le Fay?"

"No compact strong enough to save his spy's life, that's for sure," Hereward pointed out. "The question is, was he shot in the Other World, or are there elvish archers roaming the king's protected forest? Will there be more corpses found?"

"Anyone with a bow can fire an elf-bolt," Gracchus observed. "I've seen you do it, Lud."

"Aye," said Lud. "That I have—and more than one knight favored them, in days gone by. I still have a quiverful somewhere in the armory, though I don't remember exactly where. The fletchers might take offense if I advertised their merits in public."

"What's for sure, it seems to me" Gracchus said, "is that Merlin's day is nearly done. His magic is all-but-exhausted, and times have moved on. Camelot needs new alliances—and not with the bloody Welsh." He obviously felt that his was the privileged opinion within the conversation, perhaps because all the participants were fuelling their talk on his produce.

"The old man might be weak at the knees," Kay's man said, doubtfully, "but his head's clear. He'll live for ten years yet, whether he's spent the legacy of the fays or not—and while he lives, Arthur will listen to him."

"Arthur's table is round," the armourer observed, apparently forgetting whose idea that had been. "He's part of a company. The knights know what Merlin doesn't, for their families have land, and livestock. The knights know which way the wind's blowing."

"From the east," the brewmaster said. "And what it blows is Saxon planters and Saxon herdsmen. They want more land, and their eyes are on ours. If we can't force them to look north instead of west, the knights are the ones who'll lose their heritage, not Merlin. The knights know what must be done. What's the use of making treaties with the Druids? Or the Church, come to that. We need men who can wield swords and pikes."

"We need swords and pikes as well as men to wield them," Lud pointed out. "And all the mines are in the west. The Forest of Dean is ours, and Cornwall's a firm enough ally, but Wales..."

They went on, but they'd already supped too much ale to be entirely coherent. I needed insights, not opinions, and they had none to offer. I slipped away, and went back to the attic. I paused by the door, and heard the sound of snoring within. I opened it carefully and tiptoed into the room. Merlin was still fully dressed, sitting up in his armchair as if he were expecting a visitor, but he had fallen fast asleep.

I studied him carefully, wondering whether he really did have ten years left to live—and what might become of me if it turned out that he hadn't. Then I turned and tiptoed out again, determined to make myself comfortable in my alcove.

No sooner had I blown out my candle and curled up on my mattress, though, than I heard a footstep on the spiral stair. I sat up, and peered into the darkness. Someone was coming up, slowly but not surreptitiously. The glow of candlelight was reflected from the stone wall before the person moved into view.

I leapt from the alcove to a standing position as soon as I saw that it was the king.

"Amory," he said. "Your master expects me, I believe."

"I believe he was, your majesty," I admitted, "but he has fallen asleep. Will you give me a moment to rouse him?"

I was already turning away, expecting that his assent was a mere formality—but he didn't speak, and I realized that he was hesitant. I paused and waited.

"What has he said to you, Amory?" he asked.

"Nothing, your majesty," I told him. I couldn't tell whether or not he believed me.

"And what have you said to him? I need to know, Amory—what the messenger said to you, and what you told your master."

I guessed then whose spy Harl had become when Merlin had no further purpose for him. Arthur had not only decided to make use of Merlin's cast-off, but had concealed the fact from Merlin. Presumably, the spy had been intended to arrive in Camelot far more discreetly than he had, to take advantage once he was here of the secret passages he must know as well as I—but when he had been shot, urgency had taken priority over discretion.

I realized, too, that it had not been trust that had moved the king to tell Kay that I was telling the truth but anxiety as to what I might reveal. Arthur had been hoping all along, in fact, that I was lying—and now he was about to be disappointed.

"I only know one thing, your majesty," I told him, ashamed of my inadequacy. "He tried to pronounce a word beginning with the letter M. I was not the only one who heard it—the rumor will go round, inevitably, that it was Morgana, but it might just as well have been Merlin... or something else entirely."

The King of the Britons looked down at me, quizzically—but this time, he decided that he did trust me. He nodded, and went to Merlin's door. He opened it, but didn't enter. He put his head around the door and looked in. I had left Merlin's candle burning, so he could see clearly enough that the old man was fast asleep.

Arthur closed the door again, remaining outside with me. "Will you walk with me, Amory?" he said, softly. He didn't wait for a reply, knowing that I was bound to do as he said—but he didn't go down the stair the way he had come up—he stepped into a covert that gave access to one of Merlin's secret passages. He obviously knew the way quite well, although he kept the flame of his candle shielded by his hand, lest some stray draught should leave him in the dark.

I followed him along and up, then along again and up again, until we arrived at the roof of the northern tower. There was no sentry on guard there. Arthur set his candle down on the stone floor, and went to the crenellated wall to look out over the gentle hills.

13

The night was as clear as the day before had been, and the sky was filled with stars. Few of you will be able to imagine that sight, partly because you live in a very different world, where the night is lit from below and not from above. There were a hundred lantern-flames still burning in the castle and the town, but they were feeble, and carefully shielded to direct their light where it was needed. In the sky, the stars reigned supreme and untroubled. But sight is not merely a matter of light; sight is interpretation, and your notion of the stars is very different from Camelot's. You know that the stars are very distant, suns like your own lost in a void so vast as almost to be infinite. We had no idea that the stars were so distant; we imagined them to be close at hand, set in a kind of ceiling that arched over us in such a way as to confine us. On a bright night, the stars seemed oppressive, almost as if they might rain down upon us at a moment's notice to drown us in cold and silvery radiance.

I could only wonder what Arthur, King of the Britons, was thinking as he looked up at the crowded sky, studying the constellations whose march across the zodiac mapped out the cycle of the seasons while the moon mapped out the thirteen phases of the year. The moon was half-full, but it was close to the horizon; above us, there were only stars.

It seemed that a long time passed in silence before the king looked down at me again, and said: "Merlin will not live forever, Amory."

My master's mortality seemed to be on everyone's mind that night.

"No, your majesty," I said, politely.

"Time was when a day's discussions, no matter how politely veiled, would have kept him awake half the night with scheming, rather than leaving him exhausted. His mind is sound, but he is alarmed himself by the manner in which his flesh has grown weak since his magic ran out. One day, Amory, you and I will have to get by without him. Then, you will be my spy, my eyes and ears. It might be as well to bear that in mind, while you creep around those dark and narrow corridors."

"Yes, your majesty," I said, dutifully.

"I was Merlin's apprentice myself, once," he told me. "You and I have more in common than you know."

"Yes, your majesty," I said.

He frowned, but only said: "You are right to be careful. I shall need you to be careful, when you serve me." He hesitated for a moment, and then said; "Is Merlin very angry with me?"

"No, your majesty," I said. Although he might be, I didn't add, if he knew that, having already stolen one apprentice, you're now trying to steal another.

He sighed. "Of course he is," he said. "Does he know who it was that killed my secret messenger, Amory? I must know the truth. If he knows, you must tell me."

"I don't know, your majesty," I told him, truthfully. "I can't believe that he does, He seems genuinely puzzled."

"Has he sent messengers of his own to Morgana recently?"

"No, your majesty," I said. "I'm certain that he hasn't."

"Did Merlin tell you who the boy is? The boy who was shot, I mean."

"Yes, your majesty," I told him. I was tired of taking so little part in the conversation, and took the liberty of adding: "The news has spread throughout the castle. It isn't Kay's fault—Harl was recognized by servants who knew him when he was Merlin's apprentice before me. I never knew him."

"But you know that I did. You know that I recognized him as soon as I saw him, although I said nothing. You know that he had undertaken a mission for me, without Merlin's knowledge."

"I guessed as much, your majesty."

"And have you and Merlin guessed what that mission was?"

I knew that it would sound like another cautious evasion, but all I could say was: "No, your majesty."

"No, your majesty," he echoed, imitating my tone. "You're very free with the word no, Amory. Well, I suppose it does me good to hear it. I hear a thousand yes, your majesties every day. Do you know what I think when I hear them, Amory? Do you know what effect it has on me?"

"No, your majesty," I said, unable to suppress a slight smile.

He was looking into my eyes. He was looking down, to be sure, so his face was silhouetted against the stars while they filled my upturned face with pale light, but I knew that he was looking at me as frankly as anyone ever had. "At first," he said, "I was proud and delighted. I reveled in my good fortune. Now... now, I marvel at it in a different way. I marvel at the fact that it goes on and on and on, without end. I marvel at the fact that the illusion does not collapse, and that everyone around me does not simply come to his senses and say: why, that is not a king at all. It's only Arthur—poor landless, kinless, friendless Arthur. What could we possibly have been thinking, to call him majesty and do his bidding?"

"You aren't friendless, your majesty," I told him.

He inclined his head to one side, but not as if to shake it. "No," he said. "Not friendless. I don't count apparent friends, of course, or friends moved solely by a sense of duty, or those bound to me purely by their own self-interest—but when all those are excluded, I do have a friend or two. Lancelot, I think, is a true friend."

I felt a stab of alarm when I heard that. Lancelot certainly wouldn't have been on any list I suggested—but I couldn't even think of telling the king why I would have had to discount him.

The king hadn't waited for an answer. "It could still happen," he went on. "It could happen in a trice, upon the instant. They would merely have to look at me in a slightly different way, from a slightly different angle, and my crown might evaporate. I don't have Merlin's magic to protect me any more. Nor have you, Amory. We have nothing but our own wits to rely on."

I wondered how much of this he had said to Harl, and when. How long had Harl been Arthur's man, not Merlin's? I had never realized before that there might be a difference.

"You have a great many friends, your majesty," I assured him, only a little insincerely, "and a great many loyal subjects."

"Of course I have," he said. He stroked his beard with the forefinger of his right hand and looked away again, out into the darkness that cloaked his peaceful kingdom." Who shot my messenger, Amory?" he said. "Who tried to prevent him delivering his message? Please tell me, if you know?"

I wasn't surprised that he returned to the question. Arthur hadn't brought me up to that high place to flatter me with confidences without expecting something in return. I didn't know the answer to his question, but I was ashamed of my ignorance. I wanted to make it up to him, even if all I had to offer was guesses.

"Merlin really has no idea, sire," I told him. "It was no man of his—but the elf-bolt is an awkward complication. If it was not an elf who fired it, then the man who fired it must have had some reason for trying to put the blame on the elves. Given that Harl was once Merlin's apprentice, and that Merlin was once Morgana's accomplice, the opinion of the gossips is bound to be that Merlin is either the intended victim or the perpetrator of the crime. You might ask yourself, sire, whether anyone apart from yourself knew that Harl was your servant instead of Merlin's, and what message he was carrying—and whether anyone of that sort might have had a reason to prevent the message getting through."

"I have," Arthur told me. "But the only person I can think of who might have overheard me giving orders to Harl is you, Amory."

"I don't spy on you, your majesty," I told him. "I listen to discussions in the council-chamber, but I have never spied on your personal apartments. Merlin wouldn't permit that."

"And you always do what Merlin tells you?"

"Yes, your majesty."

He turned back to me, and fixed me with a gaze that reflected all the uncanny oppression of the sky." Don't try to persuade me that you're a fool, Amory," the King of the Britons said—to me! "I know how long Merlin has been waiting for you. You have been in Faerie, so it's said. Your sight and intelligence has been quickened, as his was. Even if you know nothing for sure, you're better placed to guess than anyone— even your master. Make a guess, Amory. Show me how clever you are."

I had no alternative but to do as I was asked, although I had no intention of mentioning Guinevere or Lancelot. "You must have sent Harl to keep watch on the gate of Avalon, sire," I said. "You must have wanted to send a message to Morgana le Fay, and had no other means of delivery but to wait for the elvish knights to come a-hunting. When they did come... perhaps they didn't approve of Harl's approach, and quarreled with him. Perhaps, on the other hand, they agreed to take his message into Faerie and brought word back to him... word whose delivery someone else—elf or deceptive human— had reason to prevent. I really don't know who, your majesty, but I am convinced that Merlin knows no more of this than I."

He nodded his head, as if to say that he believed me this time. He turned and placed his elbows on the parapet, looking down over the roofs of Camelot town.

"Bad timing, in every possible way," he murmured. "How could I have gone to meet her, with the abbot and the bard looking daggers at one another across my table? An expedition to Merlin's tower is one thing—a trek to the gate of Avalon is something else. But if she did get my message, Amory, and sent Harl to tell me where she would meet me, I can't send anyone to explain my absence. I'd rather think that than assume that she give the order to shoot the boy... but what will she do, Amory, if she arrives at a meeting for which I begged her, only to find that I am not there?"

"She will, go home, sire," I said, "and will not stir herself again for the sake of any mere human."

"Yes," he said, as if he dearly desired to believe it. "That is what she will do. Merlin will be pleased. That is what he has always desired her to do, isn't it?"

"But Merlin won't live forever, sire," I said, taking my courage in both hands. "He won't even live as long as you or I, let alone as long as Morgana le Fay. And when he is gone... it might be as well to have a friend in Faerie. It might be best to clear up the misunderstanding, if you can."

He saw right through me. "You're brave, or reckless," he observed. "You saw what happened to the last messenger I sent to Faerie."

"Yes, sire," I said. But if I were to find a way through the gate of Avalon, I didn't add, that would be worth almost any risk.

"Magic won me the crown," Arthur said, pensively, "and magic alone. If the spell of Kingship ever wears off, nothing will restore it but magic. Merlin doesn't seem to think so, but Merlin isn't the seer he once was."

He was right about that. I was Merlin's eyes, and my own eyes were unusually keen—but Merlin was by no means the seer he once had been, else he would have used my eyes far more cleverly than he did.

"Merlin wants to forge a triple alliance between Camelot, the Church and the Bardic Order, sire," I told him. I knew that he knew it already, but he seemed to be in a confidential mood and I wanted to know more. "He hopes that the Saxon bugbear will frighten them enough to set aside their differences, but it seems to me that it can't work—and even if it did, the harder part would still lie ahead. Magic might be a better means of securing your crown than politics, if Morgana le Fay could only be persuaded to help you."

"Merlin wants the Saxons to acknowledge me as their king too," Arthur told me. "He thinks that they'll begin to fight among themselves eventually, and might look to me for neutral leadership exactly as the Briton landholders did—but he doesn't think Morgana will help him a second time. The Churchmen have very different ideas, of course; what they want is the same privileges in Britain that they enjoyed in Rome before the barbarians came."

"Rome's old empire is crumbling, so my master says," I observed, prompting him to say more. "Gaul is lost to the barbarians, he says."

"So Lancelot says, also," Arthur agreed. "But neither of them can make up his mind as to whether the Church is to blame for the empire's disintegration, or the only hope it has to stop the rot... and even if they did, who can say whether Britain is a similar case?"

"Are there gates to Faerie in the further reaches of the empire, your majesty?" I asked. I had never asked my master

"Who can tell?" was the king's reply. "Some say that the world within the world only touches ours at a few favored points, but even if there were portals in every land on earth, men would still have to find them. The gates are protected, so they say, by spells that render them invisible as well as spells that make anyone who stumbles into them feel direly sick. Elves who visit our world are rare among their own kind; rarer still are those who take an interest in humans. Rare enough to be mad, some say, by the standards of their kind—but I met Morgana, and she did not seem mad to me. I liked her. I was young then, but I thought..."

He didn't want to tell me what he had thought. I understood, however, that he saw Faerie as a potential resource, and couldn't understand why Merlin, who had used it so cleverly once, was reluctant to do so again. It seemed to me that he was right, and that an alliance with the elves of Cokaygne was potentially more precious than any possible alliance with the church, or even the Saxon lordlings.

On the other hand, I thought, Arthur had only met Morgana briefly, in his own world. Merlin was the one who had actually lived with her in Cokaygne while centuries passed on earth. Merlin was the one who knew how things were in Faerie. If Merlin thought that Faerie now was more likely to harm Britain's cause than help it, wasn't he likely to be right? Unless, of course, he had stayed there too long, and had addled his brain more than he knew, or dared suspect.

"I shall keep my eyes and ears open, sire," I promised the King of the Britons. "When I know more, I shall tell you myself, rather than leaving it to Merlin."

"I wish you would, Amory," he said—but very softly, as if he were accepting a favor rather than giving an order. "Can you find your way back to your bed in the dark? I need to think a while, and I shall need the candle myself."

"Yes, your majesty," I said, as colorlessly as anyone else would have done.

14

Merlin slept all night in his chair. He cursed me terribly when dawn came for letting him do it, and for letting the candle burn out when there was no naked eye to benefit from its flame.

He didn't ask me whether the king had come to see him, perhaps because he hoped that I had done as he had instructed and gone to my own bed, to fall as deeply asleep as he. In my turn, I didn't tell him what Arthur had told me, and what I had told him.

I took the chamber-pot down to the cesspit, and then I fetched hot water from the kitchens so that he might wash himself and make ready for another day in close company with gentlefolk. Then I fetched our food—which was, as ever, not to his liking. He evidently felt that something was seriously amiss, and that falling asleep had only left him further behind the current of events than he already was—but I watched him collect himself, and gather his strength, and knew that he was not about to lie down and die.

No sooner had I reached the bottom of the stairs as I led him to the council-chamber, however, than a commotion began outside. We hastened to a window so that we could look out. It was a narrow window, but we were of such different heights that we could both look out together, he staring over my head. Fortunately, the window gave us an uninterrupted view of the signal-tower on the hill to the west of the castle, on whose extremity pennants were being vigorously waved.

The code of the pennants was supposed to be secret, known only to the king, his knights, the court magician and half a dozen flag-men—but that would probably have been ten too many even without the flag-men. Even I, who had only seen half a dozen exchanges of signals, had the rudiments of it—but the crowds in the courtyard and the streets of the town knew more than I did, and it was their shouts that told me how the message read.

"Morgana le Fay!" the cry went up. "Morgana le Fay is riding to Camelot!"

"Elvish knights!" the voices added, soon enough. "Avalon is coming to make war!"

"War!" spat Merlin, his wrath so intense that he could hardly let loose a single syllable at a time. "Fools! Fools!" I wasn't sure whether he meant one set of fools or two. He certainly meant that the crowds were made up of fools, for thinking that elvish knights might attack Camelot, but whether he thought that the elvish knights were foolish too, for making any approach at all. I couldn't tell.

What I did understand, though, was that I had given the King of the Britons entirely the wrong advice, I had told him that Morgana would go home if she came out of Avalon to meet him and found that he was not there. Evidently, I had made the wrong guess. There was little room for doubt, now, that Morgana had received Harl's message—in which case, she would surely not have had him shot before he could deliver her reply.

"What shall we do, master?" I prompted. He seemed paralyzed by shock.

The words broke his paralysis, but didn't move him to action. "He has summoned her," he said, wonderingly. "After all I have said to him, he has summoned her! At the worst possible time!"

I knew it wasn't true that Arthur had summoned Morgana, but I couldn't tell him that. Harl must have been waiting by the gate of Avalon for months, perhaps more than a year, so the timing of the message's delivery had to be a pure coincidence, but I couldn't tell him that either. "Yes, master," I said. "But what shall we do?"

"I must see the king," he said. "Now!"

We resumed our course, but not before I had seen Lancelot running from the northern tower, shouting for horses, with Gareth and Bors haring after him. Arthur had already given his orders, it seemed—he was sending out a party of his knights to greet his unexpected guest, presumably to add to her escort. They would ask her what her purpose was, of course, but if she told them that she had come to visit her half-brother, what could they do but make her welcome?

The cries were still echoing from every wall. There was no more mention of war, but other conclusions were being drawn that were no less discomfiting.

"The Queen of Avalon is coming to Camelot! The messenger was bringing warning!"

"Morgana le Fay has come to reclaim her elf-bolt!"

"The devil's knights are coming! Pray, Britain—pray for redemption!"

We took the most direct route available to us, which had the added compensation of requiring fewer stairs and saving us from showing ourselves to anyone who might have made the sign of the devil's horns at us. Fortunately, Arthur had retired to his private reception-room rather than remain in the council-chamber—but I was not to be privy to his conversation with Merlin. As soon as the magician was no longer in need of my shoulder he slammed the door in my face, without even troubling to reel off a list of orders to keep me busy.

I found a window from which I could watch Lancelot and his companions ride out, with half a dozen lancers as a retinue. Then I had to scamper for cover as I heard the Abbot of Glastonbury hurrying along the corridor with three of his monks.

"A catastrophe, my lord!" one of the monks was saying. "The devil has sent his temptress to disrupt our plans!"

"Don't be stupid," one of his companions replied. "We have the Lord on our side. How will she dare to face us?"

"Taliesin will be glad to see her," muttered the third. "Druids, elves... all legions of the damned!"

As they swept by, though, the abbot said nothing at all. I wished that I had been more carefully placed, so that I might see his face. I imagined the kind of expression that I had often seen in Mother Leocadia's features: half divine wrath, half holy zeal. But if Morgana were allowed to take a place at the conference-table, I thought, the balance would surely be tipped against the Christians, and whatever plans they had would most certainly be disrupted. The abbot must fear a catastrophe, even if he still had hopes of preventing one.

I made my way back to the window, and remained there even when I heard other footsteps approaching, because I recognized Sir Kay's voice while he was still out of sight around a corner.

"Not more guests!" he bellowed. "Where shall I put them? How shall I feed them? How shall I seat them at this evening's dinner? Where shall I find another cloth and forty spoons? And how shall I keep them all apart?" When he rounded the angle I saw that his face was purple. He was shouting at Hereward Wyke and another of his assistants.

I sympathized with his predicament. The southern tower was the only place left where new guests could be comfortably lodged, and it was already full to bursting with liegemen and their ladies who had been dispossessed of their usual apartments by guests already arrived. Their further redistribution would only be the beginning of the steward's problems.

"She must have heard about the conference, sire," said Hereward. "She doesn't want the king making common cause with the Christians. He is supposed to be kin to the fair folk, after all, and the Christians hate the fair folk. What a scandal there would be in Faerie if Arthur were to be baptized!"

"Shut up!" Kay roared. "You know nothing of these matters! Nothing!" Then he caught sight of me. "You!" he cried, triumphantly. "Run to the gate and tell my man there to increase his orders by a further one in twenty—and when he rolls his eyes and tells you that it's impossible, tell him that I'll string him up by the ankles if he lets me down, and use his head for a football!"

Hereward smirked, glad to have escaped the duty of carrying such orders himself. I cursed my own recklessness in staying in plain view instead of scurrying back to my hiding-place. I had no alternative but to do as I was bid—except, of course, that I had not the slightest intention of relaying the exact nature of Sir Kay's threat, lest his servant decide to take his retaliation ahead of time by using my head for a football.

By the time I had made Kay's strength of purpose clear in my own more subtle fashion, I hardly had time to sprint up the stairs to take my position at another window before Morgana le Fay and her retinue turned off the road to the west, approaching Camelot.

15

I had been expecting a glorious carriage, flanked by a dozen elvish knights in impossibly bright armor and brilliantly plumed helmets, carrying golden lances and longbows, with quivers full of elf-bolts. What I saw was seven slender figures on horseback, dressed in green jerkins and brown hose, with featherless peaked caps on their head and not a lance or bow between them. Even the daggers sheathed at their waists seemed pitifully thin. Lancelot and his companions, who rode with them on amicable terms, seemed by far the grander company.

Those aren't knights, I thought. Those are woodsmen.

I had to presume that Morgana herself was one of the riders; she could not have been either of the similarly-clad figures driving the small but heavily-laden carts that were following the troop. There were sheets drawn over the cargoes, concealing as well as binding them, but where the cloth was drawn tight I could see the outlines of barrels and bales.

Why, I thought, as disappointed as I was amazed, they're as human as we are! It was the last thing I had expected—but I only entertained the disappointment for a moment before amending my judgment. No, I told myself, sternly. They're mounting a charade. They're pretending to be common folk, putting aside their glory so that we might be lulled into a false sense of security. What need have they of lances and armor, when they have magic to defend them? Then I added, in a slightly different frame of mind: And what need have they of ostentatious carriages, when they live in a land without Roman roads or Roman cities?

When they came into the precincts of the town my sharp eyes permitted me to distinguish Morgana's feminine form and features, but her hair was tied back and her eyes were hidden behind the brim of her carefully tilted hat. She didn't ride at the head of her troop, even when Lancelot tried to bring her further forward so that he and she could ride to the foot of the castle steps together. Lancelot's expression was already thunderous, so there was no scope for his scowl to deepen when she refused to fall in with his plan, but I didn't waste time in studying his discomfort while I was still trying hard to measure Morgana's beauty.

I remembered, as I exercised my keen vision, what I said to Mother Leocadia many years before about the reason why the fair folk were called fair. The most remarkable thing about Morgana's face was its unblemished quality. There was nothing very remarkable about its form, but its texture seemed quite amazing. Guinevere was the most beautiful woman in Camelot, her face being remarkably free of scars by human standards, but even Guinevere had the occasional freckle, mole and a certain random discoloration. Morgana set a new standard of perfection, unmatchable by any mere human.

Nor was it only Morgana who was free of flaws; as the green-clad riders came closer, I was able to distinguish the faces of her male companions more clearly, and compare them almost side-by-side with Lancelot's. Lancelot was reckoned a handsome man, but his handsomeness was of a rugged kind; he wore his scars well, concealing the greater number of them with a neatly groomed beard. The male elves were all beardless, their skin so smooth as almost to seem polished. A malevolent critic might have deemed them effeminate, but they didn't seem so to me. Their features were various, but often quite pronounced by comparison with Morgana's, and considerably broader. With a few wrinkles and unruly tufts of hair, one or two of them might have been reckoned ugly—but in the absence of such spoliation they seemed magical... as, indeed, they were.

The contrast was helped, of course, by the fact that the elves were smiling—grinning, even—while Lancelot was not. Gareth and Bors seemed to have caught the mood of the visitors, and seemed to revel in the attention of the crowd, but Lancelot was not to be swayed.

The advancing company should have come through the streets two-by-two, if only to avoid inconveniencing the other traffic, but they remained ragged and unformed. The other traffic had stopped in any case; every one on the road wanted to stare at the fair folk.

Many of the townspeople must have been as disappointed as I was to find that the elves were so ordinary—but they were excited nevertheless. The news would be running through the marketplace hat the fair folk had brought two fully laden carts, and traders of every kind must have been weighing up their chances of profitable barter. None of the fair folk had come to a local market for many years, but their reputation as enthusiastic hagglers was well established nevertheless.

It was not until the elves had dismounted and climbed to the top of the steps, pausing briefly within the gates, that Morgana showed herself to be in command. She did so not by striding forthrightly into the courtyard in search of King Ar-

thur—who, for whatever reason, was not there to greet her—
but by turning to address the crowd in the street, whose members were staring at her so avidly. She untied her hair to let her
dark tresses expand, glinting in the sunlight, and raised her
delicate hands to display the palms.

"People of Camelot!" she said—and silence fell the moment she opened her mouth to speak. "Word has reached us in
Cokaygne that your winter has been harsh and the spring
foully damp. We have no winters in Avalon, and have brought
you food gathered in our orchards and meadows: barrels of
apples and pears; hares and venison; onions and lettuces;
sweet and savory preserves. There is one wagonload for the
castle, and one for the town. We have gold too, and silver, to
trade for tessera and trinkets. My brother's men will doubtless
ensure an equitable distribution of our gifts, and my friends
will visit the market in due course."

I had an image in my mind of Kay's head exploding
when she promised that he would organize a distribution of
her presents of food, as apoplexy finally got the better of him.
For myself, I only smiled delightedly—and the broadness of
my smile increased when I saw how distressed Lancelot was
that he had not been able to stop her taking control of the
situation.

"Well done, Morgana," I whispered, secure in the
knowledge that there was no spy near enough to hear me.
"That will drive the fatal elf-bolt from their thoughts, if anything can. They'll be far too busy arguing over whether faery
fruit is really forbidden, and what might possibly happen to
anyone who eats it!"

In the end, I felt sure, there would be few who would refuse to take the risk, given the scarcity of bread. If the food
really were bewitched, Morgana would have Camelot in her
grasp—except, of course, for the Abbot of Glastonbury and
his faithful monks, who would be bound to refuse to touch it
no matter how their mouths watered at the prospect.

I smiled even more broadly at that thought. I was determined to be in the dining-hall that evening, if Merlin would condescend to let me go.

16

While Sir Kay was installing Morgana and her retinue in the southern tower I went back to Merlin's attic, intending to await him there even though I was by no means impatient to see him.

It was a wise decision. He wasn't long in coming, and would have beaten me soundly when I returned had he found me missing, even though he had given me no orders.

"Is the conference postponed again, master?" I asked him.

"Most certainly," he said, as he threw himself into his armchair. "This is a matter that everyone wishes to consider in private—and we need to know what Morgana wants before we can allow her to see the king—if we can allow it at all. I have advised the king to retire to his bedroom and wait, and to put her off if she demands to see him. We must find out as quickly as possible why she has come here—not the reason that she gives out in public, but he real reason. This is the crisis of my design, Amory. I had not expected it quite so soon, but at least it has come while I am still strong enough to meet it. In any case, it has fallen upon us and we must rise up or be crushed."

He didn't sound exultant, but nor did he sound like a man defeated. However unsure he might be of the outcome of the struggle, he was ready to fight.

"Will you go to see her, master?" I asked. "She'll tell you what she wants, won't she?"

"Will she?" he countered. "Did she send me word that she was coming? Arthur swears that he didn't summon her—but he admits that he sent Harl to arrange a secret meeting. He won't tell me why, though he swears that it's a private and personal matter. Private! Personal! He is the King of the Britons! How dare he!"

There seemed to me to be a certain contradiction in the last two exclamations, but I didn't point it out. "Shall I ask her to come here then, master? Surely she will do that, if you invite her?"

"Oh yes," he said. "She'll come, if I invite her. Replete with magic, smiling all the while. She'll take a great interest in my welfare, and she'll tease me cruelly. She has the upper hand, and she knows it—but I must be forewarned, if I can. She'll have to go to the dining-hall, to watch the distribution of her gifts. But afterwards..."

"Shall I bring you some of the faery fruit for your own meal, master?" I asked. "Or should I advise everyone who will listen not to touch it lest they fall under a spell?"

He looked at me sharply, but decided that it was an honest question. "No," he said, "I shall not touch it—and I insist that you do likewise. As for warnings... they'll be drawing straws in every bedroom in the castle to decide who'll test the produce for his fellows. It's probably safe—but you and I are too precious to Arthur's cause to take the risk."

I gave no sign of dissent or disappointment.

"What I need to know first," Merlin muttered, as if to himself, "is whether Taliesin had any hand in this. He says that he has been in Faerie himself, having passed through one of the Brecon gates—I thought he was pretending, in order to increase his own mystique, but it might be true, and if it is... he might be the one who brought her here, no matter what Arthur believes... and druids might be as likely to fit elf-shot to their bows as any superstitious archer. You listened to his men yesterday—with the aid of hindsight, can you remember anything they said that might indicate an expectation that Morgana might come?"

"No, master," I said, truthfully.

"But you left your post, didn't you? You were lounging by the gate when Harl rode up?"

"I wasn't lounging, master," I said, innocently.

"No? Perhaps you were there to meet him, then. Perhaps all my apprentices have been seduced away, if not by Arthur then by someone who means us harm."

"No, master," I assured him. "I was eating a little bread before returning to my post—but events overtook my intention. Did you know that there isn't a single bowman in Morgana's company?" I pointed out.

"I know that none was carrying a bow, imbecile" he said, "and Kay's men saw none when they unloaded her luggage into the southern tower—but that tells us nothing about the elf-bolt that killed Harl." He picked up a leather cup from the table beside his chair, and cursed the fact that it was empty. I ran to fetch the water-jug, and filled it for him.

"I never had the gift of talking to ghosts," he muttered, "even when I was full of magic—but I'd be very interested to summon Harl's shade if I could. As things stand, I have only my wits to guide me. Arthur is hiding something from me, but that has the compensation of making him feel guilty, which means that he will not go directly against my advice for the time being. If she tries to see him when the banquet's done, she'll be put off with an excuse. What will she do then?"

"I don't know, master," I said.

"I wasn't talking to you, cretin," he snapped. "What would you know, who were only in Faerie for a moment, if at all? I know her better than any man alive, and better than any man who ever lived before, no matter what Mad Tom might have thought. Morgana will not wait patiently for someone to come to her; if Arthur will not receive her—and he shall not while I can contrive to keep them apart—she'll go to Taliesin. That might clear the way for the abbot to make more mischief, but he'll have his work cut out if he hopes to persuade every Christian in Camelot to let the devil's food alone, given that his communion wafers have gone moldy. She'll want to be on hand, though, to see how her mischievous gifts go down. I'll watch the dining-hall myself—you must remain on watch outside, at least while the bards are still at table. The harpers will probably play when the meal is done, for the whole evening

140

will still be ahead of us, but Taliesin will surely excuse himself and she will follow his lead. You must be waiting for them, wherever they may go—probably back to the western tower rather than the southern, but you can't afford to lose them."

When shall I have a chance to eat? I thought, bitterly. Why should I not be inside the dining-hall too, given that everything will be happening there? I knew better than to ask aloud; those were problems for the exercise of my own ingenuity.

"Yes master," I said, meekly.

Arthur had been right; Merlin's mind was still very clear. Everything went exactly as he had predicted, except that I did contrive to get into the dining-hall and see the fun. The faery food was served long before the usual dinner hour, so that those who did not wish to partake of it might have the excuse of the irregular hour—although the castle's corridors seemed quite deserted to me, and I saw many of the castle's supposed Christians within the hall.

Morgana was there, of course, with her six companions, tightly and somewhat defensively grouped. The male elves were still wearing their green jerkins and grey hose, but Morgana had changed into a white gown decorated on the bosom with gold embroidery, narrowed at the waist by a blue girdle. She had put on black court shoes, although the others still wore their riding-boots. Gawain had obviously been instructed to look after the visitors; he and Gareth fluttered around hem, paying elaborate courtesies, but none of the ladies of the court were presented to Morgana. Guinevere was absent—and so was Lancelot du Lac.

I resisted temptation for a few hundred heartbeats, but Merlin had had good reason for instructing me to wait outside. The pears were irresistible, and once I had bitten into one I could not have cared less whether it was enchanted; I even became reckless of the fact that Merlin might have seen me. I drank Morgana's wine as well, although I stopped when it seemed likely to go to my head, and took a little more food to slow its effect.

The food didn't last long, in spite of the initial anxiety of a few of the diners. As soon as examples had been set by the likes of Lancelot and Gawain, wariness was everywhere replaced by the determination to have one's fair share of the gift of Cokaygne.

When the food was gone, the bardic harpers began what was sure to become a very long evening's entertainment, while the kitchens prepared the food that Kay had bought to top up any bellies that had been too craven to consume their share of the forbidden food. Taliesin left, having not stinted himself in the least, and Morgana followed him. I slipped out and followed both of them. They went to his apartment in the western tower, not moving furtively at all; mine were by no means the only eyes that saw them together or tracked their progress.

I was at my post not long after the door had closed behind them. In spite of the difficulties of my situation, my stomach was by no means empty, nor my bladder overfull. I could see them as well as hear them, albeit from behind a blur of needle-pricked canvas.

17

I judged that Taliesin must have been handsome in his youth, at least by human standards, but he was past his prime now. He had a skin the color of fresh parchment and wrinkles like the surface of a tree-stump whose softer wood had rotted in the rain. His dark eyes had a penetrative gleam, though, and his hair and beard were barely flecked with grey.

Morgana's skin, on the other hand, had the curious quality of delicate solidity that I had observed from the window. It was preternaturally smooth and lustrous, as if it had been formed from good quality clay and very cleverly glazed. Her features were clearly delineated, but rather mask-like. It was not that they were inexpressive, but rather that the expressions

142

that showed upon them seemed more controlled than those of human faces.

Even seen from afar, Morgana had seemed unhuman, but at close range it was very obvious that she was not cut from the same coarse cloth of flesh as common mortals. Although her hair was as raven-dark as the bard's had been before the grey began its tentative invasion, her complexion was far whiter. Her lips were redder than a human's, and her teeth seemed untouchable by decay, which gave her smile an exquisite but adamantine beauty. Her golden eyes seemed unexpectedly soft at first glance, but more careful study revealed a durability that seemed as devoid of human warmth as her smile. I sensed that although I was looking at her more closely than before, with even greater concentration, I was still only seeing one element of an awesome complexity.

"Someone seems to have been expecting you, my lady," Taliesin was saying to her as I took up my position, "else they'd not have taken the trouble to send a dead man to the gate with an elf-bolt in his back. You have enemies here, I think." His accent was as foul as those of his companions, but the practice I had put in the day before stood me in good stead now.

"So it seems," Morgana replied. "I am astonished—I had always counted Arthur as a brother, and his messenger gave the impression that he thinks of me still as a sister and a friend. I cannot understand why I have been received so coldly—and then to hear that my message was intercepted, and its bearer killed... yes, it does seem that someone here thinks himself my enemy. You do understand, I hope, that it was no inhabitant of Cokaygne who fired that fatal shot. The boy was Arthur's messenger when he was brought to me, but he was mine when he passed through the gate a second time. He was under my protection, and none of my folk would have harmed him. I would like to know who did kill him, for I do not like to have my messages interrupted." Her speech was accented, though not in the same way as the Welshman's. It was no more fluid or musical than his, but it was more ca-

143

ressing—and gave the impression that it might be more deceptive.

I watched Taliesin's reaction to Morgana's speech, and saw him frown slightly, as if there were a question he dared not ask as yet. I judged that he was out of his depth, and had no idea how to proceed, although he was desperate to make the most of what might be a unique opportunity. "I never doubted for a moment that the fair folk were innocent of the boy's murder," he assured Morgana. "I am glad to see you here—very glad."

"Are you?" she queried, arching an eyebrow. "Why is that?"

"I have had dealings with the fair folk in my own country," the bard said, warily. "I have a reputation there for second sight, which some say—lightly or otherwise—must have been inherited from some other-worldly ancestor. I have only heard your own name from human lips, but I dare to hope that we might be friends."

"I fear that your name is unfamiliar to me," she said, "but I was interested to see your harpers, and I look forward to hearing them on another occasion."

"I will be pleased to sing for you, my lady," the bard assured her, "but I had hoped that we might have more important interests in common, and I feel the need of a friend."

"My lady!" she echoed, lightly, ignoring the latter part of his remark for the time being. "I am your majesty downstairs, it seems. Ever since Arthur claimed me for his kin, it seems, his loyal subjects have been obliged to reckon me a queen in my own land. That was how Arthur's messenger addressed me, when the huntsmen brought him to me. That was how the servants addressed me in the hall—but you say my lady."

"I have been assured that there are no monarchs in the Other World, my lady." Taliesin said, politely. "Am I mistaken?"

"No," she admitted. "My lady will do perfectly well, I suppose—as long as you do not mean to imply that I must be subject to a lord."

"No, my lady," Taliesin was quick to say. "I hope that I understand the ways of your world a little better than that. May I explain to you why I believe that we may have interests in common at the conference table?"

"I did not come here to take part in a conference, Taliesin," she told him flatly. "The boy who asked me to come made no mention of any such thing. I have no wish to take part in any conference. I have no wish to take sides in any human disputes. I have no interests in common with humans, save for music and the making of mosaics."

Taliesin bowed his head to signal his assent to all of that, but he was frowning again. In his understanding, the fact that she had helped Arthur to the British throne signified that she must have had an interest in his kingship—and the fact that she was here now, in answer to Arthur's summons, signified that she still did. Was it really as obvious as Taliesin thought? I didn't think so. She was an elf, after all; her reasons might be difficult for the human mind to fathom.

"If you will forgive me, my lady," Taliesin said, "I believe that your world and mine are bound to take an interest in one another, by virtue of being connected. The gates between them are difficult to find, from this side, and often hurt those who pass through them, but there is traffic between our worlds in spite of that. Even if the fair folk regard the isle of Britain as a mere hunting ground, or a convenient source of baubles and playthings, they still have an interest in the way in which things are ordered here. In my estimation, Faerie is bound to prefer the Welsh to the Romans, and druidry to Christianity."

"Faerie is not bound to deal with humans at all, Taliesin," Morgana pointed out. "We did not create the portals between our world and yours, but we can control them. If your world disappoints us, all that we require to do is hide them a little more securely. We can do more than render them invisible, if the necessity arises."

"The fact that you have not already done so, my lady, suggests that you would prefer it if the necessity did not arise," Taliesin said, his tongue almost tripping over the careful circumlocution.

Morgana refused to go any further along that road, at least for the time being. She looked away from him, studying the furniture and decorations of the apartment. "I am no queen in my own land," she said, eventually, "but if Arthur calls me queen, and sends a messenger to me, begging me to honor him with an interview, it seems rather impolite that he will not condescend to see me now, does it not? I have forgiven him for his failure to come to my chosen meeting-place, since my messenger never reached him, but my treatment here is less forgivable. He would not condescend to appear in the dining-hall, or even to send for a tray of the food I brought. Does that not seem rude to you, Taliesin?"

"Yes, my lady," Taliesin agreed, readily enough.

"On the other hand," Morgana went on, "Arthur's messenger must have been waiting by the portal for a long time. He was not to know, when it finally opened, that Arthur would have other guests in residence, and a political conference in progress. I seem to have come at a bad time."

"Perhaps Arthur intended to invite you to the conference," Taliesin suggested, "but could not delay it any longer in order to be sure of including you. If so, I am sorry that his messenger did not reach you sooner, so that he could meet with you in private and issue a formal invitation to join the abbot and myself at the table. I repeat that I would be very glad to have you there."

"I would not have agreed to attend any such conference," Morgana said, coldly. "Earthly politics are no concern of mine. Merlin knows that—and if Merlin knows it, Arthur must know it too. That cannot be why Arthur wanted to see me. Nor can it explain his reluctance to see me now."

"I am sure that he intends no insult, my lady," Taliesin said, although the tone of his voice belied his words. "It was not his fault that his messenger was shot before he could hear your reply."

"Whose fault was it, do you suppose?" Morgana asked him.

"I have no idea, my lady," Taliesin countered, smoothly. "I have no wish to be impolite, but if you really believe that you have no interest in this conference, and no interests in common with any human party to it, why are we sitting here now?"

"You invited me," Morgana said. "It was the only invitation I received, and it seemed only polite to accept. I suppose that I came to see you because Arthur is hiding from me, and I did not want to sit in the dining-hall or in my rooms, waiting for him to change his mind. I need no favors from you, and have none to offer—except, perhaps, that I would like to hear your harpers play, and to hear you sing, in a better place than the dining-hall. Although I would like to know who killed my messenger, if you can help me to find out."

It seemed to me that the discussion was becoming sterile. Taliesin didn't seem to have anything to tell Morgana that Morgana wanted to hear, and Morgana didn't seem to be prepared to offer Taliesin the kind of help he wanted—but the bard, at least, wasn't yet prepared to let go of his hopes.

18

"Tradition tells me that your folk and mine have had our differences in the past, my lady," Taliesin said, "but it seems to me that we have a common enemy now, and perhaps two. No matter why you came here, now you are here, I believe we ought to combine forces against our mutual enemies. I don't know who killed your messenger—but I can tell you who your enemies are."

"Go on," Morgana said, in a tone which declared that she was making no promises.

"Our common enemies are the Church and the Saxons, my lady," Taliesin said, forthrightly. "The Saxons may appear to respect the fair folk, and have not so far come into conflict with my own people, and they also have a religion of their own, which puts them at odds with the church—but what they have in common with the Christians is an innate restlessness, a fervent determination to change things. I assume that the fair folk cannot sympathize with any such urge. Constancy is varied in the Other World, I believe."

"Oh yes," Morgana murmured. "Constancy is valued in Faerie."

Taliesin waited for her to say more. When she didn't, he continued: "The Church and the Saxons are both intent on expansion," he told her, "but they cannot expand without eating into Arthur's Britain. I may be wrong, but I had assumed that you helped Arthur to the throne of his fragment of Britain because you favored the stability he brought to the region. I am enthusiastic to make an alliance between his domain and Wales for exactly the same reason—but my fear is that he intends to make an alliance with the Church and the Saxons instead, and to commit himself to their kind of ambition. Perhaps he will be unable to ally himself with both—but at present, it seems to me that he would prefer to take sides with either one of them than with the Bardic Order. If the Bardic Order were explicitly allied with the fair folk, however..."

Morgana cut him off. "We do not make such alliances," she told him.

Taliesin shook his head, letting his impatience show. "I beg your pardon, my lady," he said, "but the Britons believe that you do—and they have Excalibur as proof, hanging above Arthur's Judgment Seat. You did help Arthur to become king, did you not? You did consent to call him brother? If that does not constitute an alliance, what does?"

Morgana nodded her head thoughtfully, as if she really hadn't thought of that until now. Was it really possible that she had never considered the implications of helping Merlin to play the trick of the sword in the stone? Perhaps it was, given that she hadn't visited the human world for so many years. Merlin had already admitted to me that he'd tricked her, and had been very hopeful that she might never find out. Now, it seemed, she had.

"It was not an alliance," she said, eventually. "I have no power to make alliances. When I agreed to let Merlin represent me as a queen, it was a pleasant game... but I can understand how it might have seemed different to Arthur's subjects. I liked Arthur, and remembered him fondly enough to respond to his plea, but the gift of Excalibur was mine alone. The fair folk do not make alliances with humans."

Taliesin pursed his lips. The conversation wasn't going well, from his point of view—but he wasn't about to give up. "I dare say that you have your own means of measuring the situation, my lady," the bard said, "but it seems to me that now would be a good time to begin. The Church is making far greater progress than I would have thought possible ten years ago. Ten years ago, I would never have believed that Arthur of the Britons and his knights might be ripe for conversion to Christianity—but I dare say that the aristocrats of Rome thought the same about Constantine.

"The abbot offers Arthur the same seduction that his counterpart must have offered the emperor of Rome: the chance to bind a crumbling community with chains of faith and refresh its virtuous ideals. In fact, the abbot claims to be offering Arthur more than that, for Constantine's converters could not preserve his reunited empire from barbarian invasion and conquest, while the Abbot of Glastonbury boasts that if Arthur embraces Christ the Saxons will very likely follow, and Britain will be saved from devastation—assuming, that is, that Britain can be redefined to exclude the Welsh, who are, in reality, the only true Britons left in the isle. In our view, you see, Arthur's Britons are merely the shades of departed conquerors, who wish to retain and renew the legacy of Rome instead of restoring Britain to the condition it was in before the Romans ever set eyes on it."

"Is that really how things stand?" Morgana asked, wonderingly. "I had been given to understand the opposite—that Arthur's Britons were true Britons, who wanted Rome's legacy obliterated and the old ways restored." She was talking politics now, I noticed, even though she was still pretending disinterest. It must have been Merlin who "gave her to understand" that, deceptively.

"I had always hoped so myself, my lady," Taliesin said. "Ten years ago, as I said, I might have believed it. I came here thinking that I would at least be set on an equal footing with the abbot—but he seems to have come on the assumption that my presence here is merely an opportunity for yet more evangelizing, and I have not heard Arthur correct him yet."

"That must be discomfiting," Morgana observed, making no attempt to sound sympathetic. "But what of Merlin? Is he not a true Briton?"

"He seemed very sympathetic in the letters he wrote to me," Taliesin admitted, "but I can't help wondering now whether that might have been a ruse. Nor can I help wondering how much power he really has. When Arthur first came to the throne, he was a boy and Merlin was a powerful magician—now, though, Arthur is a man in his prime and Merlin seems a spent force. If Merlin does favor my people—and the fair folk—over the Christians, he has not yet demonstrated to me that he has the ability to exercise that favor."

Taliesin's opinion of Merlin seemed worthless to me—but I couldn't begin to guess, as yet, what Morgana's judgment might be. She was giving nothing away.

Taliesin must have been disappointed by her silence. "Will you tell me your understanding of the situation, my lady, in exchange for mine?" he asked.

"Your judgment must be far better informed than mine," Morgana said, negligently. "I had assumed, when his message reached me—belatedly, it now seems—that Arthur still held fast to the belief that he is Britain, and the round table, not the cross, its one and only symbol."

"It is precisely because of that," Taliesin was quick to say, "that were he to convert to the new faith, Britain would be Christian in the eyes of all believers in Camelot—and everything unchristian would become un-British by definition. Arthur has always been ambitious to be a king of kings and a maker of peace; he might be ready to forget that he became a king and peacemaker by honoring very different traditions and professing very different beliefs."

"Would Merlin allow that?" Morgana asked.

"With all due respect, my lady," Taliesin said, "the real question is: could Merlin prevent it if he would? You might have taught him well, but I fear that he is no longer able to apply his learning. I think the fair folk are sometimes inclined to forget that men grow old, and to underestimate the changes that old age brings. Whether Merlin is responsible for throwing Arthur into the waiting arms of the Church, or merely powerless to hold him back, his failure is regrettable. If there is a strategy in his silence, I certainly cannot fathom it. Perhaps Arthur was a better man when he had fewer knights, and when those he had were less eager to increase their own reflected glory by feeding his grandiosity. Sir Lancelot has not been good for Camelot, it seems to me, no matter what the ladies of the court may think."

"None of that is any concern of mine," Morgana told him.

"Is it not, my lady?" Taliesin countered. "Perhaps you're right. No one believes any longer that you and Arthur had the same father, if anyone ever did believe it. It was a convenient addition to his reputation, in the beginning, but he has been king for so long now that the fact is securely established. And even though he sent a messenger to plead for an interview with you, it seems that he is refusing to see you now. I suppose, then, that you might as well go home."

That was unsubtle, but I could see what the Welshman was trying to do. He had revealed himself; now he felt that it was her turn. He had worked hard to sow seeds of doubt in Morgana's mind against Arthur and Merlin, and he needed some reassurance that he wasn't wasting his time.

She was not about to give him any.

"Since I am here, I suppose I ought to wait a little while, in case he does wish to see me," Morgana said, with a vagueness that was surely feigned. "I ought to be polite, even if he is not. If the gifts I brought Camelot mean nothing to him, I sup-

pose I shall have to reconcile myself to the fact of human ingratitude. It is a matter of scant importance. I am unlikely to
pass through the gate of Avalon again until every man now
living has been a long time in his grave."

And that, I thought at the time, had to be the heart of the
matter. She could afford to be aloof from the petty squabbles
of men like Arthur and Taliesin, because they would all be
gone in the space of a few of Faerie's bright-lit hours.

Taliesin was not so easily put off. "I fear that you have
no effective claim on Arthur, Morgana," he said, slyly, "no
matter what lies he was once prepared to tell or what courtesies he is still prepared to offer in order to bind you to his
cause. He will continue to deny you an audience, if it suits him
to do so, and you will have no alternative but to bear the insult."

That was when I saw Morgana's eyes change color for
the first time, from gold to vivid green. I had no idea then how
much alteration they still had in reserve. She had not treated
Taliesin generously, but she obviously had not expected his
rude retaliation

"Do you think so?" she said, very softly indeed.

I watched Taliesin, to see whether he would repent his
recklessness. If he did, he felt obliged to stand his ground.

"You and I have interests in common, my lady," he said,
trying to sound confident, "whether you will recognize the fact
or not. Between us, we might persuade Arthur to resist the
pressure of the Churchmen—but if we are to do that, we must
join forces."

The truth, it seemed to me, was that Taliesin and Morgana had far less in common than he was prepared to imagine—but I could feel the desperation in him, and knew that
what he had said about his status in the conference could not
be entirely unjustified. It was not merely the abbot's arrogance
that had relegated him to an inferior situation. Arthur and
Merlin clearly hadn't made the efforts to make him feel welcome that I would have expected. I couldn't understand, any
more than he could, what strategy Merlin was following—but

I told myself that there had to be a strategy. Merlin was Merlin, after all. He must have had a plan, and no matter how awkwardly Morgana's arrival had disrupted it, he must have it still.

I made up my mind to find out what that plan was, no matter how determined my master was to keep it from me. After all, I had plans of my own to make.

19

I slipped away from the bard's chamber as cleverly as I had approached it, and ran light-footed down one secret stair and up another. As soon as my master returned from the council-chamber I repeated what had passed between Morgana and Taliesin, including the slights on his own capability. I knew that he wouldn't be pleased by what he heard, but I thought it more likely that he'd explain himself to me if he thought that I might otherwise be left nursing serious doubts about his competence.

"It tells us nothing we didn't already know," he complained. "We know what Taliesin's position is—what we need to know is what game Morgana is playing."

"We, master?" I queried. "There was a good deal in what Taliesin said that I didn't know. Had you forgotten that you hadn't told me?"

He cuffed me about the head, as I expected him to—but he rose to the bait. "Ungrateful wretch," he said. "Do you think that I ought to tell you everything that is in my mind, lest I should fall down dead and require you to continue my work alone? Do you believe Taliesin, when he says that I am too feeble to influence what Arthur thinks and does?"

"No master," I said, dutifully. I refrained from pointing out that if his influence over Arthur had been complete, Morgana would not be here. I wanted information, not a beating.

"Well," he said, eventually, "I am not as weak as Taliesin thinks, nor as unsympathetic to his interests. If I have gone out of my way to feed the abbot's arrogance, I have my reasons. If it were possible to obtain the agreement of all the sides in this dispute, I would move heaven and earth to secure that result. If it is not, I must find the solution that inflicts the least damage. If Taliesin were prepared to do likewise, we would all be better placed. He's a fool if he thinks he can win Morgana's support by such tactics—but is he fool enough to hold his ground when he knows the full extent of his disadvantage. Perhaps he is—damn him!"

"I would be better placed to do your spying, master, if I knew a little more about your aims and schemes," I told him.

"I'll be the judge of that, imbecile," Merlin replied, rudely. "It's for your own protection. If I treat you roughly, it's because treating you too kindly might put you in danger. I treated Harl in exactly the same fashion, and he'd be alive and well today if he'd done what he was told to do, instead of going into business as a spy on his own account."

I didn't believe him. It didn't make sense. If anyone were foolhardy enough to seize and torture me to find out what I knew about Merlin's plans, they wouldn't be put off by his manner towards me. What kept me safe from that kind of recklessness was the probability of retribution. I was in Camelot, after all. I was Arthur's man as well as Merlin's, and whoever struck out at me was striking out at Arthur.

On the other hand, that hadn't saved Harl from an arrow in the back.

"I do all that I'm told to do," I reminded my master.

He softened slightly—but only slightly. "I need you, Amory," he said. "You know how disadvantaged I would be if anything were to happen to you. What you need to know is that everything I do is intended to preserve Camelot, and to make Arthur safe. Whatever I need to do in that cause, I will do. If I fail, disaster will overwhelm us all—you must understand that, for I need your loyalty to my cause. You know full well that I'd rather make peace between the druids and the Christians than have them fight a holy war—but if the choice between them must be made, it must be made. It was difficult enough when there were only the Saxons to consider—now, there may be some other conspiracy afoot, which I must fathom as soon as I can. I trust you Amory. I trust your cleverness as well as your loyalty. You must help me in this, no matter who I must deceive."

It was flattery, and I refused to yield to its pressure. I was his servant, but I was my own man too. I had my own plans to make.

"Why did Arthur want to see Morgana, master?" I asked him. "Why did Morgana come?"

"He wanted to see her because he is a fool," Merlin said, hoarsely, "and so ashamed of his own foolishness that he went behind my back. Why she came in response to his call I cannot tell, but it looks bad. It looks as if he planned to invite her to Camelot, which was the last thing on his mind—but we must cope with that as best we can."

What kind of explanation was that? Could you have been satisfied with it? I wanted to know how Arthur had been a fool—but Arthur had not told me, when he had had the chance, and Merlin would not tell me either. I know now why they were so reluctant—Arthur was the king, after all, and his reputation was everything—but at the time, I was full of resentment of the fact that no one would tell me what they knew.

"That's enough talk," Merlin said, abruptly. "You've a deal of work to do before you go to your bed—you'd best get on with it." And he started making a list.

What would I have done differently thereafter, I wonder, if he only had told me the truth? If he had only confided in me more fully, would I have given him the loyalty that he expected? Perhaps. And perhaps not. I was a fool, after all—a fool like the king, with whom I had more in common than Merlin suspected.

When it was time to take the chamber-pot and water-bucket down to the cesspit I left Merlin's room carelessly, never thinking that someone might be lying in wait in one of my own little coverts—and lying in wait for me. Had I been on my guard, though, I probably would not have seen him as I passed him by, nor would I have heard his footfalls as he followed me. He had slippered feet, as I had—and other advantages that I had never had.

My pursuer had the good sense to wait until I had discharged my load at the cesspit before making his move; it's always unwise to attack a man who can wield a pot of shit against you, no matter how accomplished you might be in the martial arts. He came up behind me silently as I made sure that the vessel was empty, and clamped a cloth over my mouth.

I didn't even know enough to hold my breath, let alone how to defend myself with only a clay pot and an empty pail for arms and armor. Instead, I was moved by alarm to draw a deep and rapid breath, and promptly felt my nostrils flooded with something sickly-sweet. I tumbled an instant thereafter into a whirling dizziness that led to oblivion.

I might have fallen into the pit and drowned had elvish arms not wrapped themselves around me to keep me safe.

When I awoke, I was on the less familiar side of a sumptuous array of tapestries and silks—and could not help but wonder whether someone else might be behind them, looking in.

Morgana le Fay was seated on a stool, looking down at me. Her eyes were golden, and seemed amused. She was still wearing the white gown with the blue girdle, but it was already stained with dust.

I managed to sit up, but couldn't immediately rise to my feet. I moved instead to a kneeling position, and bowed my head as a commoner was obliged to do in the presence of a queen—even a queen appointed by incredible rumor.

"What is your name, little spy?" she said, reassuring me that even though her magic had more honest power than Merlin's she still did not know everything without having to ask.

"Amory, your majesty" I told her, not bothering to deny that I was a little spy. I was sure that she hadn't caught sight of me in Taliesin's room, but I knew that any natural or supernatural means she might have employed to spy on Merlin would have told her clearly enough what I had done when I reported my findings to him.

"Don't call me your majesty," she instructed me, sharply. "I never was a queen, and I know now that I should never have consented to Merlin's silly trick."

"Yes, my lady," I said, already wondering how an elf could be misled by a mere mortal's trick—and how, if it could be done, I might do it myself.

"As far as anyone knows, Amory." she said, "you have disappeared. No one saw you taken, or carried here, and no one is hiding behind those tapestries you eyed with such suspicion a moment ago. If you are never seen again, no one will be any the wiser. I could kill you now, or take you through the gate of Avalon to Cokaygne, and send you back a fortnight older to find that twenty or a hundred years had passed. No one here would know, and no one here would care. Merlin might guess, but even he could never be certain that you had not been waylaid by the Druids or the Saxons, or had not simply thrown his stinking pot and bucket into the pit and fled his unkind care. Do you understand that?"

"Yes, my lady," I repeated.

"Do you further understand," she said, "that I have a phial of serum close at hand which could compel you to speak the truth, a dozen times and more for every drop I cared to place upon your tongue? Do you understand that if I thought a magical substance too precious to waste on a cur like you I could take your newly-fallen balls in my own delicate hand and make you scream in agony until you begged me to let you tell me everything you know—and that I would not hesitate to do it, if I thought it might amuse me?"

"Yes, my lady," I said yet again, wishing that it were a lie.

"Good," she said. And then she stopped, and looked at me quizzically, staring into my eyes. Suddenly, I felt dizzy again—as if the drug were renewing its effect. The colored designs on the tapestries became garish, and I could hear the sound of voices from the next room: voices that were raised as their haggling became excited. A merchant was there, I realized—a lapidary, hawking his wares to Morgana's compan-

157

ions, who were laughing as they toyed with him. Those companions weren't elvish knights, I realized; they were traders. Their only purpose in coming to Camelot was to barter for trinkets and playthings. That was how Morgana had persuaded them to come with her as assistants in her own game.

I pulled myself together, and told myself sternly that I was a player too, and not a piece. No matter how beautiful my captor was, nor how much magic she had at her disposal, I was a player, else I would not be here. So I met her gaze, and prepared to play.

20

I told myself, even before Morgana spoke again, that whatever she said would be one more move in the game. I told myself that it was all a trick, a performance, a game—but I was just a fool, and Morgana le Fay was a queen among human women, whether she cared to accept the title or not.

"We have met before, Amory," she said, softly. "Do you remember?"

"No, my lady," I said, and bit my tongue to prevent myself from rushing into an explanation of my answer and an apology for its incompleteness. My determination to be a player was already under threat as she homed in on my weakness.

"No," she echoed. "You were too young to remember, and remained too young for longer than you may suppose. The legacy of your expedition is evident in your eyes, though, to those who can see it. Did Merlin ever tell you that you had once been in Cokaygne?"

"He didn't have to, my lady," I admitted. "I was abandoned to the care of the Sisters of Saint Syncletica wrapped in a shawl of elvish silk, in an elvish basket. It was never a secret."

"Ah!" she said, the syllable redolent with sweet sympathy. "You suffered in consequence. Of course you did—but the shawl and the basket served to let you know why. If there had been no such evidence, they would still have sensed a difference in you. You have been unhappy, and you blame the fair folk for your misery. You do not know, because you cannot remember, what compensation you had for your trouble—and compensation unremembered is no compensation at all. I understand. I owe you something, then—consideration, if nothing else. I accept that. I will not hurt you. No matter what you might refuse to tell me, I will not hurt you. You have my word on that."

It was all pretence, all deceptive persuasion. I knew that, but I melted anyway. She had told me what she might do to me, and now she promised not to do it. She intended that I should like her for it, that I should help her willingly because of it. She was playing with me, like a toy. But what a game it was—and how ill-equipped I was to be a player instead of a pawn!

She was still looking into my eyes, knowing that I could see how beautiful she was, and knowing what effect her beauty must have.

"You heard me talking to Taliesin," she said, her voice still ripe with kindness and concern.

"Yes, my lady," I admitted.

"I didn't know that you were there," she told me. "You're an unusually clever spy. Cokaygne left its mark on you, even though you can't perceive it. But I found out, of course, when I asked one of my companions to find out what Merlin was about. He thinks that his quarters are proof against all human spies, I suppose?"

"Yes, my lady," I confirmed.

"Elves are cleverer," she said. "You seemed to be as interested in finding out what your master is up to as I am, although he wasn't very forthcoming."

"Yes, my lady," I agreed.

"Taliesin is said to be a fine bard," Morgana observed, "but he lacks refinement in other ways. He doesn't seem to know what is happening here, or why. Do you?"

"No, my lady," I said.

"That won't do, Amory," she said. "We have no time to waste with all this yes my lady, no my lady."

"I don't know why Arthur sent an envoy to the gate of Avalon to plead for a meeting, my lady," I told her. "I don't know who killed his messenger before your reply could be delivered."

"But you'd dearly like to know," she observed. "I can see that. You'd like to find out. Why? So you can curry favor with your master Merlin? No, I think not. You have higher ambitions than that, haven't you? You want to know for yourself. So do I, Amory. Unlike Taliesin, I'm not frightened by what is happening here, because I have nothing to fear, but I am curious. I came here on a whim, in search of a moment's amusement—why else would an elf set foot in this awkward and tedious world?—but now that I'm here, I don't intend to go home with nothing to repay my trouble but an insult to nurse. I have no enemies here, no matter what Taliesin may think, but it hurts me to have my friendship thrown back in my face."

She paused, and waited for me to say something. I could still hear the dickering in the other room, as the elves closed in on whatever hard bargain they were driving with the eager tradesman.

"Taliesin wasn't entirely wrong, my lady," I told her, in a soft voice. "You may have no feelings of enmity towards any human, but not all humans feel the same way about the fair folk."

"Why should that be, Amory?" she asked.

I took the question as a test of my intelligence. "You feel no enmity towards humans, my lady, because men's lives are so much shorter than yours, even without the differences in the flow of time which exist between your world and ours. Humans can't hurt you, because you have magic to intimidate them and magic to cure any damage that humans might try to inflict on you. The worst a human might do to an elf is to inconvenience her mood—with the result that you can treat them with condescension or contempt, as you please. The condescension and the contempt seem equally insulting to many humans, and there are some who hate you for it."

"And how do you feel about the fair folk, Amory?" she asked.

"I don't know, my lady," I confessed. "I was stolen as a child, it seems, and quickly returned. I had no lasting reward from being in Faerie, and I've borne the stigma ever since. Throughout my childhood I longed to return to Faerie because I thought that I could have no life in this world. When I first came to Camelot, I thought that I had found a place after all... but now I'm not so sure. I'm not your enemy, my lady, and would like to be your friend—but I'm not entirely certain how I feel, for it's only in the last few hours that I've realized how little I know about the Other World and its inhabitants."

She didn't seem to disapprove of the answer. "And what is the little that you do know about us?" she asked.

"I've heard many tales," I said, "but I don't know which ones to believe. You steal babies, it seems, and lovestruck rhymers too—and sometimes take a liking to other humans who stumble into your realm, although you send them back as madmen or magicians. If legend tells the truth, time flows slowly in your world, the sun never sets there, and life is not toilsome. Faerie seems to humans to be a kind of paradise, from which we humans are excluded—all but a favored few— but there are also stories which insist that there must be penalties to be paid for its bounty that make Faerie far less desirable a residence than it seems. That is, however, far more than I can honestly say I know."

"It's all true," she assured me.

I had grown more confident as I spoke, and I was ready to continue. "There are those among us now, my lady," I told her, "who argue that humans are destined for a better and infinitely more desirable paradise than Faerie, if only we can be good. Anyone who believes that must also believe that the allure of Faerie is a snare as well as a delusion... an enemy to be opposed by every possible means. You do have enemies here, my lady, although you have not recognized them as such.

They have chosen to set themselves against you: they have designated you an enemy... and me too, although they know full well that I cannot possibly have chosen to be stolen away from whatever cradle was truly mine."

Was I really as eloquent as that? Well, perhaps not. I have gone over that conversation so many times in my mind that I have undoubtedly tidied up the memory, shaping and sculpting it to what it should have been—but I had practiced in advance as well; it was a matter I had thought about a great deal. So I was eloquent, by my own standards; I took Morgana's questions as a test, and I did my utmost to impress her.

It seemed to me that I succeeded, although I knew how easy it would have been for her to pretend.

"Yes, I see," Morgana said, softly. "I had not thought of it quite like that. You might be more useful to me than I thought, Amory, even though you don't yet know the answers to the questions that puzzle us both. Taliesin wanted me to help him, but I have no business with the Welsh. You and I, on the other hand, really might have interests in common. You and I might be able to reach an understanding."

It was flattery, like Merlin's flattery. It was seduction, plain and simple. But if you were flattered by Merlin, on the one hand, and Morgana le Fay, on the other, could you resist them both with equal firmness? And whether you are male or female, young or old, I ask you this: if Morgana le Fay set out to seduce you, with all the resources of Faerie at her disposal, would you have had the least desire or power to resist?

"Yes, my lady," I said, unheroically. "I think we might."

21

Morgana told me to get up and fetch a stool, so that I wouldn't have to look up at her. I hadn't quite realized before how short she was—no taller than I. As I fetched the stool I cast an eye over the various trunks and boxes she and her companions had brought as luggage. One contained more clothing, so I was reassured that she wouldn't have to wear the stained gown for much longer. There were reserves of food, kept back from the gifts she had made to the castle and the town, and wine in glass flasks cushioned by straw. There were pieces of gold and silver, too, although they were few and mostly small, hammered into discs but not stamped as coins.

"Humans fear magic," Morgana told me, when we were face to face again. She had adopted a more confidential manner, but her expression was still unreadable. "Because they fear it, they learn to hate it—and because of that, they squander even the little magic that they have at birth. Among those humans born with a glimmer of the second sight, only one out of every seven even begins by counting it a gift, and six out of every seven of those end by counting it a curse. If humans only had the knack of living longer, it might be different; had you time to come to know yourselves, you might begin to cultivate your magic, as we have always done in my world. As things are, the greatest gifts that my kind has to offer yours are never appreciated as they should be.

"Whenever we welcome humans into our world, we treat them benevolently, and it is no fault of ours that so many of them go mad. The flaw is in them, not in us. Many are so sickened by their passage through the gate of Avalon that they have to be returned immediately, if they cannot turn back of their own accord. Others stay for far longer—but in the end, they become restless. Few, if any, have the ability to adapt to our way of life, even though the rewards of such adaptation are very great indeed. In our world, even the meager resources of magic that humans have are nurtured and encouraged. Second sight has time and space to grow there, and as sight grows, mind grows with it: craft, art and native alchemy. In the human world, hands and tools have developed in similar association, but they need not have developed to their present complexity if humans had not been so willfully blind. As mind becomes more artful, so does the flesh. We are what we are because we have made ourselves what we are, and humans have no right to hate us for that while they refuse to make the most of their own admittedly meager potential.

"While Merlin was in Faerie, he became ten times the man he would have been had he stayed where he was. If Taliesin was ever there, his sojourn must have been as brief as yours, but he might have taken far more benefit from it than he seems to have done. If I take you back with me to Cokaygne, Amory, you must try to do better—not just better than Taliesin, but better than Merlin. For your own sake, you must not waste the gift. You must try as hard as you an not to be afraid of magic."

It was what I wanted to hear. I drank it in.

"I will do my best, my lady," I said.

She hadn't made me any promises, as yet, and I wouldn't have trusted them if she had—but she knew that the possibility that she might take me back to Cokaygne when she went would be enough to attach me firmly to her cause.

She leaned forward then, inviting me to savor the light in her golden eyes.

"Has Merlin told you what bargain we made when I gave Arthur the power to pull the sword from the stone and steal the kingship of the Britons from a hundred stronger men?"

"Not exactly, my lady," I said, calmly. "He has told me very little about his time in Faerie or his dealings with you."

"He asked me to make his apprentice a king, as a pleasant jest—and in return, he offered to see to it that the forest around the gate of Avalon would have royal protection, that it might be preserved as a hunting-ground for the elves. Does that seem a fair bargain to you?"

"Fair enough, my lady," I said.

"Don't be ridiculous, Amory," she said. "You mean very advantageous, to Merlin and Arthur. They gave me nothing, you see—nothing that I really cared about. Even if I, or my neighbors, had been ardently interested in the petty pleasures of the hunt, what was Merlin offering? Even in his own terms, how long could he expect their promise to last? Twenty years? A human lifetime? A hundred years? What would that be worth to me or my neighbors? A mere eye-blink, in an elvish lifetime. Do you think, if we really cared about hunting that forest, that we could not find our own means of preserving it?"

"No, my lady," I said. "Obviously, the bargain was a sham. You had another reason for doing what Merlin asked." And Merlin must know that too, I thought. But does he know the true reason?

"On the other hand," Morgana said, "What I did was very little—the sort of thing I might have done on a whim, just to please him, if I had been in a mood to please him. I had grown tired of him before left Faerie, but I did remember him fondly enough. I was pleased with him, for he had made far more of his magical resources than any other man I had welcomed to my world. I thought him an apt pupil, and liked him for it. Even whims require inspiration, though—if not a reason, then a trigger."

"You liked Arthur, my lady," I guessed, easily. "You liked him well enough, at any rate, to tell him that he might call on your aid if ever he had need of it—and enough to answer when he did call."

"Very clever, Amory," she said. "Yes, I did like Arthur. Yes, I did make him that promise—and though I made it to a mere boy, I had not forgotten it. When his messenger told me that he was a grown man now, married though childless, I was surprised. I had lost track of time in the human world, you see. I questioned his messenger very carefully as to what Arthur might want of me, but he did not know and was hesitant to guess. He had no second sight, you see—but you have, Amory. Even now, you have a little left. Can you guess what Arthur wanted from me, Amory?"

It was a sterner challenge than she had ever posed before, but I knew that it had to be met." Perhaps I can, now, my lady," I said, tentatively. "Merlin said that it was something of which he was ashamed, but I cannot believe that Arthur has any crime to hide, so I take that to mean that it was something he was ashamed of requiring magic to attain. Merlin said that Arthur went behind his back, and that too, is odd. Arthur knows that Merlin has little or no magic left, and might not be able give him what he needed, but he would have come to Merlin, even so, had it not been something that he did not want to admit, even to Merlin. As you said just now, my lady, Arthur is a man now, married several years but childless. I think he fears that he might lose the respect of his knights and subjects if Guinevere does not bear him a son, and soon. I think that is what he wanted to ask you for—in private, of course. And now that you are here, he has more than one cause for embarrassment. That might help to explain why he is reluctant to see you now."

She looked at me long and hard. Her eyes were green-tinted again, but it wasn't annoyance that had made them change color.

"Why, Amory," she murmured. "I believe you have more than a mere glimmer of the second sight. Your time in Faerie was by no means wasted, though you doubtless spent it all in dreaming. I had come to the same conclusion, but hesitated to believe it. There is no childbirth in Cokaygne, you see, and I cannot tell how important such matters might be to humans. Thank you, Amory. In return for that, I'll tell you the real reason why I made that silly bargain with Merlin.

"Yes, I liked Arthur. Perhaps it would have amused me to make Arthur a king, even if there had been no other thought in my head. But I really did it for Tom Rhymer. Has Merlin ever mentioned Tom to you?"

"Yes, my lady," I said. "He calls him Mad Tom. Apparently, they went together to a portal that stands in the same relation to your world as the gate of Avalon to ours: a portal to a Land of Darkness. He told me that Tom wanted them both to go in, but that he hesitated on the threshold and turned back. He likened the story to the legend of Orpheus, so I think he still feels guilty about abandoning his friend. He was very tired at the time, else he wouldn't have let me know that. His guard was down, for a few minutes."

"It's true," Morgana told me. "Merlin and Tom went together to the portal, but only Tom went on once they had made their way through. Merlin turned back—and left Cokaygne without ever knowing what became of Tom. Perhaps he would feel better about it if he knew that Tom had returned, but I never told him. Tom was annoyed, of course, by Merlin's failure to stay with him—but he didn't hold a grudge, and he was glad, for Merlin's sake, that Merlin had returned to his own world. He was always a fine musician, but he was even finer when he came back from the Dark Land than he had been before. He had played for the shadow folk, apparently, and the experience had changed him. It brought a new quality into the music he played for us—which, to tell you the truth, had grown tedious in its familiarity.

"When Merlin sent word asking me to help Arthur become a king, I told Tom that I would see him, and asked whether I should send his regards. Tom gave me no instruction in that regard—but he did ask me to help Merlin carry his plans forward. Tom knew more about those plans than I did, of course, and probably cared more too. When he heard about Merlin's idea—the sword in the stone, that is—he begged me to do it. He's mad, of course, but madmen can be entertaining as well as adamant, and I agreed."

"That's not what Merlin believes," I told her.

"Of course not," she said. "I never told him that Tom had returned."

"Even setting that aside," I said, "Merlin believes that you had another, quite different, reason for giving Excalibur to Arthur."

The green glint in her eye had almost given way to soft gold, but now it flared up again, almost to emerald. "Does he?" she said, her voice hardly above a whisper. "Well, perhaps I had all kinds of motives—but Tom Rhymer's request was the real reason. Now, you must lend me your second sight again, for the other matter still needs to be settled."

"The false elf-bolt?" I said, uncertainly.

"Yes. It's a trivial matter, I suppose. Why should I care, after all, whether I'm falsely accused of murder here? Why should I dignify an insult by asking who has made it? I'm curious, though—and a punishment might be in order, don't you think? Would you care to make another guess for me, Amory? I'll help you as best I can."

Her eyes, staring into mine, were still greener than a forest canopy in summer. I felt that the gaze was reaching into my mind, like a poker into a fire or a spoon to stir a cooking-pot.

"I can't do so with much confidence," I warned her. "I wondered, a little while ago, whether there might be political disputes in Faerie as there are on earth, and whether one of your own folk might have reason for making the gate of Avalon seem a dangerous place, but what you've told me makes that seem unlikely. Let's assume that someone in our world discovered that Harl was waiting at Avalon, and jumped to a conclusion as to the reason for his mission—not, I suspect, the conclusion that I suggested a few minutes ago. Evidently, Harl was shot because the person in question wanted to prevent Arthur from seeing you, and that person used an elf-bolt in the expectation that when his body were found, Arthur would conclude that you didn't want to see him and wouldn't try again. I doubt that the guilty party ever considered the possibility that you might ride out of Avalon bearing gifts for Camelot."

"Who?" she demanded, brusquely.

"I don't know," I said, frankly. "It might be the Saxons, the Churchmen, or someone in Arthur's court. Without more information, I daren't accuse anyone."

"Very scrupulous," she said. "By someone in Arthur's court, I suppose you mean Merlin?"

Actually, I hadn't—but I was reluctant to speak the name that I did have in mind.

"It might have been any of half a dozen people here at court, my lady," I said, cautiously. "I really can't tell, without further evidence."

Morgana's eyes were vividly green. She reached out to me with her delicate hand—the hand with which she had threatened to torture me—and touched me gently on the shoulder, as if by way of thanks. The contact sent a thrill might through me. I wished with all my heart that I knew the answer to her question, and that it as one I could give her without troubling my own conscience overmuch.

"If I give you the means to find out." Morgana said, "Will you bring the answer to me instead of Merlin or Arthur?"

"Yes, my lady," I said, after a moment's hesitation.

"Would you spy on Merlin for me, if I asked you to do that?"

This time, I didn't hesitate. "Yes, my lady."

"Good," she said. "I shall give you two magics to help you remain undetected."

She got up and walked away from me, smoothing down her gown as she moved. There was a trunk in the corner of the room that was full to the brim with her personal effects. She rummaged beneath the multicolored gowns and underclothes as any human lady might have done, eventually producing a sealed phial of clear liquid and a grey cap of the soft indoor kind.

"The cap will not grant you full invisibility," she said, "but it will make you very unobtrusive even to the kind of heightened senses that Merlin once possessed—Orwen has already demonstrated the capability of one like it, but he can't spy on Merlin with your educated ear, and he's anxious to be off to market. The phial is the truth serum with which I threatened you earlier. It is rare and precious even among my kind, and its power will be exhausted much more rapidly than anyone could wish. I would not want a single drop to be wasted— but I do want to know who has appointed himself an enemy of Cokaygne with such sly determination that he tries to make one of us seem guilty of his own murder. Since Taliesin thinks so badly of the Church, and your master has made an appointment to visit the eastern tower tomorrow morning, that seems an ideal opportunity to discover whether either or both of them had anything to do with Harl's murder. Find a way to prime the bishop's water-jug with this. The effect is not long-lasting, but you might get as much as an hour's continuous honesty from anyone who drinks from the jug—which is probably more than most men offer in a lifetime."

"Thank you, my lady," I said, as she gave me the two magics. "I will try to do that."

"The cap is yours to keep, in any case," she said, "but I should like the phial returned, if you can find the answer we need before exhausting its resources." She began to turn away then, but she turned back as if struck by an afterthought.

"Six men out of every seven would reckon this meeting of ours as a curse rather than a blessing," she said, "but I believe, Amory, that you're the seventh. I believe, too, that you know full well that if I had known of a human messenger who carried news injurious to any interests of mine I probably would not have hesitated a moment before slaying him—but that I would never have allowed him to reach the steps of Camelot castle with an elf-bolt in his back."

"I am certain of that, my lady," I assured her. "There are only two persons of whose innocence I am absolutely convinced, and you are the other.

I took great delight in the smile that clever answer won. Her lips were so red and her teeth were so white: unhuman in their redness and whiteness alike, in those now-distant days, long before cosmetics and dentistry. I would have given a great deal to win another like it, and Morgana knew it. It was the greatest magic she had, although it hardly qualified as magic at all.

22

I knew that it wouldn't be easy to make sure that the Abbot of Glastonbury drank the truth serum at the right moment, let alone to make sure that Merlin drank it with him. I had to be careful not to waste its effect in the production of platitudes and trivia. I knew, therefore, that I couldn't watch his meeting with Merlin from the safety of a crack beyond the wall. I would have to be in the room, close enough to reach the jug in which his drinking water was delivered. It would have been easy enough to tamper with the jug before it reached his room after being refilled, but I needed more exactitude than that.

I wasn't convinced, initially, of the potency of the grey cap—but when I tested its effect in the courtyard, I found that it really did seem to make it direly difficult for people to catch sight of me. I became more confident afterwards that I could hide effectively in the abbot's room, near enough to his arm-chair to reach his side-table. What I was able to do in advance was to make sure that he had sufficient salt and spice with his breakfast to give him a thirst—and that was easy enough, con-sidering the condition of the food that remained in the castle's stores after the previous evening's feast. Although I didn't tamper with it, Merlin's breakfast was almost as liberally doused—and he cursed me for it when I took it up to him.

"Where were you last night?" he demanded. "Do you think I'm senile, not to notice that you were gone for half the night with the bucket and the chamber-pot? Did you really think that you could hide them by the cesspit and go off in search of amusement, confident that you'd have an excuse for your absence when you brought them back?"

He'd been fast asleep when I'd finally returned to my al-cove, but he'd obviously had time to take notice of my pro-longed absence before going to his bed.

"I was listening to gossip in the kitchens and the vaults," I told him.

"And what did the gossip say?" he wanted to know.

"There's plenty of gratitude abroad on account of the faery food," I told him, "but those who wouldn't eat it are grumbling loudly about bribes and curses, magics and treach-ery. All Camelot is on fire with rumor, and the Christians are fanning the flames. There might be fighting if tempers can't be cooled. If the abbot were to preach a sermon asking for calm and tolerance, that would probably suffice—but rumor has it that he's more likely to do the opposite, and try to raise a mob against Morgana and her elvish tradesmen. If that happens, Arthur's reputation as a host would suffer irreparable dam-age." It would all have been easy guesswork, but I'd heard enough while I was testing the cap of invisibility to know that it was true.

"If I hadn't trouble enough!" Merlin groaned. "There's no meeting in the council chamber today, though. I'm seeing the abbot in his quarters. I'll try to make him see sense. No one wants violence to break out."

"Whoever shot that false elf-bolt was careless of the possibility, at least," I said. "Perhaps they intended to start a war."

"Nonsense," Merlin said. "No one could have guessed that Morgana would actually come to Camelot—and she knew nothing of the slain messenger until she arrived."

"Well, master," I said, recklessly, "given that even you were certain that Morgana had forgotten about us, and did not care about us anyway, I suppose no one else could have reached a different conclusion." As he reached out to punish me for my sarcasm, I added: "But I heard one more thing I heard, that might be relevant." That too was true, but as soon as I had said it, I wondered if I might have done better to keep my mouth shut.

He stopped the intended blow before it landed, doubtless taking note of my hesitation. "What?" he said. "Spit it out."

"I heard two maidservants chattering," I said. "They were wondering aloud whether Arthur might have sent a messenger to, Morgana... and whether Guinevere might have found out about it, and become jealous."

"Guinevere?" he said. "Why would Guinevere... ?" Then he stopped, and looked at me very sharply indeed. "Are you saying that there's speculation among the servants that Guinevere suspected Arthur of making an assignation with Morgana? That she suspected them of being lovers?"

"Utterly preposterous, of course," I said. "But the imagination of a maidservant is a wonderful thing, master, whose logic bears no resemblance at all to the workings of a masculine mind."

"And they are saying this sort of thing, in the servants' quarters?"

"Mere babble," I assured him. "They must know how ridiculous it is themselves... but Morgana is here, after all, asking to see the king, and no one knows the real reason. You might ask Kay or Gawain to inquire by the way, whether there are as many elf-bolts stored in the armory today as there were a fortnight ago—Lud mentioned that he had some in store, and he's a meticulous man. He might have made a count."

Merlin wasn't interested in such matters of detail, for the moment. "I must talk to the queen," he muttered, "as soon as I can arrange it, once I have seen the abbot. It will be a difficult interview, since she has taken such a dislike to me, but needs must. Rumors can't be stopped, but they can be countered. We must contrive a demonstration of the queen's love for the king, and her trust too. If only she had children to keep her mind busy!"

Merlin had an antiquated notion of the benefits of motherhood; he had never taken the trouble to observe that the ladies of the court handed their children over to nurses at the earliest possible opportunity, so that their social lives would not be impeded. He sighed, deeply. "As if there were not enough to do," he moaned, again.

"Yes, master," I said. "Do you want me to take a message to the queen?"

"You? Certainly not. It's a delicate matter, and must be handled delicately. You must go to the council chamber, where the king will sit down at the round table with his knights. I want to know how the current of opinion is running, and whether he can quiet their anxieties."

"Yes, master," I said, although I had not the least intention of obeying the instruction.

"Morgana will surely come to me before she attempts to see Arthur again," the wizard muttered. "I wonder that she has not come already, but I suppose she is very displeased with me. Still, it will not matter if I am not here if she does come, even if she hears that I am talking to the abbot. In the meantime, Taliesin and his friends will be growing surlier by the minute, but that can't be helped. Here, you stupid fool! Give me your shoulder, and help me to the eastern tower. I haven't got all day to waste listening to your cretinous kitchen gossip!"

I did as I was told, very graciously—gratefully, in fact, since I needed to be in the eastern tower myself. My cap was in my pouch, along with the phial that Morgana had given me. The pouch had rarely been so fully or so profitably loaded.

"I fear that you'll find the abbot's apartment rather uncomfortable, master," I told him, as he made out slow and awkward way towards our destination.

"Why?" he demanded, waspishly.

"He burns incense incessantly. His abbey must be far less crowded than any castle, else he couldn't be so sensitive to common odorous. He must be so long inured to the effects of holy smoke that he doesn't know how offensive unchristian nostrils might find it. If you will pardon me, master, I think you might be wise to make some preparation for the defense of your nose and throat. Perhaps I should go back to your attic once I've delivered you to the abbot's door, to fetch a handkerchief."

"There's no need," he said. "I'll only annoy the abbot if I start holding my nose. I can tolerate his incense if he can."

I needn't have bothered trying to find an excuse to return to the abbot's room, as things turned out. When we arrived at the door the Churchman was quick to ask my master not to send me away at once, because he had an errand I might run for him, and his own servants were all busy. Merlin didn't like it, but he could hardly refuse without giving worse offence than he might by holding a handkerchief to his nose.

"I need parchment," the abbot told me. "There is parchment to be had in Camelot, is there not?"

"A little, I suppose, my lord," I told him, feigning ignorance. "We have no clerks, but Sir Kay of Lancaster can write, I think, and keeps accounts in his capacity as steward. I think I might be able to beg a small sheet or two from one of his assistants."

The abbot looked at me with naked contempt when I told him that we had no clerks, and curled his lip into a sneer when I spoke of "a small sheet or two" but he didn't press the point. I assume that he had chosen me because I was Merlin's apprentice, and must therefore have access to the magician's own supplies, but he dared not ask me outright to plunder the materials of my master's correspondence. I was happy to play the fool—and more than happy to conceal from the haughty abbot the meager quality of Merlin's supply of writing materials.

"I'll do my best, my lord," I promised—and I did, although my objective was by no means the same as his.

I brought him two of the meanest and dirtiest scraps of parchment imaginable, but presented them to the abbot as if I were highly delighted with my accomplishment. "Fine parchment, that, my lord," I assured him. "None finer in all the kingdom."

The abbot must have known that I was being ironic, but with Merlin sitting in his armchair, ready to take offence, he dared not accuse me of insincerity without firm proof—so he only called me a cretin and ostentatiously turned his back on me.

I slipped the grey cap upon my head in a trice, and shut the door while I was still inside the room. Merlin never glanced around and neither did the abbot. They wouldn't have noticed the trick if the cap had been salmon-pink and utterly unvirtuous.

I could probably have hidden half a dozen elf-warriors as well as myself while the abbot and the magician eyed one another suspiciously, both taking it for granted that they were quite alone and that I was hurrying down the stairs.

23

My real task was only just beginning, though. I had not only to stay hidden, but to find a means of introducing the truth serum into the abbot's jug. A few moments' careful consideration informed me that it would be easy enough, if I could station myself behind the screen that hid the corner where the Churchmen's ceremonial vestments had been hung.

Under the protection of the cap, I made my way along the wall and into the covert. The vestments didn't rustle as I crouched down within their festoons.

I seized the advantage I had immediately, lest the jug be removed from my reach, and leaked three drops of the serum into the water before drawing back into my hiding-place. There was nothing more to do but hope that one or other of them would soon feel his thirst become urgent.

The burning incense was a second ally to add to the spiced food; once the polite formalities of greeting were concluded, the abbot wasted no time at all in offering Merlin water. Merlin accepted with alacrity.

Having filled the magician's cup almost to the brim, the abbot filled his own just as generously.

"I am very glad that you have come to see me," the abbot said, before he had taken a sip from the cup. "I have always thought that we might have far more in common than our different stations might imply. I know that you were a magician once, but no soul is ever lost to the Lord's mercy. I hope that we might make a Christian of you yet—and a very good Christian at that."

Merlin had not taken a sip yet either, although he had the cup in his hand. "All things are possible," he said—which could hardly have qualified as a lie, no matter what his intention was in saying it—"but I am not entirely convinced, as yet, of the church's friendship towards the king." Now he took a sip of water. "I am told that there are awkward rumors in circulation regarding yesterday's banquet, and that your followers are not helping to calm the situation."

The abbot drank from his own cup then, more deeply than Merlin had.

"We had not expected that such food would be brought into the castle," he said. "My brothers were alarmed. They could not be expected to see such things occurring without protest. Their faith obliged them to issue the sternest possible warnings. Mine obliges me to do likewise. We had not expected to find that Camelot has such close links with the fair folk."

"There is no regular communication between Camelot and Cokaygne, my lord," Merlin said. "Morgana's arrival here is quite unprecedented, and its timing is a very regrettable coincidence."

"I find it difficult to believe that it is a coincidence," the abbot said."

Merlin took another sip of water. "She was not invited," he said, flatly, "and I cannot believe that she knew that you would be here, or that the fact would have interested her in any way. The fair folk are not your enemies, my lord. They have no interest in your faith."

"That is a contradiction," the abbot told him, coldly. "If the fair folk had no interest in our faith, that would be enmity enough. We fear that the situation is worse than that. Our doctrine holds that all such creatures are the devil's instruments, sent to woo men away from the true faith. Morgana is evil—sly, seductive evil that wears a lovely face, but evil nevertheless."

The serum could only guarantee that he believed it; it was, I reflected, a mistake to call it a "truth serum" when it was really a test of sincerity. The abbot's hostility to the fair folk was honest, but that did not mean that it was justified.

"You have heard, I suppose," Merlin said, "that I lived with the fair folk for a while, and that Morgana le Fay is reputed to be Arthur's sister."

"But that was before you had the opportunity to hear the gospel," the abbot observed, implying with his expression that he was being generous. "Christ does not hold past errors to a man's discredit, if he is truly repentant. Your sins are no barrier to your baptism, provided that you acknowledge them."

I was becoming impatient. Silently, I implored my master to begin probing more deeply and more cleverly.

Fortunately, he was more than a little impatient himself, since I had given him more to think about—and he didn't want to be interrogated as to the extent of his repentance. "I merely wished to point out that Morgana has some claim on Camelot's hospitality, no matter how inconvenient her presence might be at this particular moment," he said. I thought the inclusion of the word merely must be stretching the truth a little, but sincerity is capable of a certain elasticity. "In any case," he went on, quickly, "Morgana would not be here if my former apprentice had not been killed while bearing a message from Avalon to Camelot."

""So I am told," the bishop admitted. "But I cannot help wondering why your courier was bearing messages back and forth between the castle and the devil's kin."

"It was a private matter," Merlin said, sipping from his cup but refraining from denying that the courier had been his. "It had nothing to do with the matters that you came here to discuss."

I cursed him for his carelessness in letting the abbot assume the position of interrogator again—and knew that his honesty would be wasted on the Churchman.

"Again, there is a contradiction in what you say," the abbot informed the magician. "I came here to discuss the possibility of welcoming more converts into the Christian fold. If there is traffic between Camelot and the servants of the devil, that is a matter of urgent concern to the field of our discussion."

"I do not believe that the fair folk are my enemies or yours," Merlin repeated, stubbornly. "Morgana's arrival here is an unhelpful distraction, but it is no more than that. The interception of the messenger was very unfortunate."

"He was shot with an elf-bolt, was he not?" The abbot said. He took a draught from his cup as soon as he had spoken, and I willed Merlin to abandon defensive caution and ask him a blunt question.

"He was indeed," Merlin agreed, "but I do not believe that he was shot by an elf. Elf-shot is reckoned a lucky find hereabouts, and arrows lost in the forest by elvish huntsmen are sometimes found by humans—children, as often as not—who bring them to Camelot's marketplace in order to get the best possible price. I have seen none on offer there for some years now, but I dare say that there are elf-bolts to be found in the armouries of many of the mansions in Britain."

"Including Camelot," the abbot said. "Did the bolt that killed the messenger come from within these walls, do you suppose?"

Again I cursed my master—but mistakenly. I realized immediately that he had been waiting to be asked a blunt question in order that he might counter with one of his own.

"I don't know, my lord," Merlin said. "Do you?"

"No," said the abbot, frowning. He could have answered the question with a question, or offered an evasive answer, but he didn't. He answered explicitly, in the negative. But how much, I wondered, did his answer really imply. He didn't know where the elf-bolt had come from—but did that mean that he didn't know who had fired it, or why?

I realized that truth serum might not be such a valuable instrument as commonly assumed—unless its user had the authority to ask the questions whose answers he required, and to rephrase them continually in order to counter clever evasions.

I willed my master to pursue the point as I would have pursued it, but I knew as I did so that his purpose in being in the abbot's room was not the same as mine, and that only luck would give me the certain answers that I craved.

24

Fortunately, the abbot didn't know, as yet, what Merlin's purpose was. He was toying with his cup uncertainly, as if he were less sure of his ground now that his insinuating mention of the elf-bolt had been turned against him. "Of what are you accusing me, Merlin?" he asked, after a moment's pause.

"I make no accusation," Merlin reassured him. "I merely wondered whether your extensive congregation might have given information to your priests that might be useful to us all in the pursuit of a murderer."

"I cannot believe that your apprentice was killed by a Christian," the abbot said, "and no Christian could approve of such an act. Druids, on the other hand..."

"Taliesin had no reason to want the messenger dead, even if he had known that a message was being carried," Merlin pointed out. "That is the heart of the mystery. Who knew that a message was being carried, except for those who wanted it delivered?"

They were both sipping water at regular intervals. If Morgana's report of the properties of her serum had been accurate, they had to be telling the truth—but how much truth did a statement need to contain, in order to comply with a self-determined standard of sincerity? And what, exactly, might the abbot mean when he said that he "could not" believe something?

If appearances could be trusted, neither the abbot nor Merlin had ordered Harl killed, and neither of them knew who had done it—but I wasn't yet certain in my own mind that appearances could be trusted, even with the endorsement of Morgana's serum.

"My concern," the abbot said, "is with the souls of Camelot's citizens: all of them, from the king to the lowliest serf. My concern is to bring them all to an understanding of Christ's sacrifice, and to repent their sins. Traffic with the fair folk is sinful, and it is my duty to oppose it. I am deeply disappointed to find that your links with Avalon are not entirely in the past—but it is not too late to sever them. It is never too late for a sinner to repent, if his repentance is true. Camelot and the Church may still be reconciled, but Morgana's presence in Camelot is a dire hindrance to that reconciliation."

All true, I had to suppose—and a recipe for disaster, in my master's eyes. I couldn't see my master's face, but I knew that it must be deeply troubled. He wanted to make some alliance between Camelot and the Church that did not require the conversion of its aristocracy, just as he wanted to make an alliance with the Druids on similar terms. He didn't care what gods people worshipped, or whether they worshipped any at all. He only wanted a strong and all-inclusive society, which could stand against the Saxons if necessary, or—far better— persuade the Saxons that they too might be included peacefully within it, with no necessity for conflict. He didn't need to know that the abbot's water was laced with a truth-drug in order to see clearly enough that the Abbot of Glastonbury was not about to join forces with Camelot on Camelot's terms. no matter how reasonable the bargain might be as a political expedient.

But Merlin was a hero, and he wasn't about to give up.

"You are an educated man, my lord," he said. "I think you are a man of vision too—not as I once was, aided by the gifts of Faerie, but a man of vision nevertheless. I believe you can see clearly enough how things must go in the British isles if its authorities are weak and divided among themselves. There will be conflict, and all the wealth that was accumulated here during the Roman occupation will be wasted in war. The Romans showed us how to build roads, and they showed us too what might be accomplished by such roads, if they can only be kept open as the warp and weft of a vast social fabric. Nations too must be well built, and well maintained, and if they are constructed sturdily they foster material progress. This island needs good roads, my lord: straight roads, whose network embodies the geometry of authority, power and peace. If we can only maintain the Roman roads, and extend them even further, everyone in Britain will be the better for it. You know that what I say is true, my lord. For Britain's sake, I beg you to make a pact with us, that you will not preach against us, or anyone else who will consent to join our cause."

It was futile.

"We do not preach against peace, order or legitimate authority," the Abbot of Glastonbury said, "but our first con-cern is with the souls of men, and the only roads that matter to

181

us are the roads that lead to the Kingdom of God and to damnation. The first, we are taught, is difficult and winding; the
second, easy and straight. We will never set aside our faith for
the sake of maintaining the kind of road that runs past Camelot. Our aim is to make Britain a Christian nation, and that is
the only route we can follow, no matter how it twists and
turns. If Arthur is baptized into the church, we can work with
and through him. If not... the road he follows will lead him to
damnation. The same choice faces you, Merlin, and Taliesin
too."

They had drunk their cups almost to the dregs, but the serum was still within them. They were both speaking sincerely,
from the heart. They meant every word they said. Between
their separate truths, alas, there was no bridge, nor any possibility of building one, even though they both knew that Britain—the Britain made in Rome, of straight roads and comfortable commerce—might be doomed without one.

For a few moments, I forgot why I was there, and sur-
rendered to my sympathy for Merlin, my master, the would-be
architect of future Britain.

"Is there no possibility of compromise, my lord?" Merlin
asked.

"One cannot compromise with God," the abbot told him.
"One obeys, or one does not. One accepts salvation, or one
goes to the devil." How Mother Leocadia would have admired
him!

I thought Merlin would leave, then—but he didn't. He
stayed where he was, silently sipping the last few drops from
his cup, one at a time. I realized, gradually, that he was con-
sidering capitulation. He was contemplating surrender, for the
sake of Britain. He was calculating the sum of Camelot and
Christianity, and comparing it to the weakness of Wales and
the power of the Saxons.

The abbot knew it too. "First of all," he said. "You must
be rid of Morgana le Fay. She can be sent packing, can she
not?"

Merlin set his empty cup aside. "No human can tell Morgana what to do," he said. "She follows her own whims, and she has magic to defend them—but she does not care what happens in the world of men, and cannot tolerate the pressure of its hasty time. She will go home soon enough, of her own accord, and is unlikely to return. Taliesin is a larger problem. He will feel insulted, to have been brought so far and sent away with nothing."

"He has obtained the greatest gift imaginable, if he could but accept it," The abbot said. His own cup was empty too, but he was still sincere. "He has heard the gospel. I will give him two of my monks to take back with him to Wales, if he will grant them safe passage there. No sinner is irredeemable, or unwelcome, in the house of God."

Merlin let loose a short sound, more bark than laugh. "I suppose I ought to wish you luck," he said, "and might yet be obliged to hope that their work is quickly done."

"Taliesin is salvageable," the abbot said. "As are the Saxons. The so-called fair folk are a different matter. They must be banished from the earth, extirpated root and branch. We must make men forget that there ever were such things as elves."

"Impossible," was Merlin's judgment of that ambition—but he voiced it quietly, and humbly.

I wondered whether Morgana le Fay would still be convinced that the affairs of men were irrelevant to her and all her kind, when I reported all this.

"Would you like more water?" the abbot asked.

"Thank you," said Merlin, "but I have had my fill."

The abbot filled his own cup, and I forced myself to concentrate again, in case there was more information to be gained—but it was Merlin who spoke.

"The only way to unity and peace is through a king of kings," he said, as if he were testing his own capacity to argue the case. "It is conceivable, I suppose, that I have been wrong in thinking that such a king must be found on earth, mounted on a charger with a sword in his hand. If unity and peace are worth fighting for—if Britain is worth fighting for—the idea of Christ might now be the best hope of its preservation."

"I am glad that you understand that," the abbot said. He had swallowed a whole mouthful of virtuous water, and I was perfectly sure that he was very glad indeed. "You will make sure, I hope, that Arthur does not receive Morgana le Fay? If, as you say, she will leave of her own accord soon enough, we only have to ignore her and treat her with due disdain, do we not?"

Ignore her and treat her with due disdain! I wondered what her reaction would be when I reported that.

"I shall do what I can to ensure that she does not see Arthur," Merlin agreed, having turned from hero to craven in a matter of moments—but I couldn't help hoping that it was a ruse, a matter of careful diplomacy. I had begun actively to hope that the serum had worn off, and that he was lying now even though he hadn't been lying before. "On the other hand," Merlin continued, "the king is not mine to command. Nor are his knights. My influence is on the wane. You can have no idea how difficult it is to control a company of proud and envious knights."

"Can I not?" the abbot replied. "Do you imagine that monks are easier to manage?"

"Certainly," said Merlin. "Monks are bound to consider pride, envy and anger as deadly sins, and must therefore avoid their naked expression. Knights, by contrast, are commanded by their code of chivalry to defend their so-called honor at every cost, bloody violence often being their first recourse. Arthur, alas, is not so much a king of kings as a king of knights. That is his strength, and also his weakness: his hardness and his brittleness. The idea of honor made this kingdom of which I was architect, but might destroy him as easily."

"Christendom is full of knights," the abbot said, sweating rather freely in the glow of his success. "They have their uses."

Had I been in Merlin's shoes, I would have questioned that, asking if he included assassination in such usage, and whether the abbot had any reason to believe that a knight might have assassinated Harl, but Merlin had other things on his mind and the question went unasked. Worse than that—although the abbot was primed once again to speak with voluble sincerity, Merlin stood up to go, evidently thinking that the burden of his future labors had been redoubled now that he had to change his plans.

I thought of staying behind, in case anyone else appeared to ask questions of the helpless truth-teller, but I knew that I had probably learned as much as I could. In any case, the smoke of the burning incense was making my eyes water furiously.

As soon as the abbot's back was turned I tiptoed to the door, and went out as quietly as I could. Inflamed with triumph as he was, the Churchman didn't hear me go, and never suspected that I had ever been there.

25

Perhaps I shouldn't have gone to Morgana's quarters immediately. Perhaps I should have done as Merlin had commanded and taken myself off without further delay to Arthur's council chamber, there to spy upon his patient consultations—but I was desperate to tell Morgana le Fay my news, thus to demonstrate that I could be trusted. I wanted to show her that I belonged wholeheartedly to her, and would belong to her as long as she consented to treat me kindly...whether that were a matter of mere hours, or forever and a day.

Having descended to the castle grounds I went stealthily to the southern tower, wearing my new cap every step of the way. I might have been able to creep past Morgana's companions, but that would not have been a diplomatic thing to do. There were two of them in the anteroom to Morgana's chamber, fretting as they waited there while their fellows had gone to the marketplace.

As soon as I was sure that my approach wouldn't be observed by human eyes, I took my cap in my hand and introduced myself. They obviously had orders to let me pass, but that did not prevent their looking down at me with open disdain. I forgave them, supposing that they had to take what opportunities they could to look down on men; their height was a good two inches less than the human average. Arthur and Lancelot would have towered over them like oaks above a pair of holly-bushes, but I was by no means fully-grown and was two inches shorter than they were.

I didn't kneel before the mistress of Avalon this time, although I bowed when I was first escorted into her presence.

"Thank you, Orwen," she said to the elf who had brought me in.

"Should we continue to wait, your majesty?" the elf said, ironically.

"It might be best," Morgana said, "We have enemies here, and I don't yet know who they are, or what their intentions might be."

"You might do better not to say so," Orwen observed. "Your reputation as a seer might suffer."

"Amory can be trusted," Morgana told him, sharply. "And my reputation as a seer is by no means undeserved—I shall know within the hour what I need to know. Close the door behind you, please."

The elf sighed theatrically, but did as he was asked.

"Were you able to use the serum?" Morgana asked me.

"Yes, my lady," I said. "They both drank it. They were speaking very carefully, and not as directly as I could have wished, but I'm almost certain that neither the abbot nor Merlin ordered Harl's murder, and that neither of them knows the identity of the murderer."

"Almost certain?" she echoed.

"The abbot said, in so many words, that he couldn't believe that Harl had been killed by a Christian, and was very explicit in stating that he didn't know where the elf-bolt had come from. He might have ordered the killing done without knowing what weapon would be used, and he might have ordered that it be done by an assassin who was not a Christian, but the general tenor of the conversation led me to believe that the implication was sincere even though the form of his words left loopholes. Merlin also disclaimed knowledge of where the bolt had come from, and seemed genuinely enthusiastic to find out whether the abbot had any better idea than he. The mystery is still unsolved, I fear—but there was another substance to their conversation that might interest you.

"Go on," she said.

I told her everything. I told her that Merlin had tried hard to win the abbot's consent to an agreement that would not exclude the Druids, but had failed, and how he had then appeared to capitulate with the abbot's demand that the price of Christendom's alliance with Camelot was Arthur's baptism. And I told her, word for word, everything the abbot had said about the fair folk, and the necessity of ridding Camelot of her presence and her influence. I left nothing out.

Morgana listened very carefully, but made no comment until I had finished. She seemed more amused by my news than annoyed; the golden glow in her eyes was only slightly tinted by green.

"So Merlin will ignore me," she repeated, in a soft voice, when I had finished my tale. "He will treat me with disdain— and he will demand that Arthur follows his example. Will Arthur agree, do you suppose?"

"I don't know, my lady. If he still needs your help, I suspect not—but he will undoubtedly prefer to see you in secret. I might be able to contrive that, if you wish."

"If I wish," she said. "And why would I wish it, given that I have been so grievously insulted? There is a penalty in my being here, and it was exceedingly generous of me to come at all. I ought to ride away now, and never open the gate of Avalon again, except that..."

She stopped, and waited.

"Except, my lady," I said, quietly, "that that is exactly what the Abbot of Glastonbury wants. You don't care what he wants, of course—to you, he is less than the dust on your riding-boots, no enemy at all—but if you do go, he'll think that he's won on every count. He'll think that he's beaten Merlin, and Taliesin, and Arthur, and you. You can't be beaten, but he doesn't know that...and perhaps you might find some small satisfaction in teaching him the lesson."

"And what about you. Amory?" she asked. "Would you find some small satisfaction in that?"

I was astonished that she asked, but I was ready to answer. "I would," I said.

"But you were nurtured and educated by Christians, were you not?" she said. "Are you not pleased by the abbot's victory?"

"I was nurtured and educated by Christians who told me I was the devil's child," I told her. "They never taught me to read, but they taught me to count and calculate. I owe them nothing, my lady—less than I owe the elf who carried me to their door, I think, although it has always hurt me to think of myself as a rejected changeling, thrown back into the human pool with so little delay."

She knew that I was fishing for an explanation, but she wasn't about to give me one.

"If you had not been given to them as you were," she reminded me, "you would not have attracted Merlin's attention. If you had not become Merlin's apprentice, you would not be here now. You are glad to be here now, are you not? You are content that your life has worked out for the best, and that any other pattern would have delivered you to a far less welcome situation?"

"Yes, my lady," I assured her. "I am your servant. It is all I ever wished to be, and I have no ambition but to remain in that situation for as long as you might let me."

"You are too humble, Amory," she told me. "You underestimate yourself. You will be capable of better things, if only you can develop your potential. You might make a greater impact on the world of men than you imagine, if you are clever enough and bold enough."

"Perhaps I might," I said, "if I had the kind of power that Merlin once had, and as good a teacher."

She laughed pleasantly. "Well," she said, "I am inclined to trust your judgment, given that it's aided by a little residual magic. I believe you when you tell me that the abbot did not kill my messenger, and that Merlin is innocent too. We must put our heads together, therefore, and use our powers of secret sight in combination to determine who did. Who can the murderer be, Amory? Who supplied the bolt, and to whom?"

Her eyes were green again, and for the first time I saw them flecked with red. She took a step forward, so that she was standing closer to me than ever before. She reached out and took my hands in hers. Her flesh was soft and silky, but seemed to be cooler than human flesh.

"Think, Amory," she whispered. "Think—and tell me what you see in your mind's eye."

I wasn't conscious of any supernatural inspiration. It all seemed like guesswork to me—but I was beginning to have more confidence in my guesswork than I had ever had before.

"I tested the cap of invisibility in the courtyard, my lady," I told her, "and heard two maidservants gossiping. I thought little of it at the time, and when I told Merlin he took no notice, but what they said might have been based in sound judgment."

"What did they say, Amory?" she asked.

"They said that Guinevere might have found out that Arthur had sent Harl to keep watch in the forest near the gate of Avalon in order to take a message to you, and that she might be jealous."

"Jealous?" Morgana queried.

"Yes, my lady. Guinevere is the most beautiful woman in Camelot, and is very proud of the reputation—but she also knows the reputation of the fair folk. She wouldn't easily believe that Arthur might betray her for any other woman, but a fay... might seem a plausible rival."

"Ah!" Morgana said. "I see. The fair folk do not love—but they are sometimes beloved. Humans may become besotted with elves, in spite of the fact that their love is unrequited. Arthur only saw me once, as a boy, but... yes, I understand why his wife might have been afraid. Are you why his wife might have been afraid. Are you saying that Guinevere might have had Harl killed?"

"It's possible, my lady. I suspect that the bolt came from Camelot's armory. Any of the knights might have known that it was there, and any could have taken it—but Lancelot is the best archer among them, and he is Guinevere's lover." Thus I gave up the last secret I had held back from her, and the first that my uncannily clear sight had ever revealed to me.

"Ah!" Morgana said again. Her hands pressed mine, and then released them. She seemed satisfied, and quite convinced.

"I'm not certain that they've actually lain together as yet, my lady," I went on, determined to be clear, "but I can't say that they haven't, and I'm perfectly certain that they want to. In the meantime, Lancelot would do anything Guinevere asked of him—anything at all. I saw the way he looked at you when he rode out to escort you, my lady. You were the last person he wanted to see in Camelot."

"I saw it too," she agreed, "and couldn't understand why a man I had never seen before should look at me with such loathing in his eyes."

"It makes sense, my lady," I insisted. "Who could have discovered that Arthur had sent a secret messenger to see you, when even Merlin and I had not? Only someone as close to him as his wife. And who might have cared enough about his motive to take such drastic action? Only someone who cared a great deal—and given that the queen is so deeply enmired in thoughts of infidelity herself, might she not have been exceedingly alert to any suggestion that her husband might be likewise inclined?"

"Still, it is preposterous to think that Arthur and I might be lovers," Morgana said.

"Yes, my lady," I agreed. "But how can Guinevere know that? None of the fair folk has been seen in Camelot since she arrived. She is completely ignorant of your ways, except for what legend and rumor have taught her. And what has local rumor taught her? That Morgana le Fay helped Arthur obtain the throne of England, in spite of being landless and nameless.

That Arthur set aside a forest for the exclusive use of elvish huntsmen. That Arthur once claimed to be Morgana's half-brother, although he has lately made no mention of the claim and seems content to let it be known that it was false. In addition to all that, the queen has taken an intense dislike to Merlin, who came to Arthur out of Faerie, and forged the agreement between Arthur and Morgana that set Arthur on the throne. Might she not have taken a very different view from mine, as to the likely reason why Arthur sent Harl to fix a secret meeting between the two of you? And might she not have become very determined, not only to prevent the meeting taking place, but also to make it appear that his approach had been very rudely met?"

Morgana looked at me with those lovely eyes, which seemed to burn with emerald admiration. "You do have the second sight, Amory," she told me. "Crude and untutored though it be, it has real power and insight. You have pieced all this together by yourself, with nothing to aid you but your own inspiration."

That was true—I hadn't an atom of solid evidence, as yet. But Morgana le Fay had told me that I had magical sight and insight, and I couldn't doubt her.

"It's the only explanation that makes sense, my lady," I told her. I was perfectly sincere. It did seem, at that moment, to be the only explanation that made sense.

"Thank you, Amory," Morgana said. "You have done well. I believe I understand, now, how things stand in Camelot—or how they stand with everyone but Arthur himself. I would like to know that, before I decide what to do next. I'm grateful for your offer to invite him to a secret meeting, and to make sure that he arrives unseen—but will he want to come? Will he still want to see me, now that events have moved on so rapidly?"

"I'm sure that he will, my lady," I told her. I was sure of many things at that moment, including my own genius. "Arthur is, after all, a man of honor—and Harl died in the execution of his commission. No matter what the Abbot of Glastonbury wants or Merlin might advise, Arthur is his own man. He will compromise with them, by refraining from receiving you in the council chamber, but he will try to make up for that in private, if he is given the chance."

"I shall take your advice," she said. "When can you make the arrangement?"

"The king was at the round table this morning," I told her. "He's probably still there—but he'll surely ask to be left alone for a little while, so that he might eat a meal. I might have an opportunity to see him then. I can get into the council chamber easily enough—it has more spy-stations than any other room in the castle. It's flanked by such an abundance of screens that I can set myself at his elbow, waiting for an opportunity. It will only require a moment to fix a time and a safe meeting-place, from which I can bring him here in secret. Is that satisfactory, my lady?"

"Very satisfactory, Amory," she assured me. "You will be near at hand, will you not, while I talk to Arthur? You must not be seen, of course, but we ought to see this through together and I may have further need of your good judgment."

"I shall be close at hand, my lady," I promised, "for as long as you may need me."

26

I made my way to the council chamber by a concealed route, and entered it by means of a concealed door. The meeting of the round table had broken up, but Arthur was still there, pacing restlessly up and down in front of the Seat of Judgment. Kay, Gawain and Lancelot were with him, all three standing still but none of them seeming entirely comfortable.

The grey cap was on my head; I had confidence enough in its ability to proceed as quickly as I could to the best listening-post of all, behind the silken screen to the left of the Seat of Judgment.

The screen was embroidered, in wondrous detail, with a cavalcade of animals, headed by a lion and a unicorn. I could only see the hidden portions of the threads from my side, but I knew that the peep-hole to which I applied my eye was the eye of the more fabulous of the two principal beasts.

I understand, now, that Merlin must have designed the embroidery himself, imagining the lion as Arthur and the unicorn as himself.

No sooner had I arrived at this station than Arthur dismissed Kay, who seemed to have been pestering him with complaints about provisions and accounts. Gawain and Lancelot remained behind, apparently to pester him with different petitions.

"You must send Morgana away, sire," Gawain told the king, forthrightly. "Even though she has not stirred from her rooms, she is causing havoc in the castle and the town. She has wrecked the conference with the Churchmen and the Druids, and her mischievous gift has set half the population at loggerheads with the other half."

"She meant well, Gawain," Arthur said, softly.

Gawain—unlike Lancelot, if my deductions were correct—didn't know that Arthur had sent Harl to Morgana to ask for a meeting. He shook his head firmly.

"She does not mean well, sire," was Lancelot's inevitable contribution to the argument. "She means mischief, as Gawain says. She has come to cause trouble, and that is exactly what she is doing."

"No, Lancelot," Arthur insisted. "That is not what she is doing. I ought to see the lady. I owe her a debt, and even if I did not, it would not be polite to send her away as if in contempt. Merlin has asked me not to see her until he has seen her himself, but he seems to be in no hurry to do that. He is very insistent that I should go to his attic as soon as I am finished here, so that he can give me the benefit of his best advice, but I am minded to heed my own counsel on this matter."

"You must not see the Morgana lady, sire," Lancelot said, doggedly, although he would not go so far as to preface his argument with the words Merlin is right. "The dead rider bears witness to her perfidy. He was not an official courier, to be sure, but he bore a message for you—everyone heard him say so."

I longed to be able to introduce a few drops of Morgana's serum into Lancelot's throat, so that I might force him to state the truth of that particular matter, but he had no cup in his hand. There was a stone jug on the table set beside the Seat of Judgment on the same side as the screen, which I could reach with my arm outstretched. I could see that it wasn't full, though, and might well be entirely empty. I had to little of the precious fluid left that I was reluctant to risk letting it going to waste.

"I must see her, Lancelot," Arthur said. "Secretly, if necessary. She is supposed to be my kinswoman, after all. When I took the sword from the stone to decide the destiny of Britain, its removal was a sign of the bonds linking our world to hers. You were not here then, and you are not native to this isle. You do not understand the debt I owe her."

"I was here, sire," Gawain said. "I understand." He made a show of turning to Lancelot, as if to explain it to him, but I knew that he was really talking to Arthur. "The Saxons were a very distant threat in those days," Gawain said, "and the Church seemed far less important than it does today. Alas, the British lords were quarrelling among themselves, about anything and everything, forming temporary alliances of two or three that broke apart as soon as they came under stress. The last vestiges of the order the Romans had left behind—which we had all struggled to preserve, recognizing its value—were on the point of vanishing. Everyone could see that we could not be united without submission to a single authority, but no one was willing to concede that authority to anyone likely to use it in pursuit of his particular feuds and ambitions, even though the alternative was a war of all against all.

"Merlin was the one who came up with an answer. He had abundant magic then, having recently returned from a long sojourn in Faerie. It was he who persuaded a number of us that the only king who could reign over us, given our history of disputes, was one found without the ranks of existing noble families, whose entitlement to rule was established by mystical means. He it was who devised the sword in the stone and the rumors of Arthur's strange conception. He it was who put about the notion that the idea of Britain existed even in Cokaygne, and that the fair folk would be far better disposed towards our kind if we could preserve the idea of Britain against disintegration. I helped him, as did my brothers and cousins and a dozen others you know very well. We persuaded the others to accept the king appointed by the competition to pull the sword from the stone—and I own that we used flattery to do it, suggesting to each of them, in turn, that if his own family really had the noble descent that tradition claimed, while rival claims were as false as he suspected them to be, then he might be the one to succeed. None but a few expected the outcome that Merlin had wisely preordained—but they had made promises, and kept to them for long enough to let the new order demonstrate its advantages.

"I could see why Merlin thought it wise to invest his boy-king with an authority beyond that which petty kings had ever thought to claim. I readily lent my consent to it, when he explained the idea of the round table, and the new model of kingship that he had in mind. I was curious too, to see how it would work, and what Merlin's magic might achieve if he were given the opportunity to use it on Britain's behalf. You have joined in our tale-telling often enough to inform me that in the Britannic part of Gaul, as in Great Britain, unselfish magicians are as rare as hen's teeth—but I believed in Merlin's sincerity, and I was not disappointed... in the beginning."

Here comes the moment of betrayal, I thought. Here comes the speech about how times have changed.

"But times have changed," Gawain went on, turning from Lancelot to face Arthur, who had stopped his pacing to listen. "Merlin has grown old. His magic has dwindled, and the mystical authority he gave to Arthur's throne has dwindled with it. Even if we had it still, it would not be as useful in to-day's world as it was eighteen years ago. Then, there was a confusion of faiths—the Druids were in disorder, and the Bardic Order was a mere pattern of shadows. There were Christians in Britain, but there was Cernunnos too, and Ceridwen, for whose son our guest Taliesin is named, and Jove and Mars, Ishtar and Mithras, Thor and Wotan—some of whom are already near-forgotten, thanks to the proselytizing of the Christians. Faerie was independent of all that, just as Arthur was of us: a neutral authority. It is neutral no longer; like all those rival faiths it stands condemned of diabolism in the minds of far too many of our citizens. Christians are unreasonable, I will admit—but theirs is a popular unreason, and it will break us if we cannot bend to it. We might avoid become Christians ourselves, but we cannot afford any longer to identify ourselves with Faerie, or claim kinship with it. No one really believes that you are Morgana's half-sister, sire, but that lack of belief is no longer enough. You must disown her. You must make your disassociation plain."

"Merlin would never allow it," Arthur said. He didn't know how widespread this kind of treason was. He couldn't believe that Merlin might capitulate, although I knew that Merlin had already capitulated—and I felt sure that Gawain knew it too, although Lancelot probably didn't. Gawain was preparing the ground for Arthur's painful meeting with the defeated wizard—but Gawain didn't know that Arthur had sent Harl to Morgana, or why, and he didn't know that the man who had killed Harl with an elf-bolt was standing beside him.

Gawain was too clever to tell Arthur that Merlin would allow it, and had allowed it. He took the sly approach. How I wished that a servant would come in with a new jug of wine, and that Arthur would order it to be set down on the table for a moment while he continued talking to his supposed friends, giving me the chance to pollute it before he offered to fill cups for them!

"If Merlin will not allow it, sire," Gawain said, smoothly, "then you must persuade him. And if you cannot persuade him, you must command him. I know how much you love and respect him, but you are Britain and he is not. The fate of the nation is in your hands, not his."

"And will you ask me to disown Merlin too?" Arthur asked. "Will you ask me to dissociate myself from him?"

"Only if it becomes necessary, sire," Gawain assured him. "I have faith in your capacity to persuade or command him. I believe that you can make him see sense."

I could appreciate his cunning. Arthur would go to Merlin in trepidation, anxious for their friendship, and would be mightily relieved to find that Merlin was of the same mind as Gawain—so mightily that it wouldn't even cross his mind to ask himself whether they might both be wrong. But Morgana might, if I could only do what I had promised, and arrange for him to meet her in secret.

Will all the force of my seemingly magical will, I demanded that a servant might come in with wine, so that I could introduce a little honesty into the debate.

27

Arthur began pacing again, tugging at his beard as he wrestled with his conscience. He wanted to see Morgana, but he couldn't bear to tell them why. Gawain would surely have understood, and Lancelot's mind would be set at rest, but Arthur couldn't bring himself to confess that he wanted to acquire a potion that might help his wife to bear him a son.

It would have been so simple, if he had not been so fearful... or so it seemed to me, in my hiding-place.

Lancelot was still standing very stiffly, although Gawain seemed to be at peace with himself now that he had made his speech. His body was still half-turned towards Lancelot, so that he had to look sideways at the pacing king, but he looked to me as if he wanted to reach out a calming hand of reassurance and friendship.

"I think Gawain is right, sire," Lancelot said. "I was not here when you came to the throne, and I am grateful to him for his explanation—but I have been here some little while now, and I think you know that I am as fast a friend as any you have. I never had a high opinion of magicians, or of Faerie either, and I have seen nothing in Britain to change my mind. We must live in the future, sire, not in the past. In Faerie, it is said, they have neither past nor future, but only an eternal and unchanging sunlit present, but we are human and must live as humans live, for human ends. Even if she means no harm, Morgana le Fay is dangerous to our lives and our prospects."

Dangerous to your life and your prospects, I thought. You hope that she hasn't found you out, but she has. With my help, she has found you out. She means no harm to Arthur, but you shall not escape her retribution.

"There is a rumor abroad that might work to our advantage, sire," Gawain told the king. "It is widely said that it was Morgana who put about the lie regarding your kinship to her, in order to ally her own folk with your great cause, in the hope that men might forget centuries of mischief worked by their whim."

"Gossips have short memories," Arthur said. "Merlin was once ambitious to welcome the fair folk into the community of Britain, but they remained in their own place, beyond the gate of Avalon, saying that the community of Britain was irrelevant to them. All they needed of Britain, Morgana told me, was the preservation of the forest in which they liked to hunt, against farmers who might clear it to plant wheat and herdsmen who might turn it into pastureland. We were disappointed, but we granted her wish. If only she had taken more advantage of her gift, and visited the castle sooner and more frequently...but as Lancelot says, time passes slowly in Faerie, and nothing changes there. The elves come to our world when the whim brings them, and not before."

"Merlin was once in love with Morgana le Fay, sire," Gawain informed the king, although it was a rumor Merlin had never confirmed in my hearing. "He had been to Cokaygne via Avalon, and may have dreamed of going back and forth throughout his life, a man of two worlds—but that is not the way of the fair folk. Morgana is fickle, your majesty, and mischievous."

"She treats her lovers badly," Lancelot put in, furtively following his own agenda. "She treated Merlin badly, and she could not treat any other human better. It is not in her nature. You must not see her, sire." He was not a man for subtle argument, but he did not mind repeating himself endlessly to drive his message home.

"Morgana is a guest in my house," Arthur pointed out to both of them. "I ought to hear what she has to say. No matter how delicate my dealings are with Taliesin's Welshmen and the Glastonbury monks, I must in all conscience make time for her. I will see her privately, as I said—no one outside this room need know—but I must see her."

You'd have done wisely to keep it secret from those within the room as well, sire, I said, silently

"What if Merlin asks you to send her away, sire?" Gawain wanted to know. "Will you do as he asks?"

"You are the one who reminded me just now that I am the king, not he," Arthur replied, "I am the one who has acknowledged Morgana as my kinswoman. It is my obligation, not his."

"Will you at least take his advice as to what you should say?" Gawain continued, forgetting to add any kind of formal address to his enquiry. I wondered how Merlin had won Gawain so completely to his cause, given that Gawain of all men should have recognized the obligation of which Arthur spoke.

Arthur's back was to me, so I couldn't see his face, but I saw his grizzled head fall forward a little, in evident weariness. The persuasive efforts of the two knights were wearing him down.

Then my wish was granted.

A servant came in, carrying a fresh jug of wine. He bowed deeply, and Arthur acknowledged his arrival. "Put it on the table," the king said.

The servant bowed again, and substituted the full jug for the one that was almost empty. The conversation had stopped when the door opened, and all three of them watched the servant's back as he retreated, waiting for the door to close before they resumed.

I had little or no time to think. I had hoped more than once to have the opportunity, and here it was. I wanted Gawain and Lancelot—especially Lancelot—to be forced to speak honestly, to their king and to me. The hope and the desire moved my arm while my mind was sluggish. While they watched the door close, I reached out to tip all but a few drops of Morgana's truth serum into the jug of wine.

No one could have predicted that I would do it, no matter how powerful their second sight might have been—and even if she had, how could she possibly have foreseen what would happen next?

"Would you like some wine, Gawain?" Arthur asked.

"Thank you, sire," said Gawain, "but no."

"Lancelot?"

"No, sire," said Lancelot. "Thank you."

"Will you pour some for me?" the king asked, so gently that it hardly seemed like a command. It was Gawain who bowed, and came forward to the table. He poured out a cup of wine, and gave it to the king.

Oh well, I thought, it can do no harm. The king is always sincere, and always discreet. Lancelot would never dare to ask him why he sent the messenger to Morgana, in public or in private.

Arthur took a leisurely draught, but did not drain the cup. He held it lightly in his hand, in no hurry to drink the rest. He looked down at the dark surface of the liquid, pensively. Then, absent-mindedly, he went to sit down on the Seat of Judgment, directly beneath the downward-pointing Excalibur.

Gawain left it to Lancelot to resume the discussion, although Lancelot had nothing to add but further repetition. "I beg you not to see the elf-queen, your majesty," he pleaded. "Whatever obligations you may owe to her, it is too dangerous. She should never have come here, and she must never come again. I implore you not to see her, sire. Think of your..."

He was about to say "wife"—and might, at that point, have said too much, but the door opened again and he closed his mouth abruptly.

It was the queen who came in first. Lancelot immediately lowered his eyes, and bowed in what seemed to me a very ostentatious manner.

Guinevere was not alone. She had two of her ladies-in-waiting with her, and Lady Enid. Behind Lady Enid was Sir Eric, and behind Sir Eric was Sir Kay. Even that was not the end of it, for Kay had two assistants with him, including Hereward, and Sir Sagramore was there too. The council chamber was capacious, as it had to be, but there were enough people in it now to qualify as a crowd.

The queen came forward to kiss her husband on the cheek. She barely glanced at Lancelot or Gawain as she passed them by. She seemed cheerful. Merlin must have spoken to her by now, but she seemed cheerful. The magician had set her mind at rest, it seemed.

When I had arrived in Camelot twenty months before, I had thought Guinevere the most beautiful woman in all the world, but I had begun to notice signs of imperfection about her cheeks and eyes even before I first laid eyes on Morgana. She seemed pretty enough now, though.

"Arthur..." she began—but the king interrupted her.

"I am glad to see you, my darling," he said, with all apparent sincerity. "My head is buzzing. I had never thought that there could be so much intrigue in the world. I wish you could advise me, my dear, as to whether I should see my supposed kinswoman Morgana le Fay. Everyone tells me that I should not, but how can a man refuse his acknowledged sister, even if she is not really his sister at all?"

The queen was startled, as she had every right to be. The giving of advice wasn't her prerogative.

"I hardly know what to say, sire," she said, glancing round at the crowd.

"The queen is not a party to this argument, sire," said Lancelot, intemperately—even a trifle vehemently. He took a step forward, as if to draw attention back to himself. "You must not see Morgana le Fay."

I couldn't see Arthur's face, but I could see the queen's puzzlement and I could see Lancelot's fervent anxiety.

I knew then, without the benefit of any second sight at all, why Lancelot was so very anxious that Arthur should consult with Morgana le Fay—who was also reputed to be Morgana the seer, Morgana the witch, mistress of the darkest arts. I understood, far better than before, why he had killed Morgana's messenger.

I understood that it had never entered Lancelot's head that Arthur and Morgana might be lovers; his one and only thought had been to conceal the fact that he and Guinevere were—and not for Camelot's sake, or even the queen's, but purely for his own. Guinevere might indeed have told him about Arthur's messenger, but she had expressed no terrible suspicions of her own, and had not given him any foolish orders.

Lancelot had acted alone. He had been afraid that Morgana le Fay would betray him to Arthur, and he was anxious now that Guinevere might be foolish enough—or innocent enough—to give Arthur permission to see her. Were she to do so, he knew, her mere permission might outweigh all the good advice the king had received from Gawain.

Lancelot ought have trusted Guinevere's discretion and common sense—but he didn't. Perhaps his education and experience had given him an unflattering opinion of the frailty of female intelligence, or perhaps he had a little of the second sight, even though he had never set foot in Faerie.

Guinevere was no quicker of wit than Lancelot, and she was as confused by his alarmed intervention as she was by Arthur's unusual request. I watched in fascination as she fluttered her hands, uncertain as to what to do or say next.

It was simply the need to do something that made her reach out and take the unemptied cup from the king's limp hand. It was simply the need to gain time that caused her to lift it absent-mindedly to her lips and drink from the well of honesty.

"Why should I not see her, if I wish?" Arthur asked, plaintively, well aware that he had already been given several reasons, but remained stubbornly resistant to their logic.

He must have been speaking to Lancelot, but his eyes—whose desperate expression I could imagine, although I could not see them—were still on Guinevere.

If Arthur loved Guinevere—and I'm sure that he did, although he hadn't married her for love—he did so more profoundly than Lancelot. She knew that, even though she felt differently about him. She must have felt his gaze as a form of command, because she felt obliged to answer in her knightly lover's stead even though she couldn't have known what answer she would give until she gave it.

"Because she might tell you," Guinevere said, aghast at her incapacity to stop herself, "that Lancelot du Lac has betrayed you, and that your wife loves the traitor far better than she loves you."

And thus the dream of Britain died.

28

It was to Merlin, not to Morgana that I ran first with the dreadful news. When I burst into his attic room he looked up angrily, ready to curse me—but as soon as he looked at me he realized that a disaster had occurred beyond the reach of wrath and the recompense of a listless blow.

"What have you done, Amory?" he asked—not "what's wrong?" but "what have you done?".

"Arthur knows that Guinevere and Lancelot are lovers, master" I said. "She told him herself, in front of witnesses. You must go to him, for he won't come to you. All's not lost—not yet. Lancelot killed Harl, because he was afraid that Morgana would reveal his treason to Arthur, but Guinevere knew nothing of that. The situation can be saved, master, if only you act now."

Had Merlin had any color left in his cheeks it might have drained away; as things were, he only became still, like a statue carved in white wood. The moments seemed strangely exaggerated as he went into a kind of trance, although I probably could not have counted much further than twenty before he spoke again.

"Why did she do it?" he whispered. "Why?

I didn't want to tell him. I didn't have to; I hadn't drunk any of Morgana's serum. But he was looking at me as if he already knew, and would not let me refuse to answer.

"I was a fool, master," I admitted. "But that doesn't matter. All's not lost, if you can only move fast enough."

He didn't move; he seemed incapable of rising to his feet. It was as if the awareness had suddenly seized him that he was not what he pretended to be. It was as if someone—not I!—had pointed a derisory finger at him and said: "Why, you aren't a magician at all! Architect of worlds? You're just an old man!"

"What have you done, Amory?" he asked, again.

"I didn't mean to do it," I said. "The serum was intended for Lancelot, not Guinevere. Arthur had the cup—no one could have guessed that she would take it from him, or that he would ask her such a question as she drank."

It wasn't a very coherent explanation—but Merlin had a little of the second sight within him, even if I didn't. "Morgana," he said, as he breathed out sharply. "What did she promise you, Amory?"

"It wasn't her fault," I said. "We were only trying to find out who killed Harl, and why. I intended the serum for Lancelot."

"And why," Merlin asked, "would it have been any more useful to have Lancelot reveal the truth than to have Guinevere reveal it?"

I had no ready answer to that. Why, indeed? The only reply that came into my head was that it had seemed to make sense at the time. It had seemed to make sense at the time—but it no longer seemed to make any sense at all.

Had I been duped as well as bribed? Merlin obviously thought so. But no one could have known how the drama would play out. The greatest seer who ever lived couldn't possibly have foreseen such a chapter of accidents. On the other hand, how much difference would it have made if I'd contrived to deliver the truth serum to Lancelot? How much difference would it have made to Merlin's dream of Britain?

"You must go to Arthur, master," I said. "He has retired to his room. Lancelot will be gone from Camelot within the hour. Guinevere... I don't know, but she is innocent of the murder. All's not yet lost. Arthur needs you now more than ever, master. You must tell him what to do. You must persuade him that he is still the king, still the anchor of Britain, the heart of the round table, still...

I stopped. Merlin was looking at me as if I were mad—not as his betrayer, but as a holy fool, a devil's child. His silence was more eloquent than any words he could have spoken. I had never felt like a devil's child before, but I felt like one then—and a cretin, deserving of every insult that had ever been hurled in my direction.

"It isn't over, master," I said, doggedly. "What is done is done, but the future still lies before us. Arthur is still the king. You must make him see that. He feared a moment such as this, but it was just a moment. Life must go on. He is still the king."

But Arthur was not the only one who had lived in terror of a moment that would puncture his reputation and obliterate the illusion of his uniqueness. Merlin had lived in fear of the same magical transformation, and it had happened. He was no longer Merlin, architect of Britain. He was an old man.

In truth, the had lost the battle for Britain several days before, and perhaps many years before, when the obstacles heaped up by the march of time had become a fortification that could not be scaled. It was the migrations of the Saxons, the aspirations of Church and the ebbing of his own magic power that really confounded his plans, not Guinevere's barrenness or Lancelot's flirtatiousness or Arthur's brittleness or Morgana's playfulness or my foolishness... but Merlin had lived too long in fear of the critical moment—the single instant when the tall but fragile tower of hope would be toppled by an instant of tragic stress—to take such a balanced view of his misfortune.

When I told Merlin that his precious instrument had been broken by his wife's caprice, he folded in upon himself, and ceased to be even a pretended wizard. From that moment on, he was an old, grey man and nothing more.

It as if someone more powerful than he had taken up a magic wand, and changed the world with a casual gesture.

Was I the wand, I wondered, and Morgana its wielder?

If so, how long had her scheme been brewing? Since the moment I had first been stolen from my cradle and taken into Faerie? Since the moment Merlin had asked her, as a favor he had no right to claim, to help him put his apprentice on the throne of Britain?

It seemed inconceivable. Not impossible, perhaps, but inconceivable. To her, though, the eighteen years that had passed since Merlin put Arthur on the throne, and the fifteen that had passed since I was abandoned to the Sisters of Saint Syncletica, were little or nothing—a matter of a fortnight or so, but not too long for the playing of a game, or a trick.

It made no sense, I realized, to ask what motive Morgana might have had that was commensurate with the damage she had done, as if she were some petty human political animal.

I told myself repeatedly, though, that she could not have known how the drama would unfold. No matter how powerful her second sight might be, she could not have foreseen how I would use the truth serum, nor what the consequences of its use might be.

Merlin moved at last. He didn't groan, or tear his hair, nor did he express amazement at his failure to foresee that the citadel he had armored so well without had gone rotten at the core. He didn't hit or slap me. He simply got up from his chair, and went to a shelf to fetch a stone bottle full of sweet liquor, which he poured into a cup himself. And then he drank it.

After a long pause, he said: "I don't know what to say to him."

He meant Arthur, of course. The great Merlin had no idea what to say to his apprentice king. He had been prepared to tell his prodigy how to make a bargain with the Church that might allow the crippled dream of Britain to limp a little further into the unknown, but he had no idea what advice to give a man with a broken heart. He couldn't help Arthur to come to terms with a faithless wife who would never, now, bear him a son.

"That's not good enough, master," I said. "Get up! Go to work! You have a thousand things to do, and there's no time to waste. Move!"

"I wish you would tell the king that I cannot see him, Amory," he said, casually. "Make my apologies, and say that I am not well, and that our meeting must be postponed. He will be grateful for that, I think. He will not want to see me, just at present."

29

I nearly called Merlin a cretin then, and worse. I nearly called him a coward, and a traitor—but there didn't seem to be any necessity to hurt him more than I already had.

I turned away, as if to leave the room.

"Stay a moment, please," my former master said. "Just a moment, before you go." He knew that I had no intention of delivering his message to Arthur. He knew, too, that he would never see me again. He wanted me to stay, just for a moment longer, in order that he could bring my apprenticeship to a proper conclusion. I stayed where I was, and waited.

"You're right, Amory," he told me. "It isn't over. Not yet. Camelot will fade away, now that the round table is cleft in two and its magic dispelled, but it won't disappear. It will decay, and vanish, like a thousand other dreams before, but its enemies haven't won. Every man knows his future, Amory, though none may know his past. We are born into a world we find ready-made, with nothing to tell us how it was made but legends; we look about us, and we find much that is healthy and much that is diseased, and those of us who are good as well as clever make what attempt we can to encourage the healthy and ameliorate the disease, even though we know that our own fate is fixed, and that nothing awaits us in the shorter term but old age and death.

"Camelot will die, now, slowly but irreversibly, It will age and decay, and it will be torn apart stone by stone, and even the scar it leaves on the empty hill will be buried—but it will become the stuff of legend. The straight road might be temporarily overgrown, and the arts the Romans left behind might be forgotten for a while, but they will not be lost. In time—in time, Amory, for that is what our world has in abundance, while Cokaygne languishes in timelessness—the straight road will be followed, and the arts applied.

"It isn't over, Amory. It isn't finished. She envies us that, Amory—no matter what she has instead, she envies us that. And no matter how pleasant you find things in Cokaygne, Amory, you will come back. You will age, and you will die, and you will come back here in order to do so—and you will understand, then, what I have tried to do and why.

"Britain will die too, in time—but it will be born before that, and it will live its span. Britain will grow, and become strong. One day, it will be monarch of the world's oceans, holder of an empire that will span the earth from edge to edge, greater even than Rome's. And then it will grow old, like everything else that lives, and it will die. The dream of Arthur and Merlin, the lion and the unicorn, will vanish like every other, and return to the stuff of legend whence it came. And Cokaygne will still be there, unchanged and unchanging, utterly self-satisfied and immune to alteration—unheeded, I hope, but not unknown. You will not understand, until you have been there, why I could not and would not stay—but you will. I promise you that, Amory, You will."

"Yes, master," I replied, uncomfortably. I was impatient to get away now, but he hadn't finished, and I had to hear him out. He was still my master, in a way—at least until I closed his door behind me.

"I have lost the battle, Amory," he told me, looking at me as if I were his dutiful son instead of his renegade servant, "but the world will not lose the war; Arthur and I shall be heroes in spite of everything. I have not made Britain here and now, but Britain will be made and I shall be its architect. Nothing can take that away from me, Amory. Britain is my design, and it will endure long after my death. It might not know that it was made by me, for the Church will write its history now, and will ruthlessly stamp out such rival legends as Taliesin's bards and Arthur's minstrels might contrive—but what does that matter? No man knows his past—the secret of how he came to be made as he is—and even if the Britons of the future have no memory of me, I shall be the architect of their world."

He paused, and I turned again to go, but he still hadn't quite done with me. "Could any man have done more than I, Amory?" he whispered. "Could any man have done better?"

"No, master," I replied, insincerely. "No one could have done more, or better."

He saw through my dishonesty, and roused himself to attack me one last time, though not with his hand or his stick. "You don't know, Amory," he assured me. "You're young enough and idiot enough to think that you know better than you do, but you have no idea what a task mine was. When I came back from my sojourn in Cokaygne the world I had known before was dead and gone. The younger brother I left behind had lain in his grave for hundreds of years. Everything was new, and strange. All I had to call my own were the meager gifts that life in Faerie had given me—and I say life in Faerie, Amory, not Morgana, for she had nothing of her own to give, and lies when she pretends that the gifts of Faerie are hers to bestow or withhold. I had the second sight then, until the march of time corroded and all-but-erased it.

"You have no idea as yet how cruel and parsimonious magic is, Amory, nor how treacherous its instruments and victims may become. That kind of power cannot last under the pressure of time; it evaporates like summer dew almost as soon as it is used. But I looked at the strange new world to which I had returned, Amory, and I said to myself: this is my clay; I shall be its sculptor. I shall take this world and make another. I shall take the shabby wreckage of the empire that faltered and fell while I was away, and build another. I shall take the ruins of a province and build an empire whose heart will be closer at hand. I shall build Britain, and I shall build it upon the foundation-stone of Camelot.

"You have no concept, stupid boy, of the enormity of that task. You have no concept of the ingenuity that went into my work—the ingenuity that was required to wring every last drop of effect from the magics I carried away from Cokaygne. There was a time when I hoped and believed that Morgana might give me more—or if not Morgana, some other fair en-chantress—but that is not the way of the fair folk, because it is not in their nature. They promise much, but flatter only to de-ceive. They are petty, selfish, narcissistic folk, who are inca-pable of caring for anything in our time-stressed world.

"No one could have done more than I, Amory. No one could have done better. But you will have your opportunity, will you not? You will have your time in Faerie, your magic, your dream. I forgive you, Amory. And I leave it to your own conscience and your own ambition to force you into competi-tion with me. If you think that you can do more, or better, then do it. With all my heart, I wish you luck."

"Thank you, master," I said.

Then I left him alone, closing the door behind me as I went.

I had understood something of what he was trying to tell me, but I didn't believe him. He was only a grey old man, af-ter all. I knew that he believed what he was saying—or, at least, was trying very hard to make himself believe it—but I couldn't.

I was anxious to be off, anxious to catch Morgana before she left for the gate of Avalon, anxious that she might not want me with her in spite of all that I had done for her.

I ran down the stairs and into the courtyard, then out to the roadway where Morgana's trunks were already being loaded on to one of the two small wagons the elves had brought from Cokaygne. Her companions' horses were being saddled by human grooms.

Morgana's companions weren't in a good mood. They had expected to be here a little longer, to pursue their own objectives. Orwen was grumbling, and his complaints were echoing through the band.

They looked at me without any overt hostility, accepting the fact of my arrival as if it were a dull necessity, but they looked at me as if I were a pet or a plaything, of little or no consequence at all.

I set about helping them to load the carts, focusing my attention on the work. I ran up and down the steps half a dozen times as we shifted boxes and bales, glad to be out of breath.

30

Morgana waited in her rooms until all the work was done. She was still playing the queen, although there was no need. She had changed into her riding habit before her luggage had been removed. She didn't deign to notice me until the apartment had been cleared, save for a single loosely packed sack that lay on the mat at her feet. She was still playing with me, too.

"There you are, Amory," she said, when I went back for the last time. "I feared for a moment that you had met with some misfortune. Arthur will not see me, it seems. He sent a message saying that he was profoundly sorry to have troubled me, but that he no longer had any favor to ask of me. He apologized for the treatment I have received in Camelot, and begs that I put the blame on his foolishness, swearing that he intended no insult or malevolence. It is all very annoying—but you did your best, and thanks to you the expedition has been mildly entertaining. Have you no better travelling clothes than those?"

"No, my lady," I said, meekly.

"You ought to have been given a pair of boots, at least—but it doesn't matter now. You can't ride, I suppose, but there's plenty of room in the cart now that all the food's been eaten. We have a little left, thanks to Camelot's ingratitude, so you shouldn't find the journey too uncomfortable. You've said your good-byes, I imagine?"

"Yes, my lady," I said.

"Will Merlin come to bid me farewell?"

"No, my lady. He's... indisposed."

"Of course he is, in this blighted world where disease runs riot and everything turns to dust as soon as you turn your back. I forgive him his impoliteness—I understand the frailty of humankind, you see. There are those among my kind who prefer to have nothing to do with humans, finding them offensive and annoying by nature, but I have forgotten more humans than you have ever known, Amory, and I understand the needs and desires of your kind better than you do yourself."

Perhaps she really believed that, but I doubt it. She was only playing her part, pretending to be a great enchantress and puppet-master. She knew that we would be back in Cokaygne soon enough, where she was perfectly ordinary, and that many years might pass in our world before she played the queen again.

"Well," she said, when I made no reply, "we must get on. We can't waste time with idle chatter."

She marched past me then, expecting that I would pick up the sack and follow her. That was what I did. After all, I was her servant now. I had attained the pinnacle of my ambition, and found a master for myself in the world of Cokaygne.

The pack was heavier than I'd expected, but not unbearable. I couldn't tell exactly what it held, but I'm sure that there was a chamber-pot, and a sponge on a stick—I could feel their contours digging into my back as I carried the sack across the courtyard and down the steps to the street.

Morgana was already mounted on her horse, but Orwen and two others were still attending to the packing of their goods on the foremost cart. When I had placed the sack on the second cart I climbed up after it, and took up a position behind the driver's platform, sitting with my back against the right-hand sidepiece. For the first time, I noticed the mark of Camelot's wheelwright carved into the wood. The cart had been made by men, not elves.

The driver, who was sitting patiently in his seat, saw me reach out a hand to touch the mark.

"We have no use for carts in our own land," he told me. "but we keep a few in the villages near the gate of Avalon, for the sake of our expeditions into the world of roads."

The world of roads! That was his notion of the human world.

"My name's Amory," I told him, on an impulse. "I have but the one."

"Mine's Durkan," he answered, courteously. "So have I. Can you sing, or play? Are you a craftsman?"

"No," I admitted. "I'm just a servant—Morgana's servant."

"Is that why she came? To find another servant? I thought she'd lost that habit."

"No," I told him. "That's not why she came. I wanted to be her servant, and she was generous enough to grant my wish."

"Ah," said Durkan, as if that explained everything.

The other elves ignored me. Although I hadn't taken the grey cap from my pouch after leaving Merlin's room, none of the human passers-by was taking any notice of me either.

No one seemed to think it odd that a human was going with the elves as a passenger—no one, at least, thought it worth questioning the fact. The people of Camelot all had work to do; they were just as busy as they would have been had the day's rumors been less captivating. Merlin had been right; the castle and the town would take a long time to die and decay, and their inhabitants had not the least idea, as yet, that the dream of which they were figments had begun to fall apart.

Kay was at the top of the steps, as usual. He had only to look down at me to observe that I was out of place. He was certainly capable of recognizing me as Merlin's apprentice, if only he had put his mind to it, but his mind was on other things. Even if he had deigned to notice me, he wouldn't have cared. The castle had to be supplied and maintained, whether Arthur was a cuckold or not, and Lancelot's banishment would make very little difference to the number of mouths to be fed. Kay had plenty to do, and no time to worry about the defection of the court magician's boy.

Taliesin was visible too, further along the street, at a slightly greater distance from the stables. He was making his own preparations to depart. His horses were a poor herd, by comparison with Morgana's. The largest was a full hand shorter than Morgana's smallest. Their coats were shaggy and their bellies sagged, but they were sturdy enough to carry their meager human cargo. The black-clad bards were as wiry as the elves, and not that much taller. They had but one cart, and little luggage save for their absurdly large harps, whose shapes were clearly discernible within the protective cloths that had been draped over them.

The Abbot of Glastonbury was nowhere to be seen, but there were monks among the crowds, who seemed much more at home in the vicinity of the castle than any I had seen before.

Half a dozen servants who knew my name passed close to the cart as they scurried up or down the steps, while I sat there waiting to set off—and half a hundred whose names I knew but who did not know mine. They were all about their business, but even the idlest of them sauntered past without acknowledging my presence, let alone my imminent departure. None hailed me, or even gave me a quizzical glance.

I had told Morgana the truth, I realized, when I told her that I had said my good-byes, for I had had but one to say. No matter how many intimate secrets I knew about the other residents of Camelot, I had no friends there but Merlin. The king had recognized me, on more than one occasion, and he might have paused at the sight of me in Morgana's cart—but he wouldn't have asked me where I was going, or why, and he certainly wouldn't have said goodbye.

I was glad when the wheels began to turn, and our exotic company took the road that would bear us away from the castle, across the Roman road and away to the south-east, towards the gate of Avalon. The people of the town watched us go, but their eyes were on the elvish riders, and most of all on Morgana le Fay. I was merely a churl on a cart, who didn't even own a pair of boots, standing guard over luggage.

But I was going to Cokaygne. I was going to a land of eternal summer, where food was always abundant and time wouldn't hurry my life away. I was happy to be going, no matter what price I'd paid for my place on the cart.

Interlude
The Road to Avalon

1

I hadn't traveled through the English countryside since Merlin had brought me from the convent to Camelot. I had followed a straight course on that occasion, along a good Roman road. Although the road had been long, it was so well-established that civilization had crept into its margins along the whole of its length; houses had been built near its every approach, and storage-barns not far away, and stalls along its very edge.

The road to Avalon was very different.

The road to Avalon wound across country, following the contours of the hills, skirting woods and homesteads. It went where the bridges and the fords had been established, long before it came to heavy use, and it was made of mud. The season was different, of course, and the weather had been uncommonly wet of late, but the Roman road had been immune to such trivialities because it was solidly made. The road to Avalon had not been made at all, but merely trampled out by countless booted feet and rutted by the passage of cartwheels.

It was, by its very nature, uncertain and treacherous.

For this reason, my outward journey from Camelot was good deal less comfortable than the inward one. The cart lurched continually, and frequently became stuck—at which point I had to get down, slippered feet or not, and push until the wheel was free to roll again. Durkan got down too, if the difficulty proved intractable, but none of the riders ever felt the need to dismount. It didn't help that the cart, despite its manufacture in Camelot, had a wheelbase that didn't correspond to the old Roman standard—with the result that it couldn't use the same ruts that carts made to the old specifications had hollowed out by their collective passage. One or other of our pairs of wheels was always falling into one of the deeper ruts, making the whole assembly tilt and rattle, so my skin was black with bruises long before the first day of the journey ended-although my costume was so liberally spattered with mud that I was an outward patchwork of russet and grey. But I ate well, and didn't mind my discomfort overmuch. After all, I was on my way to Cokaygne, the Land of Light and Plenty, where all my earthly ills would be soothed away.

"How long will we be on the road?" I asked Durkan, since Morgana was keeping her distance.

"As long as it takes," was his reply. He wasn't being evasive; the fair folk were unused to measuring time, and found the cycle of day and night as confusing as it was fascinating.

"Will our food last?" I asked, thinking that I might form an estimate that way.

"Oh yes," he said. "Provided that the trouble we meet on the road isn't more than we can easily deal with."

I thought he meant the mud and the awkward ruts, the fords that might be flooded and the slopes that might be slippery. He probably knew that I had mistaken his implication, but he didn't take the trouble to explain. He was an elf, after all, and I was just excess weight on the back of his vehicle.

The first night we spent in the open was cold and windy, with only a few stars peeping through the clouds, but the elves were as fascinated by its aspect as they must have been by the others they had spent in the human world. They were a little intimidated by the darkness, but they were not given to dread or superstition, and accepted their mild fear as a kind of excitement to be savored rather than an oppression from which to see escape. They posted a sentry, but didn't ask me to take a turn.

"Will we have to spend another night in the open?" I asked Morgana, thinking that she might be better able than Durkan to make a guess.

"Perhaps," she said. "The horses could go a little faster if we urged them, but they might need a little strength in reserve. We'll be there soon enough—and you'll have the opportunity to learn patience thereafter, if you come safely through the gate."

"I'll not turn back in alarm," I told her, "no matter how sick I feel."

"I know," she said. "You'll find it easier than most, given that we're with you. You might put your cap on, too. It should help, a little. Keep it close at hand from now on."

I knew that the gate was protected by magic similar in kind to that embodied in the cap of invisibility, so it didn't seem at all unreasonable that the cap might ease the disorientation of transition. I didn't wonder whether she might have another reason for advising me to keep it ready to hand, although I ought to have understood the logic of the situation.

I didn't dare to ask her, as yet, exactly how much of what had happened in Camelot she had planed in advance, or how long in advance she had laid the plan. I wanted to be safe in Cokaygne before I gave any evidence of ingratitude, and intended to be discreet even then. I tried not to think about it at all, but that was impossible.

When dawn came, I felt that I'd hardly slept at all. The elves broke camp with calm efficiency, all but Morgana and Durkan continuing to ignore me. I accepted the situation humbly; I knew that I was going to Cokaygne, where there would b all the time in the world—and perhaps more—for idle conversation.

We had been moving, not very rapidly, for three hours or so when Durkan turned his head and whispered: "Be ready, child. There's an ambush ahead."

I promptly sat up, and craned my neck to see, but he reached behind him with his let hand and pushed my head down.

"Nothing to be seen yet," he muttered, "and best not to give them any sign that we know. Have you humans no memory? Are you slaves to animal instinct, that you must commit the same follies over and over?"

"What is it?" I said, helplessly.

"How can your craftsmen and merchants be surprised that we come to trade so rarely?" he asked, without turning his head to look at me, "when we meet brigands every time? How can the brigands be so foolish, when they must know that we are exceedingly difficult to hurt? How many will they force us to kill, before they condescend to learn?"

I understood the logic of the situation then. As soon as the fair folk had arrived in Camelot—and perhaps much sooner—the word had spread throughout the region that elves had come to Camelot with laden carts, and would doubtless be returning the same way when their business was done. Everyone knew that the fair folk had magic, and were no mere mortals—but how did everyone know it? They knew it as legend and rumor—and knew, too, how much there was in legend and rumor that was mere illusion. Time passed so slowly in Cokaygne that the elves thought their expeditions frequent, but it passed so quickly in our world that they seemed rare. Rare enough, at any rate, to leave room for fools and doubters to set aside the legacy of legend, and wonder whether elves might be as easy to rob as men.

The thieves were no better equipped than anyone else to find the gate of Avalon, but the road to Avalon was a different matter, and much of it was thickly forested. Ambushes were easy to set—but pointless, against an enemy with second sight.

I kept my head down until I had pulled the grey cap on, but then I peeped over the edge of the cart. Still there was no one to be seen on the road ahead—but Orwen and another rider had vanished from the column, while Morgana and the rest had drawn closer to the carts.

I knew that the ambushers, unable to tell reliable rumor from false, would be armed with arrows tipped with iron, which was said by some to be poisonous to the fair folk—a mistaken inference drawn from the observation that they made little use of that metal in their own armory. I knew, too, that it wouldn't have mattered much had the lie been true, given that a poisoned arrow must find its target before it can do its work. I had never seen an elf in combat, or in any other determined activity, but I could imagine what an advantage it must be to them to anticipate the flight of an arrow before the bowman let it loose. I had had some opportunity to judge how limited Morgana's foresight was—but one of those things that everyone knew, except for fools and cynics, was that every elf in Faerie could anticipate a mortal strike well enough to avoid it.

I, on the other hand, was only human—and the imbeciles lying in ambush wouldn't be inclined to discriminate between the fair folk and their passengers. Even if the cap prevented my becoming a target, I might still be in danger from wayward arrows.

I crouched down, and waited, listening to the hammering of my hart. Unlike the elves, I was by no means immune to dread, or to outright terror.

I was astonished, when the arrows came, that they seemed to come from every direction. The archers lying in wait had let the carts come to within a few paces' range before letting fly, trying their utmost to make sure of their targets. I heard the shafts whistling through the air, and the impacts of two that hit the side of the cart—and then I heard the screams, of horses and of men.

I couldn't help lifting my head, when I was sure that the first volley had all been loosed. Terrified as I was, I wanted to see what was happening.

Even the keenest eyes can only look in one direction at a time, but I set my gaze from side to side as quickly as I could.

I saw Durkan, standing up in his seat, hurl his slender blade at what seemed to be a wall of green, and heard it strike flesh an instant before another scream joined the cacophony. I saw one elvish rider, and one alone, still on the road, wheeling his horse around before urging it to the gallop—and I saw one fallen. Not one had been hit, nor even an horse. The horses that had screamed had screamed within the wood, and they had belonged to the ambushers, not to us.

I saw a man stagger out of the wood with his throat cut, bleeding more violently than I would have thought possible, and watched him crumple up, lifeless before he hit the ground.

The air was full of the odor of blood and shit.

Then the fair folk came back, one by one, some still mounted and others leading their mounts. Orwen was wiping blood from his blade. So was Morgana. One, and only one, had taken a wound—slashed by a sword from his left shoulder to his hip. Durkan leapt down to help him, and brought him to the cart.

"Get down," he said to me. "You walk, now. Hadwin needs your place."

I did as I was told. Orwen came to help, and he and Durkan laid the injured elf on the floor of the cart, supine. I could see that the cut was deep—three ribs, at least, had been cut, and there was a horrible gash in the abdomen through which the guts were bulging—but Hadwin didn't seem to me to be suffering any agony. He was breathing hard, but the expression in his eyes as one of fierce concentration.

Gently, Orwen pushed the edges of the gash together, starting at the shoulder and working down. The blood flow was muted, and when the wound was closed the flesh seemed to knit almost immediately.

I went to Morgana, who had just dismounted. Her eyes, more red than green, were fixed on the wounded elf.

"Fool!" she said. "To suffer a blow like that, from some oafish human! He should not have come with us, if he could not take care of himself."

But he'll live?" I queried.

"Of course he'll live," she barked at me. "If he'd been stabbed through the heart, he'd live—but he was so slow that his head might have been struck from his shoulders. He should not have come, if he could not take better care than that." She was bitterly annoyed, but with herself rather than the wounded elf, who was only a minor player in a game that she had organized.

"How many did you kill?" I asked her.

"All of them," she retorted, brusquely. "Seven, eight... not nearly enough. But the human world has no shortage of suicidal fools, Amory—remember that. Before we reach

Avalon, a hundred more will be born within a day's ride. Were we kind, we'd steal them all as changelings, but we couldn't do it even if we wanted to. Their fate isn't ours to decide; we have our own business to conduct. Be glad you're a part of it, Amory—the luckiest of all your kind. And hope that you make better use of your opportunity than Merlin did. You can take that silly cap off now—I can see you well enough.

Yes, my lady," I said, in my meekest manner.

2

Walking was far less comfortable than suffering the lurches of the cart had been, given the scant protection my slippers provided for my feet—but my soles had been hardened by a million stone stairs, and I grew used to he damp soon enough.

I fell behind a time or two, when the carts were moving easily down gentle slops, but they never stopped to wait, because they knew I'd catch up eventually, when the horses had to toil upslope or haul their burdens through boggy ground. I didn't mind; I brought a lifetime of practice to the role of outcast. I was privileged to be part of the company, no matter how detached, and I trudged along very purposefully indeed.

When we stopped for a second night, I went to see how Hadwin was, but he was fast asleep. The wound was still horrid, but it wasn't bleeding.

"Always been idle," Durkan commented, when he saw me inspecting the sleeping elf. "Probably took the wound so he could sleep till we passed through the gate. His first time out of Cokaygne, I think—or the first that hasn't vanished from his memory. I don't think he liked your world as much as he expected to."

"Do you?" I countered.

"Oh yes," he said. "A little barter, a little murder, and a sun that ducks out of sight before popping up again on the far side of the world. Elves aren't all alike, Amory, but we all crave a little excitement. If we didn't come here from time to time, how would we appreciate the wonders of the world our wishes made in its stead?"

I knew there was an element of sarcasm in the speech, but I couldn't tell how slight it was.

Morgana's eyes were golden again; she was quite calm.

"Tomorrow, Amory," she told me. "The gate isn't far, now. This is the last night you'll see as a boy—perhaps the last you'll ever see in your entire life, if you're lucky."

"I'll survive the passage through the gate, my lady," I assured her, "Depend on it."

"That's not what I meant," she told me. "If you're lucky, you'll spend your life in Cokaygne. If not, you'll be taken by the kind of madness that claimed Merlin. Hope that you'll find more in common with faithful Tom—but don't let him seduce you into a journey to the Dark Land."

"I don't intend to hurry into any kind of madness, my lady," I told her.

"It wouldn't matter if you did," she said. "There's no hurrying in Cokaygne."

I searched about the boles of the trees for a patch of ground dry enough and soft enough to sleep on, and eventually found one. Before I could lay myself down, though, Orwen came to speak to me.

"If you want to turn back," he said, "now's the time."

"I don't," I told him. "Nor can I imagine why any man would. I'm half a day's walk from paradise, with a means of finding its invisible gate."

"That's true," he conceded. "But many do, even when they come this close, or closer still."

"The human world has no shortage of suicidal fools," I reminded him. "I'm trying not to be one of them."

"You can try," he said, "but you won't succeed. And when you've failed, you'll hardly remember your time in Cokaygne. It may be a long moment, but it's only a moment. When it's over, you'll still be human. There's no escape from that."

"I can try," I said, echoing his own judgment. "Even that makes me luckier than thousands of my kind."

"So it does," he agreed, amiably enough. "So it does."

I slept better that night, but I woke up before dawn, fearful of discovering that the fair folk had crept away under cover of the cloudy darkness, abandoning me to my dire mortality. They hadn't. They gave me breakfast, and the others followed the lead that Durkan and Orwen had provided, acknowledging my presence in their midst at least with nods and murmured greetings.

"Put the cap on when we reach the gate," Durkan said to me, before he got up on his cart. "You might need it."

"It's all right, Durkan," Morgana said. "He knows—and I'll be with him. I'll carry him through, if he falls."

Durkan only shrugged his shoulders—but he had begun to care, a little. He saw me as a person now, not as a human being.

My feet were still sore, but I kept putting one in front of another, with iron determination. Upslope and down, no matter how far I lagged behind the carts, I never lost sight of the patient riders, and they kept looking back at me to make sure that I was still there.

When Morgana rode back to join me, I knew that we must be almost there.

The gate of Avalon wasn't a cave behind a waterfall, nor a trapdoor in a hollow tree, nor a multicolored path of light at the foot of a rainbow, nor anything else that I had ever been told to watch out for as I played in the forest near the Convent of Saint Syncletica. How could it be, when we had to drive two carts and a company of horsemen through it? Nor was it on any discernible road, though the cart that now carried Hadwin made far better progress through what seemed a trackless forest than it had on the human road it had followed into the fringes of the wilderness.

So far as appearance was concerned, the gate of Avalon was a clearing like any other: an uneven patch of grasses, ferns and flowers interrupting the hectic sprawl of oak and ash, beech and willow.

"Put your cap on now, Amory," Morgana said, "and take a tight hold on my saddle-strap. It might seem that it hurts, but it isn't really pain. It's only fear—blind, irrational panic. It won't be intense for long.

I did as I was told, and instructed myself to keep on doing what I had been doing for hours already: to put one foot in front of the other, until I had left the world behind.

I watched the first cart drive into the clearing and vanish without reaching the other side. Durkan's cart followed. One moment it was there, and the next it was gone.

"Wait, Orwen," Morgana said, when all but one of the other riders had winked out too. "Let us go first."

Orwen bowed his head, with the faintest of ironic smiles, and waited for us to overtake him.

We went forward into the clearing. I was momentarily dazzled by the sunlight, and lost my bearings.

Morgana had been right; it wasn't really pain. It wasn't any kind of fear, either, that I had ever felt before. It was like being unexpectedly turned upside-down—or as if "up" and "down" ceased to mean anything at all. My head reeled. It was as if my mind exploded out of my body, wrenched apart from the flesh, although my sense of self remained behind, locked within the straining of the sinews, the surge of the blood and the churning of the gut. I had never been so intensely aware of my own corporeality—but it wasn't really pain; it was exaggerated sensation, and nothing more.

I staggered, but I held on to Morgana's saddle-strap. I was determined not to fall. I was determined to be a hero, and to walk into paradise as a hero ought to walk. But I couldn't see the ground I was walking on, and I stumbled. Morgana's horse stopped, and waited for me to recover, and then it moved on.

My head felt as if it were split in two; I couldn't see or hear, but I could feel the strap in my hand and I could taste something bitter in my mouth. I told myself sternly that it wasn't pain, merely an inability to rise above the transactions of the organism. I wasn't really hurt, or ill; I was only stepping out of one world and into another, leaving time and the night behind for eternity within the light.

I don't say that it was easy, but after all I'd been through on earth, it certainly wasn't hard.

I crossed that clearing, and came out the other side, even though I had vanished on the way.

The forest into which I walked, still clinging hard to Morgana's mount, wasn't the forest I had quit. It was composed of oak and ash, beech and willow, and a dozen other species that were familiar to me even though I couldn't name them, but they all grew differently on the far side of the gate of Avalon.

Everything grew differently on the far side of the gate of Avalon.

Part Three
Cokaygne

?

There were birds in the forest on the further side of the gate of Avalon: finches and redstarts, rooks and jays. There were animals, too: red squirrels and roe deer, slender weasels and snorting swine. But everything grew differently.

Lesser creatures than the fair folk themselves, I eventually discovered, were by no means immortal; their destiny, as in our world, was to eat and be eaten, to grow, breed and die— but everything was different.

Everything was flourishing, healthy, sharply defined and bright.

The sky was blue, except for drifting white clouds, but the sun stood still in the sky. It didn't stand directly overhead, but here as no way to tell whether it was half-risen or half-set, a pointer to the east or to the west.

The fact that the sun never moved wasn't obvious, to begin with; a human who had stumbled through the gate of Avalon wouldn't have known, at first, how radically the world of the fair folk differed from his own.

How long did it take for the truth to become clear?

I don't know. How could the interval be measured, given that the sun never moved?

In the human world, the measurement of time is built into the pattern of life. Day follows night and night follows day; the moon waxes and wanes; the seasons change as the equinoxes and the solstices alternate. Hours, it is true, had to be uneasily eked out in my world by candles or trickling water, but the progression of the hours could always be calibrated against the day, mapped out as interval of a definite whole.

In Cokaygne, there was no such defining pattern. There was no ready standard but the beating of elvish hearts—and although that beat is steadier than the ever-fluttering pace of human hearts, it is also less easily perceptible. No one in Cokaygne ever bothered to count beyond a hundred.

Cokaygne wasn't timeless; it couldn't be. Events happened in sequence, one after another, as they did in any world. Every task and every journey required its interval; every individual grew hungry some while after eating, and tired some while after waking. Time passed in Cokaygne; there was no doubt about it—but keeping accurate track of that time was impossible in the absence of such devices as my world never had, until it turned into yours: mechanical clocks, calendars, diaries and timetables.

It's possible, in Cokaygne, to keep a loose mental grip on time by remembering the order of things done and witnessed, but that grasp never holds for long. Memory can't support long sequences unaided; without the framework of hours and days, months and years, the order of past actions and events becomes confused. Lived experience ceases to resemble a river flowing steadily from past to present, and becomes instead a placid lake, or a stagnant marsh, spreading its surface smoothly across an even plain.

In Cokaygne, time is not a flying arrow but a decorated shield. When a human considers himself in the human world, he sees a creature compounded out of all the phases of his past, arranged in linear sequence like a growing tapeworm. An elf does not see himself like that at all, because he cannot organize his past into that kind of structure. Like a human, he is the sum of all that he has experienced—or all, at least, that he can remember of what he has experienced—but he sees those experiences as a formless cloud, not as a distinct chain.

I say all this now, before my account of Cokaygne has even begun, because you must not expect my account of Cokaygne to be a sequence like my account of Camelot. Nor is its failure to constitute a sequence any mere failure of memory. Yes, my memory of Cokaygne is hazy, especially as to the order of events, but that is not my fault; it is an aspect of the world in which I had come to reside.

I had heard before I ever went to Cokaygne that the bounds between waking and dreaming were less distinct there than they are in our world. There's more than one reason for that, but it's no mere matter of the idle mind failing to draw proper distinctions. Wakefulness, in Cokaygne, is more dreamlike than it is on earth because it's so much more difficult to order its experience in the store of memory. Life in Cokaygne is always dreamlike—and dreams in Cokaygne have therefore no alternative but to seem more lifelike.

Much of what I have to tell you about life in Cokaygne may seem to you to have the texture of a dream, but none of it was illusory. All of it was real—even the heart of the Dark Land and its ghostly shadow folk.

I can't guarantee the order of the things that I have to tell you now, save perhaps for the beginning of the adventure, its climax and its end. I can no longer number the chapters of my narrative with any confidence, or even be sure that I have put the text-breaks in the right places, but that doesn't mean that I'm unsure about the events and conversations I'm recording.

It all happened—and everything that happened added to the sum of what I became, to make me what I am.

The feeling of disorientation and the acute awareness of my flesh that overcame me as I passed through the gate of Avalon never went away. Nor did they ever dwindle into insignificance, although they were soothed into quiet acceptance, as everything is in Cokaygne. I gradually ceased to pay any further heed to them.

Had my panic taken the form of an urgent desire to turn and run, I would never have entirely lost that desire no matter how far its urgency relaxed. Perhaps, on some subconscious level, I did retain that desire, anaesthetized and all-but-forgotten but never set aside. Perhaps all humans do retain that desire, no matter how long they remain in Cokaygne—the great majority of the fair folk certainly thought so, and pitied poor Mad Tom for thinking otherwise.

I was able to let go of Morgana's saddle-strap after a while, but the process of putting one foot in front of the other didn't become easier immediately, even in a land where every inch of ground and every growing thing was saturated with magic.

The route followed by the two carts seemed even more tortuous than it had before, never running straight for more than forty paces. At first, the fact that we still had a way to go was uncompensated by the novelty of the experience, because I was not in any condition to study, to consider or to marvel, but I think I grew used to my surroundings before we reached Morgana's village... or not long thereafterwards.

Although the territory visible in the distance from the route we followed seemed wild, the wayside itself was crowded. One of the reasons the road wound around so intricately was that it connected countless clusters of houses. Whereas the Roman road in my world had attracted commerce to its own straight course, and organized that commerce after its own direct fashion, the path I followed on the far side of Avalon went where what passed for commerce in the elvish world had always been, long before there were any stolen carts to follow it.

I think I remember that I hadn't expected to see so many houses in Cokaygne, and hadn't imagined that they would be so very various. I hadn't expected to see so many of the fair folk, or that they would be so gregarious... but my memories are untidily heaped up in respect of those points, and such impressions are unlikely to have formed explicitly while I was still in transit from the gate to my new home.

I do know, though, that I began to interrogate myself, even then, as to exactly what I had expected of Cokaygne— and I realized that even while I had had nothing to do but sit on the cart as it progressed from Camelot to the ambush of suicidal fools, I had never attempted to calculate or take accurate account of what I thought the land of Cokaygne might be like. It had been, quite simply, unimaginable.

Had I expected to find palaces made of gold and glass, filled with plush furniture, mirrors and bathrooms with water on tap, running hot and cold?

No.

Had I, then, expected to enter a world with no houses at all, where everyone slept outdoors on beds of green moss?

Not that either.

Had I expected to encounter a world of shops and factories and thriving commerce, where the fair folk toiled as miners and cobblers, tailors and weavers, goldsmiths and lens-grinders, bell-founders and charcoal-burners, receiving wages in coin fresh from the elvish mint?

No.

Had I, in consequence, expected a world where no one worked at all, but spent their whole time feasting and laughing, playing games and playing music, dancing themselves into ecstasy and drinking themselves into a finer and more enduring state of intoxication than was ever available on earth, never polluting their fingers with money at all.

Not that either.

Had I expected that the terminus of my journey would be a castle and a court like Camelot's, where Morgana reigned as queen, with armies of armored knights and talking animals for servants?

No.

Had I, therefore, expected a world without hierarchy, where there were no soldiers or servants at all, human or otherwise?

Not that either.

And I was right. In every case, the truth lay somewhere in between—and subtly displaced to one side or another.

Did we stop for the night as guests in one of the larger houses on the route, before we reached the village where Morgana lived?

I don't think so; she lived too close to the gate of Avalon.

Did the riders and the carts leave the band one by one, until Morgana and I arrived at her house with no company at all?

I doubt that, too. But the relevant memories are half-dissolved, eaten into crooked shapes, in spite of the fact that I was fresh from my own world, full of the impetus of time.

We must have reached Morgana's house before I had even the most rudimentary understanding of elvish folkways, but as I look back now, I can't recover a state of mind unilluminated by some such understanding.

The houses in Cokaygne are made of stone, brick or wood, or any combination thereof. Their roofs are made of wood, or slate, or thatch. Few are small, by human standards, but none are fortified. They are lightly-built, for they have little to withstand the in the way of extremes of weather—but it does rain in Cokaygne, and capricious winds sometimes blow there that are not entirely gentle. Their furniture is comfortable without being luxurious, sturdy but not without elegance. They have curtains and mirrors, but no taps from which they may draw hot or cold water at any time of day or night. Most have large kitchen-gardens where herbs and legumes are grown, as well as stables, bird-houses and pigsties; many have orchards too, or groves of nut-trees.

The houses are very cluttered, inside and out, with all manner of small possessions and ornaments, which range from the very new to the unimaginably antique. Few of these objects are exceedingly precious, but all are treasured after their fashion, and they are constantly being bartered—if that is the right term, given that they routinely function as a kind of money, even though there is no fixed scale of value such as determines the worth of coinage.

The elves build their houses close to wells, pools or streams, so they tend to aggregate into hamlets and villages for that reason. They would do so anyway, for the elves like to be close to others of their kind, even though they are great wanderers, who never regard a home as something permanent.

Their communities rarely number more than a hundred individuals, but there is a near-continuous flow of arrivals and departures, so the communities are always changing, always renewing themselves.

Morgana's house was larger than many, with a second story. It was in a cluster of twelve, arranged about a circular green. It was broad-fronted but narrow-edged. Its steeply pitched roof was made of timber. It was even more cluttered than its neighbors; she had a particular fondness of seashells, of which she had a vast number, although she lived much further from any Cokaygnian sea than Camelot was from the coast of Britain. Her walls and floors were decorated with mosaic pictures, built from countless tessera. The room I was given in which to sleep had a mural on one wall representing a lion and a unicorn lying down together in an Edenic garden. She said that I might replace it if I cared to, but I never did. Her own room had an image of a crowned queen seated on a golden throne, smiling down upon a multitude. The kitchen had images of deer and boar, and a bowman aiming an elf-bolt at a racing hare.

Elvish houses have to be built by elvish hands; their furniture has to be carved, their privies dug, their mirrors polished. Elvish clothing has to be woven, knitted or stitched, and the cloth dyed; the leather from which their boots are made must be tanned; their metals must be mined and refined; their food must picked and cooked, butchered and cleaned. There is, in consequence, a great deal of labor to be done in Cokaygne, day in and day out, from which no one is entirely spared.

One of the most remarkable differences between Faerie and our worlds, however, is that in Cokaygne, labor is not thought of as drudgery, even when it comes as close to what we would consider drudgery as anything can in Faerie. Some individuals there labor longer and harder than others, many under the direction of others, for all manner of exotic wages, but elves have a remarkable capacity for absorption in whatever kind of work they happen to be doing—and whatever kind of work they happen to be doing is, of course, made easier by magic.

It almost seems that labor is, for the fair folk, a kind of hallucination: an alteration of consciousness, an experience sought and savored for its own sake. No kind of labor is experienced as an end, or a destiny, or a trap, because every experience is considered an addition to an infinite array, an element in the completion of the individual.

Morgana was no exception to this rule, but she didn't consider having a human servant as a matter of avoiding drudgery. However paradoxical it may seem, she considered it as a kind of labor in itself, a job to be mastered, and a set of duties in which to absorb herself, much like any other. Her neighbors felt no need or desire to imitate her, and probably felt free to be amused by her slight eccentricity, but they didn't consider her mad or unusual.

In fact, to the best of my recollection, none of the fair folk ever thought another of their own kind to be mad or unusual, although they never thought of humans in any other way.

The trading of the fair folk is similar to their labor. They haggle incessantly over the price of their labor and their goods, as "everyone" in the world I had come from "knew"—but they don't do so in the same spirit as humans at market, for whom bargaining is a matter of obtaining as much as one can of the necessities of life in return for whatever goods or coin they have to exchange. No one in Cokaygne lacks the necessities of life; crowded as their villages sometimes seem. Its magical soil bears fruit enough to feed its entire population, with plenty to spare—and the population never increases, for they bear no children and entertain few visitors from other worlds.

As with labor, trade in Cokaygne has more to do with the accumulation of experiences than the avoidance of starvation—but you can surely understand that far better than I could, having brought the world of men, at least in part, to a similar culmination, albeit by a different route.

Morgana was a less assiduous trader than many of her neighbors, but when she did haggle, she was the equal of any. Orwen once told me that she had the reputation of being able to buy a cow for a handful of beans—a great compliment, in Cokaygne.

In Cokaygne, attitudes to labor and possessions alike—even houses—are conditioned by the fact that all elves always know that whatever they are doing and wherever they are living is a temporary matter, from which they will in time move on. Everyone expects that in the course of a potentially-infinite lifetime, everyone will do every kind of work that there is to be done, in proportion to the general need, not because of any principle of fairness but because there is, in the end, no final antidote to tedium but to attempt every possible experience.

All the petty aristocrats in Cokaygne know, therefore—and are not in the least resentful of the fact—that the day must eventually come when they will try their hands in mining metal or digging privies, merely because it will be a novelty. By the same token, all privy-diggers and miners know that the day will come when someone else will beg them for the gift of a spade or a pick, and the need for its employment... and if their dream of the moment has added sufficiently to the stock of their being, they will hand over their tools, and wander off in search of new ones.

Cokaygne has gentlefolk of a sort and servants of a sort, but there is none entirely without privilege and none entirely without obligation, and such relationships are fluid. There is power and there is prestige; there is fame and notoriety; there is envy and cruelty... but all are temporary, in the context of lifetimes that extend indefinitely.

Morgana had posed as a queen in Camelot, but in her own village she was perfectly ordinary. In Camelot, she had been a powerful enchantress, but in Cokaygne, every housefly and carrot has its share of magic, and to be an elvish enchantress is a mere tautology. In Camelot, Morgana' beauty had been outstanding—but she had only brought male companions with her; in Cokaygne, she was as unexceptional in appearance as she was in intellect. Her intellect was not at all extraordinary, except perhaps for her taste in games.

All the fair folk like games, but they vary considerably as to the kinds of games they like at any particular moment of their lives. Morgana liked intricate games, more than any other elf I met—but no one in Cokaygne thought her odd or obsessive on that account. Her neighbors knew that they would one day discover the same fascination, if they had not already done so, and that Morgana would pass on, in time, to some other hobbyhorse.

That is the one fundamental key to the understanding of Faerie. Everything passes.

Whatever happens, the fair folk always know that it will pass, and that in the fullness of their lives it will become one more item of experience, one more aspect of their complexity. In that, they are very different from mere mortals—even from those rare and fortunate mortals who are privileged to enter Faerie as their guests. Humans in Cokaygne continue to age, though not nearly as fast as the world they have left behind. Most of them, perhaps all of them, eventually die.

Elves, Morgana assured me, sometimes die, but very rarely. I had probably been in her world a long time before I contrived to form a sound estimate of what "very rarely" might mean, in terms of time elapsed, and am not sure of its value even now. For what it may be worth, though, I believe that a thousand years might very easily pass in our world without a single elf dying in crowded Cokaygne.

The room I had in Morgana's house was far more capacious than my alcove in Camelot. It had a bed that was better than Merlin's, as well as an upholstered chair. The walls were fitted with shelves stocked with Morgana's possessions, but I didn't mind that. I was one of Morgana's possessions myself.

I was delighted to reach that destination, having traveled so far to reach it, but I could have wished for a quieter reception. The entire village turned out to stare at me. I felt horribly dirty and wretched, entirely out of place—but not for long.

I slept. I ate. I bathed in the stream behind the house. I entered into the communal life of the eternally lit green. I learned to shoot. I learned to ride. I learned to throw pots. I learned to cast metals. I had many teachers in addition to Morgana, including Orwen, Durkan and Hadwin, who all claimed a minor share of the responsibility for my presence in Cokaygne. I didn't learn to fence, though—an oversight, as things turned out.

I tried to learn to sing, and failed. I tried to learn to play the lute, and failed. There must have been other things I tried and failed, which I have forgotten. I learned to favor the things I could do and neglect those for which I had, as yet, no talent.

I learned to tell myself that there was all the time in the world to accomplish the things I needed to accomplish, and that my own magic was growing within me, subtly changing its patterns as I became more than I had been before.

Morgana presented me with a suit of new clothes, better by far than Merlin's gift, and a pair of leather boots to replace my threadbare slippers.

I made friends among the fair folk—and I made one of my own kind, who must have come to visit me almost as soon as he heard that I had arrived. That, of course, was Tom Rhymer. It was he who tried to teach me to sing, ad play the lute, but he wasn't disappointed when I failed.

Tom was a taller man than Merlin, so he towered over me, but he never treated me as a boy. I think he had been so long in Cokaygne that he had forgotten the pattern of human growth and existence.

I worked hard, by Cokaygnian standards, but I had time to spare. I had time to play, time to rest and time to wander. I had time for myself, and because I was in Cokaygne, I had the kind of self that could benefit from time. I became used to allowing whatever I was doing to absorb me, to soothe away all thought of what I would do next, or after that, or after that, since there would be time enough and more to do everything that needed to be done, and everything else that took my fancy.

Thus was I gradually fitted for life in a land of eternal summer, where food was always abundant, and no house needed a fireplace, except for cooking.

"You must not mind the curiosity of my neighbors, Amory," Morgana told me—and must, I suppose, have said it not long after my arrival in her village. "The novelty of your presence will wear off soon enough. In the meantime, though, they will want to know everything about you. They will question you relentlessly about your life in the outer world—but you shouldn't have to answer the same questions a hundred times over, for anything you say will be repeated by its hearers until it is common knowledge."

That was true. I was questioned, voluminously if not relentlessly, but the information I gave out was further disseminated by its hearers, and everyone in the village knew me soon enough. It was probably after that, when the story of my life had become familiar, that I began to tell the other stories I knew. I told Merlin's story, and Arthur's, and Lancelot's. I told the legend of Saint Syncletica and the story of the song of the Acemites. I told the tale of Orpheus. They liked them all, especially the last, because they liked the strangeness of love stories, especially when such stories also involved death. I began to make up tales of love and death, and became slightly regretful that I hadn't more experience to draw on.

Tom Rhymer, Durkan told me, had sung a great many songs about love and death once upon a time, but he didn't seem to do it any more. He composed different songs now, which the fair folk liked just as well, accepting the change in him as an understandable and acceptable thing.

"This is a wondrously peaceful and polite world," I said to Morgana, although I must have said it for the first time long before I realized how utterly peaceful and polite her world was. "Mine must seem very dangerous and violent by comparison. Mine is a world in which men may be arbitrarily and treacherously slain at any moment, casually struck down by stolen elf-bolts. That must seem a terrible prospect to you."

"No more terrible than the deaths of deer and sheep," she assured me.

"But humans are far more like elves than deer or sheep," I pointed out." In a dim light, the silhouette of an elf might easily be mistaken for that of a human."

"Do you think so?" she said. "Well, Amory, I suppose you know far more about dim light than I ever shall."

"It seems to me," I told her, that elves are merely durable humans, who live a long time and are more resistant to injury and disease."

She laughed at that.

"You are mortal too, are you not?" I said, taking slight offence. "Elves live a very long time, but you've admitted that they do die."

"We can be killed," she said, "and perhaps, in the end, some few of us grow tired of life—but we don't die or tire easily. We have the second sight to warn us of impending danger. You saw how different we are from humans when we were forced to fight in order to reach the gate of Avalon. Have you seen Hadwin recently, by the way? He's as good as new—not even a scar."

"I've seen him," I said. I'd seen Orwen, too, and Durkan, although I couldn't tell her how recently I'd seen them. None of them lived in the village, but they all passed by, and they all called to see me when they did. Sometimes, I played games with them or helped them tell the story of the epic battle in the forest, when they had killed a score of desperate humans in order to reach the gate of Avalon. In some of those tellings, I took a hand in the fight myself, but I was more often content to play the part of the helpless victim whose preservation required greater heroics than would normally have been required in the slaughter of a mere three dozen attackers.

I lied about other fights instead.

I was happy. I had every right to be. I was in Cokaygne; I had attained my lifelong ambition.

I still had the phial of truth serum that Morgana had given me in Camelot. She had told me when she gave it to me that she would like it back if any were unused, but she never asked and I never offered.

Because I prepared her food, it was easy enough to feed her the remaining drops, when I felt that it was safe enough to ask questions that I hadn't dared to ask before.

"How much did your second sight tell you before you set out, my lady, of what would happen after your arrival in Camelot?"

She looked at me very steadily, soft green glints showing in her golden eyes. "In your world," she said, "time flows too rapidly, and too strangely, for much anticipation to be possible. I felt that I would come away unharmed, with my company intact—but as to what would happen around me, there was little to be foreseen because there was so much yet to be determined, by the secret conspiracy of chance and choice."

"Forgive me, my lady," I said, carefully, "but I couldn't help but wonder, while I sat in the back of your cart, whether you knew what use I would make of the truth serum, and what effect its use would have on Camelot."

"I understand that you couldn't help it, Amory," she said. "You have a little of the second sight, but not enough as yet to know its nature and limitations. You're bound to suspect that I knew more than I could. Let's speak plainly, so that the matter might be settled. What you want to know is whether I came to Camelot in order to contrive its destruction, intending to use you as a pawn in the achievement of that result."

"Yes, my lady," I said.

"Is that what Merlin told you?" She asked. "When you went to see him, before coming to claim your reward, did he tell you that I had planned it all, at least fifteen years before?"

"He seemed to think so, my lady," I admitted, "but that isn't to say that I believed him. I'd like you to tell me the truth, if you will."

"I didn't plan it," she said, flatly. "If either of us contrived or hastened Camelot's ruin, it was you, not I. But I don't believe that you have any need to trouble yourself with pangs of conscience. You did what you did in order to bring out the truth, and it's no fault of yours that Camelot was founded on lies and delusions. You acted in your own interests, not in those of your master or your king, but that is your right. No one can blame you for it, Amory, and no one should. You were no one's pawn, Amory—not mine, not Merlin's, not fate's. It was no part of your duty, or capacity, to subvert the secret conspiracy of chance and choice. I didn't bring you here to reward you for serving as the instrument of my malice, but because you offered yourself so enthusiastically as my servant, and I decided to accept. I like you, Amory, as I once like Merlin, and still like Tom Rhymer."

She paused again, and waited. She hadn't deigned to ask me whether I believed her, but she was waiting for me to confirm that I did.

I had no alternative.

"Yes, my lady," I said, meekly.

"Good," she said. "For what it may be worth, though, you might care to know that if I had contrived the destruction of Camelot, it would not have been unjust. I didn't do it, because I didn't care enough to do it, but if I had done it, Merlin would have no cause for complaint. He tried to cheat me. In spite of all he knew, and the sight he had gained while he was in my house, he tried to cheat me. He offered me a bargain, which he always intended to break. That was the first of all the lies on which Camelot was built."

Again she waited, without having posed a question.

"What did he offer you, my lady, in return for the trick of the sword and the stone?" I asked, as she expected me to do. I already knew, but while she was in a confidential mood, I thought that I ought to take full advantage of the dose I had given her

"He gave me to understand that his intention was to undo what the Romans had done when they conquered Britain," she said. "He gave me to understand that his ambition was to return the island to its former state. He gave the same impression to Taliesin's bards, as you doubtless realized when you were listening to his conversations. But his real intention—as you must know, having served so long as his apprentice—was to preserve what the Romans had done, and carry forward the changes they had instituted. It was an unnecessary lie; I didn't care one way or the other, and that wasn't why I helped him— but it was a lie nevertheless. When the truth eventually tore the tissue of his lies apart, it was no more than he deserved."

I would have liked to comment that it was not like my master to tell an unnecessary lie, but it would not have been true. Like all great liars, he was a liar by habit, who sometimes lost sight of the truth entirely.

"Yes, my lady," I said, instead.

"Now that your mind has been set at rest," she said, "I have some work for you to do." And she made a list, exactly as Merlin used to do—except that she took the trouble to show me how to do the things she asked me to do, as Merlin never had, even when he first brought me to Camelot.

The work I did for Morgana always proved far less arduous than any I had been used to in the convent or in Camelot. Even before I had much magic of my own I had begun to understand the elvish ability to absorb oneself in any task at all, and count it a positive experience.

The fair folk are by no means always serene, but they're never despairing, or even deeply disquieted. They know, as well as believe, that in a land without natural seasons every thing may have its season, and that in a land without death, everything really does come to he who waits.

Except, of course, that their notion of "everything" excludes so many things that you or I might take for granted. Love, for instance. And sex.

Had I ever expected that I would become Morgana's lover as well as her servant?

No—but that was because I hadn't thought about it at all. Had Merlin, when he first came to Cokaygne? Had Tom Rhymer?

If either of them did, it must have been more hope than conviction. Merlin had never told me that he had been Morgana's lover, although the rumors about his time in Faerie that circulated in the bowels of Camelot took it for granted that he had. He had never told me, either, that he had wanted to be, although the rumor-mongers of all-too-human Camelot could never have entertained the idea that he hadn't.

You would probably side with them, but you might be mistaken.

Merlin might have told me the truth about whether he had ever expected or attempted to become Morgana's lover if I'd only asked him outright—though not, I dare say, until after he had kicked my shin or smacked my head for my impertinence—but I never dared to do that.

Would it have made any difference to me if he had told me flatly that he had never been Morgana's lover? Would it have made any difference to my own ambition to be her servant, if I had known in advance that I would never be her lover?

I don't think so.

Adolescent though I was, it wasn't a vital issue. I had never eaten well enough, or had the leisure, to cultivate the kinds of passion and obsession to which Lancelot fell such ready prey.

If I'd entertained such follies when I passed through the gate of Avalon, they would have been dispelled soon enough—but any disappointment would have been soothed away, as everything is soothed in Faerie.

The simple fact is that the fair folk cannot love, in any sense of the word that humans could recognize. They don't "make love" to one another, much less to humans. They don't have children, so they have no inbuilt reproductive urge to glorify into lust and passion, devotion and affection. They have their likes and dislikes, their whims and fancies, but they don't experience sexual pleasure or suffer infatuation.

I say "suffer" because they would presumably regard any such affliction as a kind of unpleasantness, or at least oddness. They are what they are, and have not the least desire to be more human than they are; they don't envy humans our ability to love.

When Morgana confirmed that the fair folk never bore children, having already admitted that they could and did die, I thought it a puzzle. Where, then, did the fair originally come from? Was their number to dwindle, however slowly, until there were none at all?

When I first asked Morgana these questions, she admitted that she simply didn't know. Neither she nor any other elf had a memory sufficiently powerful to remember a state of affairs other than the one in which they now lived. They had no notion of their individual or collective origin. Their number did not seem to have decreased markedly during the span of time they could recall, although logic suggested that it must decline in future, albeit at a very gradual rate.

Another question inevitably came to mind as I struggled with this calculation. How many of the fair folk were there, in all? Without knowing that, I couldn't form he vaguest estimate as to the likely duration of their species.

Morgana didn't know that, either.

How large, then was their world?

She had no idea. No one, so far as she knew, had ever wandered far enough to discover a boundary. Some of her neighbors had seen the sea; none had ever crossed it. So far as she knew, Faerie might be infinite, and its population might be infinite too, undiminishable by occasional death, although that notion was exceedingly strange to me.

To you, of course, these problems will seem far less peculiar than they seemed to me. You're used to dealing with the concept of infinity. You also know how large your world is, and what shape it is, and how many people it contains. I had no such knowledge. I knew that my own world must also be very large, since no one I knew had ever wandered far enough to find its limits, and probably had far more people in it than anyone could count—but I couldn't imagine it as infinite.

I couldn't think of my world as infinite because I thought of it as flat, and knew it must be bounded because I had always seen the sun rising to the east of it and setting in the west. I was tempted to think of Faerie as flat and evidently finite, by analogy—but Morgana pointed out to me that Faerie's sun neither rose nor set, perhaps having nowhere for the sun to set to or rise from, and thus might easily go on forever, in every direction.

It never occurred to me to wonder whether either world might be a sphere, let alone whether our sphere might be spinning like a top while the sun remained effectively stationary, while the Faerie sphere kept the same face perpetually turned towards its primary.

Given those limitations to my imagination, you won't be surprised that I made little progress with the puzzle of the origins, number and ultimate fate of the air folk. But I found out soon enough that I wasn't alone in wondering. Although the fair folk took their nature and mode of existence for granted, having known no other, and were happy to dabble lightly in fantasies of infinity, any humans who were guests in Cokaygne were bound to take a more pragmatic approach to the question.

There were no other humans resident in the village where Morgana lived. For a long while after my arrival, elves would come from neighboring villages to have a look at me, to interrogate me and to talk about me to my neighbors, but none of them ever brought a human being. Even so, I had one human friend and one potential confidant in Tom Rhymer.

Tom had lived with Morgana once upon a time, and he had not moved far away when he obtained a cottage of his own. He visited me soon after my arrival in Cokaygne, and I soon began to visit him. I gave him news of home; he gave me advice about life in Cokaygne; we became fast friends.

He tried to teach me to sing and play, but I never learned.

Tom told me that the cottage where he now lived had been gifted to him by an elf who had divided his time between carpentry, growing salad vegetables and duck-keeping, but had decided that the time had come to move on to a different combination of vocations. In order to have the house, Tom had promised to look after the salads and the ducks, but he had passed the carpenter's tools to someone else, except for those he needed for making instruments, in order that he might have more time for composition and performance.

He didn't seem mad to me—no madder, at any rate, than many men I had known in Camelot. All the fair folk thought and called him mad, but he didn't seem to resent that in the least. He told me that he had been madder in his time than he was now—admitting that one symptom of his earliest madness had been an unrequited infatuation with Morgana—but that life in Faerie had soothed his madness just as it soothed everything else, if one allowed it to. At any rate, he was certainly harmless.

Not everything in Faerie is harmless, by any means, but Tom Rhymer was.

We forged our friendship without any difficulty at all. We had interests in common, in spite of my failure as a player.

Tom must have questioned me as ardently as any elf in the early days of our relationship, and probably left me little time to reciprocate, but I was sufficiently acclimatized even then to know that my own turn would come, and I didn't try to hurry him.

When Tom visited me, I wasn't the only one in the village who was glad to see him. He knew everyone, and everyone knew him, because he often needed an audience and they often needed to supply one. He never came to see me without bringing one of his instruments, and he would always make time to play on the green. He never lacked for listeners, although his music seemed very strange to me, and his songs even stranger.

Sometimes, for me, he would play the songs I knew—which were, now that I came to consider the matter, all about love and death—but he preferred to play his own, which were about music, and time, and epic journeys in exotic places.

I told him, of course, how Merlin had fared when he'd returned to the human world, thinking that poor Tom was lost forever in the Dark Land. I suppose my account was terse, and self-serving, but it was true nevertheless.

"He tried to make his dream of Britain come true," I said, "but he failed. He grew old, and lost the legacy of magic he had carried away from Cokaygne. The world changed around him, too quickly. He couldn't cope with the pressure of time—perhaps because he had lost the knack while he was here. I helped him as best I could, but in the end, a fellow has to look out for himself. It wasn't my fault that he didn't succeed. It really wasn't."

I don't know why I was so insistent; Tom Rhymer hadn't accused me of anything, and never did.

"He let his dreams take hold of him," was Tom's verdict. "It's easy to do that here—and dangerous. He had no outlet, you see, as I have. I tried to teach him to play, but he had no ear for music. He had the wrong attitude to the second sight, always trying to force it. You shouldn't force magic, Amory. You have to let it flow through you, as if by nature. It's human nature to be discontented, but Faerie will soothe us if we let it."

He didn't volunteer a single word about the expedition he and Merlin had undertaken to the world of the shadow folk; he waited for me to ask..

"Perhaps Merlin should have stayed in Cokaygne," I ventured, "Our world's a poor one for the soothing of discontent."

247

"Some can't stay here," was all Tom said in reply to that. "Some can, and some can't. You'll discover which you are in time."

"You can, I suppose," I said.

"I hope so," he told me. "If I can only provide entertainment, I'll settle for that. If I can do more, I shall."

I thought at the time that by "provide entertainment" Tom meant playing his music, but he didn't. He meant dying. Elves die so very rarely that the vast majority have no memory of ever seeing one of their own kind die—but most have seen at least one human die, in their own world or the one without. It's hardly surprising, I suppose, that they regard such an event with fascination—but I doubt that any of them would go as far as to describe it as "entertainment".

It was when I did realize what he meant that I asked him what he meant by "doing more"—and that was when Tom Rhymer told me his theory regarding the origin of the fair folk.

"Elves can't remember their birth," Tom told me, "but nor can we, so that doesn't mean that they were never born—and the fact that they have navels suggests that they must have been. They're very long-lived, to be sure, but they aren't immortal. They aren't as different from humans as they like to assume, and it seems to me that the differences are imposed from without rather than being fundamental to their nature, as a result of their long existence in this world. I believe that they were human themselves once, and that the elvish condition and state of mind are largely a product of long evolution and extended maturation."

"Morgana doesn't think so," I told him.

"I know that," He said. "She wouldn't, would she? It would diminish her perception of herself were she to entertain the notion that she had ever been like you or me."

"Go on," I said.

"If all elves were human once," he said, "that could explain why the number of the elves doesn't diminish, even

248

though they eventually die. Some few of the humans who come here as their guests must eventually contrive to transform themselves into elves—not many, but a few. Most return to their own world, and most of those who don't return grow old and die—but that, I think, is a winnowing process, which eliminates those who are not capable of living as elves do."

It was an intriguing idea, but I hesitated to leap to the conclusion that it was the only explanation that made sense.

Tom had been thinking about it for a long while, though, and had elaborated his theory considerably. "That's why the youngest among the fair folk still feel the occasional urge to revisit the world of their origin, you see," he urged me to believe. "They're taken by a sudden whim to go a-hunting, or make a little mischief. They'll play fast and loose with human affections if the mood takes them, but they never actually feel anything for the men and women they seduce—it's all a game to them, a ritual whose origins are long forgotten.

"It's nearly the same with changelings, but not quite. They steal children because maternal affection is the last posthuman impulse to fade, and leaves inconvenient echoes. Babies still have the ability to fascinate and entertain them, at least for a while, just as human death does. The fair folk can't love human children as mothers and fathers do, but they can still find a special amusement in cradling infants in their arms and singing lullabies. They never call their stolen infants son or daughter, but sometimes they call them brother or sister—they haven't any sense of the human meanings of such words, of course, but they have their taboos as well as their habits."

Morgana, I remembered, had been willing to call Arthur "brother". As Tom said, it was just a word to her, an arbitrary description. No female elf has a brother or a sister, any more than she has a mother or a father, a daughter or a son.

"Did all the elves come from our world, then?" I asked him.

"It's possible," he said, "but it's also possible—and seems to me more likely—that this world was more like ours at one time, and that it changed along with its inhabitants. As the world's innate magic transformed them, they transformed the world. I don't know how the process started—with the world or with the force of their desire—but once it had started, it established a causal loop, whereby each alteration in their being was further reflected in the world, and each alteration in the world was further reflected in their being. Intercourse with our world became necessary when they had completed their self-transformation and rendered themselves incapable of reproduction."

When I put Tom's thesis to Morgana, however, she smiled.

"Now you know why they call him Mad Tom," Morgana said. "You must persuade him to tell you the remainder of his fantasy—then you'll know it for the folly it is."

I hadn't realized that there was more, and made a mental note to do exactly that—but in the meantime, I was more interested in knowing how she would counter Tom's arguments.

In the beginning, she didn't. "It's merely part of his madness," she insisted. "Humans who stay here too long always go mad, although they usually do so quietly. If a human is bent on going mad, of course, it's far better to do it here than in your world. Merlin was more than a little mad, as you know—and not so quiet in his madness."

"I know Merlin's faults," I told her. "But he was clever too—and I can't see why it's madness to imagine that elves might once have been human, or at least a little more human than they are now. What other explanation can there be of the continuation of your race in a world without birth?"

"We have always been as we are," Morgana assured me. "We are not humans grown to authentic maturity, nor are we humans transformed by subtle magic and the power of desire. We are elves. It may be that our fate is to become fewer and fewer as time passes, until we are no more; if so, we shall accept it. Can you possibly imagine that your own kind will endure forever, because it has the power of reproduction? It seems to me that the opposite is true—that the tendency of human numbers always to increase is the cause of near-universal hunger, epidemics of disease, and wars of conquest. Your world is hideously spoiled already; if its troubles do not bring it to actual destruction, they will surely secure its eternal misery."

All of which, I thought, was beside the point. But I could see why she was so resistant to Tom Rhymer's idea. If true, it would mean that the idyllic world of Faerie was parasitic upon its hideous neighbor—and the destruction of humankind would, in the end, spell disaster for elfkind too.

"Your memories are limited, Morgana," I pointed out to her. "The further ones grow hazy, and the furthest ones are lost, so you can't know that what Tom says is untrue. I'm human, but I have no memory of my first sojourn in Faerie, let alone my birth. I wouldn't know if I'd been budded from a tree and suckled by a she-wolf. All I know is what I've learned from what I saw around me as I grew, and what I was told. The same surely applies to you. It isn't surprising that you've drawn very different inferences, but surely you can see that their logic is flawed. You can't always have been what you are now."

"We don't remember our births because we had none," she assured me. "This is Faerie, not the world of men. We're closer here to the source of creation, and have no need for such follies as birth, maturation and death. I don't say that we've lived since the beginning of time, nor that we shall last as long as time endures, but I do say that we never migrated from a world as hectic as yours, or evolved from creatures like those who live in your world now."

"You were made by a god, then," I suggested, "in his own image?" I had not seen the slightest evidence of religion in Cokaygne; no elf ever made any reference to a Creator.

"I didn't say that," she said. "Perhaps we did come from elsewhere, given that we are such inveterate wanderers—but if we did, it was more likely from within than from without."

"What do you mean?" I asked. "Do you mean the world of the shadow folk, to which Merlin went with Tom Rhymer?"

251

"No, not from there. That one lies alongside ours, I suppose, as a bleak counterpart to our eternal light—but there is another world that touches both, closer to the primal fire of creation than either. That was the way we must have come to Cokaygne, if we came from elsewhere. Your world is further away from that fire than ours, and closer to the void; that's why it seems so cold and disordered. It's the rind of creation, where life abuts death and the ravages of the void must be compensated by ceaseless birth."

This astonished me, because I had heard nothing like it before from anyone in Cokaygne—although Merlin had given me what I now recognized as a garbled version of it.

"How do you know this?" I demanded.

"Because I see it," she told me. "One day, if you live long enough, you might see it yourself."

She meant the second sight, of course, not the sight of the eyes. But I had grown used to the idea that the second sight was a kind of dreaming, and I still had a human opinion regarding the unreliability of dreams.

"Tom can't see it," I told her, "and he has been here longer than Merlin was."

"But Tom's mad," she reminded me. "If you doubt me, persuade him to tell you the rest of his theory regarding the origins and fate of Faerie, and ask him why he wanted Merlin to go with him into the Dark Land."

I must have intended to do as Morgana said as soon as I had the opportunity, but she had work for me to do, and I was still content to be her servant. The work absorbed my mind as well as my time, and the matter slipped my mind for a while, as things are apt to do in Faerie. It's easy there to abandon oneself to whatever one happens to be doing—so completely that labor need not seem like labor even to a displaced human—and I'd gladly learned the trick of that abandonment.

Compared with living as a servant in Camelot, living as a servant in Morgana's house was comfortable, even luxurious, but there are certain tasks that can never be anything but onerous. I fetched and carried for Morgana as I had for Merlin, including her chamber-pot; I washed her clothes and cleaned her cooking-range. I'd known even in Camelot how much better it is to do such things in a dream than to be urgently conscious of them, but dreaming was so much easier in Faerie, especially while I was awake.

Lest this seems to you to be too good to be true, I ought to record that it wasn't without a compensating penalty.

To turn difficulty into ease, or pain to pleasure, devalues both ease and pleasure. Pleasure that is too easily available—including freedom from the burdensome aspects of toil—loses the sharpness of its contrast with its opposite. The wines of Faerie are deliciously intoxicating, and never leave a hangover—but by that very token, their delectability soon fades into familiarity, and their lack of miserable consequence takes the piquant element of bad conscience out of the temptation to get drunk.

The smoothing of drudgery and pleasure, pain and ecstasy, triumph and defeat, all assist in the process by which the bounds between waking and dreaming become far less clear when one lives in Cokaygne than they are in earthly life. I've said already that wakefulness, in Cokaygne, is more like a dream than wakefulness in the world of man because it can't be ordered within the framework of time, but that's only one reason. Another is that wakefulness in Cokaygne is so free of penalty and effort. By the same token, dreaming in Cokaygne is more like wakefulness than dreaming could ever be in a world where sleep is usually exhausted and rarely untroubled.

In Faerie, dreams are more leisured, luxurious and lucid than they are on earth.

Forgetfulness is easy, in Cokaygne—and that was why I forgot, for an interval of time I can't measure or estimate, to ask Tom Rhymer why he had gone into the Dark Land with Merlin, and what he'd found there after Merlin turned back, and how it fitted into his theories regarding the origins, nature and fate of that world.

Eventually, though, I did remember. Everything passes in Cokaygne, including forgetfulness.

"Did Morgana tell you to ask me that?" Tom asked, when I raised the subject again.

"Yes," I admitted, "but I wanted to ask you before, when I first met you. Merlin told me about the Dark Land, and how he panicked and turned back while you went further in, and that he never saw you again. He likened it to the story of Orpheus, although I couldn't quite grasp the similarity, given that you didn't go in to search for a lost love, and weren't trapped there as the result of a misinterpreted command."

"Was he drunk when he told you the tale?" Tom asked, sarcastically.

"No," I said. "Tired, but not drunk."

"Tired would probably be enough," he admitted. "Yes, we went into the Dark Land. We were supposed to remain together, but he turned back, and I couldn't go much further without him. I tried—but some adventures need two."

"Why?" I wanted to know.

"They just do," he said—but he knew it wasn't an adequate answer, so he tried again. "It's not so much that they have to be shared," he said, "but that they have to be observed... or communicated. What you do entirely by yourself is more dream than reality, even if you do it instead of merely dreaming it. What you do in company is seen and known. That's what the Dark Land's all about: seeing and knowing."

It made no sense to me, so I retreated to safer ground. "What happened to you, when Merlin turned back?"

"I went on for a while. I met the shadow folk. I played for them, a little. Orpheus played for the dead, it's said, and they were greatly impressed by his playing because it reminded them very powerfully of everything they had lost in life—but that's not why Merlin likened our story to the legend of Orpheus. Merlin thought that I really was searching for my heart's desire, although he thought I was mad. Anyway, the shadow folk aren't the dead. They did appreciate my play-ing—at least as much, I think, as the fair folk."

He fell silent then, as if there were something he did not want to say, as yet.

"Morgana says that the Dark Land is a natural counter-part to this one," I said, to prompt him. "What she means, I think, is that the endowment of his world with eternal light requires another to be eternally dark, in order that some kind of fundamental balance might be maintained. She also spoke of the primal fire of creation and the void, as if they too were opposites in balance."

"And she claims to see it all," he finished for me, "as we too might one day see it, if we live so long. She said the same to me, when I first suggested to her that Faerie might once have been a world like ours, before it was transformed by the magical desire of its inhabitants. Faerie had always been a world of eternal light, she assured me, always coupled with its shadow.

"I wasn't so sure. I wondered whether the elves might actually have created the Dark Land while they created their own, their every advantage being won to the cost of the shadow folk. I couldn't help but wonder what account the shadow folk would give of their own origins and nature—and, indeed, what their nature was. Anyway, there's a gate to the Dark Land not very far from here, although it sees even less traffic than the gate of Avalon. I persuaded Merlin to go with me. He wasn't convinced by my arguments, but he was curi-ous. Alas, he was also very jealous of the magic he had culti-vated while he lived in Cokaygne, and he soon became con-vinced, once we had crossed the threshold and his panic set in, that the darkness of the Dark Land was inimical to his second sight as well as the sight of his eyes.

"We were both carrying candlesticks, and we had more candles in our pouches, but when we had passed through the gate the flames began to flicker, and became weaker than be-fore. Merlin was afraid—rightly so, I confess—that we might not be able to find our way back to the gate if our lights were

255

extinguished. We had spare candles and the means of re-lighting them if both went out simultaneously, but he was afraid that our flints might not work in the Dark Land, and that we might be stranded there.

"The anxiety was partly irrational, but the irrational part was worse than the other. I knew what he must be feeling, because I felt it too—a pressure on our thoughts, a depression which seemed foul and deadly by comparison with the sooth-ing light of Faerie. I wanted to fight it, but he was more care-ful. He thought that I was mad, you see—and perhaps I was. We both were, I think, although our madness took very differ-ent forms.

"So he went back. I went on, in spite of the danger. I was foolhardy—but I was annoyed with Merlin too. I wanted to show him that I was braver than he. I met a number of the shadow folk, but they couldn't or wouldn't speak to me. I put my candle down, and I played for them on a little pipe that I had in my pouch. More of them gathered round, presumably to listen. When I stopped, I tried to question them again, but still received no answer."

"But your candle continued to burn," I said.

"For a while. Then it went out."

"But you found your way out anyway."

"Yes I did, although I can claim no credit for it. The shadow folk guided me out. I could still see them, even in the dark. In fact, the candlelight had made it unnecessarily diffi-cult to see them. They were more easily visible to the second sight, once the first had failed."

"Did they talk to you, once the light was out?"

"Not in words. I think they might have been able to, if only I'd had time to learn their language, but I couldn't do that alone. There was too much dream in the encounter, and not enough sequence. I could see them, though, and feel their presence... except that the seeing was more like feeling and the presence wasn't quite presence. I still dream about them, of course. Once you've met the shadow folk, you always know them. They're with me still, in a way."

He spoke in a level tone, as if everything he said made perfect sense.

"So you learned nothing new?" I said.

"On the contrary. I learned a great deal—but the fair folk have their own ideas about their nature, and the nature of their world. To them, it's all madness."

"Were you right, then, about the elves' good fortune being the shadow folk's loss, their eternal light and contentment being bought at the expense of the shadow world's gloom."

"No, quite wrong. Once I was in the Dark Land, even though I never got to its heart, I understood that the shadow folk are entirely content with their own mode of existence. I now believe that they were working with the fair folk, assisting in the process of the separation of the two worlds. I think they too were human once, or something similar. I think they too embarked on a path of self-evolution, which transformed their world in such a way as to help the world transform them... and so on, the effect multiplying as it flowed back and forth.

"In their view—which is entirely a matter of the second sight, since they've allowed her eyes to go blind—light isn't a good thing but a curse, which stands in the way of... well, what you or Morgana might regard, metaphorically, as enlightenment. They'd have to use a metaphor related to one of the other senses: to touch, perhaps, or hearing. The ultimate in feeling, the ultimate in sound... in music."

"They wanted to play for me, as I had played for them, but they had to ask my permission, because they believed—perhaps correctly, because I dared not put it to the test—that if I heard and understood their music, I would want to stay with them forever, and never leave."

"And how did they tell you that, through the medium of your second sight?" I asked, skeptically.

"We call it second sight because the elves do," he reminded me. "You have enough of it now, although you hadn't before, to know that it isn't a kind of eyesight at all, even though it helps you to see more keenly with your eyes. The shadow folk wouldn't call it second sight; they'd favor some other sensory analogy. Feeling, hearing... perhaps even taste or smell. I felt it, Amory—but if you conclude that I'm mad for thinking so, you'll merely be endorsing the opinion of everyone else, Merlin included. I certainly can't assure you that I'm not, because I've often thought the same... but one day, I'll go back to the Dark Land again, at least to learn more, if not to put that feeling to the proof."

He didn't ask me to go with him, although I saw—or felt—that he wanted to. He didn't think that I was ready, and he was right. I wasn't—but in Cokaygne, there's a time for everything, if you have the patience to wait for it. In Cokaygne, all dreams come true if you're prepared to give them the opportunity.

I was in my room on the upper story of Morgana's house, looking out of the unshuttered window, when the rider came into view. I was staring into the distance at the hills on the horizon, wondering why my eyesight—once so remarkably keen—now seemed less capable of making out the detail of their slopes, even on a day when the brightness of the stationary sun was delicately veiled by white cloud.

I hadn't consciously turned my head in the direction of the gate of Avalon, but I must have been looking in that direction, or I wouldn't have picked out the rider as soon as he emerged from the cover of the ever green trees.

I knew immediately that his horse wasn't an elvish mount; it was too massive, and its gait too ponderous. The black-clad rider was too tall to be an elf. He was tall even for a human—as he had to be, to straddle such an animal. He carried no lance or shield and his helmet bore no plume, but the fact that he was armored at all declared him to be a fighting man.

As he came closer, I saw that he wore a sword, and that the hilt of another was projecting from the pack wedged behind his saddle—but I still couldn't make out his face, half-hidden as it was by the helmet.

When he was still more than two hundred paces from the green the rider met an elf on the path, who raised an arm in friendly greeting and paused to offer him assistance. The rider brought his mount to a stop, but didn't dismount. A few moments later, the elf pointed in the direction of the village.

It appeared to me—and there might have been an element of second sight involved—that the elf was not only pointing at Morgana's house rather than any other, nor even at my own window, but actually at me.

There was no cause for surprise in that. I was, after all, the only human in the village. I had not so far had occasion to greet any human newcomers while I lived there, but it would have been universally regarded as my duty had any come along the path that the rider in black was now following. If he had come through the gate of Avalon only an hour before, whether by accident or design, he must be severely disoriented, and would need care. Even if he had paused in the woods and dismounted, and waited there until he felt a little better, he would still require advice, and food, and a place to rest.

Even so, I was surprised—and alarmed too.

I should, I suppose, have run downstairs and gone out to meet the rider. Instead, I called to Morgana, and waited where I was until she came.

"Do you see that man, my lady?" I asked. The rider had just urged his horse to move on, and the huge animal had resumed its slow but inexorable step.

"Yes, Amory," she said. "I see him."

"Do you know him?"

"Know him?" She was astonished. "How should I know him? Still, if he is coming here, we ought to make preparations to receive him. It is quite a while since we last had guests, is it not?"

"I know him," I told her. "I can't quite make out his face, as yet, but I know him. He shouldn't be here. I don't want to see him."

"How absurd!" was her reply to that. "He will have news of your world, and of Camelot. Are you not anxious to hear it? I am. I shall be delighted to hear news of Merlin and Arthur, and you should be delighted too. Perhaps he has a message to deliver, or a plea to make. Does Arthur want my help again, do you think? It would be amusing, don't you think, to return to Camelot as my servant, in all your elvish finery, with all the magic you have stored in your flesh and in your senses? To play Morgana le Fay one more time would be a welcome pleasure, I think—and the interval is just about right."

While she prattled on I was trying with all my might to make out the face of the approaching rider.

For a minute or so, I thought that I had been mistaken, and that I didn't know him at all. There were aspects of his face that seemed familiar, but there were others that seemed wrong. I had almost come to the conclusion that he merely bore an accidental resemblance to someone I knew, when I realized where the incongruity lay.

He had grown older since I last saw him—a good deal older.

I had always known that time must be passing more quickly in my homeworld than it was for me, but having no way of keeping track of time in Cokaygne I had never been able to form a sound estimate of how long I had been away. Until I recognized whose face it was that I was looking at, I had no measuring device—and when I understood who it was I received a double shock, the greater part of which was the estimation that twenty years must have passed in the world of men while I had hardly aged a day.

Twenty years!

By human reckoning, I had spent much more than half my life in Faerie, although I had done and accomplished nothing at all, and seemed to myself to be exactly the same as I had been when I first crossed the threshold of Morgana's house.

The rider was Lancelot du Lac: the man who had murdered my predecessor for fear that if Arthur met with a seeress, she might tell the king a secret that would spoil both their lives.

Now, he was coming to the house where Morgana lived with her loyal servant: the instrument who had let loose the secret, regardless of his own efforts, and who had then run to Merlin to brand him a murderer as well as a traitor.

Lancelot, I knew, was not the kind of man to seek out the gate of Avalon and cross into the Cokaygne without a very good reason—and for a man of his stripe, the only reason that would carry him through the sense of dislocation attendant on his passage through the gate was revenge. I knew him well enough to know that he must have taken dishonor twice as hard as a man who did not hold honor so high.

But twenty years had passed!

For twenty years, Lancelot had nursed his injury—and now he had come through the gate of Avalon, in search of the cause of his damnation.

Except, of course, that the true cause of his damnation was himself.

For a moment, I entertained the ridiculous hope that Lancelot might have come to seek Morgana in order to confess his sin, and ask for her forgiveness. By that time, though, he had reached the edge of the green, and I could see the expression in his grey eyes. They were not the eyes of a man in search of forgiveness; their bleak stare was questing for a very different kind of absolution.

"You had best go down and welcome him, Amory," Morgana said. "Take his horse and bring him into the house. He will be hungry and thirsty—and then he will need to rest, until the sickness passes."

"Yes, my lady," I said, meekly, although I knew that things wouldn't go that way.

I went downstairs and out of the front door. As he soon as he saw me emerge, Lancelot reined in and waited for me to cross the space that still lay between us.

"Amory," he said—just the name, nothing more.

"I'm astonished that you remember me, sire," I said, as lightly as I could. "You never remembered my name before, in the days when you saw me almost every day. How long ago was that, exactly?"

"I never saw you," he said, flatly. "You saw me, but I didn't see you."

That was presumably a veiled allusion to my spying, but I let it pass. "I stand corrected, sire," I conceded. "My mistress bids me make you welcome, and to bring you into the house. There's food and water—or wine, if you prefer—and a bed on which to rest. You'll need to sleep, and dream, if the distress of your passage between the worlds is to be soothed. We'll talk about old times later."

"Your mistress," he said, "is Morgana le Fay."

"Here," I told him, "she's simply Morgana. She's neither a queen nor a noblewoman. That was Merlin's invention."

"I too was Merlin's invention," he told me. "I too am less now than I was twenty-one years ago."

Twenty-one years had passed!

Lancelot dismounted then. I think he'd stayed in his saddle so long because he feared that he might not be able to get down without feeling dizzy, and he couldn't abide the thought that he might stumble, let alone collapse. He completed the maneuver to his own satisfaction, then drew himself up to his full height so that he could look down on me.

"I had expected that you would have grown a little," he murmured.

"Not in stature, sire," I admitted, "but I'm not the boy I was when last you saw me. I'm older than I seem."

He turned back to his saddlebag then, and unbuckled the strap holding it in place. Assuming that he was unloading his luggage so that he might bring it into the house I stepped forward to offer my services as a carrier—but when the pack was on the ground, he pulled out the sword whose hilt I had seen projecting from it.

"It must have come out as easily when Arthur pulled it from the stone," he observed, wryly.

I realized that the weapon was Excalibur.

"Are you surprised that I have it?" he asked. "I am surprised myself, although I understood the reason soon enough. I came here to make a present of it to Morgana le Fay—but you are her servant, are you not? You are entitled to receive it on her behalf?"

"She is in the house, sire," I told him. "I have only to call, and she will come out."

"There is no need," he told me. "You can take it, can you not? After all, if it were ever to be used you would have to wield it on her behalf, as her champion."

He was still speaking wryly, as if it were an ironic jest. I had never credited Lancelot with a sense of irony, but twenty-one years of his life had passed away since I had seen him last, and I didn't know how much he might have changed. I reached out, and let him place Excalibur's hilt in my right hand.

I expected the sword to be heavy—too heavy for someone of my meager stature to wield with any ease—but it was surprisingly comfortable. Being of elvish manufacture, it was made of a lighter material than iron—and my muscles had become more powerful while I lived in Cokaygne.

When I looked up from the glinting blade to meet his eyes again. I saw that he seemed satisfied with the way I held the sword.

He began to remove the glove from his left hand, loosening one finger at a time. His hands must have been damp with sweat, making the flesh cling to the leather. When one hand was free I expected him to begin on the other.

Instead, he struck me across the face with the glove he had removed.

In retrospect, I can see that I should have expected it, even without my second sight to aid me. I was a fool—but even as I realized what a fool I had been, I remained astonished by the improbability of what he had done.

I was not a knight! A man like Lancelot might strike me down quite casually; he might even shoot me in the back with a stolen arrow—but he couldn't challenge me to a duel, because I wasn't entitled to that kind of ceremony, that kind of recognition.

I realized, though, that he was no longer a knight himself, in the eyes of his own world. I realized, too, that in the eyes of his own world, Morgana le Fay was a noblewoman, if not a queen, and that I was indeed her champion as well as her servant.

And he had known my name.

When he had spoken my name aloud he had recognized me—not in the trivial sense that he knew who I was, but in the more profound sense that he had not refused to acknowledge my identity.

"Do you have armor to put on?" he asked.

"No, sire," I replied, mechanically.

"Then I shall remove my own," he said. He set to work on the buckles holding his leather arm-guard in place.

The realization sank in that Lancelot intended to fight me there and then. I also noticed that a considerable crowd had gathered on the edge of the green. The elves must have been assembling ever since Lancelot had first come into the village, moved by simple curiosity—but now that his intentions were clear that curiosity had been dramatically sharpened. I looked around for Morgana. but she wasn't there. She must have been the only inhabitant of the village who was still indoors.

Even though I was in Cokaygne—and had, apparently, been there twenty-one years—I had to fight to remain calm. "Why Excalibur, sire?" I said. "Why this sword, rather than any other?"

He had a great many buckles still to undo, and his fingers were unsteady; I could see that it would take him quite some time to unburden himself of his armor. He didn't pause in that work, but he did look at me with a puzzled expression on his face.

"Your mistress is a seer," he said, mildly. "Is she not able to keep watch on the human world, through her skrying-glass?"

I might have laughed, but I didn't. It was a mistake that he had made before, with tragic consequences. "Perhaps she could," I told him, coldly. "But she has other concerns to occupy her thoughts. No one from your world has passed this way since I first came here, and I have had no news of anything that has happened there since that day. I had hoped that you might tell me how Merlin and Arthur have fared, before killing me."

He stared at me harder, as if he couldn't believe that I was telling the truth.

"Merlin vanished," he said, shortly. "The rumor was put about that he was imprisoned in a tree by some elvish enchantress who had taken up residence in our world a hundred years before, but you may be better placed to judge the likelihood of that than I am. Arthur is dead, though the rumor was put about that he too had found a magical fate, being spirited away through the gate of Avalon so that his wounds—mortal as they were—might be healed. You have not seen him, I suppose?"

"I haven't see him," I confirmed. "I would certainly have heard about it, had he come through Avalon—but there are other gates between your world and ours."

"He's dead," Lancelot repeated, without challenging my entitlement to refer to Faerie as our world. "The rumor also said that he brought Excalibur with him to Faerie—but that, as you see, was false. Gawain brought it to me, with news of Arthur's death."

"How did Arthur die?" I asked.

"In battle, as a king should. Not that he wanted to fight, as I understand it. He rode out of Camelot at the head of an army, but he went to make peace. He met Mordred's men on a field called Camlan, and made a treaty with him that both forces would withdraw without drawing their swords—but the treaty was spoiled when a man was bitten by an adder, and drew his sword to slay the snake. The action was misinterpreted, and the fight began, so I was told—but it has the feel of a legend about it, and may be untrue. The fight was evenly balanced, so Gawain said, until Arthur fell. Had he had more knights to form a phalanx around him, or had the knights he had been more ardently committed to his cause, Mordred's Saxon mercenaries could never have reached him, let alone slain him—so Gawain insisted—but the round table had too many empty seats by then, and those still filled were spoiled by quarrelling. Had I been there, Gawain said, the battle would have had a different outcome. Do you believe that, Amory?"

"I don't know, sire," I replied, honestly.

"Arthur did. He was always inclined to think me a better warrior than I was, and a better friend. He thought the two of us kindred spirits, strangers among our own kind. He trusted me too much. On his deathbed, he asked Gawain to bring Excalibur to me, and to tell me to do with it what I must. What was in his mind, do you suppose?"

"Perhaps he had forgiven you, sire," I said, "and wished to symbolize the fact."

"Perhaps he had," Lancelot agreed. "Gawain did not think so. Gawain was jealous, of course—he thought that the sword should have been passed to him, that he might be king of the Britons in Arthur's place. He had waited long enough for the privilege, with as much patience as loyalty. His interpretation was that Arthur sought to remind me that I had broken his kingdom, and his dream, by my treachery. As if I could have forgotten! According to Gawain, Arthur wanted to make clear to me the terrible injustice of the fact that I still lived while he was dying, when he might still have been alive and strong if only I had kept faith with him. It's possible, I suppose. Merlin would have known the truth, thanks to his black magic. Do you?"

"Why bring the sword to me, sire?" I asked, for the second time. "I don't understand why you came here."

"If Gawain was right," Lancelot said, "and I dare not take it for granted that he was wrong, then I was not the only one who was responsible for Arthur's misery and death. I do not know, even to this day, how your mistress caused Guinevere to part with her secret against her will, but I do know that it was against the queen's will. I know—as you must—that I was enmeshed in a scheme beyond my understanding, and I know whose scheme it was."

"You murdered Harl," I pointed out, "and tried to put the blame on Morgana. Was that against your will?"

He knelt down then, to unbuckle the first of his leg-guards. I could have smashed his head with Excalibur while his eyes were on his work, and he would never have got up again. No one would have called me to account for it. The watching elves would only have been amused.

I didn't attempt to strike him. I waited to hear his reply to my question.

"I didn't think so at the time," he admitted, "but I wasn't certain, afterwards. If magic can make a queen act against her will, might it not alter the will of a knight? Might it not persuade him that he acted of his own accord, when in fact the plan was slyly slid into his head? Perhaps, if I had only been a little stronger, I would have been able to resist the temptation—but I was not. I am guilty. I lost everything I held dear, through my own fault. But as for Arthur's fate... I was not alone in determining that. What Arthur intended, or what Gawain intended, I cannot tell—but in my own belief, I was given Excalibur in order that it might serve as an instrument of revenge, against the true destroyer of Camelot. I could not give it to your mistress, but I could offer it to you, as her servant and champion, and that is what I have done. You must fight, on her behalf—and die, on her behalf."

As he finished, the second leg-guard finally came free. I could see, as he held it briefly before dropping it on the grass, that his hands were trembling.

He stood up, ready to fight.

Lancelot had been the finest swordsman in Camelot, twenty-one years before, and I was still a boy, who had never learned to fence. He knew where the advantage lay, in the combat he intended to begin—and I think he knew, too, how little chance he would have had if he had asked Morgana to appoint a champion from among her own people. Orwen would have killed him easily enough.

"Did Arthur have an heir?" I asked. I already knew the answer, but it was the most delicate way I could think of to raise the question of what had become of Guinevere.

"No," said Lancelot, "he did not." For a moment, I thought he was about to say something more, but he didn't. He shivered slightly, but collected himself and forced himself to stand rigid.

"I came through the gate of Avalon myself, sire," I said, quietly. "I know what effect it has on a man's head and body. You're still suffering some distress. You'll be far better able to fight if you eat a little, and drink your fill, and sleep for a while. Your head will be clearer then, your hand far steadier."

He looked down at me, imperiously. "You are afraid," he said. "I understand that. You want to give your mistress the opportunity to enchant me—to feed me forbidden fruit, and muddle my senses further with drugged wine. I cannot allow that. I must fight you while my purpose is clear, even though my head is not. But you must call your mistress so that she may watch you die in her stead. Will she care just a little, do you think? About the insult, at least?"

Until that moment, I had still been thinking of him as my superior, my natural overlord. I had still been thinking of him as a knight, a paragon of noble virtue. But I saw then that he was not my superior at all: that he was my equal, at best, and perhaps not even that. He wanted to fight me because he thought that he could kill me, and feared that he might be cheated of the opportunity if he delayed too long. We were both traitors, each after his fashion, but Lancelot's treason was by no means the nobler of the two.

I was entitled to form my own opinion as to why he had brought Excalibur into Cokaygne and placed it in my hand, so I did.

"It wasn't my mistress who compelled Guinevere to tell the truth against her will, Sir Lancelot," I told him. "I did that. I was behind the screen decorated with the images of the lion and the unicorn. I poured the truth serum into the cup she took from Arthur's hand. Until that moment, I had thought that she might have given you the order to assassinate Harl, but I was watching from behind the unicorn's eye, and I saw that you had done it of your own volition, moved by your own cowardice. I went to Merlin's attic, and I told him what you had done, and why. I also told him to make what use he still could of the information, in the interests of Camelot. I had already told him, some time earlier, that you were in love with the queen, and she with you, and that neither of you had the strength of will to set that passion aside, in spite of your obligations.

"I saw you for what you were, Sir Lancelot, and had the chance to warn the king, but I kept silent, for fear of hurting him—although, in the end, I couldn't protect him from the hurt. Morgana didn't bring you down, Sir Lancelot—I did. So you have no power to insult my mistress, no matter what you intended. Nor have you any power to insult me, given that I have but one name, and you know what it is. I know that you recognized Merlin's former apprentice when you murdered him, and I know that you were afraid of him, even as you shot him in the back, from ambush. You were right to be afraid of him, Lancelot, and you're right to be afraid of me. I thank you for Excalibur. I suppose you believe that you can and will win this fight, or you would not want to provoke it—but you don't now yourself as well as I do, Lancelot. You came here to be killed, rather than to kill. You know full well that my mistress doesn't need to feed you enchanted fruit and drugged wine to seal your fate; you're merely impatient to be dead. Who could blame you?"

He stared at me as if I were an adder that had reared up unexpectedly from the turf and pricked his boot with a frail fang. He was astonished by my temerity—but he would have been equally astonished had I really been a serpent. He was a vain man, who didn't expect to be attacked, even in such circumstances as he now found himself.

I met his gaze, trying with all my magical might to weaken his resolve. I didn't want to die.

After a minute or so, his gaze shifted, and he began staring at something behind me, with equal contempt.

I didn't have to turn around to know who was there. "I have invited Sir Lancelot to come in, my lady, as you asked me to do," I said, "but he insists that we have business to conduct that prevents him from accepting our hospitality."

"I suppose he knows his own mind, Amory," Morgana said, sarcastically.. "Perhaps he understands that if he waited a little while, until his head had cleared, he might lose the urge to fight. Anyone here would be glad to give him food and water, and a place to rest. He need not compromise himself by accepting our hospitality. But if he were to do that, the atmosphere might soothe his woes away, and he would not like that at all. Have you warned him that he cannot hurt you—that you have been in Faerie long enough not to need armor against any blow that his sword might inflict?"

She might, of course, have addressed herself directly to him, but she wasn't in a polite frame of mind. I couldn't tell whether she was bluffing, just as I was bluffing, or whether she really thought that Lancelot couldn't hurt me. One thing of which I was sure, though, was that she intended to hurt him. Morgana was more inclined to bear a grudge, and pay it out, than any other elf I knew—but how could we have come to this pass, if it had been otherwise? Merlin had done better than he knew to call her Morgana le Fay, and to inflate her reputation as a potent enchantress.

"Sir Lancelot is a brave man, my lady," I said—and I think, at some level, I actually meant it. "Once set upon his purpose, he is not the kind of man to be easily turned aside. He was once a knight of the round table, better in his gallantry than any other. He is determined to kill me if he can, and to do it now."

"Give me the sword, Amory," she said. "I'll fight him myself. Don't worry, Sir Lancelot—no one in your world will ever know that you were outfought by a woman."

She meant it—and I could tell by the expression in Lancelot's eyes that he knew it. He refused to dignify the offer with an answer; he looked at me again, and his eyes called me a coward. His expression challenged me with the idea that if I did as Morgana asked, I would be the one responsible for any travesty that might follow.

All humans who stay too long in Faerie go mad. "It's all right," my lady," I said. "He wants to be killed, and I'm happy to do it." I didn't turn my head to face her as I said it. I kept my eyes on Lancelot, waiting for him to blink—and when he did, I lifted Excalibur, and put myself en garde.

Lancelot was twenty-one years older than he had been when he sat at the round table. He was also somewhat befuddled—but he still knew how to wield a sword, and every trick that might be employed to pass an opponent's guard. I, on the other hand, had neither fought with a sword nor had an hour's training in the weapon's use. I had watched knights, squires and soldiers practicing, and knew what a sword-fight looked like, but even that was so far removed in memory that it seemed almost a dream. I had magic and Lancelot hadn't, but I didn't fight him in the expectation that I was bound to win. I fought him because I had no option. If I'd given Excalibur to Morgana, I'd have had to live with the memory of his accusing eyes for a very long time.

When he came at me, lunging as swiftly as he could, I saw how clumsy he was, not just because his head was aching and his muscles had begun to waste but because he was entirely human. My movements were rapid in comparison. Alas, they were also horribly inexpert. Lancelot's thrusts were inept, but my parries were just as clumsy. I had absorbed enough of elvish grace to evade Lancelot's awkward first stroke, but not with any conspicuous ease.

271

I saw him smile as he realized exactly how inexpert I was.

When I parried his blade with mine, though, the clank of metal on metal reassured me that no matter how light Excalibur might feel in my hand, it was a very solid weapon. Its blade was slender, and its blade was sharp, but it wouldn't break.

Lancelot's own blade wasn't the sort of weapon he would have used from horseback; it too was relatively slender, sharpened on both sides of the blade and neatly pointed, but it must have been almost twice as heavy as Excalibur. Lancelot couldn't move it as easily or as rapidly as I could move Excalibur, no matter how much skill he had. When he thrust again, I parried again, dancing out of range of his superior reach—and so the initial pattern of the fight began to develop.

Every impact of the two swords jarred my arm, but they jarred Lancelot's arm too. He knew how to brace himself against such reverberations, but he had to take their force regardless. While he thrust again, and again, and saw his blade swept aside each time by mine, I knew that each failure was taking its toll—but his eyes told me that he didn't believe he could be beaten. He thought that it was only a matter of time before his skill prevailed.

I moved before his onslaught with more than human agility. When Lancelot swept his blade in slanting arcs, it cleaved through empty air that I had vacated almost effortlessly. When he thrust for my breast or tried to catch my arm with his point, I met his blade with my own, and turned it with a dexterity as uncanny as it was untutored.

I was lucky, I suppose—but the luck was authentically mine; it was not disposed by some kindly outer power.

When two hundred hasty heartbeats had elapsed and he hadn't touched me with his blade, Lancelot became fretful and angry—but he was focusing on his work now, and becoming absorbed in it. The confusion left in his flesh by his transit through the gate of Avalon was giving way to the force of his will. He had aimed two dozen blows at me and I had escaped them all—but I hadn't aimed a single counterstroke at him, and he was well aware of the fact. I didn't know how to shape such a thrust, and he knew it.

Unlike me, Lancelot was no fool. He understood very quickly that his lack of speed would prevent him from outfencing me as easily as he had hoped, and he adjusted his tactics. He saw that I was stronger than I seemed as well as quicker, but he knew that he had two advantages that couldn't be offset: his reach and his height. No matter how fast I might be, I couldn't strike at him effectively while he could hold me at bay with a sword in his extended arm. No matter how strong I might be, I could only strike upwards at him, and would always be at a disadvantage when he rained blows upon me from above. He adjusted his style of fighting to exploit these two advantages to the full, in a more patient manner.

I saw him take note of the fact that whenever I had to hold my blade horizontally above my head to intercept a downward stroke my arm was badly jarred. He was utterly determined to end the fight as soon as he could, but he knew that he would need a more elaborate strategy to do it, and he began to plan his thrusts in combination.

I should have been able to keep on parrying his blows, using my superior speed in measured retreat until he got tired. Instead of fixing myself upon that strategy, however, I got carried away. I tried to find an opportunity to stand my ground, and turn defense into attack.

I honestly thought that I could do it—that I had the required celerity, if not the education.

I was mad, of course.

He was tiring, but so was I. I tried to find an opportunity to take the initiative, and he prepared to give me the opportunity, in order to take advantage of any attacking thrust I made with the aid of his superior skill. The unintended conspiracy of our shifting tactics brought the fight towards its climax in a hectic rush.

Lancelot's fear that he might have been bewitched if he had condescended to eat, drink and sleep in Cokaygne wasn't without foundation, of course. Morgana might not have drugged or poisoned him, but the world itself would have soothed him. Had he only let it work on him, he would have lost the waspish instinct that had driven him through the barrier in search of one last murder to commit.

Perhaps, if I had only been able to spin the fight out for an hour, or half a day, Cokaygne would have worked that magic on him—but there are no hours or days in Cokaygne, and as soon as Lancelot had realized that I would benefit if the fight were to go on too long, he had become doubly determined to end it.

The crowd was cheering. Most of them were cheering for me, but I knew that none of them held me in any real affection. From the elves' viewpoint, the duel was a cockfight, a contest of playthings; it was the spectacle that delighted them, not the hope or fear of any particular result. If I lost, the fair folk would mourn me—but only to savor the piquant sensation of being able to mourn, to delight in the novelty of burying a human whose name they had known, and to whose face they had become briefly accustomed.

I knew better than to glance sideways in search of Morgana's face while I was fighting. I supposed that she might care, a little, were I to be killed—I was her servant, after all, and in Lancelot's eyes, in spite of what I had told him, I was fighting instead of her, a mere surrogate for his hatred of her—but even Morgana, I knew, would be delighting in the spectacle, the contest, the game.

If Lancelot had put up his sword, I would have lowered mine. If he had stood back, and lowered his weapon, and agreed that he couldn't or shouldn't kill me, I would have renewed my offer to give him food and drink, and to treat him as politely as a good servant always treats a guest. I would have talked to him, about the world we had both left behind and the world in which we now found ourselves. I would have introduced him to Tom Rhymer, and advertised him as a storyteller to every elf for miles around. I wouldn't have been his friend, but I couldn't have been his enemy, because I understood far better than he did what it meant to live in Cokaygne.

It didn't happen. Lancelot had worked out what he supposed his optimum strategy to be, against an opponent of my kind, and he followed it ruthlessly and relentlessly. He bore down on me as best he could, and mingled his downward blows with occasional stabbing thrusts, no longer hoping to catch my parries unprepared but waiting, patiently, for me to initiate the next phase in the conflict.

In the end, my foolishness led me into trouble. I turned one of his not-so-desperate thrusts aside, glided past the blade as its momentum carried it onwards, and thrust the point of my own weapon into his chest with all the force I could muster.

I had assumed that my superior strength would give the blow the power it needed, but I was wrong. I had, after all, no more mass than I had ever had. Nor was the blow well aimed, for it struck him full on the breastbone, which was the best item of natural armor he had.

He laughed. There was hysteria in the laugh, but it was a laugh nevertheless. My blow didn't penetrate his rib cage— but his counterblow penetrated mine. He brought his own blade back to smash my interrupted thrust away, and the impact left me so badly off balance that I couldn't parry his next thrust. It wasn't the most powerful blow he had struck, by any means, but it was struck at close range, and guided far more cleverly than mine. It went high into the left side of my chest, to the left of the breastbone. Had he not been quite as tall, or I not quite so short, it would have cleft my heart, but instead it went clean through. A full three handbreadths of Lancelot's blade vanished into my body, and I felt the point puncture my lung and drill through my shoulder blade before making its exit.

But it didn't hurt—not for a second.

Lancelot was still laughing. He knew that he must have missed the heart, but he had no doubt that it would be a mortal blow nevertheless. He expected the shock to paralyze me, so that Excalibur would drop from my listless hand.

I knew exactly what he was thinking.

As Tom Rhymer had observed, magic has as much in common with hearing as it does with sight, but even an elf cannot "hear" another elf's thoughts. There are no words in what one "hears" by magic, nor is it really a kind of music, but there is evidence nevertheless of mood and emotion—and Lancelot's emotions were far more intense than any elf's. If Lancelot's emotions had been translated into words he would have sounded like Merlin screeching "Cretin!"

I couldn't see ghosts then, but it was easy enough to imagine Merlin voicing my own thoughts, my own instructions to my arm.

"This time, hold the blade so that it strikes horizontally," my master said, "and don't bother aiming for the heart. Send it straight through his throat."

Instead of letting Excalibur fall, I brought the weapon round again. Spitted as I was on Lancelot's blade, I too was able to strike at very close range.

With his blade embedded in my body, he had nothing to bring to his own defense.

I drove Excalibur's point into his throat, severing the windpipe. It glanced off his spin, and scythed through the artery in the left side of his neck.

Because the bounds between waking and dreaming were so confused in Cokaygne, I was able to do it entirely without malice. I did it because it was what the moment required.

I expected him to let go of his own sword at once and fall down dead, but that's not the way things happen in crude and bloody fights. He fell down, but it took him a long time to fall and he didn't let go of the hilt of his sword. He pulled me down with him.

He was still trying to laugh, even though he couldn't draw breath and the blood was gushing out of him like a fountain, dyeing both our shirtfronts red.

He fell down, but not supine. I fell down alongside him. We were facing one another, he lying on his left side and me on my right. He still had enough life in him to prop himself up on his elbow, and stare into my eyes. He couldn't speak, but he looked at me, astonished that I wasn't dead but determined nevertheless to defy me with his eyes until death delivered him to darkness.

I couldn't look away, even when I laid Excalibur aside in order to use the fingers of my right hand to explore the blade projecting from my torso. It wasn't until my fingers touched his that Lancelot finally let go, and sank back to die.

If he had been able to hold on to the idea that my wound was mortal, he might have died with triumph in his eyes, but he couldn't. He knew that appearances had deceived him, and that I wasn't going to die just yet.

Like most humans, Lancelot had always thought of magic in terms of spells and gadgets, incantations and effigies. He had thought that the second sight must require a lens of some kind, be it crystal or jet, and he had thought that magical power required ritual to incorporate and focus it. He hadn't understood that magic is something that grows in the body and the mind, little by little, until it wreaks a transformation of flesh and spirit alike.

Did he realize, before he died, how badly his assumptions had betrayed him?

I doubt it.

He couldn't maintain his smile as he died, because he was busy gasping for a breath he would never draw, but his grey face and grey eyes could still hold the ghost of an expression. He didn't want to be forgiven, any more than he had wanted to forgive.

He was better off dead. Life in Cokaygne wouldn't have been a torment to him, but there would have been no delight for him in its timeless serenity.

I thought I had time for one last word. There was little point in being discreet or dishonest, so I curled my lip, and tried to pronounce my final judgment on him.

"Cretin!" I would have said—but I had a punctured lung, and couldn't. I fainted instead.

As you might imagine, I've read the books in which legends of Camelot are nowadays preserved with extraordinary fascination. So far as I can make out, through the mists of confusion, elaboration and obfuscation, Camelot might have survived even after Lancelot's crime and Arthur's response to it. Perhaps the battle of Camlan, where Arthur fell, might have gone differently if it hadn't been for that inconvenient serpent. Perhaps Mordred might have joined forces with Arthur in the end, to keep the Saxons at bay a little longer. Perhaps, if that had happened, the Church might have saved the day.

On the other hand, perhaps not. Merlin was gone by then—dead, I suppose, although I like the idea that he might have been imprisoned in an oak by elvish magic. That would have been a fitting end for him, just as it would have been fitting for Arthur to be taken through the gate of Avalon in order that the wounds he sustained at Camlan might be healed. Without Merlin's guidance, the dream of a Britain founded in Camelot would probably have evaporated anyway. It's not so easy to turn dreams into reality in the human world.

How much time passed in the human world while I lay unconscious, as the magic of my flesh healed the wound that Lancelot had inflicted? It might have been hours, or years. Did I dream, in the meantime? Almost certainly—but I remember nothing, until I woke up and resumed my magically-preserved life in the full blaze of consciousness.

Tom Rhymer was sitting by my bed. He gave me a cup of water and offered me a bowl of cherries. I took one, chewed the flesh away, and spat out the stone.

I inspected the wound on my breast and ran my forefinger along it; the scar was almost invisible, but still perceptible to the touch. I tried to reach its counterpart, but its placement on my back was too awkward.

"That was quite an achievement, I understand," Tom said. "Lancelot's reputation had even filtered through the gate of Avalon. I'm almost tempted to step through the gate in order to carry the news to people who'll know how to spread it. You'd be a legend then: Amory, wielder of Excalibur and victor over Lancelot."

"Don't bother," I said. "Better for everyone to think that he might have vanished, like Merlin."

"Merlin vanished?"

"So Lancelot told me, before he forced me to fight."

"Arthur?"

"Dead. Camelot still stands, I dare say, but it can't be the heart of Britain any longer. Twenty-one years had gone by when I fought Lancelot, and for all I know the number might have increased even further by now."

"The castle's walls will surely endure," he said. "Merlin was an ambitious architect; he must have built it to last. What does it matter if some Saxon lordling takes control of it for a while? It will always be Merlin's pride, Merlin's glory, Merlin's monument."

"No it won't," I told him, having foreseen it in a dream, although I couldn't quite remember when. "It'll be taken down, piece by piece. He built it cleverly, but the blocks he used had to be easily carried and carefully placed. The ancient henge on the plain will outlast it, even though its capstones will fall, because it would be too much trouble to remove such unwieldy blocks. Camelot can be stolen, and will be, to build byres and boundary walls, houses and wellheads."

"Even better," Tom said. "A castle is built for siege, and reflects an unhealthy state of mind. The spirit of Camelot will be all the better preserved if its stones are dispersed and built into the fabric of everyday life. The idea of Britain will be better served by that kind of incorporation, and by the manufacture of fine legends, than it would by a castle usurped, and a name forbidden."

"Why should we care?" I asked him.

He looked at me steadily for a few moments, and then said: "We just do." But he thought better of it, as he always did, and accepted that he ought to attempt an explanation.

"Did Morgana ever tell you that I pleaded with her to have Excalibur forged by the best smith in the region, and to put it into the hands of Merlin's boy king?"

"She never said that you pleaded," I replied, "but she did tell me that the real reason she did it was to please you."

"Did she?" he seemed surprised. "Well, perhaps I helped to tip the balance, although she had other reasons too. Did she tell you why I wanted her to help?"

"No," I admitted. "I always intended to ask, but somehow..."

"Because I wanted to do something for my own world. When I heard that Merlin had gone back, I felt guilty. I thought that if I hadn't persuaded him to go into the Dark Land with me, he wouldn't have taken fright about the frailty of his acquired magic. I thought that if he hadn't thought me lost, he might have waited a little longer before gong home, until he had a little more power, and a better plan. I wanted to help him—because I cared. I had left the human world behind, and I had no intention of going back, but it was still my world. It's still yours, no matter how determined you might be to stay out of it. Did you know that you could beat Lancelot?"

"No," I admitted, "but I couldn't bring myself to run away. It wouldn't have been right. I had to face him. After all, I set in train the chain of causes that brought him here."

"That's what I thought," he said. You might forgive yourself, now, for your part in the death of Merlin's dream. You've undergone your trial by ordeal, and you've won. You've taken your punishment, and delivered your verdict. You cared enough to fight Lancelot, and I cared enough to add the weight of my persuasion to the game of the sword and the stone. I'd take some pleasure in thinking that I caused the weapon to be forged that ended up in your hand when your own crisis came, if I could only believe it."

"The legend would work out better that way, whether you believed it or not," I pointed out.

I took another cherry. When I spat out the stone, I coughed, and took a deep breath to reassure myself that my lung was as good as new. Then I flexed my shoulder-blade, to make sure that it was whole and strong.

"You're a good man, Tom," I said.

"Anyone can be good, in Cokaygne," he told me, with a sigh. "The difficulty lies in being anything else. Morgana is exceptional, though none of her friends would reckon her unusual. You don't have to be her servant indefinitely, you know. Whatever you owed her, twenty-one years is enough, don't you think?"

"It doesn't feel like twenty-one years," I said. "I haven't aged a day."

"You're wrong about that," he told me. "You can't sense it from within, but I can see it. You're older than you look. You own a horse now, by the way, and a suit of armor, and a spare sword in addition to Excalibur. Are you going to put the horse out to grass in Morgana's field and let the swords turn to rust in a dismal corner of her barn?"

"Excalibur won't rust," I reminded him. "It's not made of iron."

"You know what I mean," he said.

"What do you think I should do?"

"Whatever you like," he said. "No one knows how vast a continent this is, in any direction. Ride long enough, though, and you're bound to come to an ocean. No one knows, either, how far across the ocean the other shore might be. Wouldn't you like to find out?"

"I'd be afraid of riding forever, and never finding anything different," I said, thinking that I might as well tease him a little, since he wouldn't come straight out and say what he wanted. "This is Cokaygne, after all. Chances are I'd ride just far enough to become tired of riding, then trade my horse and swords for a cottage of my own, and become a bean-farmer, a glassblower, a quarryman, a beach-comber or a thatcher. I'd never become an elf, I suppose, but I could very easily lose the last threads of my humanity, and I'm not so sure I want to let them go just yet. I'm not like Lancelot, so scared of finding peace that I'd rather die fighting, but there's a little of Merlin in me, restless to make something of my future before I surrender to inevitability. As you pointed out, I still care. I think I might go home, one day—through the gate of Avalon and back into time. It might be amusing to be a great magician, if only for a little while."

He knew that I was only toying with him, but he'd started it. "I can offer you something better," he said. "Not instead, necessarily—as well, perhaps. Before you go back. Something even Merlin couldn't take with him."

"The Dark Land?"

"The Dark Land."

"Why didn't you ask me before? I've been here quite a while, it seems. Twenty years and more. I always expected you to ask, but somehow..."

"I've been here for more than two hundred years," he told me, "and perhaps more than a thousand. I've learned patience, and a keen enough sense of what other humans are thinking and feeling. I didn't think you were ready. I'm taking advantage of the wound that Lancelot inflicted—and the one you inflicted on him. There aren't many shocks like those available in Cokaygne, even on the threshold of the gate of Avalon. It might easily be another twenty or two hundred years before anything shakes you up as profoundly... and it might never happen at all.

"It shook me too, you know, when Hadwin brought me the news. A black knight from Camelot challenged Amory to a duel, as Morgana's champion! And Amory killed him, though he came within a whisker of death himself! What a fight it was! How far will that rumor run, do you think, before it dies in a wasteland of indifference? It's just a story to the elves, but to me...well, I'd almost forgotten what it's like to lose a friend. Almost. I lost Merlin, too. Once I was reminded...I can still care, you see. I still do, in spite of all the soothing in the world."

"Suppose I can't stand it. Suppose I can't go any further than Merlin did."

"You'll have tried, and bravely. I think you will stand it, and go further into the Dark Land with me than either of us could ever go alone. There's many a man, you know, who wouldn't have dared to stand his ground against Lancelot, even if he knew that he could take a wound like yours and live."

"I was a fool," I told him. "I shouldn't have let him wound me at all. I was stupid, as usual."

"But it was a trial by ordeal, wasn't it?" he said. "You had to defend yourself against his accusations. You even had to explain to him what you were doing, so I'm told—fighting for your own honor, that is, not for Morgana's."

"She'd have liked it better if I'd done it for her."

"Of course she would. But you don't have to be her servant forever, any more than you had to be Merlin's apprentice forever. You're your own man. What you do next, you'll do for yourself."

"Or for you, in the matter of the Dark Land?"

"Not at all," he said. "If it were only for me, I wouldn't ask you to go. It wasn't only for me that I asked Merlin, although I certainly worked hard to persuade him. If it had only been for me, I might have been able to go alone—but there are some adventures that require a partnership of equals, and this is one of them. Knowledge needs to be shared; whatever we learn there, it's important that we learn it together, else it might as well be a dream."

In Cokaygne, I thought, everything might as well be a dream. That's why it's so hard to decide where the bounds between waking and dreaming lie. If I lie here long enough, until the flesh heals over completely, I might lose the sense that fighting Lancelot was anything but a dream. But I didn't mean it. I knew that it was all real, and that Tom was right. I might never have another shock like the one Lancelot had given me. I might never be able to remember, a second time, how much I cared about anything.

The time was ripe for moving on, and there'd never be a better one for an attempt to reach the heart of the Dark Land. I let my eye travel over the shelves on the wall opposite the bed. There were more seashells than I could easily count—but Morgana had never seen the sea, so far as she could remember. She preferred to live close to the gate of Avalon, so that she could indulge her other hobby. There were more trinkets than I could count too, whose gold would be worth a fortune in Britain—but Morgana had no use for what wealth could buy in my world.

I ate another cherry, and another. I was hungry, and it was time to eat. When I was no longer hungry, it would be time for something else.

"Come and see me soon," Tom said, getting to his feet. "On foot or on horseback, with or without Excalibur."

As he left the room, he nodded respectfully at the lion and the unicorn, who lay peacefully side by side in their legendary Eden on the wall behind the bedhead. The unicorn's horn bobbed slightly as it returned the gesture—but that was something I saw out of the corner of my eye, where illusions lurk even for practiced seers.

When Tom had gone, Morgana brought me a bowl of pears. I took one, and gnawed it down to the core with considerable efficiency and delicacy.

"Does it hurt?" she asked.

"Not in the least," I told her. "Have I missed Lancelot's funeral?"

"No. We thought that you might want to say a few words—but we can't delay it much longer. The reek of decay is offensive and the dead can't be preserved indefinitely, even in Cokaygne."

"Very offensive," I agreed. "I'd almost forgotten that—but I remember now."

"You called me my lady before," she said. "It was kind of you to defend me against Lancelot's accusations, and to be my champion, but you mustn't forget who brought you here, and why."

I leaned over the edge of the bed, and pulled something out that I had hidden long before, between the mattress and the base. It was the grey cap that Morgana had given me in Camelot.

I put it on.

"I can still see you, Amory," she said, pursing her red lips slightly as she paused between sentences. "That thing has no virtue against elvish sight."

"I know," I said. "Nor had the truth serum you gave me—I guessed as much when I dosed your wine with the last of it, before you told me a pack of lies."

Her eyes, which were already tinted with green, now became uniformly and vividly emerald. "I don't tell lies," she said. "Not to you, or to anyone."

"If you really believe that," I said, "your memory is far less reliable than you think—either that, or you simply can't recognize the truth, any more than you can care whether you tell it or not."

Then, for the first and only time, I saw her eyes turn a red so deep as to be almost purple. In the world of men, it would have been a fearsome sight, but we were in Cokaygne, and I knew that the violent color would soon be soothed away. She couldn't grasp the feeling it symbolized for more than a few moments at a time, and was exceptional even in that.

"Will you tell me something truthfully, my lady?" I asked her, when the moment has passed.

"If I can," she said, cautiously.

"Whose cradle did you take me from, in order to make me your pawn in your game with Merlin?"

She looked at me with emerald eyes, still slightly stained with blood. "I can't tell you your mother's name," she told me, flatly. "She dwelt in a hovel, no better than any other and meaner than most. She had no husband; it's more likely than not that she was a victim of rape, but you might have been a love-child, I suppose. I doubt that you'd have lived six months if she'd have taken you to the sisters herself, if I hadn't built your strength here in Cokaygne. You owe me everything,

Amory. Everything. I gave you life, more surely than if I'd borne you myself."

Which meant, In suppose, that I was slightly more than an instrument to her. In her own peculiar fashion, she did care—more, perhaps, than an elf should have been able to care. I looked at the unicorn in the mural, wishing that I could ask its opinion.

I remembered the tales Sister Dorcas used to tell the children of the convent, about elves who married humans. For a while, I'd thought them fantasies, but now I understood how humans removed to Cokaygne became gradually more like elves, I wondered whether the effect might work in the opposite direction too—that fair folk who stayed too long in the human world would gradually become more human. It wasn't simply that their magic would leach out of them; they'd also become vulnerable to emotion. They'd become better able to care, to love, to be dutiful, and to be passionate.

What a shock that might be! What a torment!

The potential was there. Just as they had navels and organs of reproduction, so the fair folk had the vestiges of passion, and morality. Perhaps, I thought, Merlin really had been imprisoned by a displaced elf, fused with the flesh of some magical oak.

And perhaps not.

"I think I'd like to move on now, my lady," I said to Morgana le Fay. "I'd like you to tell me that you no longer require me as a servant, and give me your permission to leave."

"Do you need my permission?" she asked, frostily.

"No, my lady," I said, "but I should like to have it. I should like you to tell me that I've been your plaything long enough, and that you're tired of me."

"You have been my plaything long enough," she told me, "and I am tired of you."

"Thank you, my lady."

"But it was a good fight between you and Lancelot," she said, "It will be a good story for some while to come—and whatever you my think, you fought it as my champion."

"Some adventures," I told her, "must be undertaken in company. Perhaps all of them are better undertaken that way. It was a terrible fight—unnecessary, stupid, and badly wrought. Lancelot was near dead on his feet, and more than half crazy and I had no more swordsmanship than an ill-tempered rabbit. If I'd had an atom of human compassion left, I'd have refused to fight until he'd lost the urge. I killed him because I remembered having disliked him a great deal—but that was in another world, when I was no more than a boy. You wouldn't want a champion of that sort, my lady. He wouldn't be worthy of you. That's why you need to tell me to go."

"If I had some truth serum ready to hand, Amory..." she began.

I interrupted her; I wasn't her servant any longer, so it was permissible. "You have sight enough not to need any such serum, my lady," I told her. "That's the kind of thing that humans require, to aid them in their silly spying. It has no more place in Cokaygne than a cap of invisibility."

So saying, I took the cap off and tucked it under my pillow.

"You'd have died in that cradle," Morgana said, "had I not taken you out. Your mother, poor thing, might have murdered you rather than take you to the convent... and had she not, the pox would have got you, or the whooping cough, or the bloody rash, or the cholera. Had I not needed a pawn, you'd have rotted down to nothing in a corner of some field where turnips grow for swine feed. That's the truth."

"I know," I said. "Thank you, my lady, for stealing me."

She gave me another pear, and a cup of water.

"Will you say something, when we bury Lancelot?" she asked.

"Yes," I said. "I wouldn't want to disappoint the crowd, and I might never have such an opportunity again. He was the kind of man who'd shoot an innocent boy in the back with a stolen arrow, but I'll paint him a hero while you lay him to rest. This is Cokaygne, after all, and the defense of humanity is my responsibility."

"I still don't know for sure what Arthur wanted from me," she observed.

"He wanted a son," I told her. "He wanted an heir. It didn't matter, in the end. He had nothing to leave."

I was wrong about that, of course, but not in any way that concerned Arthur's desire for a child. Arthur's legacy wasn't the kind that could be handed on to a son, and his son probably wouldn't have survived in any case, any more than I would probably have done had Morgana le Fay left me in my meager cradle. Although we didn't know it, he and I were living in the Dark Ages, which were dangerous times for children, whether they were born in royal castles or wretched hovels. Nevertheless, it's a shame that little or nothing emerged therefrom but the scribblings of Churchmen, which later generations dignified with the name of history.

As I had foreseen in my dream, Camelot was torn down, piece by piece, and its pieces distributed in byres and boundary walls, houses and roads.

The stones of Camelot are everywhere—but even if Arthur had foreseen what I had foreseen, and known that he was living in the Dark Ages, he would still have wanted a son, and he would still have been prepared to go behind his mentor's back to plead with the queen of Elfland, if that would help him get one.

He cared, you see. He had but one name of his own, and he did not want that name to die with him, any more than Merlin wanted his very different dream to perish. Unlike Guinevere and Lancelot, or Morgana le Fay, and far more than Tom Rhymer or me, Arthur cared.

Tom Rhymer's gate to the Dark Land was in a cave behind a waterfall. Knowing that made me feel slightly better about the times I'd got wet looking for caves behind waterfalls

288

in Winterslow Forest when I ran away from the Convent of Saint Syncletica. Fortunately, enough light penetrated the curtain of falling water to let us see what we were doing as we tried to light our candles.

It wasn't easy. Fire isn't the necessity in Cokaygne that it is in our world, so the apparatus that elves keep for making fires is less efficient than many of their devices. Using flints to strike sparks into kindling-wool is a test of human patience at the best of times, and we'd just walked through a waterfall into a damp cave—but in the end, we got the candles lit.

Candles are understandably rare in the Land of Eternal Light, but when they're traded they can be picked up cheap. Tom had been hoarding these for a long time.

"The panic will begin to set in as you move through the narrow gap at the back of the cave," Tom told me. "It'll get steadily worse as you move through the tunnel. You'll have to tell yourself that you're in no danger of being crushed, and that the space will widen again if you just keep going. I'd best go first."

Forewarned is forearmed, they say, but it wasn't easy to hold on to the necessary beliefs, even for me. I'd spent the greater part of two years moving back and forth through the narrow spaces inside Camelot's walls, usually in pitch darkness, and had never felt the least claustrophobia, but the gate to the Dark Land struck terror even into my Cokaygne-soothed mind. The sensation that the walls were pressing in upon me, and might crush me at any moment, was almost overwhelming.

It was easy to understand why mere curiosity might be insufficient motive to drive a casual explorer on into the Dark Land— why anyone but an Orpheus in the grip of irresistible passion might have decided that it wasn't worth it. But Tom and I had two things going for us: defiant human perversity, and a responsibility to one another. A man alone might not have been able to resist, but a man observed is a different animal, especially if he's made promises that he intends to keep.

My candle seemed to be burning low, and fitfully, as if the air were bad—but I was able to tell myself repeatedly that the anxiety must be false, because Tom had been this way before, and that even Merlin had gone further than this before turning back.

I felt sick with dread, but I assured myself that it was a temporary affliction, and that things would begin to get better at any moment. I'd come through the gate of Avalon, so I could go through a thousand other gates if the necessity were there. I was a hero; I'd outfought Lancelot, and I now had Excalibur buckled to my belt. The shadow folk weren't the shades of the dead, nor were they hostile; in fact, a welcome awaited us whose warmth would be assured by Tom Rhymer's playing. We had only to carry on, one step at a time...

I lost count of the steps I took before the promises I made myself began to come true. My mind was always focused on the next one; the last was lost as soon as it was taken.

The candles were unnecessary while we were in the narrow tunnel, because we could have felt our way along it easily enough, and there were no pitfalls waiting to trap us. Once the walls began to broaden out again, the candle flames seemed pitifully weak; we had to hold them unreasonably close to a wall or the floor in order for the light to be reflected back—but at least they allowed us to see our own hands and bodies, and one another's faces.

"Rest here," Tom said, when the way had become so wide that we could no longer see both walls at once, no matter where we stood. "Drink a little water."

My clothes were still damp from the passage through the waterfall, and I felt very cold—a sensation I had not endured since coming to Cokaygne—but I did as I was told. We crouched down, setting our candle-trays on the floor, and we sipped water from our flasks.

The liquid did seem to help.

"We have to move into the open now," Tom told me. "If the suspicion that the walls were about to crush you seemed almost intolerable, the next is worse. To move into a void, which seems infinite even though you know full well that it's only a cavern, whose bounds cannot be far out of view, is more difficult than it sounds. This is where Merlin turned back. Having passed through the corridor, he was unprepared for the renewal and inversion of his terror. He felt compelled to return to the wall, then to the entrance through which we had come."

"But you went on," I said. "How?"

"I had a means of fighting the sensation of utter isolation," he told me. He meant the little pipe he was carrying in his pouch. "When we set off again, I'll begin playing. I only need the fingers of one hand to produce the notes. You might sing, if you want to."

"You've heard me sing," I reminded him. "Your playing might charm the shadow folk, but my singing would be sure to repel them. Best leave the singing till you have two hands free to play your lute, and don't need your mouth to sound the pipe."

"Even so," he said, "you might find it helpful to sing."

"How far must we go?" I asked.

"I don't know," he admitted. "I couldn't keep count of my steps last time, nor the verses I played, and I can't imagine that I'll be able to calculate any better this time. We'll need every vestige of our magic to stay focused. We'll lose all track of time—and time, I dare say, will lose all track of us."

"Time in our own world's already lost track of us," I said, thinking of Lancelot, "and we never could keep track of time in Cokaygne, no matter how we tried." I fell silent then, and stared into the candle-flame. My eyes had grown used to the everpresence of the sun, and the flame seemed more plaintive and ghost-like than any I had seen in my own world.

What, I wondered had become of Guinevere when Arthur died? Clearly, she hadn't returned to her lover of long ago. Perhaps, I imagined, she had gone to the Convent of Saint Syncletica, in order that she might spend what time remained to her as a childless mother, caring for motherless children. Mother Leocadia was almost certainly dead by now, but who had taken her place? Sister Claire, perhaps. Guinevere, given her rank, could probably obtain promotion to the rank of superior in no time at all, but would she want it? How would she feel about the politics of confession, given that the memory of that terrible moment of truth must still be a scar in her mind, a lesion in her inmost self? Once Morgana and I had left Camelot, there had been no one to tell the queen what had actually happened to make her say what she had said—and I had never spared her a thought on that account, until now.

I shivered—but the air wasn't so very cold, nor was it damp. My clothes were beginning to dry out.

"Are you thinking about Merlin, or Lancelot?" Tom asked

"Guinevere," I told him.

"Ah," he said. "She might not be the last. The shadow folk aren't the spirits of the dead, but darkness has the power to bring ghosts from within. Mine are very tenuous indeed, but you might well be a better seer of that sort..."

"Guinevere's not dead," I told him. "At least, I have no reason to think so."

"Twenty-one years is a long time, Amory," was Tom's reply to that. He meant that it was time enough for six in every seven humans to die, even in peaceful times—but Guinevere had already survived the usual killers of children, and she was a noblewoman. Arthur might have been entitled to kill a faithless queen, but Arthur wasn't that kind of man. Given that he had let her live, she was the least likely of all the people I had known in Camelot to die in a twenty-one-year interim.

Tom got to his feet, picked up his candle, and put his little pipe to his lips. The tune he played was a simple one: a cradle song. He was remembering it from a time long before mine, but I had heard Sister Dorcas sing it to younger children, and knew that she must have sung it to me, too.

I couldn't bring myself to sing the words aloud, but I sang it silently inside my head as I began to put one foot in front of the other again—just the one verse, over and over and over again.

Tom was right about its usefulness in fighting the empty darkness.

He was right about the ghosts, too.

The sickness I felt in the Dark Land was very different from the disorientation I'd experienced when I came through the gate of Avalon. Then, I had become more keenly aware of my flesh—-and although the awareness had faded the longer I lived in Cokaygne, it had never entirely gone away.

Afterwards, I'd explained that alteration to myself as an increase in awareness, caused by entering a world that was more magical, and hence more urgently real, than the one I was leaving behind. Seen from another point of view, however, it could have been represented as a decrease in a protective layer of insulation, which had preserved my mind from any excessive involvement in a body of flesh whose fate, in my own world, was to be racked and torn by pain, discomfort, injury and illness.

Either way, what I experienced in moving deep into the Dark Land was no mere reversal. As the Dark Land was a complementary parallel to the Land of Light, so the transformation that assaulted me as I entered it was a complementary parallel to the keener awareness of the phenomena of the flesh—but was, instead, a keener awareness of the phenomena of the mind.

Seen as an increase, it was an augmentation of my sensitivity to thought and feeling. My subvocalizations became louder, my visualizations more garish, my emotions more heart-rending. Seen as the removal of a layer of insulation, it permitted a new and perhaps excessive involvement in psychic processes whose fate, in my world, was to be hacked and scarified by misery, guilt, fear and loneliness.

At another time in my life, it might have been the misery, the guilt or the fear that took the most prominent role in the assault, but Tom Rhymer had chosen his moment very cleverly. What I felt most poignantly—poignantly enough to drive all potential competitors into the background—was the loneliness. And that was a curse against which I had several wards, of which the most important was Tom himself.

That was another reason why the adventure had to be shared—and I understood, as Tom perhaps hadn't, why Merlin had been the wrong person with which to try and share it. Merlin had always been a man alone, because he had always been a man obsessed. He had never been able to take comfort in the nearness of others, or the amity of others. That was why Arthur had never been able to count him a friend. I was different. In spite of living thirteen years in the company of the sisters of Saint Syncletica and all the Johns and Jameses, Judiths and Hannahs, Thomases and Bartholomews who had called me devil's child, I was different.

The ghosts might have added to another person's terror, but they didn't add to mine. What I felt, as I followed in Tom's footsteps as we walked together into the void, was a sensation of horrid isolation—but the ghosts helped to offset that, almost as much as Tom's deeply reassuring presence, reinforced by the song of innocence that he was playing. It didn't matter what they said to me, even when they were cruel; the mere fact that they seemed to be there, rising up from the moldy depths of my mind as if from the eternal grave, was far more important than anything of which they might accuse me.

They didn't stint themselves with the accusations, though.

"Stupid fool!" said Merlin. "Incompetent imbecile! Bad enough that you betrayed me, far worse that you did it so carelessly, for such little reward. Do you really think that you're a better man than me, because you can hurl yourself blithely into a deeper darkness, aimed at a non-existence more absolute than the void beyond the stars? Cretin!"

"Sinner!" said Mother Leocadia. "Were you not warned, time and time again, that you would be cast into oblivion, forever isolated from the love of God? Are you so avid to go to the devil that you'd leave earth and paradise alike, to dwell in the very essence of evil?"

"Murderer!" said Lancelot. "Do you think that you made yourself my equal in slaying me? I killed a spy and a serf, as I was perfectly entitled to do, while you killed a knight of the round table: a vile crime and sacrilege against all the laws of men and gods. Were it not for your vile black magic, you'd never have struck that final blow, for mine would have put an end to your disgusting existence, as God and logic both decreed. Go on! Go on in to the empty darkness, where you belong!"

There were kinder messengers than that, of course, but they were fewer in number and mostly less vociferous. In the end, it didn't matter. I was glad of the company, and I thanked them all for their interest in me. It was a privilege, I assured them, to be noticed by such fine individuals as themselves.

Within the cacophony of voices, however, I never lost track of the two most important. I always kept an ear cocked for the voice of Tom Rhymer's little pipe, and I savored the voice of the one ghost whose good opinion I actually valued, and whose wise judgment I was prepared to accept.

"You and I are two of a kind, Amory," said Arthur, the true king of Britain for all time. "We have but one name apiece, and we are strangers in the human world despite that we were born there. We know that we are not what we appear to other men to be, and we understand how precarious our appearances are. We have drawn Excalibur from the stone, and we have used it in the cause of Britain. You are the son I never had, Amory, and might have been my son in fact, for all that either of us knows for certain. I could not leave you the stones of Camelot for your legacy, but you have Excalibur, which is the only symbol of my kingship that really matters. Wherever you go, and whatever you do, I shall be with you in spirit, and no other magic you can ever obtain will be as powerful."

All nonsense, of course. Wishful thinking, pure and simple. Arthur's words were mine, just like Merlin's, Mother Leocadia's and Lancelot's—but I needed them, and they were more than sufficient to my need.

I lost all track of time, and time lost all track of me, but I continued singing my cradle song, albeit silently, setting one foot before the other, following the lure of Tom Rhymer's candle.

I was afraid, but I was more afraid of turning back than going on. I understood, now, how Tom Rhymer had been able to go on when Merlin deserted him, even though his light had gone out. And I understood, too, how much further he would be able to go, now that I was with him.

Ghosts came to me, and I redesigned myself as a ghost, in order to go to them.

To Mother Leocadia, appearing to her on her deathbed, I said: "I was an ungrateful child. I was a serpent in the undergrowth of your community. But I did my work, and I went on my way. I repaid your effort. I'm no longer in your debt."

To Merlin, appearing to him on his deathbed, I said: "I was an ungrateful apprentice. I was a spider in the walls of your design. But I was true to my nature, and to yours. Memory lies; speech corrupts; parchment decays—legend is the only trustworthy thing, and as an architect of legend, I was the most loyal assistant you could have wished for. Truth cannot long abide in a world like ours without being spoiled, even when it starts as truth and not as fantasy, but fantasy can abide, if it ends as legend. You always knew that. I have repaid your effort as best I cold, and we must both hope that time will do the rest. The world is in your debt, and perhaps more worlds than one, though you could not be their architect."

To Guinevere, in her nunnery cell, I said: "It was me. I did it. I put the spell on you that spoiled your marriage and your life. I'm truly sorry. But after all, it was the truth."

To Lancelot, lying in his grave, I said: "Every man knows his future, though none may know his past. You will dissolve into the soil, to nourish worms and fruit and flowers, which will nourish birds and animals and elves, and then will be excreted as piss and shit, to nourish worms and fruit and flowers, which will... but I'm sure you get the picture. It won't matter what station you once held on earth, or how you came to be incorporate in the flesh of another generation, and another and another, elves and men and monsters alike, until you have exhausted every possibility that all the worlds have to offer, from the fiery core of creation to the rind, which is also the rim of uncertainty. We can make our peace with one another, now and forever."

And to Arthur, set upon his Seat of Judgment in the fullness of his wisdom and glory, I said: "You and I are two of a kind, Arthur, true king of Britain for now and all time. We had but one name apiece, and we were strangers in the human world despite that we were born there. We knew that we were not what we appeared to other men to be, and we understood how precarious our appearances were. We drew Excalibur from the stone, and used it in the cause of Britain. You were the father I never had, and might have been my father in fact, for all that either of us knows for certain. I could not leave you the stones of Camelot as a gift, but you had Excalibur, which was the only symbol of your kingship that really mattered. Whenever you return, and whatever need you answer, I shall be with you in spirit... and no other magic you can ever obtain will be as useful."

It was all fantasy, and all rather ridiculous—but I was neither a stupid fool nor a madman for making it up.

One step at a time, we all go on into the illimitable darkness, singing nonsense all the while. There's no turning back, no second chance, no ultimate freedom from the fear and loneliness to be found. So you welcome ghosts, if you can, and you play the ghost, if you can, and you listen as best you can, and you speak as best you can, while keeping your eyes on the man in front and his flickering candle-flame. If you can't handle that prospect, best stay in your own world and keep all your layers of insulation wrapped tight about you. Be safe.

And that, to cut an exceedingly long story far shorter than you might suppose, is how Tom Rhymer and I reached the land of the shadow folk, he for the second time and I for the first.

Our candles burned down several times, but our supply didn't run out. When the time came to put them out, we weren't afraid to do so.

We didn't see the shadow folk immediately, although we knew they were there. Eventually, though, we ere able to discern them crowding around us, dark within the darkness but not in the least gloomy.

There are stars in the Dark Land, but they don't become visible immediately, even when terrestrial lights are extinguished. They're very discreet and very distant, not at all oppressive. I'm not entirely certain that I saw them with my eyes at all; they may have been the kind of stars that only second sight can see. If so, that's one of several reasons why it's so difficult to go into the Dark Land from the human world, even if you find a portal.

Once I'd been there for a while, though, my sight adapted well enough for me to make my way around, and to study the landscape and its inhabitants.

There are trees in the Dark Land, as well as grasses, ferns and flowers; there are birds and animals, insects and worms; there are houses with roofs and roads with bridges—but they're all shadows. There's no sun in the Dark Land to fuel the production and reproduction of flesh. Everything there is insubstantial—everything, at least, that remains there. Had we intended to remain, we'd have had to become shadows ourselves. While we were truly there, in fact, we did—but we did so without forsaking our bodies.

There is water in the Dark Land, but no food. A human entering the Dark Land from the human world could not stay there very long without wasting away. Humans entering it from Cokaygne, on the other hand, have magic in store to preserve their flesh for considerably longer. Such preservation isn't without cost—Merlin was right to think that any deep penetration into the world of shadows would deplete the store of magic that he could take back to earth—but it permits a far greater flexibility of choice. A human entering the Dark Land from the human world would have no opportunity to make a fully-informed decision as to whether to remain here or not; a human entering it from Cokaygne can.

Such earthly legends of the Dark Land as there are represent it as the land of the dead, implying that it is a world to which everyone who dies must go. That's false—but the mistake is understandable. A human, or an elf, who desired to live there could only do so by becoming a shadow and surrendering the privileges of the flesh. It's very difficult to imagine that any of the fair folk would ever be willing to do that, no matter how exhaustive their accumulation of experience might be, but humans only own their flesh for a little while anyway, so it's a much more attractive option for us. The Dark Land does indeed seem to humans to be a land of the dead, but if you ever go there, you're highly unlikely to meet anyone you ever knew on earth.

I know, now, why Merlin's brief adventure in the Dark Land put him in mind of the legend of Orpheus. It was because he could understand, even after a few tentative steps, what the true nature of Orpheus' quest had been. Only a motive as powerful as passion, Merlin thought, could drive a man through the kind of barrier that had stopped him short—but the quest would be hopeless, because no human who had given up the flesh to join the shadow folk could ever take back the bargain.

Perhaps the real Orpheus had invented the story of what happened to him in the Dark Land, to excuse rather than to explain his failure—exactly as you or I or any other liar might have done—but I don't think so. I think his lost lover lied to him, because it was the only way she could persuade him to go home. You might think that it would have been a happier ending if he'd joined her, becoming a shadow himself, but it wouldn't. Like the fair folk, the shadow folk are immune to passion. There in no sex in the Dark Land, and no love either. The only way for Eurydice to preserve Orpheus' love was to send him home; apparently, she thought it worthwhile to do that, although her new fellows would not have been able to agree with her. The other shadows would rather have persuaded him to stay with them, and recruit him to their choir, but she remembered life and they had forgotten it—if they ever knew it—and she took a different view.

I don't know that for certain, of course, but it makes sense—or seems to. Tom Rhymer was a musician too, and I know how they tried to seduce him. If I hadn't been with him, they'd probably have succeeded. Having been there before, he knew that.

He knew that if he went back alone, or with the wrong companion, he'd never come out again.

When we had blown out our candles and he had both hands free, even before we perceived the starlight, Tom put his pipe away and took out his lute. He began to play. He began to sing, too, with a voice a thousand times sweeter than mine.

I sat down on an invisible floor, which felt more like black glass than grey granite. I took a bag of pears from my pack, and I began to eat. I had never tasted anything so delicious, although I had been eating exactly similar fruit since I first came into Cokaygne, but—paradoxical as it may seem—I wasn't very hungry. The difference was in me, of course, not in the fruit. I was already becoming a shadow, though not irredeemably.

The shadow folk loved the music of the lute, it seemed, and the texture of Tom's voice. Perhaps, therefore, it was paradoxical for them to want him to surrender both, in favor of fingers that could only play shadow-instruments and a very different kind of voice—but genius is, at least in their reckoning, independent of the flesh, and Tom was certainly a versatile player, ever eager to try new instruments.

In Cokaygne, music is an occasional delight; Tom occasionally played and sang on village greens like the one in front of Morgana's home, but finished soon enough as his audience moved on to other pastimes, following the ceaseless hunger-cycles of the flesh. In the Dark Land, music is far more important, and there is a sense in which it's never-ending, like the legendary song of the Acemites—but like the song of the Acemites, its singers take turns, because music isn't the whole of their lives. There is silence in the Dark Land too; there is meditation and contemplation; and there is also dialogue.

On his first excursion into the Dark Land, Tom hadn't stayed long enough to learn to speak to the shadow folk. Even in the course of his second sojourn, he made little enough progress with their prosaic language, because he was too much occupied with the songs he had imported for their delectation, and the songs he had come to learn.

It was different for me. The only person I had ever met with a worse singing voice than mine was Mother Leocadia. Tom had tried to teach me in Cokaygne, but I had shown little or no improvement. Tom hadn't minded that, of course; musicians need an audience, and he was quite satisfied with my ability to listen. When he had tried to explain, in his admittedly stumbling fashion, why our adventure into the Dark Land would need two of us instead of one, he had thought of our partnership in terms of strict inequality, of the opposite but necessary pairing of performer and audience, actor and witness. He hadn't been wrong to do that, given his own nature and viewpoint, but it wasn't the whole story.

I became a storyteller in the Dark Land, as I had become a storyteller in Cokaygne and am now a storyteller in your world—but I wasn't just a performer in search of an audience, or a listener in search of a performance. I think I learned more about the nature of shadows than Tom ever would have, and more about the nature of starlight, because I became far better attuned to the subtle conversations of the shadows, the authentic dialogues of the dead.

I can't translate them as easily as I can translate the conversations I had with Merlin or Morgana, whose language was different from yours but fundamentally similar, not merely in the range and substance of its references but in the ambition of its metaphors and the polite insistence of its linearity. Someone cleverer than me might be able to make a stab at it, but the gross distortions involved would still create all kinds of false impressions. I'm not being evasive when I say that you can get a far better impression of the Dark Land from earthly music than you can from earthly prose. Some of what I learned can be restated, though, and I'll do that as best I can.

According to Tom's theory, the fair folk had been human once. Whether they were products of their own world or migrants from ours, they'd originated as beings indistinguishable from us. The magic-soaked world of Cokaygne had allowed them to transform themselves by the power of their own desire and will, into what they thought of as a far better state of being—and they had transformed their world, too, in order to make it even more hospitable to the kind of creature they were ambitious to be.

But they hadn't all agreed as to the kind of creature they were ambitious to be. Their uncertainties had polarized, drawing them apart into two camps. Why two rather than three or ten or a thousand? I'm not sure—but I don't think it was a mere fluke of chance. I think there's a sense in which uncertainties of that kind may start out as networks of winding paths, heading anywhere and everywhere, but they have an inbuilt tendency to harden into roads as they're trodden down by traffic and remade to support heavier vehicles. The ultimate extreme to which that process leads is the Roman road: the straight course that people may think of as a road to Camelot, or as a road to the west, but which must, by logical necessity, also be a road away from Camelot, and a road to the east.

Desire and goals do tend to polarize; they do tend to settle down into patterns of either-and-or, plus-and-minus, light-and-dark, body-and-mind.

The party of Cokaygne had preferred daylight to darkness, as humans generally do, so they had stopped the sun in its tracks, and held it steady in the sky, not too high and not too low, half-risen or half-set.

The party of Cokaygne had been keenly aware, as humans generally are, of their affliction by disease, pain and death, hunger, thirst and toil, so they had fortified their bodies with magic and made their world abundantly fruitful. They had become immune to disease, capable of controlling and easing pain, and as resistant to death as any creature of flesh could possibly be. They hardly ever went hungry or thirsty, and such labor as they had still to invest in supplying their various needs became a source of pleasure and fascination to them rather than a punishment.

They were, of course, required to pay a price for all these achievements, but they considered it more than fair.

You might think of their inability to make and feel love, or to bear and rear children, as a kind of penalty, exacted by way of compensation for their other rewards, but they didn't. They lost the ability to love because it wasn't something they wanted to hang on to—and once they'd sacrificed that, the rewards of sexual intercourse, and of bearing and raising children became too meager to justify the inherent difficulties and embarrassments—unlike, for instance, cooking, cleaning, digging, weaving, mining....and all the other activities which worked to more tangible and enduring ends.

Inexorable logic also requires that wishing away the ability to love disposes, too, of the opportunity to be loved, which is quite a different thing and seemingly far more desirable, but even that, I suspect, did not seem a heavy price. Many of the fair folk, I dare say, found even that easier to get along without—but just as humans vary, so do elves. Those elves who still cherished the notion of being loved, at least for a little while, retained the opportunity to be loved by humans while the gates to the human world were easy to pass through, at least in one direction. Those who retained a vestigial fascination with children had the opportunity to steal changelings.

By the same token, those elves who eventually found the elvish condition unbearable retained other options. They still had ability to become human, if they only cared to live long enough in the human world—just as humans who contrived to live long enough in Faerie, according to Tom's hopeful theory, might become elves. And they still had the ability to turn right around, and head back in the opposite way towards the other pole: to join the shadow folk.

Do the shadow folk have a similar option? Could they, if they wished, put on flesh again? I'm not entirely certain—but I suspect so, if they really wanted to. Reincarnation, into the human world or Faerie, could probably be contrived, though not without difficulty. In practice, of course, no shadow desires to be an elf any more than any elf desires to be a shadow; both parties made their choices in a past so distant that it is almost beyond the reach of legend, let alone mere memory— and the last waverers made their eventual commitment long ago.

The shadow folk had preferred transcendence of the flesh to its preservation. They'd taken a different route in avoiding its many afflictions. Light—bright light, at any rate—had become unnecessary to them. Did they actually prefer darkness to light? Yes, they did—but in accepting that, we must bear in mind that they didn't experience darkness as we do, as an absence of the solar source of all fleshy life; they still had stars of a sort, fainter by far than distant suns, so they had eyesight of a kind as well as second sight, but it was a different kind of sight than ours.

That must seem less peculiar to you than it did to me, because you know, even without ever having visited the Dark Land, that the visual spectrum is only a part of a much vaster whole, which other creatures might experience very differently. You can easily imagine that nocturnal creatures might be more sensitive to infrared wavelengths—and perhaps you can imagine too, how creatures of shadow might have senses of shadow, whose perceptions deal with other entities than mere "light", so cleverly that the merest radiance is all they need.

Tom had thought himself incapable of explaining to me in words how he had established rudimentary communication with the shadow folk. Poet though he was, he had been unable to translate what he had "seen" or "felt" or "heard" during his first excursion into terms that I might find understandable, although he had made a valiant attempt even before he had set out to educate me by example, taking me with him so that I could find out for myself.

Can I do better? I don't know, but I'm trying.

The shadow folk have more senses than we do; they retain some sensitivity to the vibrations of sound and electromagnetism, but that sensation has to be muted because they have so many others. I'm tempted to talk of "other vibrations", and perhaps I wouldn't be entirely wrong to do so, but it's too narrow a perspective.

I've read in your books that what you think of as "empty space" or "void" is actually a seething mass of potential phenomena: "particles" or "waves" that might be evident, but aren't, at least for the present.

In the Dark Land, such potentials are evident, to the senses of the shadow folk. In the Dark Land, there is no void. However empty it may seem to human or elvish visitors, at least until they become acclimatized, it's fuller than any human or elf could possibly imagine—fuller than the sea to a fish, or flesh to a parasite worm, or rock to a vein of ore.

Trying to explain it is, to borrow another phrase I've read in your books, "like trying to explain sight to a blind man"—but much more complicated. I'm trying anyway.

Like Cokaygne, the Dark Land was built by the desire and will of human-like creatures, operating in and on a world more amenable to such manipulation than ours. Like Cokaygne, the Dark Land is a kind of paradise, not a kind of hell or a kind of oblivion, forged to be as hospitable as possible to the kind of creatures its makers wanted to be.

We have other desires than those of the flesh. Yes, there's something in us that would like to live in Cokaygne: a world without darkness or evil, hunger or need, pain and old age. We are creatures of flesh and sensation; we know what health is, we know when it fails, and we know what unhappiness comes with its failure. How can we help but dream of a world in which we would always be healthy and always happy? Happiness is, admittedly, a relative thing; if we were never unhappy, we should never know how happy we were when we were not. How much more pleasant it would be, though, to live in a world where happiness was the everyday norm and unhappiness the rare exception, always available by choice but never compelled. How much more pleasant it would be to live in a world that was separated by gates from a world of misery, which we could visit as and when we wished, savor as and when we wished, play with as and when we wished, whose produce we could allow into our world by chance as well as by choice, but always in a manageable flow. All perfectly understandable. But we have other desires than those of the flesh.

I don't know whether we unremade humans are really anything more than flesh and sensation, but I do know that it's not the way we see and feel ourselves, and it's not the only way we can imagine ourselves.

Whether we have souls or not, we can certainly imagine that we do, and it's hard to imagine otherwise. Whether or not we're ghosts, temporarily housed in fleshy machines, we imagine ourselves that way, and it difficult to do otherwise. Fantasy or not, the intangible self has to be accommodated within our spectrum of desire—and if we had the power to make our wishes come true, some of us, at least, would follow the road in that direction rather than the other.

Cokaygne isn't the only other world we unremade humans dream of. Cokaygne is where our selves of flesh and sensation may live in a dream of perpetual but not-quite-uninterrupted happiness, but it has no room for our other selves—our shadow selves—which have to be forgotten there, or soothed away.

The world of the shadow folk isn't a place of exile, or a cosmic prison; it is itself a kind of shadow, a world within and beyond ours, but by no means separate from it. It's a place to which our dreams can lead us, although what we find there is far more difficult to add to the store of memory than the land of Cokaygne. It's a place where we might wish to be, even though we can't describe or articulate it.

There's no more love in the Dark Land than there is in Cokaygne. None are born there, though some occasionally die. It's timeless—even more timeless, if that admittedly absurd phrase can make any sense at all, than Cokaygne. There's no happiness there either, to the extent that happiness is part of the weather of the flesh, but the shadow folk have their own kinds of contentment, which they would not trade for happiness or for the world. It is not a joyful world, but it's a world that has its rewarding substitutes for joy. It's not an undesirable place to be, although it stands at the opposite end of the spectrum of desire to Cokaygne.

When the shadow folk welcomed us, they did so more generously and less contemptuously than the fair folk of Cokaygne. Mother Leocadia would probably say that they were merely more accomplished agents of diabolical temptation, but it's possible—isn't it?—that they were simply more comfortable with their state of being.

The world of the shadow folk is the soul of Cokaygne, in which everything abstracted from Cokaygne and negated in Cokaygne is set aside. That doesn't mean, though, that it's a place to which the evils extirpated from Cokaygne have been banished; it isn't a miserable place, let alone a place of torment. The Dark Land is a quiet and insubstantial place, to which such fleshly afflictions as hunger, disease, pain and death are utterly irrelevant; they have no more presence there than they do in Cokaygne, but nor are they conspicuous by their absence.

There's music in Cokaygne, but it's only important to its hearers while it's being played, while they can dance to it. Were the shadow folk to listen to the very same music, they'd experience it very differently. The shadow folk sing, as the legendary Acemites sang, but they don't dance. They don't need to, because the music they play and the music that is played to them are part of them forever.

The people of Cokaygne like stories, and like to re-tell the stories they have heard, but they only experience the story in the hearing and the telling, in terms of the sensations it provides. The shadow folk draw little immediate amusement from stories, but all the stories they hear and tell echo within them, transforming and recomplicating the stories that they are. To be a storyteller in Cokaygne is by no means a poor thing, especially for a servant, but to be a storyteller in the Dark Land is something else. In the Dark Land, every storyteller makes a difference, in a way that Merlin, the despiser of legend and parchment, could never have understood.

I don't mean to imply by this that Cokaygne is an empire of pure sensuality and the realm of the shadow folk an empire of pure mentality. There's no sensation without thought and no thought without sensation, and no matter how powerfully we reimagine ourselves there can be no such thing as mind without body, any more than there could be body without mind—but there's a sense in which the mind can consign the flesh to darkness, and to forsake solidity—to set it aside—just as there's a sense in which the body can set the mind aside by going to sleep. There's a great deal of sleep in Cokaygne, whose shadow is a particular kind of consciousness—an alertness exaggerated by the suppression of the senses. That, too, is an object of desire, common if not universal among humans. That, too, would give rise to an entire world of desire, if we humans had magic enough to make our wishes come true.

I couldn't explain this to an elf—but I hope that a human might be able understand it. I did, while I was there, and the memory will, survive a little longer here than it would have in Cokaygne.

Tom Rhymer and I had escaped the grip of time before we had even arrived in the realm of the shadow folk, and we remained free. We ate and we drank, for an interval, while the pangs of our difficult passage still disturbed us, but the need passed. We never stepped out of our flesh, but it ceased to inhibit us.

When Tom had done with singing and playing, for a while, I told stories, and when I had done with telling stories, we listened. I can't imagine that we heard as the shadow folk heard, or that the stories transformed our own life-stories as they had transformed their tellers, but they didn't leave us undernourished.

Little by little, we became shadows ourselves, setting our bodies aside—for an interval.

Being a shadow is being other than solid—or liquid or gas—without being other than material. Being a shadow is being other than present, without being absent—or perhaps it would be better to say that it is an absence, but an absence as full of potential as the hardest vacuum, the most absolute void. Being a shadow is like being a creature of abstract ideas, fluid and elastic and intangible but seething all the while with ambition and hope and curiosity. Being a shadow is never to have the possibility of loneliness, because a shadow can only function as part of a whole host of competing and contesting shadows, ceaselessly bringing forms out of chaos whose very essence is transience.

Some expeditions, as Tom Rhymer had wisely said, have to be undertaken by more than one individual. In the Dark Land, all expeditions have to be undertaken by everyone.

All this must seem difficult to grasp—as shadows inevitably are—but I hope it doesn't sound boring. My time in the Dark Land wasn't in the least boring. There was nothing to see, because it was dark, but there was also everything to see, by the faintest starlight imaginable. As Tom and I faded into shadows we moved further and further away from fleshy sensation, but further and further towards other kinds of experience. Our innate magic had space in which to play that it had never enjoyed in Cokaygne.

We didn't stay there as long as we could have stayed. To have stayed forever would have required us to sever all ties to our former flesh, but even to have stayed there for a much shorter time than forever would have made those ties distinctly problematic. We'd have gone mad.

By the standards of Cokaygne, of course, we did go mad—but not as mad as we might have. Even by Cokaygne's standards, we didn't make any choices that would have made it impossible to change our minds. We didn't make any commitments. That wouldn't have been possible, if we hadn't spent a long time in Cokaygne before we went into the Dark Land, but I think we were able to get the best of both worlds.

Perhaps the one penalty of getting the best of both worlds was that it made it extraordinarily difficult for us to be satisfied with either.

How long, I wonder, did it take the human-like creatures who has the power of wishing to commit to one world or the other? I don't know, but I doubt that it was any mere matter of centuries. It's conceivable, if not very likely, that our world, like Cokaygne and the Dark Land, is a product of hundreds of thousands of years of powerful wishing, tyrannized neither by the desires of the flesh nor the desires of the ghostly intellect, but by the desire to keep our options open.

Perhaps, in spite of all appearances, our world is a kind of paradise too.

That might just be an excuse, though, or a rationalization. We are, after all, here rather than in Cokaygne or the Dark Land—at least for a little while—and we're here by choice, not because it's a prison or a place of exile.

I don't remember the journey back to the gate at all, but we must have done it one step at a time, lighting our way with candles once the shadow folk had said their good-byes—or their au revoirs. It must have been easier to pass through the gate going outwards than it had been going in, but we still got wet. We had to lie on the grass beside the pool with our eyes tightly closed for what seemed like hours, until we could bear the dazzle and color of the sunlit world. Then we had to drink our fill, and go foraging for food; I doubt that anyone in Cokaygne had ever been as hungry as we were, although it had been a common enough experience in the world where I grew up.

"You're a better man than Merlin was," Tom Rhymer told me, as we began the long walk that would take us back to his home.

"No I'm not," I told him. "He had an ambition to preserve. I didn't. He felt that he'd never have a chance to build Camelot if he didn't turn back, and that was the one thing he couldn't face. I could go on because I didn't have anything to lose."

"But much to gain," he said, happily.

"Yes," I admitted, "though perhaps not as much as you. You're a musician, after all, and a poet and singer. What an artist you'll be while the legacy of the shadow folk remains powerful within you! Cokaygne will soothe it away soon enough, I suppose... but we don't have to stay in Cokaygne."

"I never wanted to leave it," Tom said, uncertainly.

"Yes you did," I reminded him. "You wanted to go into the Dark Land. You didn't know why, but you did want to. And now you've been—perhaps you're ready to go home."

"I don't know about that," he said.

"Well," I said, "you don't have to come if you don't want to. A homeward journey is one of those you can make alone, because you know you won't be alone when you get there."

"Are you sure of that?" he asked. "We've been away a very long time, and the human world always hurries on. It's not just that the people we knew will be long dead, or the stones of the castles that once protected us scattered. Even the legends might have vanished. Everything might be different, in ways we can't begin to imagine, even with the aid of second sight."

"True," I admitted. "And I wouldn't blame you in the least if you wanted to stay here. You're a man as well as a musician. I'm not just prosaic—I'm still a boy, not likely to reach manhood any time soon in a world like Cokaygne, if at all. Now I've been to the Dark Land, though, I think I might try the one thing I haven't tried so far—growing up. I think I'm ready for my own world, at last."

311

"You might not like it, you know," he advised me. "I didn't. Mind you, if I had my time over..."

He couldn't. Even in a world tyrannized by indecision, you can't turn the clock back. No matter how the young waste their youth, they're the only ones who can. Desire has its limits.

"It's a chance I ought to take," I told him. "I might make a better fist of the time I've had, if I had a second chance at it, but the fact that it's lost shouldn't make me any less eager to go forward. All the choices that lay ahead before still lie ahead now. Maybe I'll come to regret the way I took those, when I'm as old as Merlin—but I've seen the Dark Land now, and I don't think I can content myself with Cokaygne, for the present."

"There's no guarantee that we'd ever get back, if we left," Tom reminded me.

"Perhaps not," I conceded, "but we're better equipped to find gates into eternity than anyone else, aren't we?"

"So you're headed directly for Avalon, then?" Tom asked, just to make sure. "You've never seen more of Cokaygne than a few thousand paces could take you. What about the other continents of Faerie? The oceans, the mountains... everything?"

"I asked you the same question once," I reminded him. "I'd be afraid of finding it all the same. This is Faerie, after all: the land of lost content. In our world, I know where the sea begins, though I've never seen it. I know that the lands beyond are very different."

How proud that boast was—and how empty!

We walked on a little further. We ate such food as we could find, and begged a little more from houses we passed. Our hunger was quickly satisfied—-but it returned with what seemed to us to be unusual rapidity and force.

"I'll come with you," Tom said, in he end. "To Avalon, and as far beyond as we can hold our friendship together. I've done what I was waiting to do in Faerie. The kind of treasure you find in deepest darkness is only worth something if you can carry it back to world where night follows day and pain can't be wished away. In the Land of Eternal Light it would simply melt away. Our world's the rim of creation, after all: the edge of endeavor."

"I'm not so sure about that," I confessed. "Morgana was churlish to call it the rind of creation, of course, implying that what lies within is the succulent flesh of the fruit rather than a pit—but I'm not sure it's the rim either. There might be other gates that lead to worlds more hectic still, which make even ours seem slow and sterile. And even if there aren't, we might someday find the secret of their manufacture. In our world, the one thing of which we can be certain is that things won't stay the same."

"You think it might become another Faerie, in time—paired with its own shadow?"

"No—that's been done. Human nature won't always stay the same, in our world, and the spectrum of human desire is more elastic than we can imagine. Who knows what magic might one day make of our world, with wiser guidance...or wilder madness?"

The house that had been Tom's was occupied by a stranger, who made us welcome, fed us and found us places to sleep—the cycle of our hunger pangs had calmed by that time, but the naps we'd taken in the open hadn't brought a similar relief to our tiredness.

The elf claimed that he'd never heard the name of Tom Rhymer, or Mad Tom, although some few of Tom's possessions were still in the house. When Tom explained that the items had once been his the elf immediately offered to make him a gift of them, but Tom declined everything except for a flute and a fife, which he had made.

We went on to Morgana's house a while later, half-expecting that she would be long gone too. When she answered the door herself I smiled, but she stared at us both as if she had never seen us before.

"It's Amory," I said, "who was once your servant, brought from the other world after he used your truth serum to seal the doom of Camelot. And this is Tom Rhymer—Mad Tom, if you prefer—who was your neighbor for a long time before that."

"Amory?" she said, as if struggling to remember. Her puzzlement cleared slightly as she dredged up an eclipsed memory, but there was still uncertainty in her voice as she said: "Amory, is that really you? Where have you been?"

She too invited us in. She had no servant now, so she prepared a meal for us with her own hands, as skillfully as anyone could have desired.

""We've been to the Dark Land," I told her.

"You shouldn't have done that," she said. "Few go there, even though they know where the gates are, and none come back unchanged. Humans go mad even in Cokaygne, but you only have to set foot in the Dark Land to be cursed."

"We're more adaptable than the fair folk," I told her. "Humans are more hospitable to change than elves. You might call that madness, but it isn't."

"Perhaps that's true," she admitted, grudgingly. "We used to see a good many humans hereabouts, always flitting back and forth the way they do—but the gate of Avalon is narrower now than it used to be. Our horses won't go through it, so no one could hunt the earthly forest nowadays, if it still existed. The last time I was there, the trees had all been cut. That was treachery, for I bargained once for it preservation, and paid a fair price for the promise. I would have made someone pay for that, if I had found an opportunity. Humans forget their debts so very quickly, and it's up to the fair folk to remind them what they owe, to keep hem honest."

"I remember the price you paid for the preservation of the forest," I told her, sternly. "An honest judge might deem it small—and also that you took it back again, leaving nothing owed."

"I was cheated first," she said, petulantly. "Surely you remember, Amory. You were with me then, I think. You

314

helped me, as I recall—and I played fair with you, did I not? I always played fair with you."

"More than fair, my lady," I assured her. "I have no complaints at all against the fair folk, and every reason to be grateful to Morgana le Fay."

She smiled at that; her memory had only required prompting. She hadn't forgotten, and it was all coming back to her now.

"Morgana le Fay," she echoed. "Queen of the Land of Eternal Light. That was a nice part to play, was it not? I played it well, though—better than any other elf I know. Even Orwen conceded that."

"Very well indeed, my lady. You say the gate of Avalon has shrunk—is it still passable?"

"Of yes—from this side, at least, and by anyone not uncommonly stout. A slight and slender boy like you would have no trouble—nor a beanpole like your mad friend. But I'd advise you against it nevertheless, for getting back might be a different matter, and the other world is not what it was. I tried to prevent that, as you know, but only contrived a short delay. The last time I was there, the Roman road had been restored again, and there were others besides. Few fair folk have been there since, but those who have tell the same story. Even the fields are squared and hedged, and cut in straight furrows by monstrous machines. The tales they tell!"

"They still bring back the babies, I suppose," I said.

She shook her head. "Not hereabouts," she told me. "Cokaygne is not what it was, either... but there are other regions in the Land of Light. If I had not had my fill of humankind, I might move on... but I like it here, now that it's not so busy. You'd like it too, I know. Let the gate shrink to nothing, if it will—or return to its former magnitude, as chance would have it. There's no hurry, after all, and this is a very pleasant place to dwell. You're no fool, Amory—I could always see that in you. You know what kind of world you want. Stay here, until you can find a house—not as a servant, but a guest. Tom too.

He can play for us. We've always liked his playing hereabouts."

"I can't stay, Morgana," I told her. "I've been to the realm of the shadow folk. I've changed."

"That won't matter, if you stay," she told me—and I knew that it was true. "Stay here for a little while, and you'll grow to like it again. Only give it time, and you'll feel quite at home again. You'll still be changed, but you'll be content. Tom should teach you to play, so that you can play together. We have an elvish player in the village now, but he's never been part of a trio. Stay for just a while, and we'll all have the pleasure of your company."

"I can't stay, Morgana," I told her. "If I stay, I'll never grow up. I'll be a boy forever."

"That's perfection," she said. "Men grow old, and I dare say you haven't forgotten what becomes of them then. You were Merlin's apprentice before you were mine, and I see that you still carry the sword with which you slew Sir Lancelot. Where's the joy in growing old? Where's the freedom? If it's passion you fancy, take my advice and don't bother. I've never bothered with it myself, but I've seen what it can do, and so have you. You don't want to become the kind of thing that Lancelot was, or Merlin, or Arthur."

"No," I said. "I want to become the kind of thing that I might be, and never will while I'm in Cokaygne."

She smiled again, and looked at Tom. "I always told you that you were wrong about that, didn't I?" she said. "Humans and the fair folk are different kinds. I was never a human, and no human could ever be like me."

"I might have been wrong and I might have been right," Mad Tom told her, "but I'm not sure it matters any more. I can go home now. I've known passion, and I've fled passion, but that doesn't mean that I've been everything I can be, or everything I ever shall be. Like Amory, I've learned what the Dark Land has to teach, and I'm ready for the world of men again."

"I could come with you," she said, although she didn't mean it. "I could be Morgana le Fay again, one more time."

"If you stayed long enough, this time," I suggested, "you might be Morgana le Fay until you died."

"You always had a sharp tongue," she said, resentfully. "I remember that. Even when you were my servant—even when I offered to take you out of Camelot, and make you fit for Cokaygne. You always had a sharp tongue."

"I had good teachers," I told her. "Did you receive any news of the people I knew, by any chance, after Tom and I went away? Did anyone else come searching for Lancelot, or for me?"

"None," she reported. "You were forgotten already, I'm sure—it was Morgana le Fay that drew Lancelot here, and you took Excalibur as my champion. As for Lancelot... his name must have disappeared in a similar span. Camelot no longer stands on its petty hill, and the town was burned. There's nothing there at all, although the road remains. Strange traffic flows along it to the east and to the west. The henge on the plain is there, sometimes with the capstones on and sometimes with the capstones off, but nothing else that I or any other elf can recognize. Even the language has changed out of all rec-ognition. You won't be going home, Amory—you'll be going as a hapless stranger into a world you cannot even imagine."

"I won't be alone," I said. "And I'll have borrowed magic to help me find my way. The second sight will help me see what I need to see, and understand it—and my second hearing's improved a great deal while I've been in the Dark Land. I'll pick up the language in no time at all."

"It won't last," Morgana said, meaning the magic rather than the world. "Nothing does, there. Here, everything lasts. Here, everything's safe. You'd be a fool not to stay."

"I always was a fool," I told her. "Not such a stupid fool as Merlin thought, but a fool nevertheless. And Tom's always been a madman, by his world's standards. We'll be good company for one another, and we'll fit right into any world

317

that men have made while we've been away—won't we, Tom?"

"I dare say we will," he said. "As long as they still play music, and like to hear voices in song."

"Well," she said, softly, "I suppose you might get back again, if not through Avalon then through some other gate. Use your magic to seek a few out, while you have it—and when it's almost gone, remember where they are. Cokaygne will still be here, the same as it ever was. You mustn't go empty-handed. I'll give you what I owe you for all your faithful service, in good yellow gold. They like gold in your world, don't they?"

"Yes, my lady," I said. "You're very kind."

Her eyes flashed green.

"I always settle my debts, Amory, as you know very well. And if you do come back, I'll be here—or somewhere very similar. Don't come back as an old man, Amory. Don't wait that long. Old men die here too, whether they pick fights or not."

"I know, my lady," I said.

"I used to like the nearness of death," Morgana said, almost wistfully, "but I've had my fill of it now. I need no more of it. So don't come back as an old man, Amory, if you want me to let you in."

"I won't." I promised.

It's still a promise I intend to keep.

Epilogue

1

So here I am, in another Land of Eternal Light, in which the stars that used to seem so near and so oppressive now seem pale and fugitive, when they can be seen at all. Here I am, in a land more magical than Cokaygne will ever be, where the pace of change is furious and the power of artifice unfettered.

Morgana was right about the roads. They don't all run as straight as the road to the west, but they run everywhere, and they run directly. Cokaygne could never tolerate such purposiveness, such determination, such urgency. Cokaygne could accommodate a handful of carts, when the gate of Avalon was wide enough to admit them, but it could never tolerate a landrover, a tractor or a tank.

The magic I carried with me from Cokaygne was a prodigious supply, in spite of what my body lost in strength while I was a shadow. Fifteen hundred years is a long time to be out of the world, and even though Merlin's anxieties about the Dark Land draining away the charge he had built in Cokaygne were no mere paranoia, you can build a lot of potential in a span like that.

Merlin thought about such things too simply. He thought that magic was something that soaked into him while Cokaygne's eternal sun bathed his head in light, but the reality is far more complicated. There's magical nourishment for the body and there's magical nourishment for the mind. It doesn't matter where you are while you're out of the world; if you're not increasing one then you're increasing the other. Balance is what matters. I don't say that I've got the balance exactly right, but I think I'm better equipped than Merlin ever was. Wherever you are while you're not in the world, time stretches—like an elastic band or a watch-spring, or any of a dozen other wonders unknown to the Dark Ages—and the pent-up energy is yours to spend.

Magic takes people in different ways, of course. Personally, I can't bend a spoon by the power of my will, pick a winning number in the National Lottery, cure warts, concoct a love potion, cook up a truth serum or knit a cap of invisibility—but I'm an excellent spy. I only have to watch and listen carefully, and I pick things up. I can read and write now, as well as calculate, and I don't need a cap of invisibility to fit in.

Tom still hasn't mastered what passes nowadays for the English language, and I'm always having to explain to him how everything works, but he'll catch up in his own time. In the meantime, you should hear him play! In fact, you probably will, very soon. He doesn't quite understand how electronic keyboards work, and he can't read or write a note of music, but he understands sounds and his ears are quite uncanny. He loves electric guitars. He doesn't sing much at present, though, because he wants to compose some new songs, and he doesn't think he'll be able to construct the songs he wants to sing until he's rediscovered passion. Perhaps he's right; the legacy of the Dark Land, taken neat, is a trifle esoteric.

For me, of course, it won't be rediscovery. It'll be the first time. I'm trying to look forward to it, but I really don't know how it might affect me. Seeing the future is another item on the list of abilities my particular magic no longer seems to include. I don't think that's a flaw in the magic, though, or even in me. I don't think the future can be seen, in your world, the way it could be seen in mine. There's too much potential for change. The secret conspiracy of chance and choice has become so very complicated and arcane that the right hand doesn't know what the left is doing, six billion times over.

I'll be interested to see what the future brings, though. I can say that, you see, because I'm still young. In spite of being fifteen hundred and some years old, I'm still young. I have a lot of the future left to live, and I'm not afraid of variety and surprise. That's the difference between Merlin and me. He wasn't young. He came out of Cokaygne more fully charged with magic than any man before him, but he wasn't young. Like any adult, he was afraid of what the future might bring, and he wanted to take control of it. He wanted to become its architect, to make it conform to his design.

Merlin wanted to build a world that he could understand, and make it stable. Where else could he look for models but in the past? When he returned to Britain, he saw the sketch of civilization that the Romans had briefly imposed upon it, and that became his blueprint for a better world: one road, running as straight as an elvish arrow from east to west, tipped with a fragment of skrying-glass. He couldn't let go of that way of thinking, even when he'd seen Cokaygne, because he'd had to turn back from the Dark Land.

"Every man knows his future," my master used to say, "though none may know his past". He knew that he would die, and he wanted to hold the world in place, to make it steady and knowable, until he did. But he hadn't even begun to understand the hidden history of the world or the mysteries of evolution. Having no idea of the sweep and complexity of the pattern of progress that had brought him into being, he had no conception of the futility of trying to interrupt it.

I understand, now, that my one-time master repeated that particular saw so frequently because he was so very ambitious to enlarge its truth from the personal to the universal. He yearned to know the future history of the world as well as he knew the destiny of his own poor flesh, and he yearned to gain control of the development of that future history. Even at the last, when he lectured me before I left him for good, he insisted that his dream would come true, that Camelot would rise again although its stones were scattered. There is, as you will have understood while you read my report of that speech, a sense in which he was right: the idea of Britain didn't die; Arthur wasn't forgotten; the legend endured to assist in the energization of an empire. But there was also a sense in which he was wrong, because the Camelot that survived wasn't built of stone and wasn't built to last. It bore as much resemblance to the Britain that actually transpired as the Dark Land bears to

Cokaygne: it was a shadow, and abstract idea, fluid and elastic and intangible, which could only function as part of a whole host of competing and contesting shadows, to bring forms out of chaos whose very essence was transience. Because of that, it could serve as part of a progressive series; it could give way, when the time came, to something more ambitious.

Merlin was mistaken in thinking himself an architect of one world, let alone more worlds than one. He was too proud by half when he declared that no one could have done more than he, or better than he, with the start that he was given when Morgana released him from his servitude in Faerie into a world that seemed—and was—far younger than he.

When his ghost visits me, of course—and my magic is such that I can certainly see and speak to ghosts—he clings hard to his opinions, and there's no point at all in trying to convert him to mine. The dead don't change.

You and I know, however, that it was not because of Merlin that Britain came to be, or that it came to be within the embrace of Christendom. You and I know that Merlin was an old, self-deluding fool whose last speech to me was a desperate attempt to snatch some crumbs of comfort from the embers of his ambition. You and I know, by virtue of what I have confessed here, that the only edifice Merlin really did design has passed so thoroughly from actuality into legend that no one knows exactly where it was built. Even I can't find it, any more than I can find the gate of Avalon.

Camelot might have stood on the Great Ridge, or on Gare Hill. I can't be sure. The gate of Avalon was between Manswood and Witchampton, but you could walk back and forth between the two for a lifetime and never find the crack in the world, let alone squeeze yourself through it. It's not the fault or the ingenuity of the fair folk that has made it so difficult of access. Our world is the one that changes. Our world is the one in which such breaches can be healed, and sometimes are.

The reality, as I learned when I let fall that precious drop of certain truth into Arthur's cup, not knowing who would drink it, is that the fate of a world like ours might turn upon a whim of petty and absurd misfortune. I thought then, and I still think now, that Morgana could not possibly have known how that drop might go astray. Yes, she was a seer of sorts—but all she could see of the future was writ in shifting shadows in a dark glass. It wasn't Morgana le Fay who murdered Merlin's Britain. The true Architect of Worlds is the vast conspiracy of chance and choice, which can't be tracked or controlled. The future, in our world, is uncertainly sketched by shifting shadows in a glass as black as almost-starless night.

I don't expect to be able to return to Cokaygne. I can only hope that I won't ever want to.

2

I often wonder, as I once wondered in Cokaygne, whether there might be other gates. Is the human world really the rim or rind of creation, within which all others are enclosed and confined, arrayed in series all the way back to the primal fire?

Perhaps not. Perhaps there already is another, where time moves even faster, and change is more adventurous still. Even if there isn't another world outside ours, perhaps there's one— or more than one—that lies parallel to it, like a shadow or a photographic negative, as the Dark Land is to Cokaygne. If not... well, the future's uncertain, and the magic of this world makes progress with every day that passes. One day, making portals will be child's play. In the meantime, we have storytellers, not merely to remind us of our needs, our hopes and our desires but to help us reshape them.

Applaud now, if you care to.

Thank you very much, if you did.

I still look behind waterfalls and inside hollow trees, whenever I run away, although that's probably just a habit, or a silly failure of an imagination that hasn't quite kept pace with reality. The gates of your world—our world—are more probably secreted in cellars and warehouses, motorway underpasses and airports, power stations and public toilets. I haven't time to mount a serious search, though; there's far too much to see outside the murky corners, dark rooms and endless coverts.

I'm a spy, after all, trained by experience and enhanced by magic, and a spy's primary interest has to be in people: what they believe and what they know; what they hope for and what they desire. Mastering the language was easy enough, but figuring out the meanings of the words is only phase one. Figuring out the motives people have for saying what they say, writing what they write, and meaning what they mean, isn't something even I can master overnight.

I like the challenge, though—and I think I might like it even more as the work makes progress.

I've lived a long time in Cokaygne, among the fair folk, whose relative fairness was, indeed, guaranteed by their immunity to the scars inflicted on humans by the gauntlet of disease that every Dark Age child had perforce to run. I've lived in the house of the elf Morgana, who was more beautiful even than Guinevere. In today's world, Morgana and Guinevere would seem equally ordinary. In today's world, Morganas and Guineveres are everywhere.

Somehow, I don't think it'll be difficult to fall in love when the magic begins to wear off.

In the meantime, I'm working as hard as I can to bring Tom up to speed. He's a genius, but something of an idiot savant. He'd be helpless without me. We've sold almost everything we brought with us out of Cokaygne, so one or both of us will have to start making money soon if we're not to rejoin the ranks of the hungry and the homeless. Luxurious as that status seems to a Dark Age orphan, it's not one we covet.

The one thing I'm determined not to sell, although it might be more valuable than all the rest if I could only bring myself to do it, is Excalibur.

The fact that I used Excalibur to kill Lancelot is neither here or there, but the fact that Lancelot was moved by the subtle conspiracy of chance and choice to put it into my hand is a very different matter.

It's not just that Excalibur was Arthur's sword, although that counts for something, nor that it was forged in Faerie from an alloy more magical than steel, nor even that it was the crucial symbol of Merlin's dream of Britain.

It's more personal than all of that.

Excalibur went with me into the Dark Land, and came back again. Like me, it still has something of the Dark Land in it... and because it's just a rustproof sword, it will hold that aspect of the Dark Land far longer than my frail flesh, or Tom Rhymer's.

Unlike everything else that I brought out of the past, including myself, Excalibur is still what it was, and has the inertia to stay that way.

All the stones of Camelot are something different now, and the flesh of all Camelot's inhabitants has been devoured, excreted and re-embodied a thousand times over—but Excalibur is still Excalibur, and always will be. That's why I want to hold on to it.

It's irrational, I know, but some things are.

Everything else seems to make sense, more or less—and if all of that isn't enough, what is?

THE END

Afterword
by Brian Stableford

The Stones of Camelot originated as a novelette I was invited to write for an anthology of Arthurian fantasies edited by Lawrence Schimel and published in the USA by DAW Books in 1998. The short version, "The Architect of Worlds," was drastically transformed during the process of expansion, but it began with the arrival of the injured rider at Camelot and ended with the protagonist leaving the citadel with Morgan le Fay. The expansion was born of a desire to give a much more elaborate account of the inner world from which Morgan came—with particular emphasis, obviously, on its timelessness—and to develop the notion that there might be yet another world contained within that one, in which time and progress move even more slowly.

I wanted, in carrying out this mission, to explore the notion that an array of parallel worlds might be more akin to the layers of an onion than the pages of a book, moving "outwards" from a definable existential center according to a pattern of metaphysical phases. In order to facilitate that task, I fused the standard apparatus of British Arthurian fantasy with that of two Scottish ballads preserved in Thomas Percy's *Reliques of English Poetry*, "Tam Lin" and "Thomas the Rhymer," both of which make much of the slow passage of time in Faerie. I also elected to reassess the motives traditionally attributed to the inhabitants of Faerie, which lead them to steal human children.

The novel's excursion into exotic metaphysical fantasy had the inevitable effect of removing the novel from the ordinary run of Arthurian fantasies, which might or might not be seen as a good thing, depending on a particular reader's opinions and interests. The addition of so much new material inevitably exerted a strain on the traditional materials, pulling them insistently out of shape—even more so in the novel than in the original short story. That did not seem to me to be inappropriate; to treat Malory's *Morte d'Arthur* as a kind of textbook, whose version of events ought not to be violated, is to accept voluntary imaginative imprisonment. In my estimation, all the great Arthurian romances follow their own agendas with blithe abandon.

The model I had foremost in my mind when planning "The Architect of Worlds" was Thomas Love Peacock's *The Misfortunes of Elphin*, to whose influence the inclusion of a bard named Taliesin is directly attributable, although I also had Mark Twain's *Connecticut Yankee* in mind when attributing a spoilsport role to a dignitary of the church. The Sisters of Saint Syncletica, who were added to the expanded version to add depth to the protagonist's back story, have featured in my work before, in *The Werewolves of London*. According to the missal given to me a very long time ago by Father John Malone, there really is a Saint Syncletica, but she is not in *The Oxford Book of Saints* and I know nothing about her save for her name; the highly fanciful legend related in *The Stones of Camelot* is entirely my own invention.